P9-DML-877

For Fabienne
I couldn't have done it without you.

With special thanks and acknowledgment to Melody
Bowles, Kathryn Bell, Luke Hewitt and Rachel Crosby

First Published in Great Britain, in 2012

Cover designed and made by Fabienne King, on Create Space Cover Creator

Copyright © 2012 Simone King
All rights reserved.
ISBN 13: 978-1479242917
ISBN-10: 1479242918

The Underworld/ Overworld Declarations

Act 1 – No Underworld Variation and Overworld Variation shall ever possess feelings of sentiment for each other.

Act 2 – The purpose of an Overworld Variation is to obey and serve to the needs of an Underworld Variation.

Act 3 – Underworld Variations and Overworld Variations shall remain forever separated, but mutually respect each other's talents.

Act 4 – Failure to comply with any of the Declarations of is immediately punishable under pain of death. No exceptions.

The Rules of Magic (Overworld)

1) No one shall raise the dead. Ever.

2) Unless one is a Morphic, one's appearance cannot be permanently changed by magic.

3) All magic is unique to its weaver, and should be treated as sacred and sentient within and of itself.

The Underworld Proclamation

1) Barring initial deference to one's own specific race, within the greater Underworld Variation, be it under the jurisdiction of the Royal Vampires, the President of the Dark Angels, the Siren Queen or the Daemon Chief – first and foremost, Underworld control and loyalty is under the power of the Underworld Prince.

2) Current Hunting Restrictions, as dictated by the Underworld Prince, must be followed in regards to the Overworld Variations.

Chapter One – Resistance

It was the hottest day of summer so far. The air was sweltering, with only a languid breeze to offer respite. Susannah shifted uncomfortably, her shirt plastering to her back with sweat. The weather was stifling. She couldn't wait to get out of the sticky sunlight, to hide indoors in relative coolness and skulk there for the rest of the weekend. Motes of dust spun lazily in the air around her, kicked up by the sleek, air-conditioned hover cars roaring down the road beside her. She frowned, feeling irritable. No matter what Delilah said, this level of heat was intolerable. It simply wasn't possible to consider the surge in high temperature as anything other than unpleasant. She much preferred the rain of the winter months. It was cooler. She sighed, checking her watch impatiently. She should have just gone home. He wasn't going to turn up anyway. God, she hated waiting for people.

"Susannah Skelsby?" a voice asked. She spun round immediately, her magic prickling. "Whoa, hey, easy!" The boy took a step back, raising his arms in a placating gesture. He was taller than her, sinewy, with a shock of tousled auburn hair, large brown eyes and an air of authority. He looked vaguely familiar.

"Yes," she replied warily. "Who are you?"

"Oh, right," he flashed a wry grin, offering a hand. "Kriger, call me Krig...we met the other night?" She nodded. Yeah, she remembered. She'd been heading home when she came across Krig and his friends getting attacked by a Hunting Party of Dark Angels; Evelyn's crowd, and she'd never got on with them. Of course she had to get involved. A fight had ensued, and they'd driven the Underworld Variations away.

"Knight Street," she said. He inclined his head, the grin fading somewhat.

"Yeah, Knight Street - thanks for that, by the way. You probably saved our lives."

"It was nothing," she mumbled, looking away. She could feel the weight of his study, intense and assessing upon her person. "You asked me to meet you...?"

"And you agreed," he arched a brow. "You know, that's quite a dangerous thing to be doing, meeting random strangers. Do you make a habit of it? Or am I special?" She glared at him.

"I'm perfectly capable of taking care of myself," she snapped. "Probably more so than you."

"I gathered," he smiled. "The way you took care of those Carmel lackeys was pretty impressive." She stared at him flatly.

"I get by."

"Get by?" he looked surprised. "Kid, what I saw the other night was more than getting by."

Susannah scowled, abruptly slinging her school bag over her shoulder. Great, it was another one of those people. Truthfully, she wasn't entirely sure why she'd agreed to meet him in the first place, she'd had suspicions of his character – her mum and dad certainly wouldn't have been happy if they knew. She supposed she'd been intrigued, considering the circumstances of their meeting.

"I'm not interested," she stated. "And I'm not a kid - how old are you anyway, seventeen?"

"Nineteen," he replied, stepping into her way. The movement was fluid, graceful, but relaxed enough to suggest that he didn't mean it in a threatening way. It was probably the only thing stopping her from incapacitating him, and she could, they both knew it. It was why he was here, wasn't it? "You don't know what I'm offering yet," he added cajolingly.

"I can guess."

"I doubt that," he challenged. She folded her arms defensively across her chest, turning to face him once more.

"Really," she stated sceptically. "Please, don't insult my intelligence. I've seen your type before, and I'm not interested." His eyebrows arched a little higher.

"My type?" He looked faintly amused. "I suppose you think I'm a gang recruiter."

"What else would you be?" she replied. "An interested party? Because believe me when I say I've heard it before."

"I've no doubt you have," he sighed. "But I promise you I'm not a gang recruiter, well, not exactly."

"Not exactly?" she repeated. "That sounds a lot like a gang recruiter in my book." She studied him for a moment; she'd come across a lot of gang recruiters in her time, the city was full of them with the amount of street warfare that went on. If things got anymore fractionalised their Underworld leaders would start getting involved, and that wasn't good for anybody. Krig did seem a little different though; he had the qualities of a gang recruiter, but then an edge of something more which had initially caught her interest.

"You get a lot of those, I suppose," he mused. "And watching you the other night, I can see why. Your magic is..." he trailed off. Her expression darkened, her stomach tightening and twisting into suffocating knots. She could feel her heart sinking like lead in her chest, despite her best efforts.

"My magic is?" she prompted coldly. "Freaky? Abnormal? Unnatural? Is that what you meant to say?"

She'd heard that before too. He stared at her.

"Actually," he replied lightly. "I was going to say incredible. I've never seen anyone as powerful as you before, aside from Marco Carmel, and he's not exactly on our side, is he?"

"Our side? Are you sure you're not a gang recruiter?" but there was no venom to her tone. He laughed; the sound rich and warm.

"I'm sure," he said. "I mean our side as in Overworld variations generally - although that still sounds like a gang recruiter, doesn't it?"

"Yeah it kinda does," she agreed. "You're not very good at this, are you?" His mouth twisted into a grimace.

"Ha, no. Recruiting and talking to potential members is more Joel's department."

"So you are trying to recruit me." His head dropped into his hands, and she could hear him muttering darkly under his breath. She felt her lips curl involuntarily.

"Woe betide any gang who has me as a recruiter," he replied. "Can't you tell I'm terrible?"

There was a moment of silence, and she hefted her bag to the other shoulder.

"Who's Joel?" she asked finally. He looked at her.

"Huh? Oh, Joel is a friend of mine. He was there the other night."

"A gang member friend?" she questioned.

"Wow, you're like a dog with a bone on that topic," he said, swiping a strand of hair out of his face. "But if that's the way you want to look at it, yeah." She rolled her eyes.

"Well, it was nice meeting you," she said. "You seem alright, for a gang recruiter creep."

His eyes flicked to her face, before he sighed once more, appearing frustrated.

"Now I know why we don't normally work like this. I'm not a gang recruiter," he insisted. "The truth is - oh, screw it -" his magic flittered with agitation, and several privacy charms sprung up around them. "I'm the head of a civil rights resistance. I was wondering if you'd be interested in joining us?"

The sun had gone to her head, she just knew it. He couldn't have really just said that, could he? He continued quickly, as if worried she was going to storm away. Susannah didn't think she could have, even if she wanted to, at that point. She felt frozen in shock, because all she could think was 'that's illegal' over and over in her head, like some warped mantra. "We, as in the resistance, are trying to promote equality," he explained. "You know how badly they treat us - it's not fair." His voice was gaining confidence as he spoke, his previous awkwardness subsiding as he grew more passionate. "The Underworld have the best of everything, they feed on us without guilt or remorse and everyone just lies down and takes it. It's not right. They treat us like we're not even proper beings, just because we're Overworld."

"Technically, we're not..." she pointed out. "The Overworld are secondary citizens. That's the way it's always been."

"Yeah, because no one's ever bothered to fight against it before," he returned.

"Probably because it's illegal, as in, if you're caught you are dead in a matter of seconds type of illegal. Funnily enough, that's not a crowd pleaser..."

"Some things are worth dying for," he said simply. "I believe in my cause."

"And I suppose you think I should too?" she questioned,

her jaw tightening.

"Don't you?" he regarded her earnestly, his head tilting to one side. "You're powerful, you could do a lot of good in the world if you put your mind to it, I can see it and so can everyone else. You've had loads of gangs trying to recruit you because of it, am I right? And no doubt, as a result, you've had people try and kill you for it too." She surveyed him stonily, careful to keep her features expressionless. She could feel her emotions bubbling just beneath her exterior, simmering in their restraints. "You're fifteen," he began, and she shot him a sharp look considering she definitely hadn't been the one to tell him that. He ignored it, continuing. "And you live in Middle City; pretty much the roughest area possible. There's a war going on, the same one there always has been, between the Overworld variations and the Underworld variations. You've probably lost people to it, friends, family maybe. You can't remember a time when it was safe to be out at night past seven o clock." He proposed the words carefully, watching her reactions. She narrowed her eyes at him, not liking the feeling of being psychoanalysed any more than his apparent research regarding her.

"Is there a point to this?" she enquired sharply.

"You're fifteen and the Underworld want you dead. You're a threat to them. I'd be willing to wager that by the age of seventeen you'll either be the Demon Lord's marionette or dead by his hand, you attract too much attention. Your magic attracts too much attention, and I'll bet you're sick of it -"

"Shut up," she ordered, teeth gritted. Her magic was crackling, glowing barely contained beneath the surface of her skin. "You don't know me. You don't know anything about me!" Her fists clenched in on

9

themselves, her palms stinging where her nails dug in. "So stop pretending you do."

"I know you took on the Underworld, at personal risk, to help a bunch of strangers," he said softly. "Someone content with the way this world was run wouldn't do that. So yeah," he finished calmly, studying her. "I would hazard a guess that you do believe in my cause. Am I wrong?" he dared.

"Does it matter?" she returned. "You can't change the world just because you wish it to be better. If that was so, every little kid would have a secret door to sweetie land hidden in the airing cupboard." His lips twitched slightly.

"Sweetie land?" he enquired delicately, before shaking his head as if to clear the distractions away. "Look, if you don't believe in it, that's fine. I won't bother you again. But I think you do, but are just too scared of the consequences of speaking out."

"That just goes to show how much you really don't know anything about me at all then, doesn't it?" She took a deep breath, struggling to maintain a flippant, conversational tone. "Now, if you'll excuse me, I should be getting home. Don't contact me again, I'll report you to the wardens." She spun on her heel, trying to move away from him as quickly as possible, without seeming like she was fleeing. She could feel his eyes resting on her retreating form, but he didn't make a move to stop her. As if he could.

"Go ahead," he called after her. "But I doubt you will." Angrily, she tightened her grip on her bag, pointedly ignoring him.

It was not a good week.

She arrived home, some half an hour later, her hands

closing around the key in her pocket as she shoved it into the lock. She stepped through the threshold, feeling the lack of heat instantly. It was a welcome relief, though the house was hardly chilled. It was warm; bordering on stuffy. She slammed the door shut behind her, dropping her bag against the stairs with a dull thud.

Who did that boy - Kriger - think he was? How could he be so stupid to talk about resistance to her? He didn't know her. He didn't even have any reason to trust her. So what if she didn't like the way the city was run? So what if she despised the constant gang warfare? Who didn't? That didn't mean she was willing to jeopardise her family's life for it. That didn't mean she wouldn't sell him out. It was idiotic of him to take such a risk.

The house was silent; both her parents were still at work. Her mother worked in the Materialisation zone, policing it and helping beings on their journeys. She'd been there once, at the Materialisation zone, on a one off take-your-child to work day. She'd been seven, and awed by the vast white limbo. It was bustling with beings of both variations, all appearing and disappearing in the large marble arches that lined the area. Ever since, she hadn't been able to wait to learn how to materialise and get her permit - the whole idea of disappearing from one place, picking an arch and appearing in a split second in another part of the world was just so awesome. You had to be twenty-one though. She padded over to the kitchen, grabbing a glass and chugging down a drink of cranberry juice, before setting it aside to clean itself in the sink. She ran a hand through her hair, mussing the short brown strands even further. Shadow. She knew it had been a bad idea to agree to meet him. It really wouldn't be good for her to get involved in that sort of crowd, what was she thinking? She hadn't planned on going; she was just going to walk home. It was spur of the moment, her mum and dad thought she got into enough trouble as it was. She didn't, well, only a little bit, but that was beside the point. They would be absolutely furious if she deliberately set out to get herself into a life-threatening situation. Joining a resistance was a really bad idea. Why was she even thinking about joining? It wasn't going to happen. This was a mess. Why did she always attract such weirdoes? He'd just seemed so…different. He didn't act like a typical gang recruiter. Most of them were all rough, tough and forceful. They started off charming, curious with honeyed words designed to flatter; every single one of them acting like she was just an oblivious little girl. Then, when she rejected their offer, they grew menacing, spiteful and threatening. Oh, some were better than others, able to keep up a mask a little longer - but under repeated refusal, however polite or impolite depending upon the nuances of her mood, they always began to show cracks and reveal their true natures and motives. Everyone was out to get something; some people were just more skilled at hiding it. Kriger would crack too; of that much at least she was certain.

Leaving the kitchen, she headed for her room, donning her school uniform for something lighter. That done, she picked her way through the mess of the floor to reach her desk. Her mother was always nagging at her to clean up - but it wasn't that untidy. It had a very distinct order, albeit, an order that only she could decipher. It was her room, wasn't it? Her mum didn't have to enter. She let her head thunk against the table. She could feel a headache building between her temples. Unease fluttered like bats in her insides. He shouldn't have asked her to join. She didn't need to know - and she didn't need the idea of it flittering about in her head either. It would only taunt her with possibilities that logically could never come to pass. Civil Rights was more Delilah's scene anyway, her blonde best friend would have jumped at the chance of making a positive change on the world. Or, at least trying to. She was always bouncing around, smiling and ready to fight for the underdog. Susannah was happy to fight for the underdog too, but not in the same way as Delilah was. She was too busy just fighting for herself. That sounded self-centred and maybe it was, but that was the way things were. If she couldn't even keep herself out of trouble, how could she possibly do it for other people? It was wrong of him to put her in the position to consider it. Not that she was considering it. He didn't even know her. He was just another person trying to get a piece of her magic. He was not to be relied upon. She was just going to ignore it - it wouldn't happen again. Even Kriger couldn't be suicidal enough to trust a stranger twice.

Could he?

The next morning was announced by the shriek of the doorbell.

"Someone's at the door, move your butt," it screeched. Susannah gritted her teeth, unsure as to why her mother even kept the derogatory thing, aside from her claim that it was amusing. Her father tolerated it. Susannah put up with it because she didn't actually get say in whether or not they kept it. Still, it had the most annoying, shrill and frankly piercing voice she had ever heard. She took the stairs two at a time, almost skidding into the hallway mirror as she wrenched the front door open.

"Hi," Delilah greeted, smiling brightly as stepped in. "I've coming bearing gifts of sweet, icy cold, sugary goodness." She held out a carrier bag, filled with two tubs of ice cream. "You sounded like you needed it."

"Have I ever mentioned you're amazing?" she replied. Delilah's grin broadened.

"Not nearly as often as you should, but I can live with it," she joked. "You can make it up to me by coming on a picnic. It's way too sunny for you to sulk inside."

"It's way too hot for me to not," she replied. Delilah frowned. She grinned, sticking her head into the lounge. "I'm going out with Del, don't make lunch for me." Her parents looked over, away from the TV and the newspaper respectively.

"Have fun and try and stay out of trouble."

"When do I not?" she asked innocently. Her dad laughed.

"I don't think you really want us to answer that."

"Nah, probably not. Oh well, bye, I'll see you later." She summoned a couple of spoons from the kitchen, dropping them into the carrier bag and snatching her keys off the table. A moment later, they were out the front door again, the heat blasting at their faces with a blistering intensity. Delilah was watching her carefully, her azure eyes filled with concern. Susannah ignored it.

"Did you see the new episode of Dark Angel next door?" she questioned. Her friend lit up immediately at the mention of her favourite programme.

"Yeah - did you? I can't believe they brought Penelope

back in!" Susannah grinned slightly at Delilah's outraged indignation.

"I think that's kind of the point," she smirked. Delilah shot her a look.

"Well, yeah, but still. Penelope!" she exclaimed. "Bigger audience reaction, I guess."

"Still of all the characters…it just had to be her didn't it?" Susannah scowled.. Delilah made a noise of agreed discontent in the back of her throat, before glancing sideways at her.

"So, how did your meeting with mystery man go?" she teased, though her expression reflected the solemnity of the question. "Should I guess from the ice-cream that you're not calling him back?" Susannah rolled her eyes.

"Del, it wasn't a date. I don't even know him, and he was mental anyway."

"A perfect match then."

"Oi!" she drew her magic, sending a spurt of water in her friend's direction. Delilah abruptly ducked, her blonde hair flying, her skin crinkling with laughter lines.

"I jest, sunshine, I jest," she conceded. "You're not mental. Seriously though, who was he? Another gang recruiter?" Susannah shrugged, her gaze instinctively scanning their surroundings for eavesdroppers, wardens or worse.

"He said he was part of a resistance - ridiculous, I know."

"A resistance?" Delilah repeated faintly. "Isn't that -"

"Illegal? Yeah, that's what I said. He was probably just some practical joker. Nobody rebels against the Carmels." Delilah's head tilted thoughtfully.

"It would be interesting if they did," she mused. Susannah scowled.

"Not you too. C'mon! A resistance? Really?" she asked,

shaking her head. "I always knew you were slightly loopy, all this sunshine is clearly not good for you."

"There's nothing wrong with sunshine; it's nice and warm, and it makes everything look pretty, and gives you vitamin D," Delilah argued defensively. "You're the loopy one, and yeah, really. What's wrong with the idea?"

"Aside from the whole illegal, punishable by death part?" she laughed incredulously. "What's right about it? What good do resistances ever do? I mean sure, it's admirable and everything, and I do admire him for the effort, but I don't really think it's going to change anything."

"Well it won't with that attitude," Delilah reasoned. "And it could change things, if it got enough supporters."

"Sure," she agreed. "But it won't get enough supporters; Carmel would crush it to smithereens before it even got to the infancy of threatening Underworld supremacy."

"Not if he doesn't know about it," Delilah said.

"And if he doesn't know about it, it won't do anything. It's like when the werewolf strikes happened back in the reign of Contessa and Damien Carmel...they tried to make a huge underground conspiracy, then ended up being so paranoid and secretive that they all ended up bickering and accusing each other treachery. It didn't get anywhere. Then, when it was public knowledge, the werewolves just got kicked to the bottom of the food chain with even less rights than us! I call that counterproductive."

"Yeah, but they were going for Overworld supremacy instead of equality, weren't they? There's no way the Underworld would ever accept supremacy, but they may possibly accept the pledge for equality. There'd be less opposition."

"No, there wouldn't," she replied. "They would just see it working like dominoes, first equality and then, when we have that, supremacy. They treat any rebellion the same; as insubordination."

"Stop being so pessimistic! It could work."

Susannah disagreed, but at the dejected slump in her best friend's shoulders, let it be.

If Delilah still had hope in such a world as theirs, full of blood and prejudiced hate, who was she to try and take that away? Everyone needed something to cling onto, or they just stopped fighting, and in the city, the second you surrendered you were lost forever in the abyss of hierarchy and political hopscotch. You were a nobody, and you always would be. By birth, your place in the world was already pretty much marked for you unless you fought for something better. Even if you fought, you often lost - unless members of the Underworld took a liking to you.

"So, I'm guessing you told him you're not interested in joining?" Delilah asked. Susannah nodded.

"Of course, I'm not. I just want to live my life, you know that." Delilah smiled, just slightly.

"Yeah, I do...but he may not accept that - what did you say his name was again?"

"Krig," she muttered darkly. "Who's called Krig anyway? What type on name is that?"

"Wow, he has made a favourable impression on you," Delilah said, a small smile gracing her lips. Susannah narrowed her eyes. "Not like that, I know you don't fancy him," her friend said softly, quickly, all teasing gone.

"I'm not interested, in any way shape or form, and I told him that," she replied. They arrived at the central park, heading for the tiny wooded area at it centre. Soon, the green foliage would grow yellow with lack of water. She could feel the weight of Delilah's scrutiny upon her like a physical force.

"Yeah," the blonde murmured. "I'm just curious as to whether or not you actually meant it." They dropped to sit in the grass, Delilah's hands moving to unscrew a tub. She looked up again after a moment, casting a dazzling grin in her direction. "Ice cream?"

Chapter Two - Carter and Moor

On Sunday, Susannah headed for Delilah's house. It was amazing that the Moors didn't get sick to death of her; she spent so much time at Ripsol Cottage that it was almost a second home. Delilah lived in Lower City, the exclusively Overworld side of town with her grandparents and older brother Robbie. Her parents had died when she was five. The services, like the central heating, were almost always shoddy and in need of repairs, but it was peaceful and Underworld free. It was difficult to get a house there because of that: everyone Overworld wanted in.

It was nowhere near as grand or expensive as Upper City, which was the Underworld area - full of towering skyscrapers and beautiful mansions that glittered with lights twenty four hours a day - but it was the place to be. Susannah herself lived in the roughest part of the city, Middle City, the mixed Overworld and Underworld variation area. It was awful. The houses themselves were fine enough, but it wasn't pleasant to be on the same road as the Underworld. They always locked everything at night, with all the wards that they, as a family, could muster. It was the only way to have any feeling of relative safety. There had been some close calls, like the time an unkindness of Dark Angels had nearly taken the roof off and poured shards of broken glass down the chimney. She'd got used to it by now though. She'd had to.

Ripsol Cottage, Delilah's home, was on the very outskirts of the city. The garden was sprawling, and in summer full of wild flowers and berries. There was a gnarled old apple tree that swooped over the gate, and the whole building was light and open. She loved it there. It was everything that her home was not. She could hear Bilbo, the Moor's husky puppy, barking from the other side of the pea green door. She knocked.

William Moor appeared a moment later, with a tight grip on Bilbo's collar to stop the excitable fur ball from leaping up at her.

"Susannah," he smiled. "It's good to see you, come in. I was just making some tea, would you like some? - Delilah! Susannah's here," he called up the stairs.

"I'm fine, thank you. How are you? How's the garden?"

"Good, I'm good, and the garden's fine," he replied, releasing Bilbo. Susannah patted the dog tentatively behind the ears. He was only a puppy, but he was still quite big. He was lovable enough. Delilah appeared at the foot of the stairs a moment later.

"Hey Suze, I must admitted I'm impressed."

"Impressed?" she looked around her. "With what?"

"With the fact that you actually ventured outside into sunlight when you had the option of sitting skulking in your room with obscure magic textbooks," Delilah grinned. "It's miraculous."

Susannah scowled.

"Haha, never become a comedian, you're not funny. William, tell your granddaughter to stop bullying me!" Mr Moor laughed, holding his hands up in a ward as he backed into the lounge.

"I'm staying out of it."

"See, even grandpa agrees," Delilah replied smugly.

"They're interesting books," she insisted. "And I read them in the garden...sometimes."

"Rarely," her best friend scoffed. "Though I suppose that's understandable in the case of obscure magic texts, seeing as you're not really supposed to have them. Otherwise, you

have no excuse - and I never said they weren't interesting."
Susannah smirked, before turning serious. She made a slight
motion with her head and they headed for Delilah's room.

Delilah's bedroom was impeccably tidy, the walls were sky
blue and all the furniture was of a light wood variant. The
window was massive, and overlooking the garden. It was
open, and fresh – just like all of rooms in Ripsol Cottage.
Delilah dropped onto the bed, crossing her legs and staring
at her. Susannah took the desk seat, her eyes scanning
across the products of Delilah's language homework. She
was learning to speak Nymphian, the Nymph language.
"What?" she asked.
"Talk," Delilah instructed patiently. "I know when
something is bothering you; I'm your best friend. So you
might as well spill it."
"I'm fine," she said.
"Uh huh," Delilah replied disbelievingly. "Sure you are,
sunshine."
"I am!" she protested, grimacing at the endearment. The
blonde smiled at her. Susannah shifted uncomfortably. "Del,
stop looking at me like that."
"Like what?" Delilah questioned innocently.
"Like you've been secretly studying Mind Arts and are
reading my mind!"
"You didn't know about that?"
"Del!" she growled. Her best friend's smile broadened to a
grin, albeit with an edge of something, but after a moment
her gaze drifted away so that Susannah no longer felt like
she was being X-rayed. There was a silence, broken only by
Delilah's humming as she flicked through the bookcase by
her bed. Susannah rolled her eyes, her magic flittering
slightly. "So, I did some research on Kriger..." she conceded

finally.

"I knew it!" Delilah exclaimed, dropping her book abruptly back on the bed. Susannah shot her a look.

"If you already knew, why did you bother asking?" she demanded, before shaking her head. "Actually, don't answer that. Do you want to know what I found out or not?"

"That he's actually Marco Carmel in disguise?" Delilah offered. Susannah charmed the pillow to hit the petite girl across the head, ignoring the hyena like laughter that followed.

"This is serious," she snapped. Delilah sobered.

"I know, I know," she appeased. "I'm just trying to save you from your own internal angst. You worry too much sometimes. Besides, he could have been Marco Carmel in disguise…"

"Yes, because the Demon Lord is really going to be interested in me," she rolled her eyes. "I'm pretty sure he has better things to do than elaborately stalk fifteen year old girls, you know, like running the country." Delilah grinned.

"Now that was almost a joke, Suze. I'm so proud!" Susannah felt a fond smile tug at her lips despite herself.

"What can I say; your insanity must be contagious," she retorted. "Anyway, he's not Marco Carmel in disguise. His name actually is Kriger Carter…Kriger Niall Carter if you want to be specific about it. Not Carmel, or any of his Elite."

"Poor guy," Delilah murmured. "Who'd name their kid Kriger?"

"Henry and Julia Carter, apparently," she replied. "They have another child too, Cassandra." Delilah paused, staring at her slightly. "What?" she asked.

"You'd be a rather magnificent stalker," her best friend said finally. "It's slightly disturbing how much information you can dig up on someone within twenty four hours of learning their name." Susannah pulled a face.

"Full names are on public record, it's not that creepy," she dismissed. Delilah grinned.

"Yes, but what else have you found out about him in your intrepid late night hacking?"

"It's not hacking," she protested. "It's using my resources in a manner that yields more information."

"Yeah? Tell that to the Wardens when they toss you into the Anzarkledea Cells for being a trouble maker," Delilah replied, but she was still smiling.

"They hate me anyway. It wouldn't make a difference if I was guilty or not," she shrugged.

"So what have you found?" Delilah prompted, leaning forward and resting her elbows on her thighs.

"He graduated school last year, with Advanced Levels in Duelling, Political Magic and Inter-magical Relations. He also has an Intermediate Level in Warding, Mind Arts and Psychology."

"He was probably telling you the truth about the resistance thing then. Why would anyone want to take Political Magic otherwise?"

"Why would anyone want to take Inter-magical Relations?" she returned.

"I take Inter-magical Relations," Delilah said. Susannah smirked.

"I know," she replied. Delilah frowned at her.

"Did you find anything else? Besides an online dictionary of terrible jokes?" she asked sweetly. Susannah's smirk softened to a grin once more, before fading into seriousness.

"He lives on his own in Middle City, has a blog called Dream

Catchers and he wipes his internet history." Delilah opened her mouth, closed it once more, before finally speaking. "And how would you know that he wipes his internet history?" she asked.

"Cause I hacked his computer," Susannah said nonchalantly. "Obviously. But no, that's not the interesting part. He has some incredible safety and encryptions - I couldn't get anything. Normally, when people delete their stuff, it's actually just lurking in their recycling bin. Not him. It's completely gone, and I couldn't get into any of his files."

"Well, considering he's the leader of an illegal resistance, I would have been a bit worried if you could," Delilah shrugged. "I'd take it as a good thing. So, is that all you've got?"

"Yeah," she conceded reluctantly.

"Not quite up to your normal standards, you must be slipping," Delilah grinned. "I guess it's lucky that you have me then." Susannah folded her arms, tilting her head curiously.

"Oh?"

"Yeah," Delilah's grin broadened. "I know for example that his communicon code is 0872145454, that we're meeting him at Silver Hollow Park next Friday and that he works a job at Behemoth's Bar on Larsson Street-"

"Whoa, wait, what did you just say?" she demanded.

"He works at Behemoth's Bar," Delilah repeated mischievously.

"Before that," she snapped tightly. Delilah shrugged elegantly.

"Oh yeah, we're meeting him at Silver Hollow Park after school next Friday." Susannah's stomach dropped - she hadn't misheard.

"Since when?" she yelped. "I did not agree to this."

"Since I looked Kriger up in the communicon directory and arranged it," her best friend said smugly. Susannah glared, beginning to sense her magic tingle dangerously.

"No."

"What do you mean no?" Delilah replied calmly.

"No!" she growled. "You had no right to do that and I'm not going."

"You sound mad."

"I am! For Shadow's sake Delilah, are you trying to get us killed?" The petite blonde narrowed her eyes, making Susannah hesitate warily.

"No, actually I'm trying to do some good in the world because you're too scared to," Delilah said, coolly. "Don't give me that look, Suze, I've participated in far too many of your crazy schemes for you to deny me one of my own. Besides, you know perfectly well that you're interested, otherwise you would have cursed him until he went home crying, so don't you *dare*..."

"This is a lot bigger than one of my crazy schemes," she hissed. "You don't even really know anything about him."

"And he didn't even really know anything about you, but he seemed to hit the nail on the head. That's why you're scared, isn't it? It's not because his resistance is illegal at all, you spout heresy on a daily basis so it's not like you're new to the idea...you're just terrified that he seemed to understand you better than you do yourself."

"I am not-" she began furiously.

"Then you shouldn't have a problem meeting him again then, should you?" Delilah said. Susannah closed her eyes for a moment, her teeth gritted. She'd talked herself into a corner. Again.

"I'm not happy with this," she warned.

"But you're going to go along with it anyway," her best

25

friend remarked, a familiar smile making an appearance once more. "You're curious, admit it."

"I shall do no such thing," she replied, but she dipped her head slightly in confirmation. Yes, she was going to go along with it. Shadow help her, but she was.

"Excellent. I think Grandpa wants some help with the garden."

Susannah got home for dinner time, weaving through the streets of Middle City with a guarded familiarity. Her dad had made chicken curry with basmati rice, much to her pleasure. Caido Skelsby, her father, was the main cook in the house, though her mum did chip in occasionally. She was told she looked a lot more like her father - with the same silver green eyes and brown hair, same thin nose. She had her mother, Serena's, figure though.

"Get the place mats," her dad called as she entered, carrying three plates in his arms and levitating the dish of curry in front of him. Her mum was setting down the cutlery, still wearing her dark red work trousers, though she'd changed into a more casual shirt. She had another shift at the Materialisation Office coming up soon because they were short staffed for the week. One of the wardens was off sick with ghoul pox.

Unlike both her and her dad, her mum's hair was a more vibrant shade of brown and her eyes a pale blue rather than the Skelsby metallic green. Susannah summoned the place mats, catching them in one hand as they whizzed from the other room and putting them down on the dining table. Her mum raised hers brows.

"You're going to get lazy if you always summon everything," she stated. Susannah pulled a face.

"Mum, I take duelling classes...how could I possibly get lazy?

Sensei Kemp is a slave driver!" she protested indignantly. "Yet you still complain that the lessons are too easy," her dad remarked dryly. Susannah shrugged innocently.

"They are...but he's still a slave driver." They both seemed to simultaneously roll their eyes. Dinner started, silence reigning as everyone satiated their immediate hunger. She swallowed a mouthful, speaking once more about five minutes later. "You know I mentioned meeting someone yesterday?" she began casually. She'd spent a lot of time considering whether she should mention the resistance to her parents; she knew perfectly well that they wouldn't approve. However, such an under-taking was too dangerous even for them by association for her to feel comfortable not warning them. Besides, her parents had always shown a certain, guarded sympathy for resistance themselves, she was sure they would understand.

"Yes," her mum said. Her dad made a noise of acknowledgement.

"Well, I'm meeting him again next Friday, after school. I'll probably go and stay round

Delilah's house after, because of the hunting." Her mother nodded in acceptance.

"Him?" Her dad questioned. Susannah rolled her eyes.

"Dad! It's not like that. Honestly, you're as bad as Delilah," she complained. Her mum smiled slightly.

"We know, darling," she replied, giving her husband a look. Susannah felt only marginally appeased, for her mum seemed far too amused.

"It's true. He's like nineteen anyway - and don't look at me like that! Ugh, you're so embarrassing." That appeared to serve only to increase their entertainment at her discomfort. She took a drink of water to hide it.

"So, did anything happen with this nineteen year old, or are you just saying?" her dad asked finally. Susannah wrinkled her nose.

"He's in a resistance group. He wants to recruit me after he saw me take on some of Carmel's lackeys on Knight Street a couple of days ago." Her parents both froze, her mum's cutlery clattering to the floor, too loud in the suddenly silent room. Her dad set his own gently down on his plate.

"A resistance group?" her mum questioned sharply, eyes flashing. "What resistance group?"

"He didn't give me a name - just that it's a resistance group. They're looking to end the fighting, gain equal rights. A civil rights type of thing. I guess it's kind of ridiculous when you think about it." She was babbling. Suddenly, her dad's face relaxed fractionally, and her parents exchanged frantic looks for a moment.

"You said he was nineteen," he said.

"Yeah, he was. At first I thought he was a gang recruiter, but I don't know…" Susannah shrugged. "He seems genuine. Even Del thinks so." Her mum and dad exchanged glances over the table again, unreadable. "What?" she demanded. She'd expected a more explosive reaction…this was highly unusual, disconcertingly calm.

"Susie," her mum began carefully. "Are you absolutely certain you know what you're doing? There are a lot of-"

"-bad people in the world," she sighed. "Yeah, mum, I know. I'm not a kid anymore, I've come across the Underworld plenty of -"

"Susannah!" her dad scolded, hushing her warningly, jaw clenching once more. "The Prince has ears." Susannah bit her tongue mutinously. "I've come across them before," she amended tightly. There was a moment of tense silence.

"We just don't want you to get hurt," her mum continued after a while. "There are a lot of people who'd be more than happy to take advantage of your youth to use your...talents to their own gain."

"Talents," she snorted. "Right."

"Your magic is a talent, Susannah," her dad said quietly.

"Yeah, yeah," she mumbled, hoping to avoid the 'be proud of yourself' lecture. "I know." Her parents' faces told her they were fully aware of what she was doing, so she smiled back, eating another mouthful of dinner to avoid having to offer another response.

"You're meeting him again?" her dad probed. "Does that mean you're thinking of joining?" They'd picked up their knives and forks again, albeit shakily. Their countenances were grim, disapproving. Susannah shrugged awkwardly, beginning to wonder why she'd ever thought starting this conversation was a good idea. Resistance was illegal. She was basically telling her parents that she was planning on breaking the law. It was just, well...she didn't want to go behind their backs; it affected them too. If she got caught in the resistance, then her family would be dragged down with her, regardless of whether or not they knew about her actions. They deserved warning. She'd already mentioned that, but as she felt their radiated terseness on the matter she couldn't help but remind herself of it.

"It was actually Del who organised that," she said.

"Del?" her mum repeated dangerously. "Delilah's involved in this too? Do the Moors know?"

"I don't know," Susannah shrugged. "I didn't ask."

"Of course you didn't," her mum muttered, hands throwing up into the air in exasperation. "You don't think, and do you realise you didn't answer the question?"

"What question?" she asked innocently, before relenting at their stressed expressions. "Maybe. I want to find out more at any rate."

The rest of the meal passed in uneasy small talk.

Chapter Three - Extrovertai and Introvertai

Susannah came out of her Elemental Studies class feeling edgy as she hurried to meet Delilah by the front gates of the school. She had a shrunken bag of night stuff with her for when she would be staying round Ripsol Cottage later that night after meeting Krig. Silver Hollow Park, where they were meeting him, was in Lower City, so it would be alright there, but walking back to her house in Middle City could be risky. The Underworld didn't tend to attack Lower City, because it was solely Overworld and so they would be vastly outnumbered the second they stepped into that part of the city. Susannah didn't know how long this meeting was going to last - it could go on until hunting hours – in which case, staying in Lower City was the best for all involved. Delilah was already waiting impatiently when she arrived, an uncharacteristically annoyed expression on his face.

"Finally figured out that this a bad idea?" Susannah muttered, questioningly.

"Nope," Delilah replied, "so come on. We don't want to be late." The blonde skipped ahead, appearing to dismiss her irritation, before spinning round to tell her not to be such a 'slowcoach.' Susannah sighed, picking up her pace reluctantly.

"What's wrong then?" she asked. "You looked annoyed." Delilah bit her lip, before shaking her head.

"It's nothing," she said. There was a moment of silence, before her best friend spoke again. "Mrs Sullivan's just been nagging me about taking Mind Arts again." Every student had their classes at school specifically chosen for them to guarantee minimal interruptions and wasted teaching time. You were only chosen to do subjects that you had the potential to have a high aptitude for. Of course, you could take other electives, of your own choosing, but the main brunt of education was geared towards personalised learning programmes based on a series of tests at the start of every term, which decided placements. Delilah's name had consistently appeared on lists to learn Mind Arts, and her best friend had equally consistently refused to take the class.

"Well," Susannah replied cautiously. "You would be good at it. You understand people." She didn't quite understand the blonde's reluctance – surely any magic possible would be good to learn? Delilah's eyes narrowed.

"Don't you start," she snapped. "I don't like Mind Arts...I mean, telekinesis and stuff is cool, I guess, but I don't want to learn how to compel people into doing what I want, or, or reading their minds! It's horrible. It completely walks over being's rights." Susannah held her hands up in surrender.

"Okay, okay," she said. "Have you told Mrs Sullivan this?"

"Yes! And she still won't back off," Delilah replied miserably. "She's says she's going to put a request in to the board of Governors, to *make* me take her class next year." Susannah grimaced, unsure of what to say. It was rare that a student was forced to take a class, but it did happen.

"You could always go and fail," she offered. "She's pestering you because she thinks you'd be good at it, right? So if you're not, well, she'll leave you alone, won't she?"

Delilah's next words were soft, almost too quiet to hear: "But what if I find I like it?"

Krig was lounging on a park as they approached, magic swirling around him lazily as he watched the ducks.

"Is that him?" Delilah whispered.

"Yes," Susannah said. Delilah's head tilted slightly with

appraisal.

"I think I may know his sister...I've been thinking about it, ever since you said his surname was Carter and he had a sister called Cassandra....well, I know a Cassie Carter. Well, I don't *know* her, I've never spoken with her - but I've seen her around school. She's in the year below." Susannah raised her brows.

"Huh. We'll have to talk to her," she said, walking towards the bench. Delilah pulled a face.

"She seems really shy. She'd probably run away; and don't suggest we should hunt her down and corner her in an empty classroom; the poor girl would have a heart attack!" Krig's head lifted as they drew closer, his notepad and pen disappearing back into his bag.

"Susannah," he greeted. "I was wondering if you were actually going to show." He looked at Delilah, smiling and holding out a hand. "You must be Delilah; it's great to meet you. I assume Susannah has filled you in with what I said when I first met with her?"

"Hi," Delilah said, a little nervously, "and yeah, she has. I hope you don't mind me, er, organising this." Krig shook his head, waving a dismissive hand.

"Shadow, no. Not at all. I wish more beings were like you - capable of taking some initiative." Delilah smiled back, tentatively. "Sit down," Krig invited, inclining his head to the bench. "I don't bite."

They exchanged glances, before sitting down on either side of him. He studied them both for a moment, solemnly. "I know you have questions, and I will happily answer them as I believe that's the simplest way of conducting this, but first I must ask you take a secrecy ward. I have everyone involved in the resistance, member or potential recruit regardless, take one. It's standard procedure." Susannah could understand his reasoning; of course he couldn't let them walk around with their minds blaring out details of the resistance to anyone with a Mind Arts capability, but she remained wary to some stranger fiddling about with her head. Delilah, however, seemed fascinated due to her Psychology class (also taken by Mrs Sullivan.) Psychology was different to Mind Arts, its twin branch of study, in that it was all about understanding other people rather than having any active influence on them. It was passive and largely theoretical, where Mind Arts was the offensive and practical side of the art. Political Magic was similar, a cousin if you wanted to continue the familial analogy, twin to Sociology as it focussed on large groups rather than the individual like Mind Arts and Psychology.

"Extrovertai or Introvertai?" her best friend asked. Krig's eyes lit up.

"Psychology or Mind arts?" he returned. Delilah's features darkened for the briefest moment at mention of the latter study.

"Psychology," she said. Krig nodded, his delight making him appear even more boyish.

"It's an Extrovertai ward," he replied. Susannah stared on in confusion. She took a warding class, but that was focussed on physical magical warding, as opposed to mental barriers or secrecy wards. Krig glanced at her, noting her lack of comprehension as the non-Psychology student in the conversation. "An Extrovertai secrecy ward is one that is focussed on keeping other people out, rather than an Introvertai ward which is all about the individual keeping the information in. It's based on the willingness of the person taking the ward, as opposed to the intent of the warder. Both types of ward use a fluctuating amount your own magic to keep running; more if the information is being directly sought," he explained. Susannah couldn't help but find that reassuring.

"So you're not just going to messing around inside my mind then?" she laughed weakly. Krig shook his head, smiling.

"No, considering the secrecy ward is what's allowing me to trust you with information, it wouldn't be very fair of me to demand immediate trust to perform the Introvertai ward when you know nothing about me, or to force it upon you unwillingly like the Carmel brothers would. Does that mean you'll agree to it?" he questioned. Susannah considered for a moment, looking at Delilah for guidance. Her best friend smiled at her.

"An Extrovertai secrecy ward won't harm you," she said, "and it's only as binding to you as you make it," the blonde paused, looking at Krig. "Surely that would maximise the possibility of a traitor? A person could go straight to Marco Carmel and tell him everything, so long as they were speaking on their own accord rather than having the information forced out of them by magical means?"

"Yes," Krig said. "It does, but the resistance wouldn't be very successful if I couldn't trust my members not to betray me on the first instance they could. Case point, the Werewolf Rebellions-"

"-Yeah," Susannah nodded. "We know the story." Krig inclined his head in acknowledgement.

"So, will you both take the secrecy ward?"

A half hour later, with the slightest headache of pressure (which she was assured would soon fade) the secrecy ward was complete and binding. It was...strange. Her mind felt cocooned, safe. She was told she would get used to that too, and would eventually be unaware of the ward even being there. Krig's features were showing a trace of exhaustion from the sudden and detailed expenditure of magic, but also contentment at having got it out of the way. They'd moved to a more secluded section of the park, which Susannah and Krig had both warded to their satisfaction. Delilah didn't take warding.

"If you're okay with it," Krig said, "I have asked a friend of mine, Joel, to come along. Like I told you, Susannah, he normally introduces the New Recruits, so he might be able to explain things better than me. Can I tell him to come?" They both nodded, warily, as Krig sent a quick message on his communicon. "He'll be here in about five minutes, but feel free to start. I'll answer your questions to the best of my ability."

"What do you actually do?" Delilah asked immediately. "You're not militant, are you?"

"No," Krig said. "Not currently. I believe there is more than enough war in this city with the street gangs without us adding to it with extremist riots. We're kind of at an information gathering and recruiting stage at the moment, though we do occasionally have 'missions'. Missions vary in their purpose, but they're normally defensive-offensive to prevent the Underworld from gaining access to more power over us. As I've already told Susannah," Krig looked at Delilah, "the resistance's ultimate aim is to gain equal rights for the Overworld. The difficulty is, of course, that we can't afford to be largely public and do marches or anything like that. We would be annihilated instantly. Again," he smiled thinly, "see the Werewolf rebellion."

"So you don't do anything?" Susannah questioned, disappointed.

"Did I say that?" he countered. "We just don't do it publicly. We send proposals to Carmel pretty much constantly, though I'm not sure how much good those do. However, privately, we work on gaining a lot of allies and undermining

Carmel's base of operations. The Demon Lord and his ancestors have ruled for centuries and are the main pillar upholding the segregation and the hierarchy since they came into power; people are used to them and frankly, regarding Marco Carmel, they either adore him or fear him too much to speak up, as illustrated by the dramatic decrease in hostility and resistance. I'm rambling...Joel can probably explain this more succinctly," Krig shook his head. "The point is, if we can weaken the Carmel hold and thus the Underworld hold on the country, the Overworld population are going to see the situation for what it really is and rise. There are more of us than there are of them, due to their slower aging cycles. The Overworld can overpower the Underworld...we just need to get the rest of the Overworld to break out of their terror and complacency to actually do that and stand up for themselves and their rights."

"Which is where recruiting, and hence forth spreading the message of the resistance comes in," Susannah realised.

"Yes," Krig smiled. Delilah frowned slightly.

"How do you know it won't exacerbate the situation? Like with the Werewolves? They probably started out the same as you but they ended up aiming for supremacy, and then...well, bottom of the food chain."

"I'm not going to lie," Krig said. "There's no guarantee that this won't explode into something far different than I started it out as, but surely even that is better than never trying at all?" Delilah appeared pensive.

In the following pause, another boy entered their section of the park, looking around him. Susannah recognised him from Knight Street. He was hazel haired and hazel eyed, with a broad physique and a smattering of freckles. Krig smiled, beckoning the boy over. They looked to be about the same age. This had to be Joel. Her guess was confirmed when Krig introduced them.

"Susannah, Delilah, this is Joel, Joel McCann. He's in charge of new recruits. Joel, this is Susannah Skelsby and Delilah Moor, potential new recruits. Hopefully."

"Hey," Joel nodded, regarding them both curiously, holding out a hand to shake. "Pleasure. They got the secrecy ward, boss?"

"Of course," Krig said, raising a brow at the other boy, who shrugged, sitting down.

"Sorry," Joel said to them both. "Had to check." He looked at Krig again. "So, how are you doing this?"

"Basic question and answer model," Krig replied, appearing a tad amused. "I have seen you with new recruits before; I'm not completely incompetent, as you should know." Krig turned to them. "Joel was one of my first recruits."

"And honestly, boss, I'm surprised you're not dead," Joel retorted dryly, albeit fondly. "The problem is," he addressed them once more, "that Krig here gets too fanatical where his resistance is involved. Normally, he's painstaking with his security measures, but I dare say he came across you guys and got a tad over-excited with the possibilities. Hence, your rather unorthodox introduction to our cause. I'm sure he's told you that we normally work differently. So, questions?"

"How is the resistance set up?" Susannah asked after a moment. "Do you have people for specific purposes, or is it all a bit of an everyone does everything, interchangeable type of thing?"

"Specific purposes," Joel said. Krig seemed happy to sit back and let Joel do the talking as he observed. "We have four different sectors, to use the word loosely because there aren't that many of us, about eleven altogether. There's the Entry Sector, the New Recruits Sector, which is my sector, the Tactical Advance sector and Research. Each Sector has a Sector Leader, and they report back to Krig during meetings. Does that make sense so far?" They nodded. "The Entry Sector works on finding ways into Anzarkledea, the Demon Lord's mansion, and wherever else we may need to go. Despite their name, they also try and find ways out...if things should ever go wrong. We call it the E Sector for short." He paused to give them a chance to ask further questions. When they were silent, he continued again. "Then there's my sector, the NR, New Recruits Sector. As you can probably guess from the title, we deal with recruiting. In the normal way of doing things, we would scout around for potential members - beings who show sympathy or leaning towards out way of thinking."

"Troublemakers," Susannah smirked.

"Basically," Krig agreed. Joel shook his head, shooting his boss a chiding look and Susannah a contemplative one.

"No, not troublemakers," he corrected, "but people with the right attitude. If they have that, then we will proceed to make contact and spend some time around them to get a handle on their personalities and do some research into their history. If we decide that they seem like the type who would be trustworthy and interested in joining, we'll ask them to take a secrecy ward and have this type of question and answer conversation. If they decide to join then my sector will also been in charge of helping the recruits, in this case the two of you, assimilate into the resistance and pick the sector they'd be interested in working with. This process can take varying lengths of time. If they don't want to join, we wipe their memory."

"...you wipe their memory?" Delilah questioned. "And that doesn't...do any damage or anything?"

"A bit of confusion and blank spots in the memory, but nothing more serious than that," Krig replied. "We're very careful, of course, and you can understand why it's necessary."

"Yeah," Susannah nodded, in agreement. "But how do you know it wouldn't go...wrong?"

"Because we're good at what we do, and, honestly, it's not like letting them keep their memories and simply trusting them is a viable option," Krig returned, eyebrows raised. "We're risking our lives every second we spend resisting, a little memory loss is the best for everyone involved, unless you have another solution? An Introvertai Ward is potentially dangerous too." They were both quiet for a moment, exchanging glances, before Susannah gestured for the explanations to continue.

"The next sector," Joel explained, "is the Tactical Advance sector, the TA. They'll probably tell you in their own words what they do when you meet them, so I'll keep it brief, but basically they're like our strategists. They try and figure out what areas or beings it would be the most beneficial for us to target or recruit, amongst other things." Susannah's opened her mouth to speak, but Delilah got there first.

"What do you do then?" she asked Krig. Joel laughed, replying:

"Krig runs the meeting, takes the final call on decisions - he can technically veto the TA, but very rarely does - finds new meeting places and makes sure that they are secure and appropriate for a meeting, he also takes the lead if we're ever doing field work. Basically, he keeps everyone working together and the ship running smoothly. If any of us have a problem in the sector, then we go to him. He's like the glue;

keeps all the different pieces of the resistance linked together."

"Aw, Joel, you're going to make me blush," Krig teased. Joel rolled his eyes.

"Shut up boss," he said; a little pink. "The last sector is Research. You can probably guess what that involves, it's really quite self-explanatory." Both her and Delilah absorbed for a moment.

"What's the protocol if someone gets caught?" Susannah asked. "What's your security?" Delilah picked up, asking: "Yeah, like, with people's families, do they know about the resistance? Are they allowed to know?"

"I know you have the secrecy ward thingy, but what's the other stuff?" Susannah finished, with a glance at Delilah.

"In regards to your question about family, that depends on the family in question...similar process as with the recruits," Joel said. "If they're the type of family with the right, supportive attitude than no problem, presuming that they too take a security or ward and don't have a compromising job or position in society. Though, you should proceed with caution unless sharing is absolutely necessary. However, if your parents are Carmel supporters, like a few of our members' parents are, then don't tell them. They must not know. They can love you to the end of the earth but you cannot tell them. If you're not sure which of these your family fall into, keep quiet." Delilah's brow furrowed.

"No, I meant if we get caught, what's your protocol for protecting our families from getting dragged along for the ride?" she asked. Joel looked at Krig for help.

"There is no official protocol," Krig told them quietly. "All I can offer is that you try not to get caught and a promise that I'll do the best I can to protect them. However, if you have any ideas on how to improve that security measure, I would appreciate them, whether you join or not." Susannah swallowed slightly. Delilah's face was white. "This is an illegal resistance," Krig continued. "I'm not going to tell you it's not dangerous, or promise you that it's all going to be fun and easy going. In fact, I will promise you that it will probably be the opposite. If you get caught you are liable to face life-imprisonment or death."

"As for other security measures," Joel took their heavy silence as an opportunity to continue. "We wear face distorters when we go out as a resistance and there's a high chance of getting caught. Obviously, we can't wear them every time, as while most the Underworld don't have any magic themselves, they can still sense when magic is being used in glamours or wards. We also keep communicons on us constantly, and never go alone when we're doing assignments and ward all of our bases heavily."

"Okay," Susannah said. "Thank you for answering our questions...but, I need to think. Clearly, I would have to be suicidal to join you," she added helplessly, trying to ignore the part of her brain that was seriously considering it. Krig arched his eyebrows at her, challenge in his gaze, while Joel looked just a tiny bit insulted.

"Thanks," Delilah said, smiling, making a more diplomatic effort. "We'll get back to you sometime...?"

Chapter Four- Chaos Magic

All through school that day, the last day of school before the summer holidays, Susannah felt restless and couldn't concentrate. It was all his fault. Krig's words just kept running through her head, again and again. He was an alright guy, really. At this point she was pretty certain that he was genuinely trying to recruit her for a resistance, rather than a street gang or something similar. She wasn't sure if that was any better. She tapped her pen against her notepad, idly watching the clock as her Warding teacher lectured them on minor and major magical wards. Minor wards tended to be stronger and more durable, but they were small and couldn't be used to ward buildings, areas or more than one person at a time. Major wards were the opposite, shaky, requiring more power to uphold. If done well, they were incredibly effective. Did the resistance use major or minor wards? Or both? She scribbled down another paragraph of notes, wishing Mrs Wyman would just let them try the magic out already. She did like learning how the magic she was using worked, it was absolutely fascinating, but she preferred actually casting and experimenting with the magic. She sighed. It sometimes seemed like the teachers ran over everything at least three times before even letting them draw their magic in the classroom. It made her restless. It did slightly depend on the class of course, some were better than others. Nonetheless, she was pleased to hear the bell signifying break, and the end of class.

Her last lesson of the day, and the term, was Chaos Magic. Chaos had to be her favourite subject by far - it was truly challenging, and let her push her magic to the limit unlike any of her other classes did. Duelling did so, sometimes, along with the more complicated tasks in Elemental studies, but generally the magically practical side of school was tediously easy. That sounded really big headed. She didn't find all the theories and non-practical parts of class effortless or anything, there were loads of people better than her in that respect, she wasn't particularly good with theory. Using magic just came easily for her - well, most of it did. She couldn't heal to save her life, and her emotions were too untamed for Pure Arts. Pure Arts was Delilah's favourite subject, it was all about emotion-fuelled magic. It could teach you how to harness anger to explode objects, keep hope to maintain a ward...it was really awesome. She would have liked to be able to do it. Some people considered it to be a soft option, because emotions were readily available to everyone, but the hard part was controlling them to manipulate the magic safely. The highest level of Pure Arts included Morphicism, shape-shifting, but it was such a rare art that less than 1% of the population had the ability to do it.

Chaos magic was still the best though. Her classroom was large, though it held only a few people. It was rare to find a being with an aptitude for Chaos magic. It was a complex, immensely dangerous and powerful art that was based on the caster's ability to draw wild ambient magic (magic from a person's surroundings as opposed to from their internal magical core) and control it. In that way, it was a bit like her Elemental studies. However, elemental magic required far less finesse as it was more like pushing and expending your own magic to manipulate the ambient magic of the elements to get your desired result. Chaos magic didn't use the casters own magic, and didn't require the caster to mould the ambient magic with their own - as elemental magic did. Chaos magic involved taking the ambient magic from the surroundings and adding it to your own existing power and using it in that way. You didn't even have to touch your own magic reserves in Chaos if you didn't want to; you could fight entirely with ambient magic. Due to this, Susannah also lost the edge she had in her other classes, because it wasn't her own magic she was using. In Chaos, the playing field was always even and she loved it. The danger of not having an easy victory was thrilling...although the desire for danger was probably unhealthy. There wasn't a single other branch of magic that worked in the same way. It was amazing.

There were only two other students in her class, barring her teacher - Viridian Sanchez. Viridian was a sixty three year old, tiny, sprite of a woman with mocha coloured skin and dark brown, cropped hair and many wrinkles like a crumpled piece of parchment. She was extremely talented and strict, formidable to cross and liable to send you flying across the room onto your ass if you annoyed her. She was awesome, the best teacher Susannah had ever had. They all held her with the utmost respect. Susannah was the youngest in the class, the 'baby' of the group. It didn't mean any of them went easy on her though, far from it. Magically, age really didn't matter. Magic developed to its full potential between the ages of thirteen and twenty one, before settling. Before that age, magic was pretty wild, so school was all about learning basic control. Evanna Grace, the other girl in the class, was seventeen, with coal black locks that cascaded down her back and over her hazel eyes. She was very big on the gothic scene and tended to wear copious amounts of layers to hide her slim figure. As a nymph she was quite pretty beneath her heavy makeup and haughty 'bite me' attitude. From what Susannah had gathered, Jasper had quite a crush on her. Jasper Gray was the eldest of the three of them, a shy eighteen year old about to finish school, with a wicked sense of humour under his initial awkwardness. He was a soft spoken werewolf, with light blonde hair and luminous pale blue eyes. She got on okay with the two of them, all things considered.

"Hey," she greeted quietly, walking into the hall. It was quite large, because it was dangerous to try and contain Chaos, with a large glass domed roof and a small door leading to Mrs Sanchez' office.

"Hello," Jasper murmured, regarding her. Susannah could see the silver mark of a full moon shining in his gaze, as was characteristic to his variation. There were two ways to identify a werewolf (aside from seeing them transform of course). If someone caught any type of light on the eyes of a werewolf they turned luminous and secondly, they had a full moon shining in the place of their pupil. It was an old saying that eyes were the window to the soul and that was shown in almost every variation but her own. Humans were weird; they had no distinctive eye colour or characteristic. They seemed to be a bit of a mix of other things, it was why they were at the bottom of the 'intelligent creature' food chain. Well, they were until the Werewolf rebellion - another reason why resistance couldn't possibly be such a good idea as Krig made it sound... but she wouldn't think of that now. She refused. She had to concentrate.

The lesson started a moment later.

"Welcome, Jasper, Evanna, Susannah..." Viridian stated, sweeping out of her office to stand before them. "As it is the last lesson of the year, I thought we would do a review of the last couple of weeks. You may use whatever you have learned in that time, but nothing else. Focus. Your aim is to be the last one standing."

"You mean you want us to duel?" Evanna's face lit up. Jasper turned a little paler.

"Yes," Viridian said simply. "Practical application is the only way to improve and evaluate your current level in this subject. There are no ordered examinations in Chaos." That was why Chaos was so much better than Warding class; there were barely any theory lessons, it was focussed on the magic she was actually good with. Viridian had a hands-on approach to learning. For a moment, they all just stood there, thinking about what action to take, a little uncertain on whether they were supposed to have started or not. Oh well, better to ask for forgiveness than permission, right? Susannah started to concentrate. Almost immediately she felt her awareness start to tingle as the ambient magic swept over her - making impressions wherever it went. She could smell it, like salty sea air, cut grass, damp earth, darkness, light...so many smells she didn't even think were smells, but she could somehow classify. Vanilla, rain, Jasper's cologne...leather, detergent - everything in the city, all the magic, blurring together. She could taste it on her tongue, feather light and sweet, spicy, tangy... She sucked in a calming breath. In a battle, she would have been dead by now. Chaos was rarely used in duelling or fighting, it just took so much skill and concentration that you would probably be shot down before you found the right state of mind. It was ridiculously difficult and frustrating. Susannah had found that it was just so much easier just to send her own magic out and forcibly twist the world and the ambient magic to how she wanted it to be. It was much easier to find some semblance of order, rather than just let herself drift like a leaf caught on the wind, to let the boundaries on her magic that she spent so much time building disappear and go. It took a lot more control to fall into chaos than it did to remain in order. You had to have the right mind-set...otherwise you just might not find your way out of the magic again. She could hear the crashing of great waves, the whisper of the wind, the crackle of lightning...she could see colours. RedWhiteBlueBlackPurpleGoldBrownGreen...all the colours of the rainbow shifting under her eyelids. With a slight gasp, she opened her eyes again, focussing on the chair behind Jasper and lifting, before swinging at his head. He ducked instinctively, transforming the chair into a vine and shooting it back in her direction. It twisted around her ankle, yanking until she was on the floor. The vine crept over to Evanna, who transfigured it into a bunch of flowers. Susannah kicked the vine off, leaping to her feet once more. She concentrated again, aware of Viridian watching them all impassively with a notepad in her hand. Her competitive streak was rearing its head. The ambient magic swept over her once more and she struggled to control it -- time to try something a little more complex. She directed most of the magic to the floor, setting it on fire, which was the easy part. Then, feeling a tad nervous, she directed the rest at herself simultaneously. If this failed, things could go very wrong. She ordered the magic to levitate, raising herself up just as the flames engulfed the classroom floor below. Leaping back with a cry of shock, Jasper and Evanna exchanged glances, before both using chaos to send out water from their hands, to douse the fire. Susannah was aware of a sick realisation that if she lost control now she was going to plummet and burn. Still, she focussed, feeling her own magic straining for release but dutifully ignoring it, and went for the bench again. Jasper was out. Evanna immediately changed tactics, firing on her. Unable to maintain her previous use of ambient magic, and defend herself at the same time, she dropped. The flames died out as her own magic shot out, halting her one inch before she smacked into the ground. In her distraction, Evanna quickly had her disarmed with a burst energy that knocked her unconscious. It was over.

She awoke presently, sore, exhausted, but ultimately no worse for wear. Evanna was looking smug, her arms folded as she surveyed her. Susannah wasn't going to hear the end of this for months! Jasper was sitting on the bench, holding an icepack to his head and looking disgruntled at having been the first out.

"How are you feeling, Susannah?" Viridian questioned, peering at her features with a clinical concern. "Do you need the nurse? How many fingers am I holding up?"

"Three," she replied. "And I'm fine Miss, thanks." Her teacher nodded once, standing up and offering her a hand. She took it, pulling herself up with a little embarrassment. She couldn't believe Evanna had beaten her!

"Congratulations Evanna," Mrs Sanchez praised. "You may pick a lollipop." Viridian summoned a jar, holding it out to the gothic girl.

"Thanks Miss," Evanna said, selecting a strawberry flavoured drumstick. Viridian nodded once, before studying them all and reading cursively over her notes.

"Susannah, well done for taking the initiative to start first...." she began. "Evanna, you were rather late to start, waiting until you were attacked to get involved. While this can sometimes be useful in letting your enemies finish each other off, it is more often detrimental as you are not using their distraction to your advantage, your conjuration of the flowers was also rather passive. In a battle situation, you would have been dead. It has been said that the best defence is a good offence…nonetheless, you rectified this when you finally realised it would be more prudent to target Susannah, instead of wasting your time combating her spell. Jasper, a little disappointing, but you clearly have a good control of the chaos magic you do use, which is very promising. Susannah -" Viridian frowned fractionally. "That last move of yours was particularly inspired, but I feel I must press that it was very risky of you. I do remember distinctively saying to only use only what we learned in class. Also, Susannah, regarding Jasper's vine, you should have reacted instead of just letting it pull you down. Concentrate." Their teacher quietened, regarding the three of them. "However, over all, I feel you have all made extremely good progress. Well done. Next term we will be switching from external manipulation of the chaotic arts to a more introspective form of the control." Viridian glanced at her, before checking her watch. "We have about five minutes left of the lesson, so I'll let you go early. Enjoy your summers - remember to practice." Sensing the dismissal, they all moved to grab their stuff. "Susannah, if you could stay behind for a moment." Susannah closed her eyes for a moment, suppressing a sigh. Jasper hesitated a tad. He normally walked home with her; it was dangerous to walk the streets alone too much. It was always safer to travel in pairs…if you were Overworld, anyway.

"Go ahead," she instructed, flashing a smile. "I'll be fine." Jasper didn't wait, hurrying to catch up with Evanna. Susannah almost rolled her eyes. She was sure the werewolf was all too happy to have some alone time with the other girl. The beginnings of the smirk formed on her features at the thought, however it vanished as she turned to face her teacher.

At first, Viridian simply focussed on repairing the classroom to its original state, before giving Susannah her attention. "Am I in trouble?" she asked, resigned. Viridian gestured towards the seats (for the rare theory lesson) at the end of the hall. Susannah dropped into the suggested seat, suddenly nervous.

"No, don't worry," Mrs Sanchez said softly. Not sure if she should be concerned by that response or not, Susannah waited in silence. "What happened at the end there?" her teacher questioned, continuing when she didn't speak. "By all rights, you should have won...even if your methods were against the rules." Viridian arched her brows sternly, causing Susannah to grimace.

"Well, technically, you said what we'd learned in the last couple of weeks....you didn't specify that we had to cover it in class," she explained hopefully. Her teacher merely snorted at that, but thankfully didn't look too annoyed.

"Regardless, that wasn't what I was referring to," she said. Susannah frowned, tilting her head. Confusion began to trickle through her mind, stinging at her instincts which warned against being in ignorance over anything. Seeing her uncomprehending expression, Viridian elaborated. "Your magic started acting up." Oh.

"Sorry," she said. Her fingers suddenly seemed a whole lot more interesting than they had been a few seconds ago.

"I wasn't asking for an apology, merely an explanation."

"I-okay, um. I just...automatic reaction," she shrugged. "My magic didn't really like being inactive for the sake of Chaos magic, not when I was being attacked. Well, not attacked but..." she resisted the urge to shrug again, keeping her body still instead. Mrs Sanchez was quiet.

"How would you feel about some extra Chaos lessons over

the holidays?" she asked finally. Susannah's eyes widened.
"With you, miss?" That was a stupid question. Who else
would it be with? "I - that would be brilliant...er, why?"
Viridian stared at her, seriously.

"As I'm sure you are aware, Susannah, your magic is rather
more powerful than the norm." Right, of course. It would be
that.

"I don't want favouritism, miss." She rose to her feet,
grabbing her bag.

"Susannah, let me finish." Her teacher's calm voice gave her
pause. "I have no interest in giving you favouritism.
Although this has something to do with your power, what
I'm more concerned with is your control." Susannah looked
round again, intrigued, her curiosity piqued.

"My control?"

"You have issues with your control. Your magic is
instinctual; when you feel panicked, or threatened, or
angry, your magic reacts to your emotions...and from what
I've noticed, it reacts rather militantly. It tries to
incapacitate the source of your distress." Susannah
stiffened.

"Is that a bad thing?" she asked.

"Not necessarily...all magic is instinctual; however, most
people learn to control it." She could control her magic!
That was a primary school lesson. Her aura flittered, and
Viridian paused, seeming to guess what she was thinking.
"I'm not saying you can't. From what I've seen and heard in
the staffroom it is more than clear that you walk around
with permanent restraints imposed upon yourself....but, as I
mentioned, your magic is unusually potent. You have more
magic to control than most people. You're control is
impeccable in everyday life Susannah, but in any form of
battle situation, as we saw today, you lose that control."

Susannah considered this, wrapping her magic around herself defensively. Cold chilled her insides.

"So what are you suggesting?" she questioned finally.

Viridian leaned forward.

"Let me teach you how to control that magic. That fighting reaction of yours is indispensable, but if you don't learn how to manage it properly it's going to be lethal. Even if you don't mean it to be, to other people if you lose control and cause more damage than you intended, and ultimately even yourself if it turns on you."

Lethal...

"Okay then, miss," she agreed, not giving herself too much time to talk herself out of it. "I'm in. Thank you."

Viridian nodded, before gesturing that she could leave.

Susannah's head was spinning again; thoughts of resistance entwined with Viridian's words. Lethal. Was her magic really that dangerous? Sure, it could get a little out of hand at times, but that didn't mean she would accidentally kill someone like Viridina suggested...would it? Unbidden, a memory of her first time as prey rose in mind. She'd lost control then. It was the only reason she was alive, her magic had just exploded. What had happened to her attackers then? She couldn't remember. It had been such a long time ago, and she'd been so young...all she could truly recall was a sick sense of terror, of feeling her life being drained out of her mouth and the puncture wounds in her neck. She shuddered. Where was Delilah when Susannah needed her? Her best friend would know what the right thing to do was, or at the very least she would be willing to listen as Susannah ranted about the resistance and her fears. She cast a time charm as she walked out the school gates. It was starting to get late. It wasn't hunting time yet, but the countdown had begun. Talking to Viridian had taken longer than she expected. She took a shortcut through Silver Hollow Park, quickening her pace. Now would not be a good time to be caught outside by the Underworld. She could probably defend herself if they came looking for a meal, but she was tired. She shouldn't have expended so much energy in Chaos, it weakened her. There weren't many beings, Overworld, on the streets anymore - not in Middle City. In Lower City, everything would have been different. Beings would still be hanging out on with their friends, revelling in the sunshine or making plans for barbecues. The Underworld tended not to go there because of how much they would be outnumbered, thus incapable of relaxing and feeding properly. In Middle City though, most Overworld beings had tucked themselves away at home, or at friend's houses with plans for movie nights safe inside their warded houses. It left the city feeling rather eerie, like a ghost town. She almost expected tumbleweed to come blowing down the street like in an old western and there wasn't even any tumbleweed in the country. Was that a noise? Susannah looked up sharply, to see a dark shadow crouched on the top of a building, watching her. Oh no. She instantly drew her magic, but another shadow smacked her into the glass of the Grocer's before she could react. Pain exploded in her head. Her heart stopped.

Crap. She'd definitely used too much energy.

Chapter Five - Snapping Point

"Well, well, well, what do we have here?" a voice drawled. Susannah stiffened, picking herself up from the ground. She noted with unease that she was completely surrounded, backed up against the shops. There were three of them; all male, two vampires and a demon. She drew her magic again, instantly, only to have her arms yanked behind her back and immobilised in one quick blur of movement. She swore under her breath, hating the feeling of helplessness that was starting to creep on her like an insidious poison. "Try anything and you're dead," the voice hissed warningly. Susannah closed her eyes for a brief moment, carefully considering her options. She had no doubt that her new found associates would, and could, follow through on that threat. Easily. The wicked speed of vampires guaranteed that; she could be as powerful as she wanted but when they were already this close there wasn't much she could do if they were to snap her neck. Magic was only good for when your enemy was out of range and didn't already have you, hands precisely placed to kill you in under a second. If they were coming at her, she could work it. If they were trying to capture her, she could get away and out of their grip. If they had no problem murdering her when she was already in their hold - she was screwed. How had she not noticed them coming up behind her? She hated her life, and her failure to anticipate the attack tasted bitter on her tongue. It was before-Hunting Hours, they shouldn't have been doing this...but not every Underworld obeyed these restrictions, and punishment only came if there were witnesses willing to step up. There rarely were.

"What do you want?" she asked coldly. She needed to distract them. If she could distract them than she was pretty certain that she could have them on the floor whimpering at the thought of coming anywhere near her. One of the vampire's eyes widened with shock, before narrowing into molten gold slits.

"You can't talk to us like that, human," he spat. "You would do well to show some respect to your superiors."

"My superiors?" she arched her brows, forcing lightness into her tone, even as her stomach plummeted. "Can you introduce me to them?" She stifled a moan as she felt a foot smash down on her ankle with a sickening sound. That had been a stupid thing to say. She buckled slightly, a hiss of breath escaping from between her teeth. The grip on her arms tightened painfully, half to keep her upright and half to inflict further harm. She could feel an arm digging into her ribs, the definite stirrings of panic in her gut now. Some primal instinct in the back of her mind screamed at her to not to antagonise them further, recognising the very real danger in the situation. They were the predators, she was the prey. Her heart raced.

The demon smiled.

"Sure, we couldn't say no to such a pretty little face, could we boys?" An ugly laughter stained the air. Her magic prickled slightly, but she viciously constrained it. Shame at her own cowardice poisoned her insides like rancid milk; she was Susannah Skelsby, the one who never stopped fighting. She shouldn't be so scared and powerless - so useless and pathetic. She should fight back, even if it meant dying, but Shadow she didn't want to die. She almost threw up at the quick succession of strikes to her stomach, and could have sworn it was already bruised. "I'm Theron," the demon grinned sharply when she had caught her breath. "Theron Kerr, and these here are Cutler and Ordell." Ordell was the one holding her and Cutler was watching her with a malicious set to his features. His fangs were already starting to elongate in anticipation of his meal.

"I'm charmed," she deadpanned, her head whipped to the side a moment later, her cheek stinging as Theron slapped her, hard.

"We didn't say you could speak," Cutler growled. She bit her tongue, slowly straightening her neck. She could feel her heart lashing like a whip against her chest, as if her rib cage had done it a personal insult. Blood trickled down the corner of her mouth, tasting metallic. Their eyes had darkened at the sight of it, growing hungrier and more alien. At least getting killed by a Dark Angel would have felt enjoyable; they would have stolen the emotions that they fed on through kisses instead of simply ripping her throat out. It would have been horrible, worse than having her throat ripped out, but she wouldn't think it so at the time. She swallowed thickly....not that being anyone's dinner was particularly appealing.

"Enough of this," Theron said briskly. "We can teach the human a lesson later. I'm starving." She stiffened as the demon took a step closer to her, exposing her jugular with one hand, gripping her chin tightly, nails digging into her skin with a burning sensation. "Who wants to go first?" Susannah knew that she had to act soon, before she was too weak from blood loss to do so, but Ordell's and Theron's hands were too close to her throat for comfort - there was a still a very strong possibility that they would snap her head like a twig if she even drew her magic. Despite knowing it would only make it easier for them, she could feel her blood surging beneath the surface of her skin with anxiety. They were taller than her; they all were, and the exposing of her throat only served to emphasise that as she was forced to look up at them, and made her feel even more vulnerable. She could feel her magic buzzing, despite her best efforts, but determinedly kept it buried deep beneath the surface so that they wouldn't notice it. He leaned closer to her, his breath honeyed, coppery and hot on her face. "Who knows, little girl, this might be the best thing that ever happened in your small pitiable life," Cutler hissed. She highly doubted it. The next second, fangs had sunk agonisingly into her vein, as easily as slicing through warm butter, blood being pulled out with the most disgusting sucking sound. Her restraints snapped.

Susannah felt her magic bubble to the surface completely, as she temporarily transformed the blood at her throat into something toxic, poisonous, to get them off her. Her mind was wild with panic, and Cutler reared back, a repulsed grimace on his features, a choking sound issuing from his stained mouth as he clutched his throat and promptly spat out. Her blood splattered against the pavement, she felt nauseous at the sight of it.

"The human tried to kill me!" Cutler howled, enraged. Their eyes immediately turned murderous at the blatant breaking of official hunting regulations.

An Overworld variation was not supposed to fight against a hunting party, willingly offering their blood or emotions for consumption. In turn, a 'donor' should not be killed or permanently damaged from the meal. Nor, should the donor be turned into a vampire during the process.

They immediately lunged at her, a flurry of movement and flickering shadows, and she blasted out her magic to try and gain herself some fighting space. Her ankle crunched sickeningly.

There were two types of vampire; the born and the bitten. The born were higher upon leech hierarchy, and the bitten were often looked down upon as inferior, and, as such, most vampires were born. A vampire bite alone was not enough to make a being turn, their creator had to inject venom and exchange blood – but one thing all vampires shared was their pride. They were incredibly vain creatures, and she'd just badmouthed them!

Susannah lashed out automatically as they lunged again, her magic snapping out, teeth tearing at her skin, not drawing blood anymore, just intending to wound. They were fast, but her magic was surging now, spinning around her like a whip, inflicting as many injuries as she took in response. She could feel the poison in her blood weakening her, burning her, but recklessly maintained the bizarre sensation to keep them at bay. If they properly started feeding, she wouldn't stand a chance, quickly drained. She missed her first few shots as they quickly dodged, panicked, before she forced herself to get a grip and concentrate. A calm slid over her, any distant sounds seemingly fading away as she focussed her attentions entirely on her opponents. Cutler, the closest, fell first when she successfully sent a blasting hex at his knees. He buckled, screaming with pain and Ordell spun to try and help him. She took his split second distraction to transform his hands into spoons, only to be smacked across the face with one of them. She hit the far wall, head throbbing, tears springing automatically to her eyes. She sent out another blast of magic, scrambling to her feet, setting Ordell's clothes on fire as he shrieked and struggled to put it out and promptly fled. Theron paused as the screams died out, warily, eyeing her with more caution than before. Susannah was breathing heavily, her vision tainted by black spots, but held firm, not allowing herself to show her weakness. Blood was gushing from her numerous wounds, and Shadow, normally they wouldn't even have gotten close enough to scratch her! She was off her game and not exactly in the best situation either. She pushed everything to the side for later analysis, calling her magic to mute the pain and warning signals of her body. She felt lightheaded; it was probably the blood loss. She straightened her spine, acting as if this was no bother to her, knowing a display of confidence was more likely to guarantee her safety. The Underworld weren't used to their prey challenging them.

"My father could have you in court for this," he spat. "You *stupid* human, I should kill you."

"Second time lucky?" she returned mockingly. His eyes narrowed to slits. Her tone steeled, her jaw clenched, partially to hide her pain. "Take a hint from your friends and *go*," she ordered. "Or you'll be the one dying tonight, or any other night you cross my path for vengeance!"

He stared at her, incredulously, his lips drawn back in a mean snarl, almost white with rage.

"You'll pay for this," he warned, circling her, scooping up a whimpering Ordell. "I've seen that type of wounds on your kind before, girl, you won't last the night, however wily your petty magic tricks are."

"I'd go heal your pet leech. He's got *human* venom in his system – wouldn't want him to get infected by lesser beings!"

She flared her magic, watching him pale.

He was gone a second later, and she almost collapsed in relief. Poison. She turned her magic inwards again, picturing her blood free and clean of anything that shouldn't be there. She prayed it would work, as it was more in the branch of healing magic and, admittedly, she was better at destroying stuff than fixing it.

Then, she stumbled off home.

Susannah felt distinctly nauseous. The world was slipping and sliding beneath her feet, and she felt like the earth would at any minute just split open and she'd fall into a gaping abyss and never come back out. She'd released the block she'd had on her injuries, and now they were rushing on her. Her ears were ringing. Shadow, she couldn't believe she'd let them get the better of her! It was humiliating. Everything hurt. Damn it, how could she walk home like this - her parents would absolutely freak. Stupid gang warfare, stupid hunting; it had to stop. It just had to. They couldn't go on like this, bruised, beaten and perpetually preyed upon. It was wrong. Something had to give. She gritted her teeth, suppressing a whimper. She was so pathetic. She'd gotten overly confident about her magic, so much so that she'd failed to take the exhausting effects of a prolonged use of ambient magic - Chaos - into consideration. How could she have forgotten to consider it? Sure, she'd won relatively easily, but in normal conditions she wouldn't have even got into the situation in the first place. They should never have managed to sneak up on her. She'd just wanted to get home. It probably hadn't been a very good idea to antagonise the Underworld further, but she simply hadn't been able to quell her tongue. They just made her so mad, creeping under her skin with their casual dismissal. It was her own fault; she shouldn't have stayed out so late. She should have got her dad to pick her up, or something. If Jasper had been there, he would have walked with her and the whole situation might have been avoided, but he hadn't been there. Shadow, this sucked. She hated what ifs. She bit back a rough curse as she closed her eyes for a moment, her head spinning. Blood loss. Her skin felt clammy and she no doubt looked like absolute crap. She staggered, reaching out a hand to steady herself against the street wall. She drew her magic, wrenching at with desperate pleads to stop the bleeding of her neck. The crimson flow immediately grew sluggish, before stopping entirely. At least that was one good thing. She breathed a silent sigh of relief that her healing attempts had worked for the second time that night. She normally ended up doing more damage than good; she was too volatile for such a calm, precise form of magic. Damn. She felt like she was going to faint, but she couldn't, not here and not now. It was far too dangerous. Collapsing alone in a battered state was pretty much asking to be murdered and robbed.

"Susannah?" a voice questioned from behind her. She whipped round, her magic lashing out. The sudden movement threw her balance completely off, and she felt herself pitch forwards. A strong pair of hands caught her by her upper arms, steadying her. She winced at the contact. "Holy...what the hell happened?" She looked up wearily. Krig.
"I think I screwed up. Look, it's noth-"
"Don't you dare say it's nothing." His voice was tight and carefully controlled. "Damn it! You look like road kill." She laughed faintly.
"You sure know how to flatter a girl..." He ignored her, his eyes scanning across her injuries. His grip shifted as he abruptly pulled her arm over his shoulders. "What are-"
"You're coming to my place," he said, seeming to guess the question. His tone was blunt, accepting no refusal. "There is absolutely no way I'm letting you walk across the city like this." His gaze paused on the recently closed puncture wounds on her neck, his jaw growing taut. "How much did they take?"

"Not that much. Really, there's no need -" she began.

"No need?" he snapped. "Of course there's a need. Don't be so stupid Susannah." She frowned slightly. He kept interrupting her. "Can you walk?" he asked, his voice growing softer. She nodded, feeling hot tears ridiculously begin to prick at her eyes. The shock was setting in.

"Yeah," she replied. "Yeah, I can."

"Good," he smiled encouragingly. "Just lean on me, okay? That ankle of yours looks pretty shaky."

"I think it's just a sprain," she concluded.

"Let's not take any chances though," he said. "C'mon, I live just round the corner."

"What were you doing out?" she questioned, wincing as they started to move. The ringing in her ears was growing, and the edges of her vision still had suspicious black spots.

"Had a meeting," he glanced at her, a small sly smile curving his lips, before it vanished. "What about you? What's your excuse?"

"I had," she winced as her body jolted with their movement. "I had a Chaos magic class that ran late."

"You take Chaos magic?" he looked impressed. She nodded.

"Yeah, it's my favourite subject. Difficult as hell though."

"I can imagine," he agreed. "Here we are." He slowed to a stop in front of a tiny, red bricked block of flats with a blue door. It looked squashed in its row, all the houses on either side exactly the same but for slight variants in door colour and curtains. Krig fished for his key.

"Won't your roommate mind?" she asked nervously. She suddenly felt very self-conscious about the grime and blood that was caking her person. He shook his head, though his eyes pierced her for a second.

"You know, most people would ask about my parents," he said.

"I'm not most people," she muttered.

"Clearly," he gently eased away his grip to open the door. It took a moment, of shoving and kicking the bottom, but it opened to reveal a dark, thin hallway with several rooms.

"You hacked my computer." Susannah froze. He knew about that? She glanced up to gauge his expression.

"I have no idea what you're talking about," she lied nonchalantly. Krig raised his eyebrows at her, appearing vaguely entertained.

"I'm on the first floor," he said instead, quietly. "Can you make the stairs?"

"Yes," she replied. "Look, are you sure -" He looped her arm over his shoulders once more, lifting most of her weight onto himself.

"I'm sure," he said firmly. "If you insist I'll walk you home once you've cleaned up a bit." She felt heat rising on her cheeks.

"You don't have to, I can -"

"Take care of yourself?" he smiled. "Yeah, you've said, but it would ease my conscience." Maybe so, but it wouldn't ease hers if he got attacked on the way home for being out in Hunting Hours. He shook his head, seeming to guess what she was thinking once more. "Kid, I may not be at your power level, but as the head of a resistance group give me some credit on being able to defend myself." Susannah flushed. Okay, he had a point. It wasn't like he was completely defenceless or anything - he'd survived the first nineteen years of his life after all. Then again, she hadn't thought the Underworld would ever get the jump on her after the first few times. They hadn't for years. She wasn't exactly what you would call the easiest target.

"Sorry," she mumbled. They arrived at the top of the flight of stairs, in front of a door that had the label *Carter, Kriger* stuck in with black block capitals. He opened the door, flicking a set of lights on and leading her in. He immediately shut the door behind him, locked it and slid the bolt across. Susannah could feel her magic tingling, sensing the protective wards surrounding the flat. They were, if she admitted it to herself, quite impressive. The flat was small, with a strip of a kitchen and a lounge that doubled up as bedroom and any other room. There was also another door, opened a crack to show a bathroom. There was a toilet, sink and a shower stall, all crammed in. There was no room to do anything but stand. An old takeout lay on the table at the foot of the bed, surrounding by over spilling, but relatively organised stacks of paper and notepads.

"Sorry about the mess," he apologized, grabbing the takeout and tossing it into the bin.

"It's fine," she said, awkwardly. He cleared some space on the sofa, pushing aside some more papers and books.

"Here," he helped her sit down.

"Thanks." He turned his back to her, pulling two mugs, an icepack and a battered first aid kit out of his cupboards. He set the tea to boil, before making his way over to her.

Ten minutes later, most of the blood and filth had been washed away. He'd lent her one of his shirts, and her own was swirling about in his washing machine. She pressed an icepack uncomfortably to her swollen ankle. He leaned his elbows forward onto his knees, studying her. His mouth opened to speak.

"I should probably call my parents," she said before he could do so. "They're probably worried."

"Of course," he replied. "Do you want to borrow my communicon or -?"

"I've got it, thanks." She pulled her communicon out of her

now tattered school bag. She was just glad that she'd managed to head them off before they really got to it, or to her. For that, at the very least, she was grateful. She dialled the code; her father's face appearing after only two buzzes. "Susannah, is that you?" her dad demanded. She swallowed.

"Hey Dad, yeah, it's me."

"Where are you?" the fear had only somewhat faded from his voice at the confirmation that she was still alive.

"I'm at a...friend's house. You know Krig, I mentioned him?" she glanced at the nineteen year old sitting next to her; he looked faintly amused.

"The res...the one with the club?" her dad asked warily.

"Why?" She could hear her mum talking in the background, her voice an octave too high. "She says she's at that Carter boy's house," her dad explained, presumably to her mother. "Susannah, are you okay?"

"I'm - ah, fine," she said. She saw Krig shoot her a look, but she pointedly ignored him.

"Do you want me to drive over and pick you up?" her dad asked worriedly.

"No, no, it's fine. It's almost Hunting Hours, I'll -"

"-You're not walking home," her dad said sharply. "Not at this time." She winced. Krig was watching her, his features unreadable. "Will you pass me over to your friend?" She froze at the request. "Susannah?"

"Uh, yeah..." she looked away from the orb. "My dad wants to talk to you," she cringed. He held a hand out wordlessly for the communicon.

"Mr Skelsby," he greeted calmly. There was a moment of silence. "She got into a bit of trouble with the Underworld, it's nothing serious." Susannah glared at him for the disclosure. It would only worry her parents further. He

66

glared back. "Yes sir...she can stay here if she wishes, of course, I'd be more than happy to take her home...of course. My pleasure. It was nice talking to you." He handed the communicon back to her.

"Dad?" she questioned.

"Was there something you forgot to mention, you said you were fine?" he demanded. She grimaced.

"I am Dad, really. I've had worse. It's just a scratch," she reassured. He didn't sound completely appeased. "Look, I'll explain when I get home," she said.

"Yes," he agreed. "You will. Tomorrow."

"Tomorrow?" her eyes shot to Krig.

"It's too dangerous to be on the streets now," he said, not sounding remotely happy about it. She nodded nervously. Why did that have to make sense? It wasn't often that she allowed herself to get caught outside after Overworld hours – it was one of the strictest rules they had. She was going to be in so much trouble tomorrow.

"Um, okay. Tomorrow then?"

"Yes. Take care of yourself," he instructed.

"I will," she promised. "You too."

"Goodnight."

"Night." She ended the call, looking at Krig. His gaze didn't waver. "So, um..." she twisted her hands in her lap. "You're, uh, okay with this?" she asked. "I don't want to be any trouble." Her cheeks were flaming with mortification.

"It's no trouble," he assured her. "Really. It's better than getting ripped to pieces out there."

"Are you sure?"

"Yeah, no worries," he dismissed, moving forwards. He took the icepack from her hand. "You were right, it's just a sprain. I'll bandage it just for good measure, and you should probably try and keep off it, but you should be fine." He glanced up, checking she was listening.

"Sure thing boss," she saluted slightly, in a joke. He stared at her for moment, shocked, before grinning, and then turning serious again.

"So what happened to you?" he asked. She shrugged, before closing her eyes with pain and deciding that moving all too much wasn't a good idea. Her ribs felt sore. She could see the concern in his gaze, and shifted uncomfortably. He pushed a couple of painkillers in her direction.

"It's stupid," she muttered finally. "I just forgot how tiring Chaos could be and..." she trailed off.

"You could have died," he noted flatly. She flinched.

"I gathered that, oddly enough," she hissed, before widening her eyes in horror. "Oh, crap, sorry - I didn't mean -"

"It's fine," he said, offering her a wry smile. "Try and be a bit more careful though, okay?"

"Okay," she swallowed. Her stomach was knotted. He stood, his gaze mercifully releasing her from its hold. "Is there anything I can do to help?" she asked. It was so awkward just sitting there in his flat, on his sofa. She didn't even really know him, and he was nineteen. He probably thought she was just some little kid who couldn't look after herself now.

"Are you any good at cooking?" he replied lightly. She laughed, wondering if it sounded as forced as it felt.

"No. I'm terrible actually," she admitted. "Much to my dad's dismay." He chuckled.

"Yeah, same here. Cassie says it's amazing that I've survived the year having to feed myself, but cooking is not one of my talents – unlike protecting my computer files." He glanced behind him at her. She presumed he was teasing her, but

68

remained straight-faced.

"Cassie's your sister," she confirmed. He didn't look surprised at the lack of question in her tone.

"Yeah, she's about your age." Susannah nodded. Her hands were still twisting in her lap. She took a deep breath.

"Is she in the resistance?" He looked at her over his shoulder once more, sharply this time, assessing her intent with a dangerous protectiveness. "You don't have to answer," she added quickly. He regarded her carefully for a moment.

"Yes, she is," he said simply. Silence filled the room, punctuated only by the clatter of plates and the opening and closing of cupboards.

"Do you parents know about...you know?" The resistance.

"No, they don't...are you okay with immediate-meals?"

"Yeah, anything is good. Thank you." The truth was that the thought of food still made her abused stomach lurch a little. She cautiously pulled her knees to her chest, wrapping her arms around them. He turned around to face her five minutes later, two steaming bowls of chicken fried rice in his hands. He handed one to her and she cupped it gently in her hands, revelling in the comforting warmth the bowl emitted. He slumped down onto the sofa next to her, eating absently with one hand.

"You're shivering," he stated. She looked down at her hands.

"I'm crashing from an adrenaline rush," she replied. It was probably true, because she didn't feel cold.

"I've no doubt," he said dryly. She felt the barest hint of a smile touch her lips. "Eat," he instructed after a moment, also tossing her a blanket. She speared a piece of chicken and popped it into her mouth, surprised that it instantly made her realise how hungry she was. The nausea was starting to fade, thankfully. He turned back to his own food, seemingly satisfied for the time being once she'd also wrapped the blanket around her shoulders.

"Krig?" she began hesitantly. His eyes flicked up from his bowl, his hands stilling at the seriousness in her tone.

"Hmm?"

"I want to join the resistance."

Chapter Six - First Meetings

It had taken a while to sort everything out, but today was the day: she and Delilah were joining the resistance. Her parents weren't aware of this fact, as of yet. Still, Susannah didn't consider that to be a wholly bad thing. The less they knew, the less danger they were in. It was strange though, when she'd first met Krig and heard about the resistance she'd never thought she'd be joining it only a month later. She supposed some part of her had wanted in when she first heard about it, and Krig had picked up on that. Or maybe she was just too impulsive for her own good. He had assured her that he on no accounts went declaring knowledge of resistance to most people, that would be a fatally huge security risk. It kind of felt nice to be singled out for something good. Of course, she had spent a large majority of her life being singled out due to her high magical proficiency, but that hadn't been the most positive experience. Actually, it tended to be negative as people either wanted to use her for it or just wanted nothing to do with her because an aura such as hers was 'unnatural'. The Underworld certainly hadn't viewed it as good, hell, most of them had seemed more partial in trying to squash the potential threat it posed. She'd always been led to believe that her power was something to be restrained and controlled, directed under the orders of her superiors and then caged once more. Krig, somehow, didn't appear to be the same. He'd said her magic was incredible. Of course, he probably only wanted to use her and her magic to further his cause just like everyone else, but at least it was a cause that she believed in. She did believe in it. It had taken a while to admit it to herself, but she did. The Overworld deserved better rights, she deserved better - to be more than free food, fun and workforce.

"Nervous?" Delilah asked. They were sitting on the kerb of the park, waiting. The air had finally dropped from its previously unbearable level of heat to something tolerably cooler. It was still warm, t-shirt weather, but not as oppressively hot as it had been the past weeks. Susannah was more than welcoming to the change.

"No," she replied. "Are you?"

"Yup," her best friend said cheerfully. "Slightly nauseous as well." Susannah was silent for a moment, studying the blonde.

"Same here," she conceded quietly. Delilah shot her a comforting smile.

"I'm sure they'll be nice."

"I hope so," Susannah shrugged uneasily. "You'll get on with them Del, you get on with pretty much everyone halfway decent." It was the truth. Delilah was good with people; everyone just seemed to like her. Susannah didn't have that same skill, unfortunately.

"So will you," Delilah frowned at her. "Don't worry. You've got on with them so far, haven't you?"

"Yeah..." she agreed. So far. They waited in silence for a few minutes, breaking from their individual thoughts at the sound of footsteps. It was Krig and another girl. She looked similar to him, with the same chocolate eyes and auburn coloured hair. It had to be Cassie, his little sister. Susannah glanced at Delilah to confirm it, and the blonde nodded minutely. It was Cassie. They both stood up as the pair approached them.

"Hi," Delilah smiled brightly.

"Hey, she greeted impassively. Krig's head tilted slightly, before he smiled.

"Nervous?" he asked.

"No," she lied; ignoring the amused expression Delilah sent her way.

"I am," Delilah said cheerfully.

"We're very scary," Krig grinned. "It's part of the requirements of being a successful...club." He paused, turning serious. "I joke, we're all friendly. Are you both certain that you want to join? Susannah, don't pout. I know I've already asked you this a dozen times, humour me."

"I wasn't going to," she said, her cheeks burning. Delilah laughed.

"Already figured out that she's not good with authority and orders then?" she asked.

"Of course. She wouldn't be joining otherwise, would she?" Cassie replied, flashing a shy but impish smile at the small blonde. Glancing at Krig, who looked entertained, Susannah folded her arms dramatically.

"I see how it is, just gang up on me. Thanks. I feel loved." The other two both grinned in response. Krig shook his head, smiling faintly.

"Come on," he interrupted easily. "Let's go. You don't want to be late to your first meeting."

About a quarter of an hour had passed and they were nearing the outskirts of Middle city, mainly trying to avoid the use of public transport. Krig was looking around himself casually every few seconds, scanning their surroundings. His features were cast in a shadow of seriousness. He'd stopped fooling around now, no more jokes. He was completely, single-mindedly, focussed on the security of the resistance. Susannah would have expected no less. The illegality of their actions ensured she felt no humour for someone not heeding caution. Even the thought of someone revealing the resistance out of stupidity or inattention made her temper begin to rise with a restless fury. The street they entered was characterless; grey, with each slab of building no more distinctive or memorable than the ones it was squashed between. It was derelict, abandoned and absolutely perfect for a secret meeting. The sign said Tilleway Road. Krig checked to see if they were all still following him, the beginnings of a smile gracing his lips once more before he crossed the street to a battered old café - Le Café Noir.

"Ladies first." He wrenched the door open in a sweeping gesture. Cassie laughed, entering the building without hesitation. Susannah paused a moment, only moving forwards when Delilah tugged gently at her sleeve. Krig's expression softened.

"Relax kid," he said. "It'll be fine." He didn't mention what he thought would be fine, but she thought he knew. Delilah certainly did, if her expression was anything to go by. Then again, Delilah knew exactly why Susannah was apprehensive of meeting new people as well. Everyone in the city was wary to a certain extent - you couldn't fully trust anyone but yourself - but still. Not everyone had to suffer being gawked at and shied away from the second they walked into a room. It was depressing. It did mean public speaking at school was no problem though, she'd had to get over fear of crowds at a young age. She took a deep breath, nodding tightly, her magic flittering with a carefully concealed agitation. She stepped over the threshold as Krig closed the door behind them. She felt her skin prickling immediately under the scrutiny of the eight new, curious gazes in the room.

"So these are your mysterious new recruits," a boy remarked. Susannah's eyes zeroed onto the speaker, her mind instantly beginning to catalogue what she was seeing. Spiked black hair, with a few strands of blonde at the roots so clearly dyed. Punk style clothing, lean figure - probably accustomed to combat - a problem with authority and a bucket load of self-confidence too if that careless posture was anything to go by. Boots were propped up on a chair, arms were folded and dark blue eyes were surveying her with the same air of assessment that he himself was under. She couldn't help but wonder what he was thinking. After a moment the boy grinned, pushing to his feet and holding out a hand. "David - David Black. I'm head of the Entry sector. Pleasure to meet you both I'm sure."

"Hi," Delilah said brightly. "It's nice to meet you too. I'm Delilah, Delilah Moor"

"Hey," Susannah murmured. Entry; if she remembered rightly that meant he was one of the people working on finding ways into Anzarkledea, the Demon Lord's manor house and base of operations. "Susannah Skelsby."

"I know," he smirked. "I've heard all about you from boss man over there." Susannah's eyes shot to Krig, who didn't look the slightest bit abashed.

"All good, I hope?" she questioned, arching her brows.

"Nope. Apparently you're an absolute nightmare and your friend's the nice one," David winked. Susannah gathered that he was joking, or she hoped so anyway. She wasn't a nightmare...was she?

"Anyway," Krig said loudly, stepping to the front of the room. Everyone in the room automatically looked away from them to give him their full attention. "As you all heard, this is Susannah and Delilah. They're joining the resistance - try not to scare them off." There was a round of laughter and promises that none of them would do anything of the sort, although David said "Damn you, always ruining my fun." There was some more laughter to that. David had smiled at them both though, suggesting that he was only teasing. Susannah wasn't quite sure what to make of the punk just yet.

"Introductions," Krig began. "Don't worry if you can't remember everyone's names at first. It took me a while too…"

"It really did," said a girl with long blonde hair and lots of makeup. "He kept calling me Leanne."

"You weren't supposed to tell them about that, Leola," Krig teased. He looked at them. "See, this is what I have to put up with. Blatant insubordination! Leanne is pretty similar to Leola anyhow…both have a Le at the beginning." Leola snorted. Delilah beamed, beginning to look a little more relaxed, her fingers loosening from their anxious twisting.

"Leola," she repeated. "I'll try and remember." The one called Leola flashed them both a smile.

"You better," she said. "I'm head of the TA, Tactical Advance sector." Susannah glanced at Krig; he'd said the TA would probably explain themselves.

"Basically," Leola continued. "We - my sector, Leon Daggey, Alice Hull and Cassie, who I'm sure you've met," she gestured to each person as she talked. Leon was a rather haughty looking boy who was eyeing them as if they were some particularly disgusting but fascinating specimen in the science lab. Alice was a cappuccino coloured girl, with large hips and a single plait that hung over one of her shoulders. She offered them a wave, as Leola continued. "Do research and tell him," Leola inclined her head at Krig, "what the resistance should be doing."

"You love me really Leanne," Krig smirked. Leola rolled her baby blues heavenward, as if praying for patience. Susannah decided that she liked her. She didn't like Leon so much, but would reserve judgement for more than just the contemptuous way he was studying her.

"We're kind of like Vanessa Cobre, (you know the Demon Lord's PR?) of the resistance, but we're nicer and Overworld," Alice added to Leola's explanation. "And there are more of us. And Leon's not female."

Leon snorted at that.

"I'm Joel, as you know," Joel continued after a moment, letting them absorb the TA's words. "Good to have you both here, especially after you near swore you wouldn't do something as stupidly suicidal as joining us." Susannah grimaced.

"What can I say, you're just extremely persuasive," she replied.

"What and I'm not?" Krig huffed mockingly. "Oh, you're going to fit in with these guys perfectly, don't worry."

"You're very persuasive too," Delilah assured him. Krig grinned.

"Why thank you," he said. It was true; Krig did have a certain compelling charm to him. He wouldn't be running the resistance if he didn't. He'd managed to get her to join after all – with a bit of help from Delilah.

"In my sector is Mica O'Brian and Jessica Du'vont, but she couldn't make this meeting. I'm sure you'll get to know us better in the next few weeks though."

A boy waved at them, Mica she presumed. His most noticeable feature was a near afro of wild honey coloured curls. "Oh, and this is Jamie Cutta," Joel said clapping a boy her age on the back. "He's a newbie just like you. Joined last week." Susannah stared, only breaking her gaze away when Delilah jabbed her side with a subtle elbow. How come Krig hadn't mentioned another new recruit?

"Hey," she offered lamely. "It's nice to meet you." She really hoped she wasn't blushing from gaping at him like some idiot. He was just...rather handsome, with dark brown hair that whispered black, tanned skin and the most beautifully unusual amethyst eyes. He probably had a girlfriend, a pretty one who helped old people cross the road. Or something.

"You too," he nodded easily, studying her. "Both of you."

"Are you in the New Recruits sector too?" Delilah asked. He shook his head.

"No, I haven't picked a sector yet," he replied. "Still trying to get to grips with the whole illegal thing."

"I know the feeling," Susannah admitted. "When Krig told me about the resistance I thought I'd misheard him or started hallucinating." Jamie grinned, his teeth gleaming white against his lips.

"That's quite common actually," David said, drawing her gaze back to him. "It's why we try and keep boss man away from the new recruits. He's our brilliant founder and I don't know what we'd do without him, but his recruiting skills are pathetic."

"Thanks Black," Krig said dryly, though he was smiling. Susannah was starting to get the impression that David was one of those people who showed affection by insulting you.

"They're always like this," a girl with copper hair and a fashion magazine style said. "I'm KT, by the way. I'm in Entry with David."

"Hi, it's nice to meet you," Susannah replied. It was going to become her automatic response soon, she just knew it. It wasn't that it wasn't nice to meet them though, it was. Why was she describing everything as 'nice'? It was such an empty adjective. She looked around herself, her gaze resting on Delilah for a moment. The petite azure eyed girl looked like she could have been in the resistance for years;

there was no trace of the awkwardness that Susannah herself felt. Delilah probably wouldn't have any trouble remembering most people's names. No, it was only going to be her who made a total twit of herself. Krig offered her a discreet smile when she looked at him. He was lounging against a large armchair at the front of the room, lazily.

"Hi, I love your t-shirt - Leiko?" Delilah said. KT smiled, shyly, looking down at her top. It was cream, with a picture of the infinite forest.

"Thanks, and yeah, it's Leiko."

"I love that shop," Delilah nodded. KT's smile widened some more.

"Same." There was a moment of silence.

"So, are you not a Leiko Girl then, Skelsby?" someone asked. Leon. The haughty one.

"No," she replied, trying to tell herself that she was simply imagining the snideness in his tone. "What about you?" she returned.

"I'm not a girl!" Leon snapped, sounding outraged. Leola seemed to hide a smile; it seemed to be bit of a joke among the TA if the earlier "and Leon's not female" was anything to go by. Krig's lip twitched slightly, as if he too was suppressing amusement.

"I'm sure Susannah didn't mean it like that, Leon," he appeased. Leon scowled, but didn't say anything further. His eyes were grey slits in her direction for a moment.

Susannah felt another surge of dislike. Delilah shot her a look, reproving.

"Of course she didn't," Delilah murmured, offering a small polite smile. "Daggey, isn't it?"

"Yes," he drawled. "Remember it new girl." Susannah resisted the urge to roll her eyes.

"Wouldn't dream of forgetting," her best friend replied.

Leon stared at Delilah suspiciously, trying to suss out if she was being serious or mocking.

"I'm Cade," another boy declared when Leon didn't respond. "Unspoken Research - the UR, though we normally just call it Research - it would be a sector too, but it's just me at the moment." Cade shrugged. "Basically, if there's anything that we need to know, from telephone numbers to obscure Underworld rites and the like, I'm the go-to. Any questions?"

"Why is it unspoken?" Susannah asked, even as Delilah enquired "Are you related to Mica?"

They glanced at each other, and there was a small round of laughter around the room. Delilah smiled too, while Susannah flushed slightly. Now she thought about, Mica and Cade did look similar, though Cade was older and didn't have quite so wild hair.

"It's Unspoken because we figured that my research is so important that I shouldn't have to be told to do it...though Krig still does," Cade explained. "He's like a mother hen. And yeah, we're brothers."

"Speaking of mother hens," Mica said loudly. The resistance laughed. Susannah raised an eyebrow.

"Inside joke?" Delilah questioned uncertainly. Leola took pity on their confusion.

"Cade's a mother hen. He fusses terribly," she said. "As I'm sure you'll come to see." Cade opened his mouth, presumably to protest against this statement.

"This, as you know, is Le Café Noir," Krig cut in. "We currently have three bases in total. Here, the Stage...that's the old theatre on Wharton Road....and a disused fire station on Janus Street." Delilah's face twisted a little with puzzlement, and Susannah frantically wracked her brains.

"It's in Upper City," Krig added, somewhat knowingly.

Susannah nodded. That would explain why she didn't know it. "I'll get someone to show you how to get to all our bases the first couple of times," he said. "Where do you guys live? A vague 'lower city' or 'middle city' will do."

"Lower City," Delilah said.

"Same as me," Joel grinned. "Meet me outside Leiko next time, I'll make sure you don't get lost." Delilah smiled.

"Thanks." They all looked at Susannah.

"Middle City." There were several winces, as suddenly everyone was eyeing her with a mixture of pity and understanding. .

"I'm sorry," KT sounded distressed. Susannah shifted uncomfortably.

"Guys, you're such wusses," David rolled his eyes. "Save your sympathy for those of us living in 'Demon Land' will ya?"

"You live in Upper City...?" she guessed. David nodded. "Sadly so. Leola and Leon do too...ha, maybe it's a 'Leo' place..."

"That's a terrible joke," Leon scowled. Susannah's lips curled slightly.

"Alice, Jess, will one of you show Suze the way?" Krig glanced at her, not bothering to otherwise comment as he already knew where she lived. "I'd offer to do it myself, but my schedules are rather different."

"He practically lives at base you see," Leola 'whispered.' "I personally think he migrates his bed to whichever base we're not currently using." Susannah bit back a laugh. Delilah didn't bother.

"Yeah sure, I will," Alice said, studying her curiously. "I'll meet you at Central Park. Don't be late, or I'll leave without you." The laugh was startled out of her this time.

"Okay," she agreed. Alice grinned back.

"Well, I guess that's the formalities out of the way. On with the actual meeting - and don't hesitate to ask questions."

"So long as they're not stupid ones," Mica added, winking.

After about three quarters of an hour or so, the meeting came to a finish. Susannah still couldn't quite believe that she'd just had her first resistance meeting - it felt so bizarre. She'd slightly started to pick up on people's names, but she wasn't very good yet. Joel had promised them a tour next time, to introduce them more to the individual sectors so that they could begin deciding which of them they would be interested in working with. Susannah thought that the TA looked quite cool, but she didn't think that she could suffer through working with Leon on such a regular basis. She also liked the look of Entry. Wow. It just hit her again that she'd just had a resistance meeting. It felt surreal. In a good way. In a scary, good way. Her stomach twisted.

"Excuse me," a smooth voice said, touching her shoulder as if to stop her. Susannah froze, tingles shooting like fireworks across the skin as she turned around.

"Oh, hi," Delilah smiled, apparently having also been stopped, "Jamie, wasn't it?" Jamie nodded, smiling back that dazzling smile.

"Yeah, and your name was Delilah, right? And you're Susannah?" he questioned, studying them both intently.

"Nice to meet you," Delilah stuck out a hand, which Jamie shook after a moment.

"Hey," Susannah murmured; certain that she must be sounding stupid.

"Hello," he replied, before shrugging with a strange elegant awkwardness. "Look, the thing is, I was kind of wondering if the two of you wanted to go for a drink with me...seeing as we're all new recruits and that. Share stories, that type of thing?" he proposed.

"Sure," Delilah agreed brightly. "So long as you're not some creepy psycho, are you?" Jamie blinked slightly. Susannah could feel heat rising in her skin. She couldn't believe her best friend had just said that!

"Nope," Jamie replied thoughtfully, shaking his head with a surprised laugh. "I think I can safely say that I'm not a creepy psycho…what about the two of you? Are you secretly going to murder me when my back is turned?"

"Possibly," Delilah grinned mischievously. "But probably not, so I reckon you're safe."

"Well, that's sorted then," he returned. "Drinks on me? Are you in, Susannah?"

"So long as you're paying," she managed, praying inwardly that her teasing came off as just that, teasing, rather than plain rudeness. He laughed again, before tilting his head towards the door.

"Deal," he said. "You can pay me back next time." She exchanged a glance with Delilah, torn between smiling and scowling slightly at the amused smirk the other was sending her. 'Next time?' She mouthed, deciding on smiling. Delilah grinned back, winking.

He led the way, weaving through the streets with a confident ease, before stopping at a small, obscure side café that she didn't even know existed. It was crammed between a bookshop and a Tailor's. It was called the "Cup and Saucer." It wasn't hot, like the rest of the city, but pleasantly cool and classy with an all glass shop front and glass counters and tables – the chairs were like brightly coloured stools, which were far more comfortable than their initial appearance gave them credIt.

"What are the two of you having?" Jamie instructed, with a smile, pulling out a discreet black wallet with dark blue stitching. He leaned forwards confidingly. "The smoothies here are *amazing.*" Delilah laughed, and Susannah found herself relaxing at the engaging gleam in his gaze. She studied a slip of menu on the table for a moment.

"I'll have the apple and raspberry smoothie," Delilah said, cheerfully.

"An excellent choice," Jamie grinned. He looked at her, an eyebrow raised.

"The, um, chocolate and banana one," she said. "Thanks."

"Coming right up – save our seats," he instructed, rising again.

"Hold on," Susannah said, pulling out her own purse, despite what she'd said. "It's not fair if you pay." He laughed.

"Hey, none of that, Susannah, really," he said. "I don't mind."

"It wouldn't feel right," she said, stubbornly. He exchanged a look with Delilah.

"I'm trying to be a gentleman, here," he said dryly. Susannah blushed, and he favoured her with an amused expression. "Indulge me."

He returned a few minutes later with the drinks.

"What did you get?" Delilah asked.

"Chocolate and raspberry," he said, setting the glasses down with a flourish. "Best of both worlds."

"Yeah," Susannah smirked. "I figure the fruit cancels out the chocolate."

"Exactly," he said. Delilah rolled her eyes. They all spent a moment drinking.

"This stuff is good," Delilah exclaimed, happily.

"Told you," Jamie said, with a hint of an endearing sort of smugness, which in itself should have been an oxymoron, but seemed to work for the boy in front of her as much as elegant awkwardness did. "So, how did the two of you get involved with Krig?"

Susannah glanced around the café, trying not to look paranoid. He caught her wrist, reassuringly, the pad of his thumb tracing soothingly across her pulse point.

"It's alright. Everyone here knows how to keep their mouth shut, and they won't bother us. Trust me. I wouldn't have picked it otherwise." Susannah stared at him.

"Should we feel suspicious about why you would be in the know-how for discreet café's where people know how to keep their mouth shut?" Delilah questioned. "What do you *do* in your free time, Mr Cutta?"

"That which would get me invited into an illegal resistance," he winked. "It's my job to know any and all rebel hot spots in the city by default." Susannah smirked.

"How did you get involved then?" she asked, curiously. He took another swig of his smoothie.

"I've been friends with Leola for a while, and hence have hung around with Krig before – they're dating-"

"Awww, they're such a cute couple," Delilah beamed.

"-So I got to know them that way," Jamie said, with a smile for Delilah. "And I guess they must have seen something in me. I helped them out with the Underworld a couple of times. The rest, well, the rest is history. What about the two of you? Leola tells me it was a somewhat unorthodox recruitment."

"I ran into Krig on Knight Street a while back," Susannah explained. "Helped him out, and he contacted me again and told me about the resistance."

"Just like that?" Jamie questioned, head tilting as he surveyed her.

"She saved his life," Delilah said. "And took out an entire hunting party nearly single-handedly."

Susannah flushed, ducking her head as Jamie's appraisal became even more intent.

"How powerful are you?" he questioned, softly. Susannah shrugged helplessly.

"I'm not sure. I haven't experimented all that much – mum and dad told me not to, said it would bring too much attention. Like, Carmel, as ridiculous as that sounds." She laughed, nervously.

"No doubt," Jamie murmured. "You don't think he's noticed you before now?"

"No. Why would he? I'm a fifteen year old school girl, and he runs the world."

He blinked, but didn't say anything in response, turning to Delilah.

"What about you?" he asked. "What's your story?"

"I tagged along with Susannah," Delilah said, running a finger around the rim of her glass. "And arranged another meeting with Krig cause she told him to get lost or she'd set the wardens on him the first time...went with Susannah to meet Krig. Here I am."

"He saw something in you though," Jamie said quietly, causing Delilah's head to snap up from her smoothie-watching. "You're not just Susannah's shadow."

"Of course she's not," Susannah replied, defensively, anger swelling in her aura. "Del's brilliant!"

"And she's *your* best friend," he returned, evenly, not flinching. "Which makes it very easy to get overlooked a lot, and that's not your fault, it's just the way it is." Susannah frowned, staring at Delilah, who looked down again, biting her lip.

"What, you think Krig only recruited you because you were with me? That's total rubbish!" she exclaimed. "How can you not see that? You're like a kick-ass healer; you've healed me enough times for me to know that! And I've never seen *anyone* as good with Pure Arts as you, not even Sensei."

"You're going to make my head swell," Delilah mumbled, blushing.

"Not possible, apparently," Susannah said. "How come you never said anything?" She paused. How come she had never *noticed* when Jamie had noticed upon his first time meeting them? Her magic prickled uncomfortably. Jamie surveyed Delilah calmly, before picking up his glass and holding out to chink.

"To quote Marco Carmel," he smiled, wryly. "Everyone has something to contribute; you just have to find that something and use it."

"I'm pretty sure he didn't mean it in a fluffy way..." Delilah laughed.

Chapter Seven – Tours and tests

Alice was waiting as Susannah entered Central Park. The TA girl stood with one hand resting on the large curve of her hip, while holding the other wrist up every few moments to impatiently check the time. As far as Susannah was aware, she wasn't late; she may even have been a little bit early. Alice looked up as she approached, nodding in greeting and swishing her caramel coloured plait over her shoulders as she set off at a brisk stride. Susannah quickened her steps to catch up, and they settled into a somewhat comfortable pace. The other was glancing at her curiously every few minutes.

"So, you live in Middle City?" Alice asked after a while, presumably to start a conversation. Susannah nodded.

"Yeah, have done so long as I can remember. What about you? Have you always lived in Middle City, or…?"

"For as long as I can remember," Alice shrugged. "Though I think my dad moved us there when I was about three."

There was a small silence.

"How did you meet Krig?" Susannah asked. Joel had said something about her and Delilah's recruitment being unorthodox, so she was interested to see how the other members' introduction into the resistance varied from her own experience.

"Well, Leola was in my Alchemic chemistry class at school, and she mentioned it to Joel. It was just her, Krig, Joel, David and Cade when I joined," Alice explained. "She got talking to me over a couple of months, before asking me about it and introducing me to Joel…and here I am," the girl finished. "I was always in trouble with my Alchemy teacher because I didn't want to give up the potions I had made; I never understood why we couldn't just keep them instead of putting them into Carmel's collection. What about you? I heard something about Knight Street?"

"Does everyone know about that?" Susannah muttered, groaning. Alice grinned.

"Krig was dazzled. It was all he would talk about, though he was spectacularly fuzzy on the details. It got rather annoying actually," she replied. "Joel was almost as bad." Susannah grimaced back apologetically, causing Alice to wave a dismissive hand.

"Um, well, basically Krig and Joel seemed to be having a bit of trouble with some Dark Angels - I think it was a Coming-of-Rage hunting trip - and I gave them a hand." Alice folded her arms.

"Oh COME ON," she said, rolling her eyes. "Give me a little bit more than that, I'm dying here."

"Nothing much more happened though. We had a fight, we won, and we went different ways." Alice looked highly disappointed.

"Aw man, and Krig had me thinking that it was something cool. You a good dueller?" the TA girl eyed her in a speculating manner. "You probably are, you've got the magic for it." Susannah deliberated for a moment on whether to play modest or give a more arrogant reply.

"Yeah," she replied finally, proudly. "I am. Top of my class." Alice's brown eyes gleamed.

"Ooh, get you," she returned, smirking good-naturedly. "Big words, we shall see if you live up to them. Maybe I can get Krig to give you a spin sometime - now, come on, through here, we're almost there." They dodged through a small alley, arriving on Wharton Road with the large theatre directly in front of them.

There were lots of peeling posters for old and forgotten

shows plastered across its walls and the words 'the Phoenix Theatre' were emblazoned above the double doors in dull large letters that had long since lost their shine. Though she knew of the place, Susannah had never been there or had reason to come to this part of the city. It was right on the borderline between Middle City and Lower City. She glanced at Alice, only to find the other already watching her expression.

"What do you think?" Alice asked, her tone suggesting that anything less than awe would be insulting. "Krig found it for us; we call it 'The Stage.' It's been empty for years."

"It's cool," Susannah replied. "Very grand looking." Alice smiled.

"It is, isn't it? It's my favourite base, I love the theatre..." she seemed to shake herself. "Now anyway, let's not stand out here like a pair of lemons. The meeting will be starting soon, come on in."

The inside of the theatre was just as grand and faded as the outer building, with thick, plush red carpets and wood panelling. It was dark, and everything valuable had long since disappeared into the hands of thieves and plunderers, leaving only the occasional splash of graffiti or litter. The building wasn't impressive in regards to Underworld standards, because the Underworld had almost double the money to put into a single, small house than the Overworld would ever have for an entire theatre, but it was spectacular for an Overworld building. They soon arrived at another set of doors, before walking through them and along a ground level slice of aisle wedged between rising stands of seats, which led to a the stage itself. Susannah could hear a low murmur of voices ahead of her, and heard the resistance before she saw them. They weren't on the stands themselves, but by thick, musty velvet curtains adorned with a phoenix weaving, which pooled at the corner of the stage.

"We don't use the stands themselves much," Alice explained to her. "Cade gets vertigo, he doesn't like heights, and we're not sure how stable the seats are anyhow." Susannah nodded in understanding.

"It's easier to escape from an open space," she added. "The seats would hem you in, especially against Underworld speed." Alice regarded her with surprise.

"That too," the TA girl agreed. The rest of the resistance noticed them as they approached, giving several forms of greeting. Delilah was already there, talking with Leola and Joel. Her best friend smiled at the sight of her, waving cheerily, before going back to her conversation. Krig was talking with David and KT, greeting them with a smile as they approached. Their leader began when everyone was there - Jamie had dashed in last, giving a rushed apology that he'd got "caught up" with some "stuff."

"Okay," Krig said, when everyone was silent. "This meeting, I will happily admit, is for the purpose of assimilating our new recruits. By all means, get on with your on-going tasks, but Susannah, Jamie and Delilah will be coming around for, shall we say a tour? Joel, if you could..."

"I could," Joel said placidly. "Jamie, Delilah, Susannah, over here. I can pitch for you to join the NR sector."

"Make sure you give the rest of us a go too," David reminded, grinning. "Remember children, you have to visit us cool kids at Entry before Joel can snare his grubby little claws into you. And TA - right princess? - Leola?" David looked around him at the lack of reply from the blonde haired girl. Mica prodded her side, causing the TA sector leader to start, magic flaring slightly.

"What-oh, sorry, what did you say?" she asked. Krig frowned, studying her worriedly.

"Joel needs to give us a go with the new recruits too," David repeated. Leola nodded, before her face seemed to brighten.

"Yes, you better give us a go, Joel, we know what you're like...hogging the new recruits...."

"Hey, it's not my fault they like me; you two probably scare them!"

"Don't be silly," David rolled his eyes, before looking at Susannah, Delilah and Jamie and raising his brows. "Am I scary?"

"Not nearly as much as you'd like to be," Susannah smirked, before she could help herself. To her relief, David just laughed and wandered away with a gesture at KT to follow him. The rest of the resistance slowly dispersed to different areas of the room while Mica and Jessica came over, as the other two members of the NR.

"Okay, Joel began, smiling broadly at the three of them.
"We don't really have a specific area to tour, in any of our bases, because our job is largely done outside of the HQ."

"Obviously," Mica said, "as we're recruiters." Joel dismissed the interruption easily, merely inclining his head to acknowledge the point.

"Do you have any other new recruits you're considering at the moment?" Jamie asked. "That's how you work, isn't it, picking out someone and...researching them? Like you did with me."

"Yes," Joel agreed. "And we do have a couple of potentials we're looking into - potentials is our name for, well, potential recruits."

"Do you have potentials often then?" Susannah questioned; her brow furrowing. Most people seemed to like the

Carmels...

"We normally have one or two, but they're normally long term" Joel said. "They don't always amount to even being told about us."

"We have to be very careful about who we trust," Jess said, studying them all almost pointedly. Susannah frowned.

"Of course," Delilah smiled, dispelling any tension before it could even consider settling. "That's very sensible of you." There was a slight pause.

"How do you know when potentials are ready to become recruits?"

"Well, first they have to pass extensive background checks, and normally give some indication that they're interested in resistance...after that, it's a matter of all of us in the NR approving them. We don't take a recruit unless everyone approves."

"Normally, anyway," Jess added, with a smile.

"Normally?" Susannah felt a sinking feeling in her chest, the urge to frown increasing.

"Though we do largely work on a somewhat democratic basis, Krig does have veto if he wants and a capacity to...suggest either plans to the TA, or in our case, recruits," Joel said, smoothly. "And it's nothing to worry about; Krig's a good judge of character."

Jess's eyes were hard.

"Anyway," Mica said, perhaps a little too loudly. "That's the New Recruits sector. It's all pretty self-explanatory really-"

Jamie's head tilted.

"-Would you ever recruit the Underworld?" Delilah asked.

Jamie's face went rigid, just for a second, the stillness of his expression there and gone so quickly that Susannah almost thought that she may have imagined it. Joel spluttered, seemingly choking on air in his shock. Mica blinked. Jess looked absolutely bewildered.

"The Underworld?" Joel repeated.

"Yeah," Delilah flashed a smile. "Would you recruit them?"

"I highly doubt there would be a member of the Underworld who wanted to join us, it's not like supremacy as opposed to equality is a bad thing for them," Jess replied.

Joel's surprise faded to thoughtfulness.

"I suppose we would, theoretically, if they were ever interested," he said. "Although I'm not sure how good it would be, practically, in terms of the actual recruiting...firstly because if they were interested in resistance, they could hardly afford to be open about it for us to discover their sympathy...secondly, because our methods are obsolete against them because we can't get to know them and do any form of personal background check that way, like we normally do, let alone get a strong judge on their personality, which would lead to the question of how we would contact an Underworld variation in the first place without raising suspicion...we wouldn't even know where to start."

Delilah bit her lip.

"It would work if you had one Underworld variation on side to act as a go-between to the others," Susannah murmured, "but getting that first one would be tricky...if any of them, as Jess said, are even interested." It was possible; she'd never met a decent Underworld variation who gave any indication of empathy or sympathy for Overworld plight, but that didn't mean there weren't any...though she very strongly doubted it.

"What about magical creatures, non-human Overworld variations like the Werewolf packs or the Nymphs...do you recruit any of those?"

Joel shook his head, mutely, staring at Delilah in

astonishment. There was a marginally awkward silence.

"No, we don't," Jess answered, finally, seeming to compose herself the quickest. "That's a good idea though. You should mention it to Krig sometime." Something in her features had softened as she surveyed the blonde with open curiosity.

"...any other questions?" Joel asked.

The second sector on their 'tour' was the TA, Tactical Advance. Leola, Alice, Leon and Cassie were in what looked to be a converted storage room and were leaning over tables, poring over thick sheets of documents as well as newspapers. She felt Delilah pause hesitantly on the threshold of the door, before continuing with only the smallest falter in her confident step. She tucked a strand of hair behind her ear, watching the proceedings with sharp eyes. Jamie had approached as if he belonged there, with not even a hesitation to mark any worries he may or may not have had.

"See if you can beat our pitch," Mica challenged, grinning, but Joel was quiet, with a level of amusement that made Susannah think he was wondering what her best friend might ask the TA. Seeming to notice his awareness, Delilah blushed. The TA members had all straightened, glancing up as they entered.

"What are you guys working on?" Joel questioned easily. "Can we cut in?"

Susannah's attention was drawn more firmly to the numerous maps and documents spread across any available surfaces, and she studied them with curiosity. There were a lot of clippings from newspapers, more than anything else, and then around them annotations and observations. It looked to be...

"You think there's another resistance group out there? Are you planning to contact them?" she asked.

"Gold star to the girl who can read," Leon drawled, surveying her.

"Ignore Leon," Cassie said, shaking her head. "Yeah, we do. Maybe more than one."

"How do you think we should go about such contact?" Leola questioned, with an air of test in her voice. Susannah noticed Krig had come to lean in the doorway, watching the proceedings. She suddenly felt under pressure, and shot Delilah a glance. Her best friend offered her a reassuring smile. Jamie, too, was watching her with intent inquisitiveness, the piercing quality of his gaze at war with his relaxed demeanour.

"Um, well, firstly you'd have to try and research everything about the resistance group...how many there are, what their characteristics are, like if they're militant...which is what you guys seem to be doing right now. Once you've found out everything you can about them, you need to find a way to contact the targeted resistance group, which will be easy or hard depending on whether or not you know any of the members. I'm going to presume you don't know, considering most resistance groups are secretive about their names and membership, they could all use aliases for example, because otherwise they have to live at their base or something...and there's nothing about it in your notes. Er," she paused, thinking, watching their expressions. "If you can't contact them directly, and are willing to take the risk, then I suppose you could get a message out to them in some other way that everyone could see...except that would also have its own problems...but it might be the only option available if you don't expect them to contact you. Then you'd open negotiations to see if they were interested in teaming up." There was a silence. "But that's just a rough idea," she added, nervously.

"Huh," Leola said, leaning back against a filing cabinet. "Not bad, Susannah, not bad at all."

"Thanks," she replied. Leon rolled his eyes.

"Yes, well done for being able to deduce the obvious," he muttered, under his breath. Susannah arched her brows, but squashed the extremely tempting urge to say something scathing in response.

"Is that what this resistance group's main plan of action is at the moment?" Jamie asked, as if to verify. "Aside from recruiting more members, obviously. Uniting with another resistance?"

"Yes," Leola said. "A united force is always stronger than a house divided...of course, we are open to deviations if something comes up, but that's our current plan...spread the rebellion and all that."

"So the resistance is a bit like a pirate radio or something?" Delilah asked.

"That's a good way of putting it," Leon replied. "We'd do more, but we can't go around campaigning openly, or holding a march or anything like that. It would be a bloodbath. So, it's small steps to the overall plan."

"Overworld equality," Jamie confirmed.

"Yes," Leola said.

"And in the TA, the main thing is analysis, at the moment? You don't have any concrete plans to contact a resistance group?" Susannah questioned.

"We don't just do nothing," Leon snapped.

"I'm sure she didn't mean it like that," Cassie said, placing an appeasing hand on the brunette's shoulder. "She's only making sure." Leon's eyes were narrowed to slits, and she couldn't help but wonder what his problem was.

"Yeah," Alice said. "That's our main angle at the moment, Susannah. We're working a lot with Cade to see what we can uncover, though, if the opportunity for action arises, we'd sure take it." There was a moment of silence.

"There's not much we can do at the moment," Krig said, quietly, speaking for the first time. "We're not adults, and so the best thing we can do is raise awareness for when we can make more of an impact, to drum up support and try and encourage everyone else to stand up for themselves, until our words have more weight and we can actually do something."

"Krig's planning on being a lawyer," Jess added, shooting him an admiring expression. "Then he'll try and get some precedents down and fight this de jure - legally start fighting for our rights - find all the loopholes in the law and use them. Carmel can't argue against his own constitution." Delilah frowned.

"But the courts are corrupt, they wouldn't listen to you," she said sadly. Krig's lips twisted.

"They may be corrupt, but if the case is public...which any court case that challenges the Underworld supremacy would inevitably be, they can't rule against us if they're backed properly into a corner." Their leader sighed. "It doesn't mean anything would change in reality, but it's a start, and it means acknowledgement."

"You'd be removed," Jamie said bluntly. "No offence, but the Demon Lord would have his assassins on you the second you accepted the case, if you were good. Either that, or he'd find your weak point and use you."

"You can't use someone without their consent," Krig replied.

"He can," Jamie rebutted. "If there's anything that would sway your opinion, anything at all, he would find the chink in your armour and shred you from the inside out. No one challenges him."

"You sound like you have some experience with that," Delilah noted.

"My family loves the Carmels," Jamie's nose wrinkled slightly in disgust. "I have to listen to it."

"How did you get into rebellious circles, then?" Susannah asked, leaning forwards.

"How did you?" Jamie returned, with a smirk. "I fell in with the 'wrong' crowd."

There was a small burst of laughter. Jamie's expression grew downcast, subdued. "I reckon my family would roll in their graves if they ever thought I was seriously into resistance."

"They don't ask you where you go all the time, to meetings?" Susannah questioned, beyond fascinated.

"They're dead," Jamie replied, "so I'll hazard a guess that they don't ask me all that much generally." No one else seemed surprised about that, except her and Delilah, so she figured it was another fact the NR had turned up in their 'recruit research.' She supposed being an orphan was a pretty big background check to miss. She winced; she supposed they'd literally roll in their graves then, not figuratively like she'd assumed.

"I'm sorry," Delilah said softly. "When?"

"Don't worry about it, we didn't really get on that well," Jamie shrugged. "And it was a long time ago. My brother and I have got on fine without them, better, in fact."

"And he doesn't ask either?"

"He's not around most days - he's got to work."

Susannah swallowed at the lump in her throat. How lonely it sounded; she couldn't imagine not having a close family.

"E sector?" Joel prompted, uncomfortably.

"'Sup ladies, and gentlemen, of course," David saluted them as they walked in - the E sector didn't seem to have so permanent a base, and there were no huge diagrams or anything out of the ordinary at their corner of the stage.

"Hi," KT smiled, somewhat sheepishly. "Are me and David the last ones?"

"Cade hasn't pitched them to Research yet," Joel replied, sounding somewhat amused.

"No threat of a better last impression then," David retorted, cheekily.

"Oi," Mica laughed. "That's my brother you're talking about - and I'm pretty sure he could leave a lasting impression on *you* in a duel. Only I'm allowed to insult him!"

David waved a dismissive hand, but Susannah couldn't help but notice the sudden green tinge to his skin. Delilah bit back a smile, exchanging an entertained glance with her and Jamie.

"I could-" the punk began, stopping when KT clamped her hand playfully over his mouth.

"Stop it," the Entry girl chided, not looking particularly annoyed. "You're supposed to be a professional. Don't stir."

"Yes ma'am," David grinned, promptly, tipping an imaginary hat to her. He folded his arms neatly behind his head, sprawled lazily. "Well, anyway, here be where all the best people reside, kids. We get everyone in, and we get everyone out safely, or so is the plan...we are your human navigations systems of awesomeness, and warders extraordinaire. Join us." KT shook her head in mock despair.

"The TA had pretty diagrams," Susannah smirked. "What do you have to prove your claims of worthiness?" David's grin widened.

"Nothing, because that is the superiority of our sector." He tapped his head. "It's all in here." The grin faded a bit. "Having information for entry and vanishing acts only works if it is in the long term part of the brain, it wouldn't do to frantically start wondering which exit we're supposed to be using in times of trouble. Therefore, we have it memorised, and hold no notes and pretty diagrams to prove our illegal involvements once we have."

"Wow. I want your memory," Delilah said, eyes sparkling. "You can remember the whole city?"

"Every nook and cranny," KT replied shyly, proudly. "That's our job."

"Wow," Susannah repeated. She suddenly felt a bit intimidated.

"Haha, my teachers just wish I'd apply myself at school," a grin was tugging once more at the corners of David's mouth. "They think I'm stupid. Reckon it's the piercing...that always seem to give them the heebie-jeebies for some reason...of course, we try not to flaunt our brilliance in fear of unwanted attention, but sometimes it just slips through. That guy-" David jerked his head at Joel, "stalked me for weeks. Desperate to have me, is all I'm saying."

"I did not *stalk* you," Joel rolled his eyes. "I'm in your class."

"He stalked me," David told them, as if that settled the matter, but his eyes were glittering with mirth.

"Stalking..." Mica mused, chewing his lips. "I reckon that was the time Cade almost took your head off your shoulders, wasn't it David?"

"I was only going to surprise you guys," David sighed plaintively. "It aint my fault your brother freaked out and thought I was a bloodsucker." Susannah snickered.

"You must be talented warders," Jamie said, surveying the two E sector members. "You say you have knowledge of the city, what of Anzarkledea?"

"We don't know that quite as well," KT admitted. "Mostly, we know the ground level, before it gets to Carmel's private home section, that's the upper levels - the first and second floors."

"We know the ways in and out," David said. "Probably not all of them, but a fair few."

"The thing is," KT's voice lowered. "And this is going to sound *crazy,* but we think the house...moves."

"Moves?" Delilah repeated, edging closer with interest.

"The corridors, the doors, the rooms," David explained, sounding absolutely intrigued. "We think, well, we think the building itself might even be sentient, linked to the Carmels."

"Do you mean like how wards are linked to the 'Lord of the manor' or whatnot?" Susannah questioned. "Only the people in charge of the house can manipulate them?"

"Exactly like that," KT exclaimed. "It sounds absurd, and we've never seen anything like it, but I swear it's true. The house is alive."

"That would make sneaking out difficult," Susannah remarked dryly.

"If the house moves, how can you know the way in and out of it?" Delilah questioned worriedly. "I mean, surely, the exit would just move."

"It's not that obvious," David replied. "It's more...shifts, from what we can gather. Like, an extra door appearing, a door locking on its own or disappearing, a new corridor, a sudden lack of stairs – that kind of thing."

"How do you know about it?" Susannah asked.

"It's documented; visiting dignitaries have made reference to it, a slight change in the house. We think that's where the whole idea of 'you can't leave without permission' comes from, because you literally can't. They could have you wandering around in circles for days."

"Creepy," Delilah shivered.

"That's incredible magic," Susannah muttered, not wanting to express her awe of anything Underworld too openly.

"So yeah," David summarised, "when we're not actively looking for ways in and out of places, or planning for such occasions, or practising our warding skills...we're studying Anzarkledea...rumour has it took over ten architects to make. That's the Entry sector for you." There was a moment of silence. "Bet Cade can't beat that."

"*David!*"

Cade was sitting at another corner of the stage, a small, thin, musty smelling book in his hands, and a pen in the other, while a notepad rested, precariously balanced, on his knee.

"Cade normally heads off to the library, or into the depths of cyberspace," Joel stated, as her, Delilah and the rest of the NR Sector (Mica and Jess) approached. "But he figured he actually had to be around if you guys wanted to talk to him."

"I figured nothing," Cade mumbled, casting his honey-coloured gaze up as they got close. "Krig told me to stay put for a bit."

"Socialising will do you good," Krig clapped the other boy on the shoulder, grinning.

"I have plenty of friends," Cade grumbled.

"Fictional ones?" Mica returned, smirking, only for his brother to shoot him a foul glare, to which he held up pacifying hands. "Relax, I know you have friends, it's just my job to piss you off." Jamie looked amused.

"Yeah," Krig's grinned broadened. "You still have me, after all."

There was a burst of laughter, and Cade rolled his eyes. "Ignore them, they're giving a false impression of me," he told the three of them. "I have friends and a perfectly adequate social life. For Shadow's sake," he cursed, "I'm not some type of hermit; I'm captain of the Tackleball team!"

"Your proudest moment."

"Sod off." There was a moment of silence. "Anyway, I'm research, that's all there is to it. If anything needs to be researched, I do it. I could appreciate some help, but if you do join my sector, remember that caffeine is your friend. I record everything in a notepad, as opposed to a computer that could be hacked from a distance, or crash, or have any number of problems. I collect and trade rare books on the black market of information, and have several contacts across the city who I probably shouldn't go into too much detail about. Just to annoy David, I'll shake up my 'pitch' a bit and say that research is like the spies and secret service aspect of the resistance, and I have to remember far more than his little geographical map."

"Sounds like a dangerous preoccupation," Jamie noted. "Information pays a high price in this city. The Carmels would love to get their hands on you."

"Precisely," Cade said, staring at Jamie with a greater appreciation. "Thank you! I've been telling David that for years."

"Are they always this competitive?" Delilah asked.

"David and Cade?" Jess confirmed. "Yup. I don't think David ever quite forgave Cade for beating him in a duel – we'll have to tell you sometime, it's a hilarious story!"

"David glosses over it," Joel smirked. "But anyway – us, the TA, the E sector and Research, there's your tour, and our modest company."

"So," Alice began, with a sly glance at some other members of the resistance, who seemed to lean forwards in anticipation. "Why don't you ask Krig to duel with you, Susannah?"

Susannah froze, her mouth running dry. Krig paused, looking at them. They'd all settled back together into a group by the curtains again, going over threads from previous meetings.

"What's this?" their leader asked.

"Skelsby wants to duel you," Leon drawled. She could feel heat rising to her cheeks.

"I didn't say that-" she started, uncomfortably.

"Well, no," Alice shrugged easily. "But I want to see what all the fuss is about and why Krig's so amazed with your duelling skills that he forewent normal recruiting procedures to have ya."

Delilah had an amused expression on her face, and everyone else had started to look between them.

"Come on Krig," David smirked. "Don't tell me you're chicken."

Joel started laughing quietly at that, but Krig didn't look goaded.

"You just told me I fast tracked her because I was so impressed with her skills, and now you're wondering why I might be reluctant to duel her?" he returned, brows raised.

Jamie was slumped gracefully in a chair, one arm resting on his knee, then his chin resting on his hand. She could feel his eyes fixed on her again with a burning, curious intensity, though he didn't speak. Leola's head tilted.

"Krig...you were the best dueller in our year," she reminded. "It's just a bit of fun."

Susannah felt slightly unnerved – hadn't Viridian said she could kill someone with her magic by accident? It wouldn't be 'a bit of fun' if she killed their leader. Hell, it wouldn't be fun if she lost either...he was an illegal resistance group leader, he was probably a really good duellist. What if she lost and everyone started doubting her? Being a good dueller was kind of her thing...

"It's fine," she said hastily, insides knotting at the thought. "Really."

"Oh don't tell me you're scared too," Jess snorted. "You're powerful, aren't you? And Alice said you were top of your class."

Nice to know Alice and Jess were talking about her. This just made the possibility of losing worse.

"Best in the school, actually," Cassie chipped in. "Sensei's got her to do demonstrations for my class before."

"Okay, now I see why you might not want to duel her..." Mica said, shooting her a wary look.

"I still reckon you're chicken," David muttered, with a grin. Krig rolled his eyes, meeting her gaze for a moment, as if he were searching for something, checking for something.

"I'm up for it if Susannah is," he said finally.

"I don't know," she hedged. They immediately stated coaxing her, tugging at her like they had Krig. In a way, she really wanted to duel Krig, because he seemed like he might be a challenge at least, but in another...what if she lost control? What if she lost and they just assumed she was a fluke and tried to remember why they recruited her?

"If she doesn't want to, she doesn't have to, leave her be," Krig added firmly, with a ring of finality in his tone.

She heard Leon mutter something about all bark and no bite, and she surged up onto her feet before she was fully aware of her own actions, determine to prove herself.

"Come on then," she sighed, though she could feel her excitement building, along with her grin. "What rules are we playing by?"

David cheered, conjuring mini flags, waving them madly, before enquiring about bets, even as Cade told him off.

"I want popcorn. Does someone have any popcorn?" Mica asked cheerfully.

They stood facing each other on the stage, the rest of the resistance drifting back to the stands (though not very high up.) Krig had an indulgent gleam in his eyes when he looked at them, protective too, but she could see a hint of nerves on his face. Joel was shaking his head, having seen her fight once before already, but refusing to give David any tells on which of them would be his best bet against Leola and Mica.

"Sorry about this, Susannah," Krig told her, glancing up. "They act like children when they get a new recruit, I swear. This is just them trying to get to know you and make you feel welcome."

"Like a shiny new toy?" she replied, but she smiled, softening it. She did like the resistance, and, despite her fear of harming Krig among other things, the familiarity of magic and duelling *was* putting her at ease. Most people tended to prefer she didn't play with her powers around them, so it was nice to know that here it seemed to be viewed as a gift rather than a horrible abnormality which should be tamed for the uses of the government.

He smiled back at her, reassuringly.

"Don't embarrass me."

"Try and keep up," she teased, not letting her doubts show. He laughed – and then, they were duelling.

She let him take the first shot, but dodged it, calling the curtain to wrap around him, but he banished it back to its spot easily, pinning the drapes to the roof so she couldn't use them again without great effort. He was good, and his magic was strong, even if he was currently on the defensive. Her heart started to speed up, her body shifting to a greater alertness. She followed her curtain spell immediately by turning the ground beneath him to ice with elemental magic, the ambient magic tasting deliciously frosty on her tongue, crisp, like a winter's morning with the same freshness. She had the advantage as most of her talents – Duelling, Chaos Magic, Elemental Magic specifically – were based on offensive and fighting. His was more judicial, more to do with compulsions and subtlety than all out fighting. He nearly slipped, before narrowing his eyes upon her, still grinning with exhilaration, not breaking a sweat just yet. She could feel their magic flaring, clashing and tangling, testing and pushing as they twirled around each other in dangerous choreography, trading and dodging spells, testing each other out. He was talented and decisive with his magic, shaping his attacks carefully rather than simply trying to destroy her with blunt force, which wouldn't have worked. He was a clever fighter, Susannah herself was an instinctual one – for now, aside from her having more power, they seemed pretty evenly matched with his greater experience and opposing tactics. She prepared another line of attack when, suddenly, an odd calm came across her mind, insidious, soft. *Surrender, Susannah...surrender, concede...you know you want to...let the ice melt...it's alright...*Susannah relaxed, feeling her control slipping, the ice melting from beneath his feet, the wintry taste departing from her mouth. Yes, she did want to relax, and she opened her mouth to say so, her magic dying out - Mind Arts! She snapped back to herself, throwing herself to the side to avoid his next spell, as he'd taken advantage of her distraction. It grazed her, and she hissed with pain, before closing her eyes, struggling but unable to push the voice out, and just about able to keep dodging his spells. She couldn't combat this magic head on, she had no Mind Arts skill, and so attacked the root of the problem, slamming her hand forward in an explosion of pure power, knocking him off his feet and breaking his concentration. It was a bit of a cheap trick, but one she found herself using increasingly often. She pulled the curtains into her control once more, pinning him down to the floor, before walking over. There was a shocked, breathless silence, their audience silenced a long time ago. They stared at each of for a moment, panting for air.

"Concede, boss?" she smirked.

"Yeah," he winced. "Nice one."

She offered a hand to pull him up, relieved when he took it, showing he wasn't angry with her. They shared a grin, before turning to their audience.

"Erm. Wow," Alice breathed.

"-That was incredible, Susannah!-"

"-Ha, Krig got his arse handed to him!-"

"-Where'd you learn to duel like that?-"

"-I so thought the Mind Arts would work-"

Susannah grin widened.

She could get used to this.

Chapter Eight – Control

Susannah walked towards Mrs Sanchez' house. It felt odd
visiting a teacher when she was on her summer holiday, as
if the natural order of the world had somehow been
disturbed. It wasn't necessarily a bad feeling, but it was
awkward. Her mum said she was just being paranoid, as
there was nothing wrong with the situation if Viridian
herself had offered, but it still felt strange. Her Chaos Magic
teacher lived, according to the address in her hands, in a
house just off the heart of Lower City. It was a red brick
building, on the large side for an Overworld area but quite
plain. It was nice enough. Her nerves increasing, she
dithered outside for a moment before ringing the bell. After
a moment, the door opened, revealing the sixty-three year
old.

"Hi," Susannah greeted, clutching her bag tighter. "You told
me to come about the Chaos lessons...?"
"I know," Mrs Sanchez said, smiling slightly. "Come now,
let's not stand on the doorstep, enter, please." Susannah
stepped in, looking around herself with curiosity. She'd
never been to a teacher's house before. It was rather
normal looking all things considered. She didn't know why,
but considering that Viridian was a Chaos teacher, she'd
sort of expected her house to be really wild and chaotic. It
was actually rather boring; mainly done up in creams and
blues.
"Would you like anything?" Mrs Sanchez asked. "Tea?
Juice? Coffee?"
"Er, no thanks," Susannah said, clutching her bag tighter to
her chest.
"Then let us move to the workshop." It turned out that the
workshop was a stone basement room, heavily fortified and

largely empty. It was huge. Viridian must have caught her expression, for she smiled slightly. "Being a Chaos teacher, I have certain privileges." Susannah grinned back. This was more what she had expected. There was a plug in one corner, but that was about it. Viridian conjured herself a chair, pulling it up. Susannah took it as invitation to make one of her own. Her teacher's eyes twinkled lightly at her actions. She pulled an innocent expression in return, before turning serious.

"The purpose of these lessons," Mrs Sanchez began, "is to teach you how to control your magic, both ambient and normal. Do you have any questions regarding that?"
"Why now?" she asked, before grimacing. "I mean, you never mentioned my needing extra classes before." Surely they could have waited until next term? Not that she minded the extra Chaos. Viridian was silent for a few seconds.
"I already confessed my concern over the militant nature of your magical reactions," she said. "What I didn't mention was that left unchecked it is possible that the extremity of that reaction may only increase, especially if you were to get into a situation that would require you to fight. The sooner you begin learning to control it, rather than letting it control you, the less danger you will pose to those that you do not mean to harm." Susannah stilled. Hadn't Viridian last said her magic could be lethal?
"In other words you want to pre-empt me from murdering someone," she verified tightly.
"Or hurting yourself, yes," her teacher said bluntly.
Susannah sucked in a deep breath, squeezing her eyes shut as her magic flittered. "Susannah," Viridian stated quietly.
Susannah clenched her aura down, chanting song lyrics in her head. Every being with magic had a magic medium, (a

certain habit or object that was calming to a person's aura) hers was music. Ever since she was little and her parents had figured it out, they'd always played music in the house to stop her magic from being too wild. Apparently, once, when the music player had broken she'd been almost impossible to live with as a toddler. Locks were nothing to her uncontrolled, childish aura, and if she wanted anything she just summoned it. She must have been an absolute nightmare. After a moment, she felt her magic simmer down to a controllable level.

"I understand," she said. "How are we doing this?"

Susannah stood in the middle of the hall, the chairs vanished. She wasn't frightened

"Okay," she stated warily. "What do you want me to do?"

"I want you to try and resist letting your magic attack me," Mrs Sanchez replied. "I will be firing spells at you, do not let your magic lash out."

"Do kyou want me to use Chaos?" she asked, getting ready to concentrate.

"No," Viridian said quickly. "With your magic, it would be horrendous if you lost control of the ambient magic as well as your own magic at the same time." Susannah swallowed, hard. Now she felt scared. She was basically opening herself up to getting the spit beaten out of her. She wasn't sure if she trusted herself to speak, her mouth felt a little dry actually, so she simply nodded once. She saw a flash out of the corner of her eye, and before she had even thought about it her magic had whipped out violently. There was a smash. Her eyes widened in horror as her teacher picked herself up of the floor, dusting herself down.

"I'm sorry!" she cried, moving forwards to help. Viridian shook her head, freezing her on the spot.

"Again," her teacher instructed simply.

"B-but I just -" she pointed helplessly at the floor her teacher had just crashed into.

"Again," Viridian repeated firmly. Susannah sighed, nerves fluttering in her stomach. She fell back to the centre of the room once more. She found herself tensing, ready to flinch before her teacher had even drawn her magic. Her insides were restless and twisting with anxiety.

"Susannah, relax…" Viridian ordered calmly. "Your magic is spiking." She started to concentrate fiercely, trying to lose herself to the world. If she wasn't aware of the magic, then surely she wouldn't attack it? She managed three attacks, gaining herself a tiny cut on her shoulder, before she lashed out again, without permission. Her teacher narrowly ducked a rather less tiny cutting curse. Susannah winced.

"Maybe we should take a break -" she started. She didn't want to hurt Viridian. She was being so nice about this, and she wasn't exactly in her prime, was she? She was sixty three. Her teacher's glare pinned her to the spot, before softening once more.

"There was a slight improvement that time, what did you change?" she asked encouragingly.

"I tried to drown the world out?"

"Are you asking me or telling me?" Viridian asked, arching her brows. Susannah realised that was the second time her teacher had asked her that in the space of as many conversations.

"Telling you, miss," she sighed. "I tried to drown the world out," she explained. "I thought that, maybe, if I wasn't thinking about the attacks I could ignore them and not attack."

"Sometimes I forget you're still so young," Viridian said, the barest hint of a smile gracing her delicate features despite the situation. "Remember, your magic is instinctive, Susannah. In duelling class, for example, out of ten, how many times are you actually thinking about what you were going to do?" Susannah paused, tilting her head. She didn't, how could she? Magic was supposed to be instinctual...oh.

"I just react," she realised. Her teacher inclined her head.

"Exactly. Drowning the attacks out will do your control little good in the long term. You will still lash back eventually, perhaps with even less control than before."

"What can I do then? Just try and ignore it? I can't!" she said. It was ridiculous, she was frustrated at herself and her failure before she'd even started properly. Disappointment burned in her gut, a bitter mixture of vinegar and lemon juice.

"Temper, Susannah," Viridian chided lightly. "What's your magic medium?"

"Music," she said automatically. "Anything to do with music - listening, writing song lyrics, playing."

"What instrument do you play?" her teacher questioned.

"Guitar, mainly. It annoys the neighbours though," she said. Viridian nodded.

"Do you take lessons?"

"In school. I take music as a class - there's a lot of stuff about how you can create spells through lyrics and that type of thing. I just like the playing," she explained. Her teacher nodded, slowly.

"Hmmm. Bring your favourite CD for the next lesson, or your music player, I presume you have one?"

"Yeah," she said. Viridian looked thoughtful, before disappearing out of the workshop.

"One moment," she called. Susannah stared at her fingers. Before this, she'd thought her control was quite good. She'd thought magic was just her thing, effortless as breathing. Apparently not. She had lasted an appallingly little time when her magic instincts for fight kicked in. In her mind, she knew that everything was fine and that her teacher wouldn't hurt her, but her magic just didn't seem to want to differentiate. She couldn't control it. The realisation was horrible, a black dawning. She'd always, arrogantly, considered her control over her magic to be impeccable. Viridian walked back in, shutting the door behind her. Susannah knew now why they were in such a reinforced room - her magic was too volatile to be put into an easily changeable or damaged environment. She didn't know how it would react to attack. Viridian did, it seemed.

"In the meanwhile," her teacher said, strolling towards the plug behind a hefty looking, levitating music player, "how opposed are you to the classical works of Patrick Daniels?"

"Okay," Viridian said finally, when Susannah was nearly keeling over from exhaustion, her muscles trembling. "I think we're done for this lesson." Unable to care about decorum, Susannah slumped onto the floor, panting. The stone felt so lovely and cool against her skin. Who would have thought it was so much more tiring to avoid using magic then it was to actually use it in the first place? Even her bones ached. Her teacher appeared at her side a minute later, offering her a glass of water. She almost inhaled it in her eagerness. Her throat felt scorched, as rough as sandpaper in its thirst.

"Thanks," she set it down again.

"There's more if you want it," Mrs Sanchez stated with a small measure of humour.

"I'm okay."

"If you're sure," her teacher said. "As for the lesson, I think that was an improvement. You went from being able to ignore no attacks, to being able to ignore five of them...with a little cheating." Susannah grimaced; she'd dodged a couple of the attacks.

"The music helped," she said. Viridian nodded.

"That is to be expected, though I will eventually have to wean you off it as you will not always have music to help you control your magic." She'd figured as much. "Nonetheless, well done. That wasn't too bad for a first attempt, even though it is clear that more work is needed." "I did rubbish," Susannah scoffed.

"I didn't expect you to get it immediately," Viridian said, dismissing her reply. "This is going to be a long, difficult process. It would have been remarkable if you'd grasped it instantly." Susannah nodded. "Now, homework," Viridian said, causing Susannah's head to shoot up. Homework? On summer holiday? "Yes, Susannah, homework," Viridian repeated. "Firstly, I want you to loosen the restraints you have on your magic, not completely, that would be...unwise, but a little bit. Secondly, I want you to find a place where you can use it freely without constraint, at least once a week."

"Why?" she asked, even as her magic stirred at the thought. "Because I believe that part the reason you have such difficulty controlling it is because you lock it up so much, leaving you unpractised with using the whole of it for more than minor, occasional tasks. Magic is a naturally wild; it does not do well to chain it. Thus, when your magic does leak through, it is all the more fierce. That is why I have set you the homework, to assimilate you into being comfortable with your power - *all of it* -" Viridian stressed, at her expression, "and because I think it will do you good. Understood? Good."

Susannah blinked.

"How did your lesson go?" her father asked as she walked into the lounge. "You look tired."

"Thanks," she said sarcastically. Her dad shrugged, unrepentant, though there was an edge to his movements that made her frown. "It went okay," she replied.

"What did she have you do? Your magic seems a little less volatile than usual."

Susannah's magic flickered slightly with pleasure, the lights in the room glowing brighter in their bulbs.

"Really?" she grinned despite her aches. "You think so?" He nodded, smiling a tad tightly.

"Yes. Not much, but a little bit. What did she have you do?" he asked again.

"Try not to attack her," Susannah grimaced. "I was supposed to stand in the room and not let my magic lash out when she attacked me." His gaze shot up worriedly, protective. His aura flared.

"She attacked you?" he demanded, starting to rise from his seat, shoulders tensed. Susannah waved her hand in a dismissive and hopefully placating gesture.

"Not seriously," she replied quickly. "It was needed. It was mainly just itching hexes or slight electric shocks and that type of thing. I'm afraid I did worse to her." Her tone dropped a bit, but her dad seemed appeased as she'd hoped, for the moment at least. "I was terrible," she continued, her facing falling, fists balling with frustration. "My magical control really is terrible. I'm bringing my 'Right Freakuency' album next week. It got a bit better when she put music on - by the way, have you ever heard of Patrick Daniels?"

"He's a pianist, very famous. Why?" her dad questioned, disregarding the helpfulness of the music as obvious. Susannah shrugged.

"Miss played it during the lesson."

"Which one of his works? I went to one of his concerts once, back in the day."

"Classical," she said. He nodded.

"Beautiful pieces. He used to be very popular," he

remarked.

"What? Doing classical?" Susannah questioned, "not that I have a problem with classical music or anything, but..."

"He did other styles too," her dad smiled wistfully. "Your mother and I danced to his fifth sonata at our wedding."

Susannah grinned.

"Well, I thought the lesson was good," she said. "Incredibly frustrating, but good."

"I'm glad," he stated, studying her closely.

"Do you really think my magic seems calmer?" she asked.

"Yes," he replied. "It's...nice to see." Her grin broadened. That was good. The smile soon faded though.

"You don't *seem* very happy about it," she said, trying not to feel miffed about that. He shot her a sharp, somewhat weary look.

"Another Underworld Variation has gone missing. The office has been hectic as they tried to get the story into immediate print."

Susannah immediately went still, dropping to sit on the other end of the sofa. Underworld Variations had been going missing for two years now, seen one day and the next – vanished. It was causing a lot of trouble, and she held out a demanding hand out for a copy of the paper. Her dad passed it over, watching her expression as she read.

Disappearances Continue!

Judith Stuart, a young demon, vanished from her home yesterday and not been seen since.

Only 173 years old, she is believed to be the latest victim in the string of hate-inspired disappearances which have been periodically occurring every three months for the last two years.

The eighth victim, Miss Stuart appears to have been tragically stolen in the same manner as her predecessors, somewhere between midnight and dawn. Similarly with all the previous cases, there are no witnesses to the disappearance, and the victim in question is an Underworld Variation, whose absence was only noted and reported the following day on her failure to arrive at work.

Whilst no leads have yet to be found as to the full nature and significance of these disappearances, authorities are doing everything possible to catch the culprit, whom is thought to be an Overworld Variation with great powers of compulsion as no Underworld Variation would otherwise have been so easily subdued, and the lack of witnesses suggest that a larger group could not have been directly present in the kidnapping.

Vanessa Cobre informs us that "Lord Carmel is now looking into the matter personally, and hence not to worry, as he is confident that the culprits will soon be brought to criminal justice."

In the meanwhile, we ask that anyone with information on this matter should step forward, and to remind all of our first citizens to remain extra vigilance.

More on page 3...

Susannah folded the paper up, looking up at her dad again. "We're going to update the wards again?" she confirmed. This would only create a greater viciousness within the Underworld in their area, and a renewed flood of attacks upon Overworld variations and houses. Her dad nodded once, tightly, in agreement. Susannah found herself tapping tunes on her knees in an effort to calm herself and her magic.

"Who do you think is doing this?" she asked. "I mean, they would have to be really good, wouldn't they? What do you think they want? Are they killing them?"

"I don't think they're killing them, no," her dad murmured. "There wouldn't be a need for disappearances, if this was a political murder. The bodies would be left to be found, a taunt. I don't think this is a traditional attack, whatever it is."

"You think they want the Underworld variations for something?"

"I don't know," her dad said, more sharply now, shaking his head. "And I don't want to know, you shouldn't look into this either. I don't care if you're interested, leave it alone, do you understand me?" he demanded.

Susannah paused at the terseness of his tone.

"Yeah," she mumbled, holding her hands up. "Not going to do anything, I'm not stupid."

"Good," his expression relaxed marginally. "You give your mother and I enough grey hairs already."

Susannah snorted.

"But you think it's a political thing?" she frowned, after a moment.

"It has undertones of that – all the victims are Underworld, and seeing as Lord Carmel has involved himself, that makes it political by default."

"And the compulsion part?" she murmured. "Do you reckon

that's true?"

"I think it's highly plausible."

Her dad stood, as if to signify the end of the conversation, rather abruptly.

"Dad?"

"I need to talk to some people, think no more on this and hold your tongue. The Prince has ears."

Susannah's nose wrinkled.

Chapter Nine – Emiah's Cause

"So," Krig looked around at them, specifically her, Delilah and Jamie. "Have you decided which Sector you want to join?" Susannah bit her lip. She thought she might have done, and nodded back cautiously.

"I think so, yeah," she murmured. Jamie and Delilah both gave their agreements too. Krig raised his eyebrows back at them, as if to encourage them to tell.

"Research," Jamie replied quietly, glancing at the elder O'Brian brother. "If Cade doesn't feel like I'm intruding?"

"Nah, not at all, mate," Cade shook his head. "Be nice to have some help. Great to have you on board."

"Research it is," Krig muttered, scrawling something into a battered planner. "Excellent." He flashed a smile.

"Hope you don't mind long hours and lots of dusty books and obscure topics," Mica joked. "Seriously, it's a wonder we get Cade out of his room! I think Mum thinks he's got a secret online girlfriend or something."

"You didn't know about Laura?" Cade returned, deadpan. "You've done that joke already, by the way." They laughed. Susannah assumed it was something to do with the joke that Cade had no friends cause he spent so much time around 'dusty books' and 'obscure topics.'

"I thought she was called Amelia," Leola smirked. "You hadn't forgotten Amy, had you? Ooh, you player." Delilah's head tilted, her brow furrowed. KT glanced over at them, smiling, laughter lines crinkling her porcelain skin, taking pity enough to fill them in.

"It's a standing joke," she explained. "Cade doesn't actually have a new internet girlfriend every week, he just...well last week he was researching Laura Carmichael."

"The vampire who came up with the theory of shadow-flitting?" Susannah and Jamie questioned, simultaneously, only to stare at each other. There was a moment of calm. "Now I feel stupid for not reading obscure textbooks," Delilah remarked mildly. Susannah shrugged awkwardly, and Jamie laughed.

"Don't worry," Leola said, grinning. "Most of us don't raid the rare, illegal book section either. I prefer the romantic fiction aisle, personally."

"I know," Krig groaned, before adding in a horrified mock whisper. *"She forced me to read the Paper Hearts!"*

"It's a great book," Leola declared empathetically. "You loved it. Don't lie."

Cade, Joel, Leon and David all snickered at Krig's expression. Susannah's lips curled.

"But yeah, anyway," KT said, shooting the boys a disapproving look. "Basically, Cade and Mica's mum doesn't know about the resistance, and so she believes Cade must either have a secret online girlfriend or hole up in his room playing videogames all the time...it changes...and so that led into the joke that Cade has a new online girlfriend every time he switches topics."

"Right," Susannah grinned. "I see."

"What sectors are you two planning to join?" Krig questioned, bringing the meeting back on track. "Delilah, you mentioned the MA...?"

"What's the MA?" Leon questioned. Delilah blushed; her skin colouring as red as KT's hair. Krig smiled, reassuringly.

"Well, when I was having my tour," Delilah began, appearing calm but for the way her fingers twisted into her hair. "I noticed you guys don't really do anything with other magical creatures, like, the non-human Overworld Variations like the Nymphs and the werewolves. So the MA...Magical Alliances...I thought could recruit them? Kind of like a subsection of the NR? I talked to Krig about it; I don't necessarily have to do it myself-"

"I - and Mica and Jess- thought it was a great idea," Joel said. "Delilah's right. We don't do anything with other variations, mostly because we haven't the time or the resources...and with the Tree Spirits for example, I don't know their etiquette and wouldn't have a clue where to begin without offending them."

"Does anyone object?" Krig asked. No one said anything, and their leader smiled again. "Brilliant. You are now in charge of the MA Sector, Delilah. Co-ordinate with the TA and the NR, come to me if you have any problems. Susannah?"

"Entry," she said. David whooped and gave KT a high-five, who laughed at the punk's antics. Susannah grinned, but caught a flicker of something in Krig's eyes. She dismissed it as nothing, for it lasted only a second.

"Welcome to the team," KT said. "Try not to let David wind you up too much and you'll be fine."

Susannah was sitting with David and KT, poring over documents. Her first priority as a new member of the E Sector was to learn and memorise most of the city, its shortcuts, and all the ways in and out of noteworthy places such as Anzarkledea manor. It wouldn't be an easy task, she knew, but she was determined to succeed with it. David and KT dropped to sit in front of her.

"Alright, listen carefully, young grasshopper," David said. KT was sketching something on a large piece of paper, her fingers light and nimble.

"This," the punk flicked his fingers at the forming drawing. "Is Anzarkledea, the lower levels – as stated, we don't know as much about the upper levels. Now, there are four ways, that we so far know of, to get in and out of Anzarkledea...five if you count jumping out a window."

"But you know, that's never been tested," KT added. "So I

wouldn't recommend it."

Susannah was startled, but amused, to hear such as David-esque (or so she had come to consider them) type of comment coming from her lips. She seemed so polite and lovely. It was like hearing Delilah cuss, it didn't quite ring properly. It was strange.

"There is, of course, the front door and the back door," David continued, with a small grin for his willowy sector member. "Those are rather obvious, but not always the best for sneaking in due to Charlie Edwards, who's the Gate Keeper, and the general security around the back...though if one had an initially legitimate and official reason for entering the manor, then Charlie can buy you time because you'd be on the gate records, even if you happened to get 'lost' whilst wandering around Anzarkledea."

"You researched him?" Susannah questioned, referring to the Gate Keeper.

"Her," David corrected, with a smirk. "Vampire, Charlotte Edwards, prefers to go by the name Charlie." Susannah blinked.

"Oh."

"And yes, we researched her," KT said. "She's two hundred and ten years old, ambitious, and wants to join Carmel's secret police. On the way to that, she is using her job as Gatekeeper to get noticed."

"She's good, then?" Susannah asked.

"Well, she's not thus far been promoted, but she's very vigilant."

"Anyway," KT said. "Apart from the front and back doors, you get the secret entrances and passageways."

"I dare say we know barely any of those," David muttered, sounding a bit dejected.

"But the ones we do know," KT continued, brightly, squeezing her sector leader's hand, "is Hangman's Bridge and the 'Bookcase passages.'"

"Hangman's Bridge as in the old bridge between Upper City and Middle City?" Susannah verified. "The one where they apparently used to, er...dispose of political prisoners?"

"That's the one," David replied cheerily, seeming to shake off the remnants of his negativity. "There's a loose stone underneath it, and through it, a passage leading to one of the Anzarkledea cloakrooms."

"We had a heart attack the first time we tried it out," KT admitted. "Nearly got caught – thought I had for a moment. It was horrible. I pretended to be a servant."

"And they didn't question that?"

"It was a Daemon who found me." That explained it; they weren't the brightest of Underworld variations, but made up for their lack of intelligence with their ability to morph between a humanoid form and that of some monstrous creature. She shuddered. They were, perhaps, more obviously frightening than any other variation.

"We'd need to time an entry very carefully if we went through there," David said. "Depending upon whether or not the Carmels have any particularly big political thing going on...if so, it would be near impossible to navigate through them. If it was a quiet night, however..."

"Does Carmel not know about these entries?" she asked, her brow furrowed. "It's his home, surely he would know, and have them guarded?"

"Guards have to switch shifts sometime," David said simply. "And if they don't, you can always stun them from behind." She studied him with a bit more of a wary eye than before. Most of the people in the resistance so far seemed so...nice, funny and relatively ordinary that it was easy to forget that in some way or another they were all dangerous, and in no way simply kind people. They were in an illegal resistance, after all, and she had no doubt they all knew how to fight...you did need a certain toughness of character to have the motivation to do something like this, after all. Someone content with life wouldn't be risking it in severely punishable mutiny.

"The bookcase passages are harder to enter, but it's easier once you've managed to get into them to slip into Anzarkledea unnoticed," KT stated. "They come out in the library on the upper floors of Anzarkledea, which is how we figured that was where the Carmels actually live...and barely anyone goes up there now except the two remaining Carmels - not that we've ever actually seen them – and sometimes, the Demon Lord's elite if they're reporting to him late at night."

"I thought Demon Lords didn't need to sleep," Susannah said.

"They don't," David agreed. "At least as far as I know, but as much as I'm aware, Carmel does business by day, and then whatever else he wants or needs to do at night, be that attending notable Underworld events or parties, or...well...studying."

Studying? Of course, one of the few confirmed facts about their youthful overlord was that he was a stone cold genius. None of the Carmels had ever been stupid, but Marco Carmel was off the charts with his intelligence and power levels. The Underworld weren't even supposed to have magic! Magic was an Overworld gift, where the Underworld had gifts such as increased speed, strength and lifespan. Marco Carmel, and Demon Lords or Ladies, were the exception to this for their ability to use magic as well as having all the talents normally granted to Underworld Variations. She would have called them Hybrids, if the idea wasn't so blasphemous and absurd. No one knew why the Demon Lords had magic, but as the generations came on, their power only grew, and Marco Carmel had been born powerful for even Overworld standards. It was bitterly unfair, all things considered, and had no explanation that she personally knew of.

"And what about the wards he has? For both places, surely they'd go off?" she asked.

"I'm a very good ward breaker," David said quietly.

Susannah blinked, the significance of that statement, and ones he'd made before, beginning to register.

"When you say very good..."

"I've never come across a ward I can't open. I'm a Locksmith."

Oh. Wow. A Locksmith was someone with a natural warding ability; they could ward and ward-break with barely any effort, easily unravelling the layers without a trace of their entering. It was like they had long nails to pick off the sellotape on wrapping paper, while the rest of the population had sausage stubs for fingers. They were key holders, and so largely viewed with suspicion.

"That's incredible," Susannah exclaimed, fascinated and awed. "Your parents-?"

"Signed me up for Carmel's Locksmith league and summer internship as soon as they could," David replied, smiling. It wasn't a nice smile. "How do you think I know so much about Anzarkledea considering the beings who visit that place either don't come out or don't blab, and certainly not to seventeen year old boys?"

"But, you...Carmel doesn't-"

"Locksmith's aren't that rare, sure he keeps an eye on us, but he's a busy man, he's got everyone else to keep track of too. It's easy enough to slip through the cracks if you know how."

"Are you a Locksmith too?" she asked KT. The girl shook her head.

"No, but I have a good memory and my sister works in the Carmel Kitchens."

"...but Demon Lord's don't need to eat?"

"They do before they turn," KT replied. "And the youngest hasn't turned yet. Besides, I think they enjoy the taste, more than anything, and then there's when they're hosting, which is at least once a week."

"It's strange; you never see the littlest Carmel...how old is he?"

David shrugged.

"I've heard Marco Carmel's overprotective, he probably doesn't let his baby brother outside the grounds," he said instead.

"Yeah, I've heard that too - the overprotective thing, that is," KT said. "Kind of hard to imagine the Underworld Prince caring for anyone." Susannah snorted at the mental image. She couldn't picture it. He was like the epitome of everything wrong with the world.

After a while, she turned back to her notes, trying to visualise walking through all the streets, picturing the houses, shops and parks as if she was there. She rubbed at her temples, not sure how she was going to manage to memorise every nook and cranny. Her own memory was pretty average, and though she could remember things well, they tended to not always be the things she was supposed to be remembering. For example, she could remember every lyric to every V.A.M.P song, but she could scarcely remember any of the numerous case studies she was supposed to have memorised for Duelling class. Still; she wasn't sure she could stomach working with Leon (and what did he have against her anyway?) every day. She was good with escaping and escape routes, and she already knew the city well, especially Middle City, so she would do her best with Entry. The resistance…

"How did the resistance start?" she asked, curiously. "Krig never actually told me the story." They turned to look at her.

"Well, he's modest like that," KT smiled. "He wouldn't."

"You know he founded us, right?" David verified. Susannah nodded. "Well, about three years ago, his eldest sister – Emiah – was, well, wraithed."

Susannah's blood chilled. 'Wraithing,' or being 'wraithed' occurred when a Dark Angel devoured all the emotions in their victim, hence feeding to full consumption levels. The end product was a wraith, a shadowy, emotionless figure that served the Dark Angels as part of their brood. It was really a rather horrible process. A wraith would do anything for the Dark Angel they were sired to, often fading away in the process. She swallowed the sudden lump of pity in her throat.

"Does he know the Dark Angel who did it?"

"Yes, he hunted them down, tore the pigeon's wings off in bloody vengeance and barely escaped a stint in Anzarkledea," David replied flatly. Susannah blinked.

"But he seems so nice."

"Krig's nice until you harm someone he cares about," KT said quietly. "Then he goes ballistic. Especially after Emiah."

"But how did that lead to a resistance on equality? How come he's not aiming for supremacy, not that I'm complaining but…"

"Because Krig has a very strong moral code and sense of justice which wouldn't allow him to do that, and Emiah was kind of like Delilah, I guess, and hated all that stuff. Her best friend was a Dark Angel."

"Emiah's best friend was a Dark Angel?" she repeated, incredulously. "How on earth did *that* happen?"

"I can't claim to know the full story, but she was," David

shrugged. "And that same Dark Angel paid for the funeral and all the arrangements. I guess Krig came to the conclusion that the world's not black and white, and to be honest, winning and enslaving the Underworld in turn just makes us as bad as them, don't it? It certainly don't help anything."

"So, Krig just upped and created a resistance group in response?" Susannah gaped.

"I think Emiah's death was the final straw for him, though he's always been on the wrong side of the law," KT murmured.

"To give you the simple version – I don't know everything, like I said - it started small, more remembrance and tribute to Emiah," David continued, "and grew from there when the court cases and everything started going to hell in a hand basket. He started working in rights, got himself roughed up several times as far as I know, nasty stuff..."

"How come none of this is in his records?" she frowned, puzzled, and disconcerted as to why she hadn't come across it before.

"Because Krig had a strong case," KT snorted. "Dark Angels aren't supposed to feed to full consumption, it goes against the hunting restrictions, but to admit the mistake would be to admit a problem in the system. The Carmels – not Marco, his parents in their last term of office and life - completely blanked it out, total media block. As far as anyone who doesn't remember her specifically knows, Emiah Carter doesn't exist. Krig's parents kind of...shut down after, they don't care what he's doing anymore, hardly look out for Cassie, it's appalling, anyway...Krig started firming his ideas up and then, eventually, recruiting...and the resistance began. Emiah's cause."

Susannah was silent for a moment, absorbing this.

"And the Dark Angel, Emiah's friend....what happened to

her? How come she's not part the resistance?"

"Kitty? She's probably long dead for being friends with a human; it's against the Declarations after all. Probably why Emiah got wraithed too…"

Bile clawed up her throat.

"Cheerful story, ain't it?" David said. "I wouldn't bring it up with Krig, it hurts him to remember too much."

"I can see why," she murmured. "The Carmels never brought him in? If he tried a court case then surely-" she paused, realisation dawning. "They died. The elder Carmels died, and Marco succeeded to become overlord." It had been a messy time, three years ago, the streets in simultaneous upheaval and celebration as the Underworld Prince came to power, after the couple of century's long reign of his parents.

"You know what it was like," KT shrugged. "Things were bound to slip through the cracks. One grieving teenager wasn't going to rank on the Prince's list of priorities – he had the werewolf rebellions to crush at the time anyway."

"And so here we are," came a new voice. They all whipped around to see Krig standing in the doorway, an unreadable expression on his face. "I see you've filled Susannah in on our history."

David nodded, eyeing their leader with a slight nervousness. "She asked and I didn't know if-"

"It's fine," Krig reassured. "Thanks, David."

"Anytime boss-man," David replied, the tension seeming to visibly drain from him, before he straightened again with a level of professionalism...or as close as David seemed to get to it anyway. "What can we do for you? Our skills of awesomeness are at your disposal."

Krig handed a sheet over to David and KT, with a strained smile.

"We need some more warding done on the Bristox safe house...could you take care of it? And I need to borrow your new recruit quickly..."

Susannah looked up at him, slightly startled. Krig shot her a quick smile, inclining his head at the door before walking out again with thanks. KT poked her when she didn't move. She followed.

Chapter Ten – The Ichtaca Ruins

"You wanted to talk to me?" Susannah questioned, as they sat down on the edge of the stage, legs swinging over the edge.

"Entry," Krig murmured. "Why Entry?"

"Was Entry a bad choice?" Susannah's brow furrowed. He studied her for a moment, arms folded across his knees.

"Entry is great; I'm just surprised *you* picked it. I would have assumed you to pick Tactical Advance."

"I like Entry," Susannah replied, a tad defensively.

"I'm sure," he said. "Doesn't mean you wouldn't be more suited to the TA-"

"-Are you ordering me to change sectors, boss?"

He looked at her flatly, at the interruption. She met him head on, defiance and challenge in her own eyes.

"No, I'm not a dictator, I value you your opinion," Krig replied. "*However*," he continued, "this is only to the extent that it doesn't damage the resistance as a whole. If you make it clear to me that you are better off in the TA, I will switch you. Is that clear?"

"Did you have this talk with Delilah and Jamie too?" Susannah asked, after a minute or so. "Or is it just me?"

"You're the only one who didn't pick the sector obviously most suited to you," Krig responded. "But my real question, right now, is why?"

"What makes you think I'd be so terrible in Entry?"

"If I thought you were terrible, I wouldn't allow it," he raised his brows. "I just think you're better suited to TA."

"And why's that?" she dared.

"For crying out loud, Susannah, now you're just being unnecessarily defensive. Cease and desist." He stared at her, his gaze unyielding, until she nodded in acceptance, unfolding her arms and taking a small, calming breath.

"Sorry."

"Apology accepted." His manner turned light again. "As for why TA over Entry...you take warding class, and your warding skills are strong, and made only more convincing by the amount of power you have to tap into and although I have nothing to account for how good you are at getting into places and escaping thereafter, I would assume you're not untalented at the art. This means you'd make a fair sector member in Entry, and certainly not the worst possible. Nonetheless, you would still be better in TA. I saw your 'interview'; you have a natural talent for deciding what to do. You know how the world works."

"It's called common sense and initiative," Susannah replied dryly.

"Yes," he agreed. "And you'd be surprised how many people lack those. Your duelling skills also far surpass your warding skills, and your instincts are razor sharp. You'll do well enough in Entry, I'm sure, but in TA you'd be phenomenal...not in the least also because you seem to like deciding what to do for yourself instead of following other people..."

She stared at him for a moment, before laughing quietly, even if she blushed at the last part.

"In all seriousness though, kid," Krig continued, "why Entry? I'm curious."

"Not a kid," she reminded.

"It's a nickname," he returned, patiently, before nudging her shoulder with his own. "Come on – tell me, that's what I'm here for."

Susannah bit her lip. His head tilted.

"Is it Leon?" he questioned, after a moment. She looked at him, stunned. "I see everything," he smirked, before shaking his head. "It's not difficult to see the tension...I hope that won't be a recurring problem?"

135

"I have no problem with Leon when he's not being so — *annoying*! Seriously, have I done something to offend him?" she asked, before she could stop herself.

Krig sighed, leaning back on his arms, scratching his head in an absent sort of way.

"Leon's story is not really one I can tell you," he murmured. "But it's not *you* so much that he's got issue with, rather your...power level."

"It's not like I can help it," Susannah muttered, staring at the floor. Wow. That...wasn't nice to hear. She was used to it, of course, but everyone else in the resistance seemed so nice and accepting that she'd thought, for once, that she might be okay.

"I know, and you shouldn't have to," Krig said, simply. "I'll be having a word with him-"

"-No!" Susannah interrupted quickly, turning to face him more directly again. "Don't."

"...and why not?"

"I don't want nor need special treatment," she mumbled.

"Are you suggesting I wouldn't look out for anyone in my resistance if I thought they were being treated unfairly?" he questioned mildly. Susannah winced.

"No, but..."

"But *nothing*, Susannah," Krig said. "Relax. It's fine."

"But people already think you've given me special treatment due to my magic, fast-tracking me in!" she protested.

"Then they'd be right," he replied evenly. "Whether you like it or not, you are special circumstances. People are always going to treat you differently, and that's a part of who you are, it's not necessarily a bad thing."

"Aren't you supposed to be for equality?" Susannah returned, though a faint smile tugged at her lips.

"Oh, I am," he grinned. "But there's a difference between

allowing everyone the same basic rights and opportunities then there is to thinking everyone is squarely equal. In a battle, for example, you'd prioritize and value people who could fight, or healers, over plumbers or secretaries. Equality as and of itself doesn't work, it needs to be more structured than that."

"So, like...equal opportunities for everyone, putting everyone on the same starting point, and then letting them branch of into their specialist fields and what would be best after that? Equal rights...but then judge on the basis of talent, rather than anything else?"

"Precisely," he murmured, flashing a smile.

"Reckon Carmel would let you take over from him?" Susannah asked, after a while. He smiled again, before squeezing her shoulder.

"Go find your sector again. I'll see what I can do about Leon."

"Does he just not like power?" she questioned, as she stood, inquisitive. He studied her for a while.

"Control, Susannah. Sometimes people want control in their lives, and your power can be perceived as a threat to that. Leon's had a hard life, and I know he's got some family issues, and his sister's sick...he simply wants more control over his life, and you, with your magic, are not easily controlled or categorised." Krig cleared his throat after a moment. "Don't go talking about that though, Susannah, I'm completely serious." He straightened, getting to his feet, levelling her with a look to express how much he meant the last part, before softening once more. "Now...I need to talk to Delilah about running the MA..."

On that note, he left, leaving her mind spinning more than it did before.

It was only a week or so later, after another lesson with

Viridian, that it occurred to Susannah that David and KT may have known somewhere she could practise magic. Now, it was just a matter of plucking up the courage enough to actually ask them about it. Thankfully, it was easier than expected, as they seemed to notice that something was bothering her. They sat down on either side of her, in an almost unnerving unison, leaning in. She paused in her memorisation, looking up at both of them. David beamed a bit too brightly.

"Susannah, we cannot help but notice that you seem a bit...distracted."

"Is something wrong?" KT asked. "Anything we can do to help?"

"Erm," Susannah wetted her lips, a bit awkwardly, before figuring she might as well just speak. What was the worst could happen? "I need to find some place to practise my magic."

"You can do that everywhere in the city, that's the beauty of magic," David replied dryly. KT shot him a look.

"I think she means somewhere a bit more private to practise *properly*," she said, mildly. "As in, with *all* of her magic. Where she won't get caught."

"Right..." David was quiet for a moment, giving her a considering look. "Obviously not in Upper City, or anywhere near Anzarkledea."

"Yeah, I gathered that bit," Susannah said. David rolled his eyes at her.

"We'll see what we can do," he agreed. KT was silent, her hazel eyes distant.

"What about the Ichtaca ruins?" KT questioned. "You ever heard of them, Susannah?"

David's head snapped to her, a gleam in his eyes, a smile curling relentlessly at his lips.

"Of course – KT, you're brilliant!" he murmured. KT blushed, smiling back, before looking at Susannah again.

"The Ichtaca ruins, they're about two miles outside the city, on the Overworld side. You ever heard of Ichtaca?"

"Nope," Susannah said, waiting for explanation.

"Ichtaca used to be the royal house, right back at the beginning, before the Carmels took control….Polo and Shadow's palace." Susannah's eyes widened. Polo and Shadow had been the establishers of the city and the original rulers of their world – though little else was known about them. All any of them really knew was that it was around their time that the Declarations were made, and the Underworld/Overworld hierarchy was established, as was the segregation between them. The rest was lost in history.

"How do you know this?" she asked. In all her reading, she'd never come across Ichtaca or its ruins. She'd have thought it would be common knowledge, a tourist attraction. Apparently not.

"Cade discovered it in some old records," KT said. "David and I went and found it. They're well hidden, in the Infinite Forest. It would be easy for you to miss them if you didn't know they were there."

"We can give you directions, if you want?" David offered. "The place reeks of magic and wards; you should be safe to practise there."

"Does Carmel not know about it?" Susannah questioned. "Doesn't the magic draw him in?"

"He knows about it, probably, but it doesn't bother him much I don't think. The point is, if he can already sense the magic of the place, and there is a *lot* of magic in that place, your power will be hidden among it. It's not really active anymore, and the magic and everything has stagnated, old, but…"

"Thank you," Susannah murmured. "You said you'd give me directions…?"

"Yeah, just a tic," KT conjured some paper and a pen, hastily beginning to scrawl, her copper locks falling over her face. David watched her with a small smile on his face. "Here you go," KT declared. "Enjoy yourself."

Susannah grinned.

Well, that had been a stroke of luck!

It took her some time, and getting lost, but Susannah eventually found the ruins about a day later. She'd never particularly liked the Infinite Forest, called so because of its size. It was the largest forest in the world, and curved all the way around Lower city, up the flank of Middle and Upper city, before coming to a stop in the back garden grounds of Anzarkledea.

The Ichtaca ruins were some way into the woods, where the trees grew particularly thick and gnarled, catching on her clothes, almost seeming to move. There were a lot of tree spirits around; she could hear them on the whisper of the wind. They didn't reveal themselves though, and she made an effort not to disturb them either.

The ruins themselves really were ruins – the upper floors had largely crumpled, and there were only the shapes of the bottom floor. No furniture remained, and the stone was ancient and worn, weathered and battered by the elements. There was a hum of magic around the place, deep-rooted, twisting into the very foundations of the earth around her, looping around the spiralling piles of rock that formed the ruins. There were the walls of the bottom floor, a hint of a staircase, but little else. Doors, too, had long since rotted away. Amazingly, no weeds were crawling out the stone, or the earth. It was entirely clean, and so was the clearing around the ruins. The trees formed a thick canopy above, almost bowed over the remnants of the building, concealing it effectively from a birds-eye view.

Delilah would have loved it; her best friend adored old places, they fascinated her. Beautiful wasn't quite the right word for it, but there was something enchanting, haunting about the location. For a while, she simply wandered around, stunned. Before, finally, coming to a stop in what seemed to be the remnants of an entrance hall. It opened up to the sky, as did all the ruins mostly; with only a few places that held any cover should it rain. Experimentally, she sent out a dart of magic, a blast with no particular intention. The walls seemed to simply draw it in, absorbing it without taking any damage. Susannah's eyes began to gleam, though she was still wary. She couldn't think of a time she'd ever been encouraged to just use her magic – all of it – without caution or restraint. Perhaps, as a kid, she had, before she was old enough to understand her parents when they told her not to.

Her parents hadn't necessarily been the strictest parents, outside of vague rules of doing well at school and being home before the Hunting Hours. They'd been dedicated to patching up her injuries when she got them, and being fiercely protective in the meanwhile. The one rule, however, that they had always crashed down on, and that she'd ever seen them losing their temper over, was the 'don't flaunt your power' rule.

It felt odd to break that rule now - the thought of dropping all her restraints both terrified and exhilarated her. What if she didn't manage to put them back? It had taken her years to build and perfect her self-control. Except, if Viridian was to be believed, her self-control and restraints weren't as good as she'd once thought either, and this could help. She drew a shaky, calming breath, before just letting everything explode. Hopes, dreams, fears, worries – everything. The sky roared, and the ruins didn't shake, and her mind was almost spinning at the rush of power that flooded through her. It raced through her veins, burned in her heart and behind her eyelids, tingling. It was more than she could ever have imagined, but it felt so right, so perfect. It was like a dam that had broken, and now it was gushing out...even if she had wanted to stop it all from spilling over the edges, she wasn't sure she could have stopped it. It was frightening, there was so much of it, and alarmingly only a bit above half of it felt familiar to her. The rest was raw, wild, untamed and almost alien to her – and yet, not at the same time. There was fury in that side of her magic, as if it were sentient and railing against being locked up, but it was welcoming at the same time, swirling around in ferocious embrace. She could scarcely breathe.

She didn't make any effort to perform any specific magic or spell, she didn't feel she could, there was too much for her to try and grab at. It poured through her metaphorical fingers like sand when she tried. So she just let it out. It was like thunder in her ears, lightning in her blood - magnificent, wonderful, but so very, very frightening. She never wanted to let it go, and could already feel herself regretting having to cage it all again...because she had to contain it again, at least for a little while. She wasn't in control. The magic was in charge, and she was just getting dragged along behind it, a vehicle.

She thought she finally may have known what Viridian was talking about.

What she didn't notice was the forest green eyes that watched her movements curiously, before disappearing, because her communicon started to buzz, shakily, as if the ruins had a bad connection...considering how old the place was, it wasn't implausible. She darted out the ruins, into the trees, shaking the little orb a bit to try and clear the signal, finally getting through.

142

"Hey, Del, now's not a good time-Del?" she paused. Her
best friend looked on edge, and Susannah's heart sank.
"What's the matter? Has something happened?"
"I'm at your house; can you come back from wherever you
are? I want to talk to you," Delilah said. Susannah struggled
to rein her magic in again, and it cut off easily enough,
where before it had been resisting, as if understanding her
need to go and see Delilah.
"I'm coming now."
Delilah nodded, smiling shakily, before hanging up.

Susannah nearly sprinted home, the euphoria of released
magic dimmed in the face of the greater urgency. She
arrived on record time, slamming the door behind her,
finding Delilah sitting in the kitchen cradling an empty mug
of tea.
"Del? You okay?" Susannah asked, dropping her bag
instantly, striding forwards. Delilah gave her a small smile in
response.
"Fine...might just be being paranoid," her friend muttered,
rubbing her nose tiredly.
"Do you want to talk about it?" Susannah offered,
awkwardly, wondering what was going on. Delilah nodded,
moving towards her room.
"Thanks for the tea, Serena," she said, to Susannah's mum.
"You're welcome sweetheart, anytime," he mum replied,
looking after her with a worried expression, before turning
to Susannah and mouthing 'is Delilah okay?' Susannah
shrugged in response, shaking her head, helplessly,
following.
Delilah sat down on her bed, grimacing at the mess, pushing
some clothes off and onto the floor, her hands folding
neatly into her lap. Susannah leant against the desk, eyeing
her.

"So…everything okay?" she asked again.

"Have you ever based your life on something, some assumption and fact, and then just had it all come crashing down when that one something, a keystone, is shook?" Susannah blinked.

"Does thinking I have control over my magic, but then finding out I don't, count?" she offered. Delilah snorted.

"I don't know, I suppose so." They sat in silence for a while, during which Susannah fought not to fidget. Finally, she sighed, breaking the quiet again.

"Del, what is it?" she asked. "I don't have awesome mind arts powers, remember? Can't read what you're thinking if you don't tell me. What's the keystone?" Delilah's mouth twitched in the direction of what could have been a smile as she glanced over, before sighing too.

"I think my parents were murdered."

It took Susannah a few seconds to even begin processing the statement.

"They died in a hunting accident…you think it wasn't so accidental?" she questioned, confused, and a bit skeptical. Delilah bit her lip.

"Do you think that sounds stupidly paranoid?" she returned. Susannah shrugged.

"Depends on your reasoning for thinking so and changing your previous opinion," she replied, reservedly. "Do you have any new evidence or anything?"

"Kind of," Delilah mumbled. "It's just that – you know – none of the vampires were ever convicted for their murder."

"Del," Susannah said, as gently as she could. "That's not exactly unusual, especially not under Contessa and Damien Carmel. Most the Underworld get away with these type of thing-"

"-Please hear me out," Delilah said quietly, not raising her voice. "I've always listened to you." Susannah obligingly fell silent, and Delilah continued. "I just started researched it because of that...and...well, you know they said there were no witnesses?" she asked. Susannah nodded, her mind spinning. "Turns out...there was. It was just covered up, or maybe not even covered up, Grandma and Grandpa just never told me...I don't know"

"And this witness told you it was murder?" Susannah verified. Delilah paused, before shaking her head.

"No. I haven't ever met her."

"...then why?" Susannah began, brow furrowed. This made no sense, there was no logic to it, she didn't see why Delilah seemed to genuinely believe this new theory.

"She's in the trauma ward at the mental Hospital. Checked in about a month after it happened," Delilah said, eyes wide and meaningful.

"And you think there might be a connection," Susannah stated. Delilah nodded, firmly.

"I think that I want to have a look, just to be sure. It never sat right with me, you know it didn't...Grandma and Grandpa won't talk about it, but sometimes they just get the oddest expressions and..." Delilah trailed off, powerlessly. "I think there's more to the story. Robbie told me I'm just being mad, cause I want there to be more...but I have to *know*...you don't believe me, do you?"

"I think it's a little sudden and farfetched," Susannah allowed. Delilah's lips pressed together in a thin, unhappy line, and Susannah hastily continued. "But if you think there's something to it, I'll help you investigate, of course. You're my best friend! Do you want me to go with you to see if you can try and talk to the witness...who is she anyway?"

Delilah hesitated for a moment, still looking upset, but there was a hint of something else to it now too, a different sort

145

of reluctance.

"Rebecca Daggey."

Chapter Eleven - Explosive beginnings

Keeping a careful eye on her surroundings, Susannah darted across the street to Le Café Noir. It had grown to be a familiar haunt in the last month or so. This particular meeting had been called rather suddenly; with only a small envelope sliding through her letter box a half hour earlier to signify her of its happening. Something big was up, of that at least she was sure. She closed the door behind her with a soft click, studying the scene before her as she did so. Delilah was sitting with Joel, talking animatedly, presumably about the, still work in progress, Magical Alliances sector. Her best friend smiled in greeting when she entered. Krig was at the front of the room, deep in conversation with Leola and the TA; his expression was serious. Something was definitely going on. He too glanced at her when she entered the room, before his gaze flicked away again. Susannah couldn't help but feel a slight, ridiculous disappoint grow in her stomach, though she could scarcely fathom why. She brightened when Jamie hailed her over, ignoring the smirk on Delilah's face at their interaction. She weaved her way over to him. He was in the far corner of the café, observing the proceedings with interest.

"Hey," she took the seat beside him. "What's going on?"

"I'm not completely sure," he replied, leaning towards her marginally. "Something's happened though..."

"Krig looks stressed," she noted, frowning. Jamie's head tilted to once side as he surveyed their leader. He hummed quietly in agreement, before his gaze rested on her again, appraising.

"What do you think's happened?" he asked after a moment. Susannah shrugged.

"No idea," she said. "It's bad though, whatever it is." It had to be, everyone looked apprehensive and on edge now;

even David, which was saying something as the punk had so far seemed pretty unshakeable. An instant cathedral-like hush fell as Krig called for silence.

"We have a mission," he announced. Susannah felt a strong thrill of excitement burst like confetti in her insides at his words, it streamed through her veins like a shot of electricity, despite the abruptness of the announcement. Her magic prickled with anticipation as she exchanged an excited look with Delilah, before glancing at Jamie. His features were arranged in an unreadable, stony composition. "A man named Remasso Sklis is set to be assassinated today, you might have heard of him. He invented Gossamer." Susannah's eyes widened with recognition. Her magic began to ache on principle, fearing the substance in question, reacting instinctively and causing everyone's gaze to flick to her, before returning to Krig.

"What's Gossamer?" KT asked blankly.

"It's a rare substance that locks your magic up in three out of its five forms so that you can't use it," Krig said bluntly. There was a moment of silence, shocked, and people glanced at her again, as if suddenly noting why she'd reacted so badly.

"That's barbaric," Mica snarled. "Why on earth would anyone invent that?"

"Cause they're Underworld lovers," David replied conversationally. "Boss, no offence or anything, but why do we care if the douche-bag dies? I say good riddance."

"Because," Krig began in a disapproving tone of voice. "If Carmel's assassins get to Sklis before we do then they get his supply of Gossamer, and the procedure for how to make more of it. He may be an Underworld lover – not that we have any proof of that - but I doubt even he would give the Underworld Prince a weapon like that." Susannah personally thought Krig was being a little optimistic - it

148

wasn't that she doubted his judgement; it was more that she thought he might underestimate the dark allure of the Demon Lord. There was a reason behind the dramatic drop in resistance or resentment since the time of his parents, other than the fate of the werewolves. He was supposedly very charming; dangerous, probably psychotic and certainly ruthless, but charming nonetheless. Also, why would anyone who wasn't an Underworld Lover make a substance like Gossamer? Unless Gosammer was an unexpected by-product of another invention? It made no sense for Sklis to be an Underworld Lover after all, he was a Werewolf!

"Okay," David said after a moment. "Save Remasso Sklis. Got it."

"Do you know the forms?" Jess questioned.

"Fabric, spray and liquid," Krig said. "The fabric must be touching your skin and in doing so locks your magic in your body, if the spray is in the air your magic is similarly unable to have any effect on the physical world, much like if you swallow the liquid form – in which case, you would not be able to use magic until the gossamer has been purged from your body."

"That's sick," Joel muttered. "I-shadow-I think I might actually be sick."

"How do you know he's going to be assassinated?" Jamie asked. Krig inclined his head in the direction of the TA.

"Leon overheard one of Carmel's servants talking about it...they were drunk."

"If they were drunk, how can we trust them to be reliable?" Delilah enquired, brow furrowed. Krig smiled wryly.

"We can't, but can we really afford ignore the implications if it is?"

"I guess not," the blonde murmured, looking troubled. "So what are we doing?"

"We're going to see if we can relocate Sklis and his family

before Carmel's lot get to him."

"All of us?" Jess wrinkled her nose. Krig shook his head.

"No, we're splitting up," he said. "Joel, Alice and Delilah, I want you lot to go Pembroke Street and organise the safe house - make sure it's still secure and can be lived in for a short duration of time, go now, this is urgent." Joel stood up with a nod, quickly motioning for the other two to follow him. Delilah looked nervous, her hands twisting against the hem of her t-shirt. Susannah offered her what she hoped was a reassuring smile as they left, and Krig was already continuing without pause. "Cade, Leola, Jamie and KT, I need you to create some false IDs for Sklis and his family. Quick as you can, but make them solid, realistic and forgettable. They need to be able to fool the wardens. Hurry," Krig ordered. "We've lost too much time already."

Leola smiled at Jamie.

"C'mon gorgeous, let's see if you're any good. Who knows, I might even let you join the TA if you get sick of Cade and his dusty old-"

"-*Leola,*" Krig cut in. "Less talking, more moving please." Susannah's stomach squeezed "David, Leon, Susannah - you guys are with me. Let's go. Cass, stay here at base in case anything goes wrong, you too Jess. Keep us connected with the others - okay? Don't let the connection fall." Cassie agreed immediately while Jess scowled.

"You mean I can't come?" she whined.

"No," Krig said tightly, no compromise in his voice. "I need people here in case of emergency, and I'm not leaving anyone on their own."

"Susannah could stay," Jess began. Krig was already out the door. Leon followed him promptly, while David frowned at Jess, before he too left for the door.

"Come on, kid," he called.

The door slammed shut behind them.

150

Soon, they were in Upper City, Underworld territory. Susannah felt distinctly uneasy, her magic crackling at the automatic danger of the location. It was beautiful, there was no denying that, but it was unequivocally dangerous. It wasn't official hunting hours, but many of the Underworld variations weren't adverse to bending the rule if a 'lower being' dared enter their part of the city. It wasn't forbidden for Overworld variations to go or live there, she knew some of the resistance members did, but the Underworld didn't like it and were liable to attack. The four of them made their way to Mellington Street, just on the edge of Upper City. There, instead of skyscrapers and obscenely expensive penthouse flats, were the smaller, but infinitely more private and still obscenely expensive houses and cottages. Every building was isolated from its neighbours by towering, immaculate walls or fences. No place in the city matched Anzarkledea, the Demon Lord's mansion and base of operations, but Susannah still felt her jaw drop at the sheer grandeur of it all. They crept along the streets, hearts pounding, trying not to be seen by anyone. There were a few close calls, in which they had to frantically scramble for adequate hiding places, or in one case, even an excuse as to what they were doing there. Finally, however, they hid crouched across the street from Remasso Sklis' residence. "How the hell do we get in there?" she whispered. The security was prevalent. Despite herself, Susannah could feel a slight admiration grow for Carmel's unknown assassin; he had to be brilliant at his job to be able to get into this building without drawing attention. From what she'd been told on the way over, Sklis was an extremely paranoid (not surprising considering his living area) and a bit of a hermit. Susannah was frankly amazed that he'd chosen to live in Upper City at all, but she supposed the houses *were* nicer here, and that it was a mark of wealth and status, especially if he didn't plan on going out, it was more private. Also, wherever he'd intended to create Gossamer or not, the Underworld favoured him for it, so he was safer than the average Werewolf or even the average Overworld being of any variation. Yet…if he had created Gossamer by accident…why had he published the invention? None of this made sense, and it just heightened her unease.

"David, can you take down the ward?" Krig asked. David's features were uncharacteristically grave, his expression thoughtful.

"You doubt me, boss?" the punk replied, eyebrows arched, voice a bit too light to be truly casual. "Give me a moment." Susannah's attention zoned on him; immensely interested to see the Locksmith in action, even if she was on edge. Krig smiled just faintly at her, a somewhat strained smile, but didn't say anything. She watched, curiosity burning, as David closed his eyes, his aura flaring and searching out the protective enchantments around the building. Ward breaking was a rather delicate operation; the slightest mistake would bring the protections raining down on the intruder, and numerous alarms ringing. Warding itself didn't require as much finesse, as a person was essentially layering up ambient magic to create a wall of sorts. She was better at Warding; she didn't have enough control over her magic to be a proficient ward breaker. Warding was just layering magic and spells, at its essence; though it got trickier the more intricate the ward and whether or not it was playing off and needed to be balanced with other wards. Ward Breaking required an intense amount of concentration, because there wasn't room for the slightest slip. A few minutes later, she felt the Sklis' wards beginning to silently unravel, much to her amazement. There was a small hole, an invisible tunnel in the magic. "It will stay open for ten minutes," David muttered, looking slightly strained, beads of exertion forming on his forehead. His knuckles were white as he struggled to temporarily control the wards. "Hurry. This dude has some good works."

"Come on," Krig instructed, moving forwards. "Keep in my footsteps no matter what, or you'll trip something, and keep an eye out for any traps." They edged forwards in silence, taut with tension. Susannah's heart was pounding in her chest, her magic flickering with nerves. She worked on keeping it still, under control. Leon was behind her and David behind them both, keeping the wards unravelled in a little bubble around them. She could feel the wards pressing against them, not quite oppressively, but a constant itch that wanted to turn into a searing pain but couldn't. The rooms of the house were elaborate, well-furnished and lavish. She didn't get to see much; they weren't exactly there for the scenery. She did note a large, intricate star constellation painted across one of the rooms though, and the deep scratches gouged into the walls on the stairs. Leon stopped to examine them, but didn't touch under Krig's hissed instruction. A few minutes later they were nearing the top of the house, and there was no sign of Remasso Sklis, or any life outside of them really. It was eerie, like a ghost house. There were no signs of his children, no shrieks of laughter or noises otherwise. Were they all out? Had they screwed up on the mission already? Susannah couldn't help but feel uneasy nonetheless, and think otherwise. There were games half played with a plush dragon and a princess on the stairs, and the communicon in the living room had been smashed. She feared they were too late. They finally reached the bedrooms and Krig abruptly stopped in front of her, frozen.

"What is it?" Susannah whispered. She tried to peer around him, pausing when she caught a glimpse of the bedroom

Krig was staring at. Her heart ground to a halt. Remasso Sklis was lying on the floor, spread-eagled with blood pouring from his chest. The werewolf was ashen and stiff, white as sheet. Dead. There was an expression of great horror and pain on his face, a twisted grimace, mouth half opened in scream. She felt nauseous, her hands trembling unperceivably. Then she noticed the other presence in the room, suddenly, with a jolt. It was as if someone had slammed a stop button on her circulation. Her insides flooded with ice. The figure was the assassin, it had to be! He definitely wasn't what she expected. The Dark Angel was tanned and broad, with muscles bulging beneath his tight white t-shirt – he looked more like a surfer than she had imagined the third most dangerous being in the city would. He was regarding them with the copper eyes characteristic of his variation, a cruel smile distorting his lips, just sitting there, on the bed, casual and completely silent. He must have been watching them. Susannah felt bile claw a path up her throat, terrified by his presence and the fact that she hadn't noticed him immediately. He was a killer. He killed people for a living. He enjoyed it. She was standing across the room from him. Her back stiffened, her magic curling instinctively in anticipation of a fight.

"Well, if the little humans haven't come out to play," he drawled lazily, straightening off the bed. "You're too late, you know." The Assassin waved a thick sheaf of documents in the air. "Mr Sklis was most co-operative in the face of death."

"Yet you killed him anyway," Krig spat, eyes tight with rage. The Dark Angel shrugged, before studying the papers in his hands once more; the secrets of Gossamer.

"Are you going to kill us?" the words slipped past Susannah's lips like vomit, distasteful and without her permission, following the tendrils of their panic. Surely he wouldn't let them know his identity if he was going to let them live? Krig, David and Leon all glanced at her, aghast. She ignored it, her stance ready to attack or defend on a split second basis. For the first time, the assassin looked at her, gaze searing through her skin. His head tilted with interest. She felt Krig step just very slightly in front of her, inducing the barest flash of annoyance as much as gratitude. She could look out for herself! He didn't need to coddle her.

"You were not my primary target."

"No, but you seem like the type of sick freak who would kill beings for pleasure regardless of your orders, so I figured it would be prudent to check," she replied coldly, before she could stop herself.

"New girl," Leon snarled, under his breath, warningly. The assassin smiled; a horrible twisted imitation of a smile.

"Is that so?" he drawled. "Rather bold assumptions that you're making there, Susannah. I could be offended." She froze for a moment, as did the rest of them. What? He *knew* her? "Really, little girl," he continued mockingly. "Did you think we weren't aware of you and your...exploits?" The assassin's grin widened, grotesque. "You're making quite the name for yourself in our circles; the Kerrs especially have friends in high places." Susannah resisted the urge to blanch, her mind spinning back, wondering where she recognised the name from. Kerr...Kerr...bloody hell. The demon! Ordell, Cutler and Kerr, who'd attacked her! Krig's stance shifted further in front of her, fiercely, and David stepped closer too. In direct contrast, Leon seemed to want to edge away. "I'd make more of an effort to watch my tongue if I were you, darling, if you want to keep it," the assassin finished. He was in front of them in a flash, causing them to automatically jump back away from him, alarmed. Susannah's magic flared, warningly, but he ignored it completely.

"I'll bear that in mind, thanks," she replied tightly.

"Do," he purred, but he'd dismissed her now, his attention turning solely to Krig. "How's your sister?" he grinned. Krig's expression twisted, and, the next second, he was on the assassin, fighting, blasting magic out ferociously, temper snapped. The second after that, the assassin, with a hiss of pain and blood pouring out his nose, had a tight hold on Krig's throat, pulling up so their leader's toes were just skimming the floor. Susannah darted forward, in unison with David and Leon, only for the assassin to constrict his grip. "Stay back..." he warned, "unless you want Mr Carter here to die."

The three of them froze on the spot with a mutual horror, watching as Krig's hand automatically closed around the Dark Angel's wrist to try and pull the suffocating fingers away. Krig's eyes were wild, defiant, unafraid and more dangerous than she'd ever seen them. His hand moved to press flat against the assassin's chest.

"I'll take you with me," Krig threatened, tone ice-cold. "You don't scare me, you're pathetic!" But then, as the grip constricted once more, before the Dark Angel's attention shifted again and he put his other hand to his ear. For the first time, Susannah noticed an earpiece, now buzzing in a low murmur. The assassin's features contorted, but remained concentrated on whatever he was hearing, before going utterly blank. They all held their breath, as if they were the ones with a restricted passage to their lungs, magic geared to attack if they had to. Krig was the only one who seemed perfectly calm now, a deadly gaze fixed on the Dark Angel holding him, even as his lips started to turn blue. After a few seconds, the assassin let Krig drop to the floor in a coughing heap, releasing him almost reluctantly. David immediately dragged Krig back and further away, and the

Dark Angel did nothing to stop it. Krig's gaze still hadn't moved, even as he pulled air into his chest again, gasping.

"Seems it's not your day to die by my hand today *Krig*," the assassin said, tonelessly, eyes hard, burning with an almost personal vengeance. Had he received new orders? Susannah's magic was surging, wondering if making a shot would ultimately worth it, but the Dark Angel was doing something else now.

He pulled a small round object from his pocket and what looked like a controller, simultaneously tucking away one copy of the gossamer notes. Susannah took another unconscious step back, instinctively - the ball was an incendiary bomb. The assassin glanced up, meeting Krig's eyes with a pitiless smile. Then he held up the controller.

"There are bombs all over this house, they will detonate in about three seconds when I click the button," he informed them, with a malicious amusement. "Run." Krig gaze flicked to the controller, then without pausing to see if the assassin was bluffing, he shoved them all in front of him towards the door. Susannah twisted her head to see one copy of the Gossamer notes placed next to the body of Sklis, before the Dark Angel disappeared in a flash of large, white wings. Her eyes widened.

"Out! Everybody out!" Krig roared, giving her another push that had her stumbling into action.

The next second, the rooms were exploding beside them.

The world turned black and red as thick, clogging smoke streamed through the building and fire devoured everything in its path in a blistering hunger. The one copy of Gossamer notes rotated in her mind, taunting her with its knowledge, even as she was being swept forward relentlessly. She opened her mouth to point this out to Krig - because the information was still available! - before realising that probably wasn't the smartest thing to do in a burning building. Her eyes stung, everything a blur. The next second they were bursting, light headed and coughing, onto the street. Susannah's head was spinning. David instantly fell to his knees, heaving for air as ash clung to his clothes and face. Leon's arms were burnt and cut by splinters, his normally impeccable appearance dishevelled and dirty. Krig swore loudly.

"They knew we were coming," he cursed. "They must have; it was a bloody trap!" David stared at the other, ashen faced and trembling. His aura felt exhausted, from having kept the wards from imploding on them. They were all but disintegrated now; they're foundations burnt and their master dead. Susannah spun to face Krig, unable to think clearly. The communicon was making an irritating, buzzing noise.

"Were those notes really important?" she demanded, a scheme already twirling fixatedly through her mind. "Cause the assassin copied them and there's one copy still in there on the floor." They all gawped at her as if she'd gone mad. "Yes, but -" her boss began, pulling his communicon from his pocket. Not listening to more, Susannah sprinted back into the crumbling building, her magic surging to protect her from the blasting heat, water spurting from her hands. "Susannah!" She heard Krig scream. "Get back-" his words were drowned out by the hiss of flames. She couldn't see properly, her eyes streaming, feeling dizzy. Frantically, she dodged her way back up to the bedroom. The assassin was gone, vanished without a trace. The final incendiary bomb was counting down next to the sheets of notes. She scrambled across the wreckage, lunging for the papers. She dropped them once in her fumbling panic, before crushing them to her chest and sprinting for the door. She glanced at the incendiary - fifteen seconds. Heart in her mouth, she raced out the room, flinching as the house fell into ruin around her. Even with magic, it was getting difficult to breathe. She was at the hallway when the final bomb went off; the explosion large enough to reverberate through the building to lift her clean off her feet. She was aware of nothing. Spinning in the stars. Endlessly. Then she hit both reality and the roadside with a sickening thud.

The world realigned itself in what could have been both seconds or an infinite amount of time later. Hands were hovering tentatively above her head, before swooping down to keep her still when her eyes cracked open. "Easy," a voice warned. David. She blinked blearily, dazed. Her ears were ringing and his voice sounded as if it were being issued from underwater. She moved to sit up, cautiously, looking around her. She didn't recognise where they were. They must have still been in Upper City, albeit away from the scene of the explosion. "Alright?" David demanded roughly.
"Fine. Peachy," she replied numbly. Her voiced sounded a tad croaky. Leon was scowling at her.
"What were you thinking, Skelsby?" he snarled. "Krig told you not to go in there!"
"Where is Krig?" she asked, worried. "Is he okay?" Leon didn't reply, merely stalking away with a withering expression marring his features. She followed his gaze. Oh. Krig was standing a few feet away, talking furiously to Jess and Cassie through the communicon, the gossamer papers clenched in one white-knuckled hand. His face was livid with rage and concern, white as Sklis' had been. She caught only a few words - "attacked" "trap" and "injured." Fear swelled inside her gut, indefinable terror that smothered all other emotion. She looked at David, uncomfortably. Her sector leader's gaze was hard, relentless, disappointed. Her throat

felt dry. "Where are we?" she asked after a moment. How had she got here? How much time had passed? What HAPPENED?

"About ten minutes away from Mellington Street," David replied tightly, after a pause in which he seemed to be debating on whether or not to answer her. "You were unconscious." She nodded. Right.

"Yeah, I, um, remember that bit," she said. His jaw clenched. Susannah wasn't sure whether or not to be thankful that Krig seemed to have finished his conversation, striding over to them, Leon at his heels. His eyes were scanning across her to check her general state of wellbeing, but he didn't meet her stare, concentrating on putting the communicon and the notes away instead.

"Can you walk?" he questioned tersely. She nodded.

"Yeah, no harm done really." That seemed to be the wrong thing to say, for her boss stiffened and David glared. Leon merely rolled his eyes, derisive as always. She opened her mouth to apologise.

"Come on," Krig interrupted, before she could. "We're going back to Noir."

Chapter Twelve - Just a little girl

Susannah followed Krig nervously, kept at bay by the alarmingly cold set to his features. All traces of a smile had gone; it was as if the warmth and friendliness on her leader's face had never even existed. He still hadn't met her eyes, and she couldn't quite decide if that was a good thing or not. It was good, because it meant that she didn't have to witness the rage and awful disappointment that she knew would be searing in his gaze, but it was bad too...because all she was now left with was the vacuum of uncertainty regarding just how badly she had screwed up. He seemed so angry. She didn't understand it. They'd needed that information, so she didn't see what was so terrible about her actions. Silently, she willed him to spare her even a glance - even fury would be preferable to this all-consuming sense of unknowing. Her insides twisted. *Let him look round.*

"Is he going to kick me out of the resistance?" she whispered. David flicked his eyes at her for a moment, before looking away again with a terse irritation.

"I don't know," he said shortly. Nausea bubbled in her gut.

"You're mad at me too," she noted quietly. David swore under his breath, darkly.

"Let's just get back to the Café," he snapped. "Now's not the time." That was a yes then, resounding. Her magic flickered, wrapping around her form in a familiar comfort. It drew David's attention once more, and her sector leader sighed. "You gave me a bloody heart attack Susannah. Cassie and Jess were having a meltdown on the communicon; Joel, Delilah and Alice had just faced down a hit squad and we've got nothing from Leola! They could have been dead, and as far as we knew so could you. Yeah, I would say I'm mad at you." His fists were clenched, his aura spiking every now and again. Susannah felt a fresh pang of guilt curdle her blood, rancid in its expressive shame.

"We needed the information," she said. "You know we did."

"It was a stupid thing to do," he growled. "Stupid and reckless."

Silence reigned.

They soon arrived back at Le Café Noir. Krig wrenched the door open without a word, standing against it to hold it open as they all traipsed in. Susannah hesitated, uncertain on whether it was a good idea to get within touching distance of her boss. His expression was unusually grim. David regarded her for a moment, taking in her stillness, inclining his head that she should go in before entering himself. The last one outside, she considered running...but then it would be even worse once she came across Krig again. How could she show her face at the next meeting if she fled like a coward? Besides, his gaze was fixed on her rather pointedly now. The moment was gone. Steeling herself, she slipped past him. The door shut behind her. He crossed the room, brushing against her unmoving form, and dropped onto the armchair at the front. It was battered, but the best one and everyone automatically reserved it for him. Even Leon. Everyone else was already there; Leola, Jamie, Cade and KT included, all looking slightly confused and fearful.

"Well, that was illuminating," Krig remarked after a moment. The tension in the room broke a little at the comment. "You guys did well today," he continued, more sincerely now. "You got into a tough situation and pulled yourselves out of it. None of us could have predicted what happened today. Good job."

"Aw, boss," Mica sniffed. "We love you too!" There was a chuckle of laughter around the room.

"Oi, back off," Leola ordered with an uncertain grin. "He's mine!" Krig smiled, though his expression remained slightly strained.

"Seriously, I'm proud of you," he said. "Now go home and get some rest. I don't want to see you until the next meeting. We'll talk about today then - okay?" There was a clatter of chairs at the dismissal. "And stay out of trouble." Susannah rose, stopping under the glare Krig sent her way. Instead, she watched as the rest of the resistance left. Jamie and Delilah were walking together, talking quietly. Delilah shot her a highly venomous, disappointed look when she opened her mouth to speak.

"Don't," her best friend warned, "I heard what happened…and just…not now. I can't talk to you right now, Susannah." Susannah fell silent again. Her stomach was churning. She heard Krig telling Cassie not to bother waiting outside, because he would be a while. She considered running again, under the pretence of failing to understand that the glare was a silent order to stay put. Slowly, like a train moving away down a tunnel, the noises and conversations of the others faded into silence as the door shut behind them.

No more witnesses.

Krig was motionless, regarding her with an intensity which would make a basilisk proud.

"What were you thinking?" he demanded harshly. She didn't flinch, staring at him impassively. It wasn't like she wasn't capable of defending herself if things turned ugly. She hoped they didn't though. She'd grown to respect Krig. She didn't want to hurt him.

"I was thinking that we needed that information," she replied evenly. His magic crackled, harnessed lightning and Susannah realised suddenly, for perhaps the first time, that it was powerful - by normal people standards. If they fought, she knew she would win every single time, however arrogant that may sound, but it wouldn't be easy. Their duel had proved that. Looking at Krig now, there was a wildness to his magic and posture that she'd only ever caught glimpses of before. He was a resistance leader, an illegal resistance leader; she was only just beginning to see the implications of that. He was dangerous.

Of course, she'd thought of that before a few times, but it was times like this that reminded her once more. She also found her magic was automatically cataloguing what she knew about him, in anticipation of threat. There wasn't all that much, only the snippets she'd gathered from that one time she duelled him.

"You deliberately disobeyed my orders," he said flatly. "And almost got yourself and the people around you killed in the process." Susannah could feel her frustration beginning to surge. Everyone kept acting like she'd done something terrible. Sure, she hadn't obeyed orders, but it had worked out well, and what the hell was this about the people around her? She drew a calming breath.

"I apologise for disobeying your orders, but it worked out, didn't it? If I hadn't done it we would have lost the information and Carmel would have won. Besides," she picked up heat. "It's not like I dragged anyone in there with me, so I seriously do not see what your problem is!" Her magic was curling, itching to lash out.

"My problem," Krig snapped. "Is that you almost died. *We thought you were dead.* David was about a split second from running in there after you to check for a body."

Susannah blinked. What? "But, hey, you didn't actually drag him in, so everything's cool right?" Krig continued acidly. "If David got himself burnt alive looking out for you because you couldn't wait for orders, it would all be fine, wouldn't it? I might have a couple of dead recruits on my hands, but that's okay, we needed the information. Pity it burnt along with David Black and Susannah Skelsby!" Her boss came to an abrupt halt, before looking away from her as he paced - a trapped tiger. After a moment, he turned to face her once more, noticeably more collected. "As surprising as it may be to you, Susannah, there is actually a reason behind my orders." She felt like she'd been hit by a hover car. Crap. She hadn't...what if?

"I-" she stammered ridiculously, any frustration draining out of her. "You wouldn't have let him run in after me, would you?" She tugged a hand through her hair. "Shadow, no wonder David was mad at me."

Krig's made a curt, angrily jerky gesture at one of the chairs. Sit," he instructed. She surveyed him for a second, and then dropped into a seat. He pulled up a chair too, sitting opposite her. There was an uncomfortable pause, at least on her behalf. Krig sighed, with a constrained rage still present, though he was obviously making an effort to *sound* calm. "Kid, do you understand now why I'm so furious with you?"

"Because I almost got David killed," she mumbled.

"And?"

"I disobeyed your orders?"

"Are you asking me, or telling me?"

"Telling you," she said, mustering a little more conviction into her tone. People had the horrible habit of questioning her on that; Viridian did it too. His head was tilted back slightly as he surveyed her. When the silence dragged on, he spoke again.

"You're still missing something," he prompted. She frowned.

"I can look out for myself," she said. "You don't need to worry about me getting myself killed. It's not your responsibility anyway."

"I've no doubt you can," he responded. "Doesn't stop me worrying though - don't give me that look, you can tell me it's not my responsibility all you like but that won't change my opinion. I'm an adult, you're not, and you're in *my* resistance group. That makes you my responsibility."

"I'm not a child," she snapped. He smiled, faintly, without mirth.

"You're not quite an adult yet either, especially not legally, however much you seem to dislike the fact." She folded her arms.

"Is there a point behind this?" she asked.

"I would also have had to tell your parents that you got killed in my resistance," Krig bit out, his expression flat. Susannah paused at the statement, and the other continued, unyielding. "I would have had to go to your house and explain to your mum and dad why their fifteen year old daughter will not be coming home to them, will not be graduating, or ever getting married and exactly how and why she got herself burnt to death. Did you consider that, Susannah?" he demanded. "Did you even consider the effect your death would have on the people you left behind? On your parents? Delilah? *Me?*"

Susannah swallowed. Preferred

"But it all turned out okay-"

"-It could have just as easily, if not more easily, gone wrong," Krig returned. "The truth of the matter is, however much you try to justify yourself, that you did not think. You simply sprinted into a burning building without any serious thought of the consequences, and that is absolutely unacceptable when you're in my resistance." He eyed her for a moment. "I'm not saying an instinct reaction isn't good, and that you should never go with your gut, but don't...don't ever throw your life away on a whim, do you understand me? Information is always available somehow, there's only one of you."

"Oh, so sorry that I don't analyse every single little thing I do," Susannah muttered defensively.

"Little?" Krig replied, raising his eyebrows pointedly. "If almost getting yourself killed is a 'little thing' I would hate to know what you classify as a big thing, Susannah." He shook his head after a moment, looking tired, stress lines tucking the corners of his mouth. "Look, I understand that you're someone who goes by their instincts, but sometimes there's a thin line between gut instincts and recklessness, which you crossed today-"

"I didn't have time to think everything through, the house was about to explode!"

"And it never occurred to you that I might value your life over some information?" he questioned. Susannah's mind ground to a halt again, and she studied Krig almost warily.

"I did the right thing," she insisted, though there was less vehemence in her tone now. He sighed.

"You have trust issues."

"Trust issues?" she repeated.

"I think you could be a great, a brilliant, addition to this resistance, Susannah, but not if you don't trust me. If you can't do that, this isn't going to work," he said bluntly.

"I do trust you..." she frowned.

"No, you don't," he disagreed, more mildly now. "If you did, you would trust me to be able to lead this resistance, call the shots and *do the right thing*...because, whether you like it or not Susannah, in regards to this resistance I am in charge."

"So you're not annoyed at what I did in itself, but because in doing it I didn't follow your orders," she said flatly. He shot her a chastising look.

"I'm annoyed at both," he replied. "Frankly, because as long as you can't follow my orders, I am never going to be able to trust you on the field." A shock ran through her system, like ice. He held up a hand to forestall her interruption, expression firm. "I have to be able to trust that you will do what I tell you to do, not just rush in headfirst like you did today, regardless of your opinion on the matter. Outside of this room, I cannot afford to have to keep a constant eye on you, to check that you're doing what I requested. I have plans behind my orders; I pick people to do certain tasks for a reason. Yes, today ended well, I can admit that, but it could have been a disaster...do you understand what I'm trying to say at all?"

Susannah thought she finally did.

"There's a reason behind your choices, you do actually know what you're doing."

He nodded in acceptance of the answer. "But what if your orders are wrong?" she persisted, backtracking quickly at his expression. "Not *wrong*, but...like today. We needed that information, and you didn't technically tell me not to by the way..."

"If you have a problem with my orders or plans, or find them somehow inadequate, take it up with me before we leave base. If we're in the middle of something, I still expect you to mention it to me for a little forewarning...the ONLY time I would not have you do that is if someone is about to die if you don't react immediately. Okay? Does that sound reasonable?" He once again seemed to be making an effort at composure.

"Yeah," she conceded. He nodded.

"I'm going to have to tell your parents about this, I hope you realise that," he said. Susannah froze.

"What?" she protested. "You can't! Do you have any idea how angry they would be at me for risking my life like I did?"

He didn't seem the slightest bit moved by that statement, his expression becoming slightly pointed. Susannah grimaced, reminded of his earlier words.

"So you do have some awareness of how your actions affect others. Good." He fixed her with a hard stare. "They seem okay, and willing to accept the resistance, so you should give them a chance. You're very lucky to have the type of family who would support you in this, a lot of us in this resistance group don't. This is dangerous...and they have a right to know that, and what you do. Furthermore, maybe, if I can't get through to you on this, they can."

"You can get through to me," she mumbled. "I am...sorry, about today. I didn't mean to cause trouble; I was just trying to help." His expression softened, and he reached forward to squeeze her shoulder gently.

"I know...but we're still going do this."

"But-"

"Susannah," his tone was uncompromising, final.

Damn it.

The night air was blissfully cool as she stepped outside of the base, Krig at her side. His posture had somewhat eased, leaving no fury, only a grim determination. He seemed to have mostly forgiven her.

"You really don't have to do this," she tried again,

helplessly, feeling like a child coming home with a bad parent's day report. She was thankful that the night helped hide her blazing, heated cheeks.

"No, Susannah, I really do," he replied softly. "You almost died, and I would have had to tell them anyway, like I said. It's better this way." A lump grew in her throat. Shadow, she hadn't thought about how her parents would react, at the time, until Krig brought it up. She opened her mouth to argue further, and then closed it again at the look he gave her. "Right," she mumbled. "You're the boss." Susannah couldn't help but be thankful that she had at least mentioned the resistance to her mum and dad before, even if she hadn't since told them that she'd specifically joined. They approached her street some time later. Susannah's stomach began to ache, her magic flickering with her discomfort. Krig walked up to the door, waiting for her to pull out a key. Reluctantly, she did so, calling out as she entered.

"I'm home!"

"Good, you're just in time for dinner," her father called. "You can help set the table." Susannah winced, shooting Krig a pleading look. He ignored her, striding through towards the dining room. She hurried after him.

"Suzie," her mum began as 'she' walked in, turning around to face her, before freezing. Her dad set the cutlery carefully down on the table. They both stared at Krig, not quite hostile, but making no effort to be welcoming either. She stepped up next to him, resisting the urge to cringe, shrink back and hide in her room. Her mother's lips pursed.

"Hello, it's nice to meet you. I'm Krig, Kriger Carter," Krig began, directing himself more to her father. "We spoke on the communicon…?"

"Yes," her dad said, not elaborating, looking directly at her.

"Something you wanted to tell us, Susannah?" She glanced at Krig for help, but he merely raised his eyebrows at her. She searched for a good way of saying it, then soon realised that there was none and that she'd just have to go for it. "Uh, yeah…well, I…er. I joined the resistance," she said finally. There was a moment of absolute quiet.

"*You did what*?" her mother questioned dangerously. Susannah swallowed.

"I joined the resistance," she said. "I just had my first mission actually."

"And when were you planning on sharing this without being forced to?" her dad asked shrewdly. His voice was calm, too calm considering both the illegality of the situation and his normally animated state.

"I, um, wasn't," she said. She hastened to elaborate as her parents' magic began crackling ominously, especially her mum's. "It was too dangerous for you to know! I wanted you to have plausible deniability if I got caught -"

"If you got caught?" her mum shrieked. "That is exactly why I didn't want you in that resistance! It's dangerous! What happens If you get caught, Susannah? Do you expect us to watch and lie and - plausibly deny- as the Demon Lord murders you -!"

"I think what your mother means to say," her dad interrupted tightly. "Is that it would never be a question of plausible deniability if you got caught."

"I'd kill him," her mum hissed, looking truly menacing. Susannah's eyes widened. Krig seemed to be wondering what he had gotten himself into with this conversation as he held his hands up in a placating gesture.

"Mrs Skelsby," he started, "I assure you I would do everything in my power-"

"Don't you talk to me," her mum rounded on Krig, pointing

an accusing finger in his face. "You recruited my daughter! You talked her into this suicidal crusade. Exactly how young do resistances take them nowadays? OH I bet you had a field day didn't you..." her mother trailed off, seemingly too livid for words.

"Of course I had a field day," Krig replied, with a quiet firmness and determination. "Your daughter is exceptional; anyone would have a field day if they could get her support on anything. I am not alone in that."

"The difference is that your organisation is illegal and punishable by death," her mum said coldly. "Resistance is not tolerated, and neither is challenging the declarations – from what little I've gathered, you aim to do both."

"And so you believe, Mrs Skelsby, that the Overworld should simply accept their situation?" Krig demanded incredulously. "I find that hard to believe considering the way Susannah seems to have been raised!"

"That does not mean I would put my only daughter on the firing line! I know how these things work-" her mum came to an abrupt halt. Susannah blinked.

"You know how these things work?" Krig repeated. "That would imply you had previous experience with a resistance, Mrs Skelsby?" Susannah stared as her mother flushed, turning away from them. Maybe, if she hadn't, she could have bluffed it, but her flustered state revealed her.

"Mum?" Susannah questioned incredulously.

"It only proves that I know what I'm talking about," her mum stated firmly. "You don't want to get involved in that type of thing." Susannah gaped.

"Dad - did you know about this? How come neither of you ever told me?" Her mum folded her arms, unspeaking.

"Dad?" she questioned again. Her dad merely nodded at her, once, moving from his spot to go over to his wife.

Susannah dropped to sit in on one of the dining chairs, stunned. How had she not known this? Her head lifted with an idea.

"But then, surely," she said slowly. "You must know why I have to do this...the resistance isn't a bad thing," she grasped at the argument. "Isn't it kind of hypocritical of you to try and forbid me to do this?" One of the dinner plates cracked as her mum whirled round again, temper rekindled, where it had previously started to brood rather than flare. "That was different!"

"How?" she demanded, surging to her feet herself. "How is it any different?"

"I wasn't fifteen!" her mum snarled.

"Oh like that matters!" Susannah rolled her eyes, infuriated. That was such a flimsy excuse. "Besides, you didn't have a problem when I mentioned it earlier."

"That was before you joined," her mum spat, glaring at her father, who'd stopped again. "Caido, back me up here. She's not joining...not continuing with that - that thing. It's outrageous! She's just a child - our child, you cannot possibly condone-"

"-I'm not a child," Susannah hissed. "And Marco Carmel started ruling the bloody country when he was seventeen, and that's only two years older than me, if that!" She looked at Krig. "Help me out; you were the one that wanted me to tell them." He frowned at her slightly, in reprimand for her tone, but spoke up.

"I understand your concerns, Mrs Skelsby, Mr Skelsby," he started carefully, inclining his head at each of them. "Really, I do. I worry about Cassie, my baby sister, nearly constantly...

"And you want to involve Susannah in that?" her dad demanded.

173

"*But,*" Krig stressed, regarding your daughter; it's not a matter of attracting attention. She already does that." Her leader paused. "She had her first mission today," he said after a moment, skilfully ignoring the whitening of both her parent's faces. "And, though I took issue to her rather reckless judgement, she didn't do half bad considering the circumstances." She could practically sense Krig debating something in his head. "During the course of our mission, we ran into Carmel's assassin-"

"-And yet you still think this is a good environment to drag my daughter into?" her mum interrupted icily. Krig's gaze was piercing as he continued, relentlessly.

"He knew her, Mrs Skelsby. He knew her name. The Underworld are already aware of your daughter. When I first met Susannah, she took down an entire unkindness of Dark Angels near single-handedly, and I don't even know about half the things she's got herself into...her being in the resistance isn't going to make the blind bit of difference. So, considering she's already on black lists, are you really going to discourage her from trying to use her power to do some good in the world? Good that I *know* you can emphasise and sympathise with."

Susannah folded her arms triumphantly. That was settled then. Her mother tightened her lips in response.

"I don't want my little girl in your resistance, but," her voice shook tremulously as she threw her dad a betrayed look. "I can see that I am to be outvoted."

"Serena-" her dad began, helplessly. Her mum shook her head, angry tears welling in her eyes as she walked out. The bedroom door upstairs slammed shut. There was an awkward silence. Her dad's jaw was tense.

"I think you should leave now, lad," he told Krig quietly. "We all need a little space to think over these…developments. We will, of course, take a secrecy ward on this."

"Of course, sir," Krig replied, dipping his head in understanding. "Thank you." He squeezed her shoulder encouragingly before he left. Susannah sighed, hesitating for few second before darting after him with a sign to her dad that she'd be right back.

"Krig - Krig!" she caught up with him, dodging into his path. He stopped, waiting for her to speak. "Did you know about my mum?" she asked, having to ask, needing to." When you recruited me?" He studied her for a moment.

"No," Krig shook his head, a wary respect gleaming in his countenance. "I didn't. I was initially just clutching at straws, I didn't expect her to confirm, or even be involved in that type of thing." Susannah nodded, thoughtfully. He smiled, briefly, if not quite with his previous warmth yet. "I suppose I'll see you at the next meeting, then. Stay out of trouble, kid, I mean it. I'm *this* close to putting you on a suspension or – something."

"I said I was sorry."

He shook his head again, looking tired.

"Take care, Susannah."

"Bye."

"She watched as he disappeared from sight, before walking slowly back into the house.

Her dad was sitting at the table, head buried in his hands, seemingly lost in thought. His gaze flicked up as she entered, over the discarded pots of dinner, his fists clenched.

"Well, that went well."

Chapter Thirteen – Dragons, Sky Cats and Bluebirds

"So," Susannah said awkwardly, sitting down next to Delilah and Jamie. "How much trouble am I in?" Delilah said nothing, so she figured that meant a lot. Her best friend's gaze only darted to her, briefly, before she returned to her previous conversation. Jamie looked marginally awkward, and shot her a look too, reassuring, sympathetic. This was the worst thing about upsetting Delilah, her best friend didn't talk about it, she just let her feelings silently boil until she exploded. "Oh, come on Del," Susannah continued, insistently, moving around into Delilah's eye line again. The waiting had always been the worst, the stiff silence that locked her out completely, painfully. "I talked it out with Krig, its fine!"

"You could have died," her best friend said flatly, lips white with rage.

"...but I didn't."

"That's not the point!" Delilah exclaimed, and Susannah found herself on the receiving end of a rather ferocious glare. "You can't just do stupid stuff like that!"

"We needed the information," Susannah protested, again. "Besides, I do loads stupid things – that one was hardly the worst."

"It was near the top of the list," Delilah muttered angrily.

"-I'm sorry, alright!" Susannah put her hands in the air in surrender. "I'm sorry. I didn't think everything through, it won't happen again."

"You said that last time," Delilah replied, not yielding an inch.

"Krig forgave me," Susannah muttered.

"For Shadow's sake Susannah!" Delilah exclaimed, fists clenching fiercely, eyes suddenly wet. "This isn't about you being forgiven! Do you have any idea what it was like to hear over a Communicon that my best friend had run into a burning building and could be dead?!"

Susannah's mouth felt a little dry. "How would you have liked it if it was me?" Delilah continued. "You wouldn't have!"

"Yeah," Susannah tried to joke, "but you wouldn't be that stupid..."

"That's not the point!" the blonde hissed. "You need to start thinking, you scared me half to death." She felt awful to see Delilah wiping away hot, furious tears, and shrank into herself, her bravado disappearing.

"I'm really sorry, Del," she murmured, looking at her shoes. "I was just – reckless."

"Incredibly."

"And I shouldn't have done it."

"But you would do it again," Delilah said quietly. "That's the worst part. You always say you're sorry and you *always* do it again." Susannah squirmed, not knowing what to say to that.

"Will you forgive me?"

"You're an idiot," Delilah muttered, but she made an effort of flashing a weak smile. Susannah relaxed marginally, more at ease once again. It was just as well that Delilah didn't tend to hold grudges, or there was no way they'd be friends still.

"Yeah, well, I mean it this time," she said, smiling back, "when I say I won't do it again." Delilah just rolled her eyes, irritably. Susannah grimaced.

"She normally does stupid things then?" Jamie asked, regarding them both curiously, obviously trying to move the whole thing to less dangerous waters.

"Too much," Delilah said curtly. "It's a miracle she isn't

dead."

"I didn't do it to spite you, you know," Susannah couldn't resist adding. "I was just doing what I thought was right." Delilah shot her a warning look, and Susannah shut up.

"Oh?" Jamie questioned, his eyebrows rising, a smirk capturing the corners of his mouth, albeit a forced, uneasy one. "Do tell?"

"No, Del-don't-" Susannah tried. Delilah ignored her.

"I wouldn't even know where to start," the blonde said, though not maliciously. "She does a *lot* of stupid things, as she said. What is there? Oh, so many things...constantly picking fights for one thing-"

"-I don't pick fights, people pick fights with me!"

"It takes two people to fight, Suze," Delilah dismissed.

"Do you expect me not to defend myself?"

"Defend yourself...you tend to simultaneously insult and taunt your opponents," her best friend returned. "It's not very nice."

"Only the Underworld ones who try and kill me," she mumbled. "I'm nice in duelling class."

"Is that why they're all too scared to fight you?"

"They don't fight me because I always win – and that makes me sound like an arrogant twit, sorry! – But it's true. I don't taunt them or anything. I *try* and be nice, as nice as you can be when the aim is to beat them in battle."

"Yeah, except duelling class isn't a battle...it's a class," Jamie said, with some amusement.

"Not you too! Does anyone here think I'm not a total screw up!?"

"We don't think you're a screw up," Delilah said instantly, exasperated. "It's just that sometimes you screw up, like everyone does. Seriously, you need to learn to balance things a bit. You're either way too hard on yourself, or think you're completely blameless when really it's somewhere in the middle."

"I, personally, think you did right on the mission too," Jamie added. Both of their heads snapped to him, Delilah's incredulous, and Susannah's pleased.

"Really?" she asked hopefully. He smirked at her.

"Really," he said. "With time pressure opportunities like that you have to react one way or another, and as far as I'm aware your actions led to the best possible outcome. I see no problem."

"At least one person agrees with me," Susannah said, smiling relentlessly.

"Oh, don't encourage her!" Delilah murmured. "Please." They ended up talking for quite some time and, too her happiness, Delilah seemed to have softened up again too. It would take time still, of course, but they would be okay. Then, they finally breached the topic Susannah had silently been dying of curiosity about – Jamie himself.

"Well," Jamie began, looking awkward. "I live with my brother, as you know. My parents are both dead...the Underworld killed them." Delilah winced with sympathy, her eyes filled with a terrible sort of understanding that Susannah couldn't help but be glad to be excluded from.

"He's busy a lot of the time – I also told you that, and he, along with the rest of my family, have always been Carmel supporters."

"Even after your parents died?" Susannah questioned, brow furrowed.

"Act two of the Declarations: the purpose of an Overworld Variation is to obey and serve to the needs of an Underworld Variation. They considered it an honour, and so do the rest of my family," Jamie replied.

"But you don't?" Delilah asked softly.

"I'm here in a resistance, aren't I?" he returned; his eyes dark. "I mean, I get on well with my brother, I always have, but...you know. He doesn't exactly know about this, so..."

"What do you reckon he'd do if he did know?"

"Kill me," Jamie laughed shortly. "No, I don't know. Let's just say I'll be keeping it a secret. He certainly wouldn't support the idea."

"And I thought my parents disagreed with the idea," Susannah murmured. Jamie grimaced.

"Your parents don't like you being in the resistance?" he verified. "Why not? Too dangerous?"

"Yeah," Susannah agreed. "Too dangerous. I know they mean well and all that but, really, I can look after myself."

"Know what you mean," Jamie rolled his eyes. "Whilst my brother has the utmost respect for the Carmel name and the Underworld, he's frightfully overprotective. You'd think he'd just invest in bubble-wrapping me, it's insane! What about you, 'Lilah? Are your parents okay with all *this?*"

"I wouldn't know," Delilah replied mildly, a bit too mildly. "They're dead. Hunting accident, like with you."

Susannah couldn't help but notice her friend made no mention of her suspicions of murder, but, then, it wasn't exactly the type of thing one threw into casual conversation either, certainly not with someone you were just getting to know. It wasn't that she didn't trust Jamie, he was in the resistance she trusted him with her life by default; it merely wasn't something you really talked about. At least not without proof, and Delilah had always been cautious with her words in comparison to Susannah's own hot tongue and temper. The blonde tended to think everything through before speaking, and similarly tended to reserve judgement on people until she knew them better. Susannah had always admired the trait, and had on some levels assimilated as much of it as she could by association. Whilst she still said thoughtless things, or acted recklessly, she now did so with a simultaneous analysis of the situation rather than jumping in blind. Or, at least, that was what she tried to do as much as possible….sometimes, like with the mission, she just forgot or didn't have time for it.

"I'm sorry," Jamie said quietly. "Was it recent or…?"

"It was a long time ago, I never really knew them," Delilah responded, shrugging. "I miss them, but I never knew them – though I wish I did. Grandma and Grandpa always say how much I remind them of my mum, though apparently Robbie, my brother, is more like my dad."

"At least Carmel put in all those new hunting rules and restrictions," Jamie said, with a twist of his lips. Susannah snorted.

"Only works if people follow them. Not everyone does."

"It's the thought that counts…?" Jamie offered, with a smirk. Her and Delilah both laughed, before glancing at each other with some awkwardness.

"So," Susannah returned to their previous conversation, another point of curiosity striking her. "What do you do when you're not lurking in rebel hot spots?" she teased. He raised his eyebrows at her.

"Is this twenty questions?" he returned, though he was smiling. "Not much. I *don't* read obscure magic texts illegally under my duvet. Um. I do read though…I write? Fence, sword fight, hang out with my brother, go flying-"

"Go flying?" Delilah repeated, her eyes lighting up. "What do you mean you go flying?"

He looked at them both, taking in their expressions, before grinning.

"I can show you if you like..?"

A few minutes later they were peering into the tiny, pocket-sized Dragon sitting in Jamie's palm. It was a dark green colour, scaly, with an almost pearl like sheen and eyes that were blacker and darker than Jamie's own. It was stunning, really. Delilah gave him a hesitant look, silently asking permission to touch. After a moment, Jamie nodded, and Delilah reached out.

"...you have a pocket dragon?" Susannah questioned, torn between incredulity and impressed awe. Jamie chuckled.

"Well, it's a Flight, actually. Just so happens to be a Dragon – you guys ever heard of Flights?"

"Nope," Susannah said, immediately.

"Might have vaguely heard of them," Delilah replied, the Dragon preening under her soft touch. "It's kind of like an obscure branch of Internalised magic, isn't it? Bit like a pseudo Pure Art? But more subconscious, unlike Pure Arts which is consciously using emotions to channel magic." Susannah's face dropped. She wasn't good with Pure Arts. At all. Did that mean she couldn't make a Flight?

"Yeah, kind of," Jamie agreed. "It's easy really; I don't know why more people don't have one, my friend Raphael taught me. I'd probably put the whole art of it more in the category of mild Soul Magic though, instead of Pure Arts. Basically, you just sort of...dive into yourself, and ask your magic to make you a Flight. The Flight will then externalise, shaped under your magic, into a shape that best represents you at the time you were making it. Then, obviously, you go on it and fly – it will grow bigger when you need it, and can be summoned because there's an automatic link, or soul bond, between yourself and your Flight. It's a bit like having a familiar, really, except one that is inactive and limited to flying."

"Pretty cool though," Delilah beamed. "I've always wanted to be able to fly like that."

"I can teach you if you like?" Jamie offered, with a smile. "*Both* of you."

And that was how they ended up spending the next day making Flights.

"I can't do it," Susannah exclaimed, resisting the urge to tear at her hair in frustration. Delilah was sitting serenely, cross-legged, on the floors some metres away, the air around her swirling with the formation of the Flight. It seemed to come so naturally to the blonde, Susannah couldn't help but be a bit envious. She was proud, of course, but still a little envious. Delilah seemed to have calmed down even more from their fight, but still wasn't as casually affectionate or cheery as normal.

"Yes, you can," Jamie said, watching them both.

"Easy for you to say," she replied. "You've already made yours! I have no idea *where* to even start."

"That might be the problem," he said dryly, appearing to be smothering a smile. "It's called your subconscious for a reason."

"Oh. Right. Yeah. Sorry," she mumbled. He just chuckled, shaking his head, but nonetheless regarding her with a considering expression.

"How good's your relationship with your magic? You block it out a lot, don't you? Restrain its power?"

"Yes. But, really, it's not like I can leave it wild, can I? I don't have a choice in the matter," she added defensively. "There's too much of it."

Jamie hummed slightly in agreement.

"It's soul magic, Susannah....hate to be the one to break it to

183

you, but you're going to have to loosen those restraints a bit, just a bit, to be able to get to the core of your magic. Just for a moment. I think, right now, you're more tentatively poking the edges…?"

Susannah swallowed.

"I can't loosen my magic, not right now. It's too dangerous," she replied. "It'll attract all the wrong sorts of attention. Like, I don't know, killer moths or something."

"Bit of a problem there, then," Jamie stated.

"You're telling me," Susannah muttered. She supposed she could always try making her Flight at the Ichtaca Ruins instead…

"Does your aura still attract so much attention when its passively out?" he asked.

"I don't know," she said. "I never have it passively out. I don't even tend to have all of it out, only as much as I need in day to day life, really."

"And then a bit more," he teased.

"It spills over," she mumbled. "Doesn't like being trapped."

"I would imagine not, it's unnatural," he said. She looked at him sharply, her jaw tightening, hurt beginning to blossom. He caught her gaze, before pausing, quickly shaking his head. "Don't mean the magic itself, Susannah," he reassured. "I mean the keeping it trapped part. It's unnatural for magic to be trapped. It's supposed to move, flow and be free…you know that."

"Yeah, sorry – force of habit," she blushed.

"No worries," he dismissed. "You probably get a lot of the other type of reaction, I'd imagine."

"Yes," she said, a bit tightly. He studied her for a moment. "Do you know why?" he questioned. "It's not because there's anything inherently wrong with having that much magic, it's because the level of power is threatening to those around you, especially under consideration of what you'll do with it."

"What I'd do with it?" she returned.

"Yes," he murmured. "You've joined an illegal resistance, haven't you? Power like yours, it could shake stuff up. A lot of people don't want things shaken up, especially when it doesn't benefit them. People fear change, Susannah. Any new player on the board, particularly one of unseen power, is bound to be intimidating. The unnatural part is what you could propose with your power."

Susannah was silent for a while.

"I never looked at it like that before," she admitted. He shrugged.

"Try again with the Flight, okay? Just long enough to flash through, your magic understands you, it doesn't want to cause unnecessary problems. If it did, there's no way you'd be able to restrain it."

"How do you know so much about magic, Jamie?"

"I read a lot."

She chuckled, and he grinned at her.

"Thanks," she murmured.

"Just make the damn flight."

She dove.

It was a rather strange feeling, Susannah thought, to go through her own magic. It gave her a sort of tingling feeling, not good, not bad... just *glittery.* It was weird. Some parts of her magic were dark and throbbing, others gold and pulsating...not that any magic was light or dark, it was the intent that mattered. People could still be more inclined towards some arts rather than others, but no magic was specifically good or evil. Someone with a lighter aura could say, be more partial to pure arts but still favour the darker arts (not evil) due to personality, upbringing and situations in life. It was the same with someone with a darker aura; they could just as well never cast anything but light magic their whole life. Most people had a mix between the two, a sort of marble cake mix. The magic surrounded her on every side, intense – a shimmering maze that seemed so familiar and alien to her all at once.

It was especially strange, as, with her eyes open, she could still see Jamie too. She realized, now, why Delilah had closed her own. Jamie had an odd, almost transfixed expression on his face as he stared at her. If she wasn't so swept up in the magic, she would have blushed. As it was, she simply shut her own eyes, entirely focused on the task at hand.

She wasn't completely certain how to go about *asking* her magic for help, as it was supposedly such a subconscious art, but it seemed she didn't have to. It engulfed her, piercing more tangibly across her mind and body than she'd ever been aware of before, appearing to vibrate in her very bones. When she next opened her eyes, overwhelmed, exhilarated, her Flight was next to her.

It was some sort of cat, its coat a golden brown in colour. Its eyes were held the same metallic green shade as her own. It was lithe, but not without muscle and couldn't be considered slim, but nor did it have any fat. It was a wiry creature, and far larger than her when it was grown to its full height, as opposed to pocket-sized and transportable. It was absolutely beautiful, though she suspected she was personally biased.

Delilah had finished her Flight too – a bluebird. It was a deep azure, the same colour as Delilah's gaze. It possessed the same dainty elegance its owner did, along with a barely visible iron-willed core, a hidden internal strength. Its feathers gleamed, glossy, catching the light, and its eyes were kind, playful and shrewd. She couldn't help but smile to look at it.

"I picked a bluebird, is that okay?" Delilah was asking Jamie, who'd torn his attention away by now, and whose eyebrows arched at the question.

"You *picked* it? As in, consciously? It didn't just form on its own accord?" Jamie enquired. Delilah bit her lip.

"Is that wrong?"

"No, no…" Jamie said quickly, a speculative expression on his face. "It's just interesting. It suits you well."

"I like bluebirds," Delilah replied cheerfully. "They're my favourite animal." She was practically hopping one foot to another, bouncing with excitement. "Ooh, you're a cat, Susannah – I can see that. Does it make a difference if the creature is a magical creature or not?" she rattled off, spinning to face Jamie again after a moment.

"No," he smirked. "It just means I'm more pretentious than you; because I wanted a Dragon…read too many fantasy books as a child, and all that."

"Awesome, just wondering," Delilah said, turning to her bluebird once more. "So, er, can we pretty please go flying now?"

Susannah and Jamie exchanged entertained glances.

Chapter Fourteen - Day of the Demon Lord

When another resistance meeting was called, abruptly, with little warning, Susannah thought it was more than a little reasonable to be worried. They had a meeting planned for tomorrow anyway, to discuss the mission, so whatever this unexpected get together was about, it probably wasn't good. She wasn't sure if she wanted it to be another mission or not. On one hand, they were exciting and made it feel more like the resistance was actually doing something, accomplishing something...on the other, they were dangerous and increased a person's chances of getting killed or imprisoned for life. Her first mission hadn't exactly ended in smiles, had it? Her parents glanced up when she entered the room, sorting out an emergency bag with one hand and clumsily trying to eat lunch with the other.

"Going somewhere?" her dad asked. "I thought I was meant to be teaching you how to make potato omelette?"

Susannah winced.

"Oh god, yeah. I'm so sorry - Krig-"

"Called a meeting," her dad finished. She hesitated, dithering helplessly on the spot. "Go on," he urged. "Try and stay out of trouble."

"Excuse me?" her mum snapped, eyes flashing. "Caido!"

"Seri, she's going to go anyway, whether we tell her she can or not," her dad replied wearily.

"No, she's not," her mum hissed. "She's going to get herself killed - you're going to get yourself killed Susannah - you're not going."

"Mum-"

"No. I said no," her mum's magic was beginning to prickle. "That's my final answer."

"You can't tell me what to do!"

"I'm your mother." Susannah scowled at the statement, her magic blazing.

"Dad?" she turned to her father, beseechingly. Her dad exchanged a long, meaningful look with his wife. Susannah folded her arms restlessly, before letting them swing to her sides only a moment later. "You didn't have a problem with the resistance earlier," she pointed out, once again. "When I first told you about it."

"Before you joined and almost died," her mum retorted. "I thought it would be-"

"Different?" Susannah offered incredulously. "What were you thinking of when I said resistance? A little phase of mine, soon over? Or a nice club where we drink tea and munch on biscuits, maybe cocoa if we're feeling hardcore, all while we sit revelling in our own sense of rebelliousness? For crying out-"

"Susannah," her dad said sharply. "That's enough. There's no need for that type of tone." She fell silent at the grim inflections in his voice, before glancing at her mother who appeared horror stricken. She felt a pang of guilt and affection, Infusing with her frustration. "Sorry," she mumbled. "I just - I love this, mum."

"You've only just joined," her mother argued, "You're fifteen, how could you possibly know what you want or the full consequences of your actions?" Susannah grit her teeth, feeling her temper bubble once more.

"I'm not a child," she retorted, before taking a deep breath to calm herself. "Besides, Krig seems more than happy to teach me about consequences." The last part was a mutter, inducing raised eyebrows. There was an awkward lull in the conversation. "I really do love this," she began when the silence continued, growing ever heavier. "I didn't think I would, I was uncertain...I was scared, but I do! I love this resistance, for once I feel like I actually belong somewhere and…" she puttered out, uncomfortable with the attention. "Don't try and take it away from me. I won't let you," she finished fiercely.

"You don't know what you're getting yourself into," her mum replied, magic crackling. Her parents both exchanged looks again. Before, she would have been confused, now she bet it was to do with her mum being in a resistance group. Hypocrite.

"I'm going now," she said softly. "And Dad, I really am sorry about the potato omelette - tomorrow?"

"Tomorrow," he agreed. She shut the door to the sound of waspish whispers and a brewing storm.

All the way across the city, her thoughts would not stop swirling around in her head, incessant. She didn't want to be in the resistance without her parents' approval, it affected them too after all, but…she couldn't just give it up. Her own words had hit home sharply, burrowing straight through her skin, slicing through her bones like butter to settle upon her very core. She did love the resistance. She hadn't thought she would, she hadn't ever admitted to herself how very much she believed in it - to be unreserved was a dangerous thing in the city, it only got you hurt as you displayed your weaknesses out for the world to see. Yet…she'd never belonged anywhere before. Not really. No one wanted to get too close to the troublemaker with the 'freaky powerful' magic. In the resistance, after the initial staring and a couple of questions, no one seemed to care. Well, no one seemed to see it as a bad thing at any rate. Maybe they were just using her, like the gang recruiters had tried to, but at least if they were they were nice about it…aside from Leon, but the arrogant fop didn't really seem too fond of her anyway, magic or not. She sighed softly, scanning the area around her. Ever since the incident with Kerr and his Underworld buddies she'd been hyper vigilant. As far as she was concerned, she never wanted to get into that type of situation ever again, not if she could help it. Seeing the coast was clear, she moved to the abandoned fire station. Everyone looked up when she entered, the meeting having started.

"Sorry I'm late," she apologised. Delilah frowned, shooting a questioning 'what's the matter?' look in her direction. She shook her head slightly in response. Now wasn't the time. Krig waved a hand dismissively.

"Apology accepted, at least you made it. Take a seat," he said. She slunk over to sit with Jamie, not wanting to give her best friend the chance to question her lateness and - no doubt, if this was Delilah - the nuance of her countenance that revealed her tumbling emotions. The amused, but worried, expression she received told her that the other knew exactly what she was avoiding,

"As I was about to say," Krig glanced at her briefly, before fixing his gaze on everyone as a whole, "Marco Carmel is holding an audience over at Central Park later today." Susannah felt her insides freeze up a bit. The Demon Lord rarely descended out of Upper City, or out of Anzarkledea, his manor home and base of operations. Central Park was in Middle City, not far from where she lived. She knew this wouldn't be good. "I've heard he's doing a speech of some sort, open invite." That meant everyone in the city was going to turn up, like lemmings, once the news spread...

"You think he's doing a speech?" Cade questioned sceptically. "Surely he could call a press conference for that?"

"Unless he wants to see the reaction directly," Delilah said quietly. Everyone's head twitched in the petite girl's direction.

"That's what I thought," Krig replied seriously. "So I figured I'd warn you beforehand...brace yourselves. The secrecy ward should prevent him from plucking the memories of these meetings out of your head, but I can't guarantee that he won't notice that there's a ward present...just try to take your cues from the crowd, and for Shadow's sake, don't broadcast your thoughts, any person proficient at Mind Arts would pick up on it, let alone him." There was a tense silence. "I'm not saying he's going to be searching our minds," Krig continued carefully. "He doesn't have a specific reason to try - but I figured it's better safe than sorry."

"Do you know what his speech is about?" Leola asked. "How do you even know he's doing a speech?"

"If it's another servant in a bar..." Jess muttered.

"No, I'm afraid I don't," Krig replied. "And as for how, I was up at Anzarkledea the other day, a mate dragged me there to scout for job vacancies."

"Were there any?" Susannah asked curiously.

"Why, do you want to work for him?" Leon sneered.

"Oh of course," she drawled sarcastically, glowering at the grey eyed brunet. "It's my life time wish, didn't you know? Those black eyes of his make me go weak at the knees, really. I tremble." Delilah bit her lip, rolling her eyes while David snickered and Krig glared at both of them.

"Enough," he said dangerously. "I won't have you arguing within the team."

"Sorry," they both mumbled, temporarily abashed. He stared them down for a moment, then seemingly satisfied, continued.

"The whole place was buzzing with hype over it,

speculation...he doesn't seem to be making any efforts to either hide or promote it. That's how I know about it." Jamie looked pensive. Susannah stiffened, after the last mission had been a trap, surely that wasn't necessarily a good thing; it could be another trick. "Yes, I know it's suspicious," Krig added, before she or anyone else could point it out. "But seeing as everyone is going to be attending anyway, it might not be as ominous as you're all thinking." She couldn't help but wonder if he was putting on an optimistic front, of he really meant that.

"Oh sure, unless he's setting up a public execution...namely for us," Jess scowled. Krig grimaced.

"Thank you for those encouraging words, Jess," he said. Jess flushed slightly, pouting sullenly.

"Well, it's a valid point. If you're giving us pre warning of our own deaths it would have been kinder to let us be oblivious. I think so anyway." A sense of annoyance bubbled briefly in Susannah's gut, before she quelled it, smiling at the brown haired NR girl.

"Would you like me to make you forget then?" she offered politely. Jess blanched, shooting her a nasty look.

"Krig! She's just threatened me - did you hear her? - she just threatened me!"

"No she didn't," Delilah sighed, patiently. "She was genuinely offering, if that's what you want."

"Genuinely - ?"

"She is sitting right here, Del," Susannah deadpanned. Delilah glanced at her, admonishingly.

"Yeah, genuinely," she continued. "I don't know why you'd want to forget though, personally. At least if you know you can say goodbye or explain to your loved ones..." the small blonde trailed off as everyone stared at her.

"Assuming he's even planning an execution," Mica

commented cheerfully. "You never know, we could just be traumatising ourselves for nothing. He might be announcing a special new law or something."

"Cause those are always so good for us," David muttered. Krig was silent.

"Anyhow, I thought a warning might be prudent," he said finally. "Tomorrow, we will discuss the mission and, possibly, the fruits of Lord Carmel's speech, if it is viable. Okay?"

There was a murmur of agreement. The dismissal was clear.

She and Delilah both arrived back at the Skelsby house, mutually deep in thought. Even if the whole speech was a trap, a set up for a public execution, it didn't mean they could afford to avoid it...if everyone was going (as they would be, once they heard that the Underworld Prince was actually making a public appearance himself) it would be more suspicious if they didn't turn up, eager eyed and drooling, for the occasion. Marco Carmel ruled over them all, advocating Underworld supremacy like all of his family before him, yet some of the Overworld as well as the Underworld still loved him. It never ceased to amaze her. Sure, she remembered a time when as a kid she too had been enthralled by the otherworldly beauty and power of the Carmel family, but that was before she was old enough or smart enough to be able to hold her own opinion or understand the situation. Back then, in those innocent days, the Underworld were just the monster under her bed, the warfare not tangible in her world. She knew about it, of course, but it had seemed distant and unrelated to her day to day life. That changed instantly the first time she became prey. There was little about that awful day she didn't regret. She sighed inaudibly. This thinking was getting her nowhere.

It didn't matter why beings adored the Carmels, especially Marco, all that mattered was that they did, despite how he was more than happy to throw them, the Overworld, to the beast with only smiles and the occasional hunting restriction to appease them. People were so easily bought. She dug in her pocket for her key, unlocking the door and gesturing for Delilah to enter first. A languid pair of Dark Angels eyed them hungrily from the roof of Mrs Denvers house across the street. She slammed the door shut, locking and placing a quick ward, trying to resist the temptation to walk out again and knock them off their perch.

"I'm home!" she called, receiving two murmurs of response from somewhere in the house.
"So, what's up with you?" Delilah asked after a moment, watching as Susannah walked to the kitchen to grab a drink ("want one?" "No thanks.")
"What makes you think something's up?" she returned, leading the way to her bedroom. Delilah gave her an unimpressed look. Susannah frowned.
"You were late," Delilah clarified. "And though you make a habit of acting very cavalier and devil-may-care about everything, you're normally pretty punctual."
"Mum isn't happy about me being in the resistance..." she mumbled at last, shutting the bedroom door firmly behind her. Her best friend winced sympathetically.
"You know, she's probably just worried about you."
"Doesn't stop it being annoying," she muttered, debating and deciding against telling Delilah about her mum's resistance. "Have you even told your grandparents about it yet?"
"Yes, actually," Delilah snapped. "And I didn't wait until I was forced, either." Susannah faltered at the unusually

harsh tone.

"That was uncalled for, I'm sorry," she murmured.

"Yeah, just a little bit." Her expression had softened somewhat from their uncharacteristic hard lines though, at the apology. The blonde shook her head. "Just forget it. You're stressing. You always do this when you're stressed. You should take up yoga, or something."

"You can picture me doing yoga?" Susannah laughed. Delilah's lip twitched in the beginnings of a smile.

"Well, I'm not going to suggest that you take Martial Arts - you hardly need any more encouragement to rush head first into danger, on the basis that you'll probably come out relatively unscathed."

"Ouch. Now that was uncalled for," she teased. Her best friend scoffed.

"Don't think I didn't notice the evil eye you gave those Dark Angels outside." Susannah smirked in response, but didn't say anything. She still remembered the mission.

"Do you reckon we should tell them about the upcoming speech?" Delilah asked after a pause, 'them' presumably meaning their respective families.

"Most likely," Susannah groaned, growing sombre. "They'll find out anyway, but I guess it wouldn't hurt...might convince mum that the resistance is useful, not just dangerous. Then again, perhaps we should keep quiet...I'm sure they'd take Jess' suspicions of a public execution spectacularly." Delilah's eyes narrowed.

"You shouldn't joke about that," she said mildly. Susannah shrugged awkwardly.

"Do you reckon the others have told their parents?" Delilah accepted the change in subject, shrugging back.

"I don't know, some of them maybe. It's kind of a varied topic, isn't it? Krig wouldn't have, would he?"

"Jamie wouldn't have — it must be so odd not having his parents, and I doubted he told his brother, he's an Underworld supporter, isn't he? That's what Jamie said?"

"Yeah. I mean, Grandma, Grandpa and Robbie are okay with me being in the resistance...not happy, definitely not, but they've accepted it. I can't imagine what it must be like for him, or the others. They must be so scared to be found out." Delilah brushed over the possibility of a clogging silence before it could settle, with a grin. "You were just so eager to get Jamie into the conversation, weren't you Suze?" Susannah's cheeks flamed, heat rising from her skin. "Del!" she protested. Delilah's grin broadened mischievously.

"You're blushing," she remarked.

"Shut up," Susannah moaned, burying her face into her hands.

"No, really," Delilah continued calmly. "Like a tomato." Susannah threw a pillow at her.

It was about eight O clock, and the whole city was buzzing and migrating towards the Central Park. Susannah avoided her parents' eyes, feeling self-conscious ever since her mum had rushed in, exclaiming that Marco Carmel was giving a speech. All traces of amusement, or even embarrassment, had vanished from her mood. The atmosphere was excited, yet uneasy. Fear pressed down from every side; Overworld or Underworld. Marco Carmel, or any Carmel, were not the type you wanted to mess with. It left for the feeling that you were heading towards the edge of a cliff; when you got there, you would either see the most beautiful view or you would go tumbling off the edge with the momentum of the movement. The congregation was thickening already when they arrived. She caught sight of Delilah, her grandparents

197

and older brother, Robbie, coming into the park, and pointed it out to her mum and dad. They made their way over.

"Bells, William," her dad greeted solemnly. Isabella "Bells" Moor nodded back, pressing air kisses to all of their cheeks and sweeping them up in a puff of her floral perfume. The normal exuberance was, however, drained from the action. Robbie nodded at her, also subdued.

"Caido, Serena," William returned, tipping his head, eyes sharp. "Do either of you know what this is about?"

Susannah felt the adults' gazes flick over her and Delilah.

"No idea," her mum said, only a second later. They continued towards the growing crowd, getting a place somewhere near the middle - still able to see the podium, just about. It would probably be the closest she ever got to Marco Carmel anyway...not that staying back was a bad thing. Marco Carmel was fire, getting too close was mesmerising, but liable to get you burnt or even dead.

There were lots of official looking beings milling around at the front: no bodyguards though. Marco Carmel was too powerful to have to rely on them, and no one was stupid or brave enough to attempt a fight.

There were no props, no slide show; he didn't need them. There was nothing but a screen to magnify his image so that everybody could see, and a single microphone. The Press closed in like sharks on the scent of blood. Susannah could feel her stomach knotting, hard balls of lead dropping in her gut. She dared not look around the crowd to see her friends, classmates, or fellow rebels. She glanced at Delilah, who was staring intently at her feet. Robbie was watching his younger sister carefully. Sometimes, she wondered what it would be like to have siblings. Marco Carmel had two of them, though only his little brother was still alive in the family. She wasn't completely sure what had happened to the rest of the family; it was a most fiercely guarded Carmel secret. Maybe he killed them? Her thoughts were rambling. Crap, she felt slightly nauseous. It wasn't like anything was going to happen...Jess was just overreacting. It wasn't actually a public execution.

"You okay?" Robbie questioned. She waited for Delilah's answer, hoping the answer was yes. "Susannah?" Her head jerked up at her name.

"W-what?" she asked. Both the Moor siblings were regarding her closely, eerily similar with their sandy hair and blue eyes, despite the age and gender differences.

"Are you okay?" Robbie repeated.

"Uh, yeah," she replied airily. "I'm fine."

"You look green," Delilah noted flatly. Susannah scowled.

"It's my eyes. They're reflecting," she said through her teeth. Delilah smiled, just a little. The smile disappeared when a familiar, unfamiliar magic swept across the park - drawing sighs as the magic coiled teasingly past.

The Demon Lord had arrived

Marco Carmel was tall and ivory skinned, with eyes like liquid shadows and hair as equally black. He strolled towards the podium with a careless, debonair confidence, clad in a dark, expensive suit and boots. His image was immediately magnified by at least ten. His lips were curled into the beginnings of an alluring smirk. Damn it all, but Susannah felt her knees turn to jelly. His magic, shadow, that *magic* - there was nothing quite like it. It was powerful, graceful, all consuming. She sounded like a bloody fan girl. He stepped up, instantly taking the microphone out of its rigid holdings. His features were cold, inhumanely beautiful, adult beyond their nineteen years of life.

"Ladies, gentlemen, and variations beside," he began. "I feel I must thank you for joining me on such a short notice." A collective shiver ran through the crowd at the smooth, enthralling voice. Susannah loathed herself for feeling affected. A glance at the crowd saw nearly everyone leaning just marginally towards him, as if he were a magnet. She decisively kept her posture straight. "I'm sure you are all curious as to why I am holding this gathering, so I will get straight to the point." His voice grew serious, his dark gaze scanning over the crowd with a casual, frightening intensity. "Rather disturbing news has reached me, as of late," he paused. "News of a new resistance group."

Susannah stiffened, holding her breath along with anyone else; thanking any possible deity she could think of that freezing in fright was considered the appropriate response to his words. She dared not glance at Delilah, or her parents, in fear that their expressions would tip her over the edge into hysterical laughter. Obsidian eyes scanned the crowd once more, leaving no face untouched in their quick study. "These self-named 'freedom fighters' will try and tell you that they are right in their rebellion, that they are right to break our laws, that they are right to promote the equality of Overworld and Underworld." There was a sharp intake of breath, almost collective, from the Demon Lord's spellbound audience. "They are wrong." Susannah noticed the Underworld glaring at them, the Overworld variations, with a renewed hatred, a fearful mistrust and repulsion. Her heart sank. The two variations seemed to inch apart without even moving, furthering the resistance from its aims. "These rebels are not freedom fighters," the Underworld Prince declared. "But the masked terrorists of our society. They are dangerous miscreants who will use any means to fulfil their goals. They are the disease that will infect your mind....it will start with equality, with their righteousness, only to mutate as they grow hungry for their own superiority. Trust me when I tell you that, for I would never lie to you." Rage surged in Susannah's stomach - he was twisting everything around! Yet, it seemed that the large majority believed him. Of course they would. She struggled to keep her features composed, her magic still, her expression adoring. His gaze flicked over their section. "I've no doubt that the rebels are amongst you even now- waiting for their chance to seize this world as their own." There was a murmuring of harsh whispers, falling into silence when the Demon Lord raised a hand for quiet. "Yes, it distresses me too...to have traitors amongst those who should be loyal is unforgivable." His tone had hardened now, icy and unyielding. "So now I speak directly to those who would seek to usurp me and my own: disband, or I will make you." The Central Park rang with silence, a sick anticipation for elaboration. "Have a good night." Without another word, the Underworld Prince swept off stage and disappeared into the dark.

Chapter Fifteen – Traitor

Her parents hurried her back towards the house, their countenances grim. Delilah's parents were shepherding Delilah along hastily too. Robbie's face was rigidly expressionless, only the depths of his eyes even hinted at the intense fear they were all feeling. It was the only reason their family's actions didn't look suspicious - everyone Overworld was acting the same, fleeing as if they were leaving the scene of some hideous crime. Mothers clutched their children close; fathers glared accusingly at anyone who made eye contact with their household; teenagers were numb with shock and terror. The Underworld were in direct contrast, noisy in their outrage at the resistance and their love of the Prince who had just left the location. Susannah struggled not to let her magic flicker. Now really wasn't a good time to attract attention. There was a sense of enormous, mutual relief when they entered their warded home once more, though the air remained strained with the weight of storms to come. Her mother rounded on her.

"That's it," she said, flatly. "You're leaving that resistance."

"What?" Susannah protested. "NO! No, I'm not."

"You will do as I tell you-"

"-Then tell me something different," Susannah snarled, her magic unsheathing like claws. "Can't you see this means he's worried? We're getting somewhere-"

"Oh yes, you're getting very far, sweetheart, a whole six feet into a grave if you continue down the road you're going," her mum snapped. Susannah threw her hand up in frustration.

"You understand, don't you dad?" she asked. "Dad?" Her father was silent.

"Your mother might be right," he said finally. "You heard

what the Demon Lord said; the resistance is going to disband anyway, so if you leave now he-"

"What do you mean it's going to disband anyway?" Susannah spat. "We're not disbanding. Carmel can go to hell-"

"-Susannah!"

-For all I care. Him and his stupid speech and his *stupid* laws. I can't believe you're telling me to give up! You're the ones who always taught me to fight for what I believe in...or does that only apply when my belief is the same as everyone else's?" she demanded.

"Sometimes it's important to fight for your own survival too," her mum said tiredly. Susannah snorted.

"Oh yeah, is that what you told your resistance when you abandoned them?" There was deathly silence.

"Go to your room," her father ordered. Susannah sighed heavily, unbelieving.

"Yeah, just send me to my room because you can't handle-"

"*Go to your room!*"

Susannah's head tilted back at the steel in his tone, before glancing at her mother who was as white as sheet. Actually, her dad looked pretty white too. Without another word she spun and stormed up the stairs, making sure to slam the door to show how disappointed she was.

The atmosphere at The Stage the next day was tense and oppressive, made only heavier by the weight of stagnant, decade old air. Krig was late. They were all slumped restlessly in the moth devoured chairs, near the thick velvet curtains at the front of the theatre. The normal conversation was muted and subdued. Susannah had snuck out; her parents had later grounded her, but considering they were at work they couldn't actually enforce that punishment.

"Do you think something's happened?" She whispered to Delilah. The blonde bit her lip, before shaking her head with a reassuring confidence.

"Nah, if it had we'd know, wouldn't we?" Susannah glanced at Cassie, whose eyes were flicking feverishly to her watch every few seconds. Every time the younger Carter looked down, her face dropped and bleached even further in colour. Leola was observing Cassie too, with a concerned expression on her face. Every so often, the TA leader would exchange a look with Cade or Joel. Susannah suddenly wasn't so sure that they would know.

"Shouldn't we be starting the meeting anyway?" she asked uncertainly. "The later it gets, the harder it will be to avoid the hunting..."

"Would you like to run the meeting then, Skelsby?" Leon sneered. "I bet you would. You're not really a fan of the chain of command." Susannah winced. Jess perked up eagerly. She hadn't thought anyone was listening to the two of them. Jamie was sitting with Cade. Delilah frowned, face flushed, opening her mouth to respond.

"Leave her alone, Leon," David ordered tiredly. "She's got a point."

"Of course she does," the grey eyed boy muttered sarcastically. "I forgot, Susannah 'I'm-so-powerful' Skelsby can't do anything wrong. Why don't you just ask her to lead us then? I'm sure Krig wouldn't mind!"

"I would never replace Krig," she snapped. Her magic crackled, but she wrenched it back with shame.

"No," Leon replied smugly. "You wouldn't."

"I don't know," a voice remarked. "I reckon she'd be quite a good leader, all things considered." They all whipped around to see Krig descending down the aisle towards

204

them. Spots of colour stained Leon's cheeks.

"I don't lead people," she said, before arching her brows as she reigned in her emotions. "Probably best if you stay in charge." Krig merely shrugged in response.

"We should start the meeting - sorry I'm late by the way."

"Why are you late?" Leola demanded, fiercely, fists clenched.

"Got stopped by the Wardens at the metro."

"Are you okay?" Cassie asked, her nails bitten down to the skin.

"I'm fine," Krig smiled gently. "Don't worry Cass. They just wanted to know where I was heading to. It was a routine check, nothing more."

"Sloppy, boss," Mica remarked, grinning crookedly. "They shouldn't have seen you."

"I had a lot on my mind." The mood instantly sobered, and Krig sighed, dropping into his customary seat. "I'm guessing you guys want to start with yesterday," he stated. There was an affirmative mumble.

"What are we going to do?" KT asked. "I mean...he was referring to us, wasn't he?"

"Yes," Krig replied. "I believe he was."

"He knows about us then," David scowled. "How the hell did he find out?"

"I have no idea," Leon drawled. "Aside from running into burning buildings and back chatting assassin's we've been rather discreet." Susannah's magic flared, the curtains shaking in their rusty hinges. Everyone glanced up at them nervously, and she forcibly restrained her aura, breathing deeply.

"You prat," she hissed. "He already knew. The whole mission was a trap-"

"-That you decided to play with-"

"-Hey," Krig cut in, glaring it both. "Stop it. Both of you. No fighting on the team, I won't tell you again."

"Sorry," she said. Krig's 'talk' was still fresh in her mind. Leon was silent. Jess shot the TA boy a sympathetic look.

"I assure you, Leon, I've dealt with Susannah's actions. There's no need for you to keep bringing it up - though I'll come back to it one last time later in the meeting," Krig said. "For now, I need to hear what happened to all the groups. In detail. Leave nothing out." Delilah's eyes closed with a momentary shudder, as she looked at Joel. Those who had not been present for the two disastrous parts of the mission leaned forwards with ill-disguised curiosity, drawn by a car-crash watching fascination.

"Well, we went to Pembroke Street to create the safe house, like you said. Everything seemed calm enough - we were wearing face-distorters just in case though."

"There was nothing odd, nothing that stood out to you?" Krig pressed. Joel shook his head, licking his dry lips.

"There was a woman," Delilah murmured. Joel's head snapped round.

"There was? Why didn't you say anything?"

"I did," Delilah protested. Joel's head tilted as he thought, before clearing.

"Oh...that women. I still maintain it was nothing."

"The weird one with the shades, big headphones and pink hair?" Alice asked.

"Back up," Krig instructed patiently. "What women and what happened?"

"It was nothing," Joel said. "There was just this girl sunbathing on the little hill by Pembroke."

"Was she Underworld?"

"Couldn't see her eyes...no wings and she looked human." Joel seemed a tad disturbed now. "Could have been a vamp." There was a pause. "Damn, she probably *was* a vampire - I can't believe I missed it."

"She was sunbathing," Jess dismissed. "Vamps don't like sunbathing. Their skin is too sensitive. And, it was lower city; the Underworld don't go there."

"What happened when you got to Pembroke?" Krig prompted.

"We started up the street, to the safe house. Everything seemed pretty normal. Then-" Joel's gaze flicked to meet Krig's. A look passed between them, and the NR leader continued resolutely. "We noticed something wrong, Alice did anyhow..."

"The house was swarming with Spectres," Alice picked up the narrative. Krig's attention switched to her, with a lingering concern directed at Joel. Susannah kept her features carefully composed, watching Delilah and Jamie; trying to gauge if either of them saw the relevance of the comment. Spectres were invisible, ghost like creatures - like Dark Angels, they fed off emotions. Unless...Alice could see Spectres, in which case she would apparently be able to see a reflection of the emotions in the area, from which the Spectres were currently feeding from.

"You're a Distributor?" Jamie questioned, before she could. "You can see them?"

"Yeah," Alice's chin jutted out. "That a problem?"

"More like amazing!" Delilah exclaimed. Alice blinked, startled.

"You think so? It's just that most people-" the Latino halted abruptly. Susannah smiled bitterly.

"Find it unnatural?" she offered. Alice stared at her.

"Yeah," she said. Susannah could feel the other girl's brown eyes digging at her skin, as if it were her first meeting all over again. Krig quietly brought them back of track, and

Alice continued hastily. "The house was swarming with Spectres, they were black - I've normally found that means there's a large concentration of hatred in the area...and I knew it wasn't coming from us, so...I told Joel and we stopped. It seemed they'd realised that we'd somehow noticed them, because the next second they were charging out. Demons, Vampires, Dark Angels...all of them." Alice stopped, her hands curling tightly in her lap. "We ran for it."

"But obviously you can't outrun the Underworld," Joel murmured. "They're faster than us...especially Vampires. So we had to fight."

"You managed to beat Marco Carmel's hit team?" Jamie's eyebrows rose. "Aren't they known for being really good fighters?"

"No need to praise them too much," Jess scoffed.

"No need to act like it's easy either. If you think it is, you're an idiot," Jamie snarled. "Whatever else you might say about him, the Demon Lord is brilliant at his job."

The NR girl looked chastised, averting her gaze, unable to meet the other's dangerous expression.

"No one said he wasn't, pretty boy," Leola appeased.

Jamie's features smoothed over, as he grinned abashedly. "I know, I know," he sighed heavily. "It's just...sorry. Puts me on edge."

"It's fine," Krig said. "We get it. He shouldn't be underestimated." Jamie was quiet and Joel took the opportunity to continue.

"It was luck, really," he told them. "They had us at their mercy, could have ripped our throats out...and then in the last second they just withdrew." Krig frowned, troubled.

"I was worried you would say that - not that I'm not overjoyed to see you all in one piece."

"Why?" Cassie asked.

"Because it means he's toying with us," Krig replied bluntly. "Instead of a hit team, we (David, Leon, Susannah and I) got the assassin."

A troubled silence choked the room.

"So, where does that leave us?" Leola questioned cautiously. Delilah's jaw was clenched. Susannah didn't want to be the one to say it. A traitor made a horrible lot of sense, how else had the Underworld known that they were coming? It couldn't be a coincidence, especially with their rather toying actions. The assassin had known them, and not seemed surprised to see them, whilst the same seemed to be espccially true of the hit team. They'd know about the *safe house* even! And, in both scenarios, been called off at the last possible moment.

"As playthings," Mica replied, his tone drowning in false cheer.

"Oh, for Shadow's sake," Jess snapped. "I'll say it if the rest of you are too chicken - we have a traitor, clearly." The brunette flicked irate eyes at her in a pointed manner. Susannah's aura flared, causing the other to shrink back slightly.

"Oi, you can't assume that," David snarled. KT nodded resolutely, her hands curling into delicate fists, glaring.

"That we have a traitor?" Leon said coldly. "It seems like a plausible assumption. In the same manner, it is reasonable to assume that some 'possible suspects' are more plausible than others."

"And who would you argue are plausible suspects then?" David responded dangerously, voice scarcely above a growl.

"Let's not jump to pointing fingers -" Cassie pleaded. Delilah opened her mouth to speak.

"Skelsby," Leon replied bluntly. "She's a new recruit and we didn't appear to have a mole problem before she joined.

Jamie and Delilah are also possible, for the same reasons as above. However, Delilah doesn't seem to have such a...reputation."

"You like reason, Leon" Jamie stated. "Then surely, if I was the traitor, or if Susannah or Delilah were, it would be more reasonable of us to bide our time so it would not be so obvious that either of us was the betrayer, and to wait until there was another *convenient* new recruit to blame?"

"If you're suggesting that I'm simply trying to hide my own guilt-" Leon began, his nostrils flaring with rage.

"I'm suggesting nothing," Jamie replied calmly. "There's no need to look so...flustered." Susannah hid the strained, impulsive smile that threatened to grow at his defence.

"You-"

"Enough." Krig's order was quiet, but his words rang across the room like a pistol crack. Silence descended upon them instantly. Susannah's head whipped to him, still seated in his chair. He didn't glare, but there was a weight to his gaze that made her gut squirm in hot shame at their bickering. He leaned forward fractionally; seemingly nonchalant to the fact that he had everyone's undivided attention. "Have you ever considered that this petty pointing of fingers is exactly what Carmel wants?" He paused, staring at them all. "He said 'disband, or I will make you.' Perhaps this is his way of disbanding us? Because at this rate he doesn't have to lift a finger to wound us - you lot are doing a fine job at tearing this resistance apart by yourselves."

"Exactly!" Delilah exclaimed. "That's what I was going to say!" Krig smiled at her, faintly.

"I'm more worried about why the Demon Lord is playing with us, actually," Joel said seriously, after a moment. "If he's got a traitor he could have already rounded us all up and tossed us into the Anzarkledea cells for insubordination, so why hasn't he?" There was a pause, as everyone digested the question.

"He could be lulling us into a false sense of security," Cassie offered.

"But why would he need to?" Krig countered, the barest frown creasing his features. "Why would he want to? The whole idea of the public speech was to scare us into stopping; lulling us into security would then be contradictory."

"Maybe the traitor isn't well...completely traitorous," KT said.

"That's an oxymoron if I ever heard one," David muttered. "You're either a traitor or you're not, there's nothing else to it. You can't be half a traitor, that's ridiculous!"

"Oh please, you don't really think it would be that simple, do you?" Leola questioned acidly. "People aren't black and white. You don't know why the traitor turned, what his or her motivations were - how do you know that the treachery isn't a forced one?"

"Because treachery is a choice," David replied. "Everything's a choice, especially with boss man's mind block. Sure, the traitor could have a 'compelling' reason for being a backstabbing b...for turning traitor, but they still turned. They could have ignored the motivation, whatever it was."

"Yes, but even if they were incompletely traitorous, if that's the right way of saying it," Alice began, in a frustrated voice. "Carmel would still have been able to kill us or capture us during the last mission. He had the assassin and the hit team out, and as Jamie said the Demon Lord's hit team is really good. He could have finished it, even if he didn't have all the information. Him playing with us is nothing to do with the traitor: it's *his* choice. The traitor's just going to be following orders."

"Why on earth would he do that though?" Mica scowled disgustedly. "You'd think he'd have nothing better to do."
"Of course he's got nothing better to do, I mean, it's not like he runs the country or anything," Susannah replied, in a falsely bright tone of voice. Cade snorted. She caught Krig regarding her with speculation, and grew serious. "Maybe he's bored - he's a genius, he probably gets bored easily," she offered, though she wasn't really convinced with that.
"Fabulous," Jess sneered. "So by your estimation we're alive so long as we're interesting enough."
Susannah had to bite down the cruel impulse to reply 'yeah, so you should probably write your will now, shouldn't you?'
"Possibly," she said instead. "I don't pretend to know how a psychopath's mind works."
"But I thought you knew everything," Leon muttered. Susannah's eyes flashed.
"I give off that impression? Wow, thank you very much," she forced a smile to her lips.
"Cade," Krig said pointedly, as if to remind them not to argue. "Can you and Jamie do some research?"
"Sure thing boss," Cade agreed. "Already thinking on it." Krig nodded.
"Moving on then, unless anyone else feels they have any answers to offer?" There was silence. "Okay; then I would like to return to the mission for a moment." He pulled out the sheets on Gossamer.

Krig had asked the TA to, amongst researching other resistances, to team up with Cade once more to see if they could do something with the Gossamer – find some way of neutralising its effects, as they had the details for how to make it since Susannah had got the sheets. He, too, said he'd have a look at working on something about the

212

Gossamer, and offered it as a 'free time, extra-curricular' project to anyone. If she had time, Susannah vowed to look over them and see what she could do, though this type of invention and trial and error practise had always been more Delilah's forte...Delilah who was now dragging her over to talk to Leon about going to go see the mysterious Rebecca Daggey. Susannah suspected the conversation would not go over well, and certainly not with her presence involved.

"Could we talk to you for a moment, please?" Delilah asked the brown-haired boy softly, with a pleasant smile. Leon came to a stop, regarding them warily.

"What is it?" he returned, not exactly hostile, but not in a particularly friendly manner either.

"Okay, this may come out a bit of a strange request," Delilah said, biting her lip, "but are you related to Rebecca Daggey?"

Leon immediately stiffened, his eyes flashing dangerously, his aura flaring. Susannah remembered Krig had mentioned Leon had a sick sister, and not to bring it up at any costs.

"Why do you want to know?" he demanded.

"I need to talk to her," Delilah replied.

"Why?" Leon folded his arms, radiating aggression. Susannah felt her own magic flicker in response, and he shot her a sharp look.

"Because I think she was there when my parents were murdered," Delilah said quietly, "and I need to know the truth. Leon – please. That's all I want, just to ask her."

"You do know she's in the CCC mental hospital?" he questioned. Delilah nodded. "And that doesn't bother you?" Leon continued sceptically. Delilah shrugged.

"I *need* to know," was all she said. Leon's jaw was tight.

"She's my sister," he replied, finally. "Becki's my sister."

"Would you let us see her?" Delilah persisted.

"*Us?*" Leon snatched upon the word. "I might consider letting *you* see her, because I understand needing to know something like that, but *Skelsby?*"

"I'm not that bad," Susannah growled, before she could stop herself, annoyed and maybe a little hurt though she'd never admit it. "For crying out loud, can you stop making out like I'm some horrible disease or something?"

Leon surveyed her flatly.

"It's just for moral support," Delilah murmured, resting a hand on his arm. "She's my best friend, and I-she won't judge you for anything. Neither of us will. We won't judge your sister either. *Please.*"

"And I'm supposed to take your word on that?" he questioned tersely.

"We won't tell anyone else anything either," Susannah added, after a moment. "You have my word. I can make a magical oath on it too, seeing as we both know that in your eyes my word counts for next to nothing."

Leon's fists clenched, and he stared stonily into the distance for a moment.

"If I say no, you'll just be finding some other way to talk to her, won't you?" he asked, his gaze moving to Delilah again. Her best friend smiled, a little awkwardly.

"Probably?"

He sighed.

"Fine."

"Fine?" Delilah's expression brightened. "You'll let me see her?"

"Don't see how I have much choice in the matter, really," he muttered.

"*Thank you!*" Delilah exclaimed, pulling the startled boy into a hug. Leon blinked.

"…just don't make me regret it, Moor."

Susannah crept back into the house after the meeting, willing her parents to still be at work. The doorbell screeched as she entered, and she slammed it with a piece of magic in hopes it would shut up. Horrible doorbell. She turned around again, only to freeze. Her mother stood before her, still in her uniform, probably between shifts. Susannah swallowed.

"Oh, hi…I thought you were at work?" she asked.

"Where have you been?" her mum demanded. Susannah pulled a puzzled face.

"I was at the park with Delilah," she lied. Her mum's eyes narrowed to slits.

"You were grounded," she accused, "and so was Delilah. I had a very concerned communicon message from William." Susannah resisted the urge to shift uneasily. Her mum placed her hands on her hips. "You were with that resistance group weren't you? *Weren't you?*" Susannah tightened her jaw, staring back, neither confirming nor denying the answer to the question. Her mum tossed her hands irritably.

"Susannah, for shadow's sake," she hissed. Susannah rolled her eyes, frustration boiling in her chest.

"Well, you didn't actually expect me to stay at home, did you? Quitting the resistance is what you want, not me!"

"It's going to get you hurt."

"Everything can get me hurt," Susannah retorted, angrily. "And I can look out for myself."

"You're just a child -"

"-I'm not a child! I'm fifteen; the other Carmel would be my age and he helps the Underworld Prince rule the country, I doubt Lord Carmel grounds him because he's too young to do anything."

"The Underworld are different," her mum replied stubbornly. "They age differently - and they're not my daughter." Susannah gritted her teeth, her magic flickering dangerously.

"Funnily enough I was aware of that by now," she said.

"Don't take that tone with me," her mum snapped. "I'm trying to help you." Her face was pale, eyes starting to appear red rimmed. Susannah felt a cramp of guilt, and sighed.

"I know," she said quietly, "but-" she shrugged helplessly.

"You're still not going to leave it," her mum finished.

"Never."

Her mum went back to work soon enough, leaving Susannah alone in the silence and the tension. She did feel bad about making her parents worry so much about the resistance, but it was the right thing to do. How could she possibly go back to the meaningless, purposeless way of life she'd had before? It would all seem so empty in comparison.

Her dad found her in much the same state of contemplation when he returned home some hours later. She held her guitar across her lap, absently plucking at the strings to soothe her magic when her thoughts got her too stressed. He paused in the door of the lounge, dropping his keys into the bowl with a jangling clink.

"I got a message from your mother," he stated, disapproving of her actions. She looked up, daring him to give her another lecture. He didn't, merely loosening his tie and walking over to sit next to her on the sofa. "You know, we're only worried about you, don't you Suzie?" he asked. She nodded. That didn't stop it being annoying though.

"Your mother and I both joined the Starlight Resistance

when we turned twenty one," he continued, causing Susannah to watch him curiously and set her music aside to listen. "It's how we met, actually."

"You mean you were in a resistance group too?" she asked disbelievingly. She couldn't believe it. How come they'd never told her before?

"Yes," he replied patiently. "As were Robyn and Joseph Moor." Susannah's eyes widened with shock, as she froze entirely for a few seconds.

"Delilah's parents?" she demanded, leaning forward. "Does Delilah know? Is that how they died?"

"No, I don't believe she does know," her dad said softly. "When we left we hoped to put everything in the past, behind us, none of us talked about it."

"But why did you leave?" she asked, unable to comprehend why someone would. If you swore to a cause, an illegal cause, why would you just back out? It made no sense. Her dad was silent for a minute, his features haggard.

"You must understand, Susannah, the Starlight resistance was not like yours. They were militant, extremists, with a rigid system designed for efficiency."

"And you joined that?" she questioned, arching a brow.

"We were young," her dad sighed. "We wanted to get something done; Contessa and Damien Carmel were not as skilled in public relations as their son is, times were different...and it wasn't always like that. It started out okay, better, but then...things changed. I don't know what it was, a lack of progress, impatience or just chance, but they changed. To put it simply, there was a shift in the government of the resistance."

"Like a new leader?" she asked. She couldn't imagine the resistance without Krig being in charge, it would have been too weird, and the idea of Krig one day not being there was even stranger, too odd to even consider thinking about. No one could fill the shoes he'd created - he'd founded them!

"Yes," her dad said. "A new leader, though I cannot share names with you."

"There's a secrecy ward?" she guessed.

"Yes," he said. "Introvertai, if you're familiar with the type..." she nodded. "Whilst our old leader was efficient, also rigid in his hierarchy and determined to a fault, he did care about things outside of the cause. However, his deputy," her father smiled bitterly, "was of a different make. He was ruthless, thinking of his recruits as little more than tools to fulfil the resistance's aims." Susannah frowned.

"What were the aims?"

"What is the aim of all resistances?" her dad returned. "To overthrow the Underworld supremacy." Susannah's head tilted to one side, her brow furrowing.

"How can you be telling me this now? If there's a secrecy ward?"

"Because it's been weakening over time; magic does if it's left alone, it has to be renewed every now and again to maintain its potency. Magic isn't made to be still and stagnant." Right, of course, she should have known that – she *did* know that. She was silent for a moment.

"But what about Delilah's parents? What happened to them?" she asked again. "Were they killed in action? Delilah thinks they were; that it wasn't just a hunting accident." Her dad drew a hand over his face, shooting her a sharp look.

"I don't know," he replied. "The bodies were never found. Probably."

"Shadow," she cursed, voice a murmur. That was awful.

"You can't tell Delilah," her dad warned. Susannah's head shot up.

"What? Why not?" she demanded. "Surely she has a right to know what happened?"

"Not if it will lead her to Starlight," her dad said.

"You mean they're still around?"

"Yes, somewhere," her dad said. Susannah plucked at a guitar string again.

"Is that why mum's so touchy about the resistance? Does she figure the same thing will happen? Because Krig's not like that! Not at all." Her dad sighed once more, heavily.

"I think that's a conversation you'd be better off having with her," he said. Susannah stared at her fingers, watching them curl and uncurl like flower petals.

"So the deputy took over?" she verified. "That's why you left?"

"Among other reasons," her dad said, though by his expression Susannah had a feeling there was stuff he was leaving out.

"And he just let you leave?" she questioned shrewdly. "I thought you said he was obsessed."

"He was," her dad replied tersely. "And I wouldn't know his feelings about us quitting, I haven't seen any of them since."

"They didn't hunt you down?"

"We still had a couple of friends in the resistance to help us hide."

"When was this - roughly?" she asked, frowning.

"Fifteen years ago. We never looked back. We had you to think about, you were only little, bless you, and he...even then your magic was powerful, Susannah...if he *ever* knew about you..."

"The deputy?" Susannah's throat felt dry. "He'd..."

"Recruit you. Use you. Train you as weapon," her dad said flatly.

"Is that why you taught me about everything so early on,

recruiters and stuff? People who would want to use my magic? To keep me away from Starlight?"

"And the Carmels," he agreed. Susannah was silent.

"Are you disappointed that I joined the resistance? My resistance, I mean," she asked, finally, quietly, plucking at the guitar strings again, discordantly. Her dad sighed, running a hand across his face once more, tiredly, as if to soothe away a headache.

"I'm concerned," he said after a while. "As is your mother. These things can start out…good, but they can spiral and before you know it you're stuck in a situation you don't want to be stuck in."

"But are you?" she persisted.

"No," he said, adding gruffly: "I'd never be disappointed in you for following what you believed in."

Susannah felt a small smile curl her lips, her chest feeling a bit lighter. Then she frowned.

"Dad, Delilah already suspects her parents were murdered, she told me. She's looking into it all now…"

"Then I suggest you try and prevent her from doing so," he replied. Susannah stared at him.

"I can't sabotage her!" she protested.

"Well, for crying out loud, don't encourage her," her dad muttered. "They'd love to…never mind."

"Dad?"

"I said never mind, Susannah," he said, more abruptly now, standing. "I'm going to make dinner."

Susannah watched him go, still frowning.

Something was *definitely* up with this whole story.

Chapter Sixteen – CCC

"Leon, Susannah, I want you to both work together to research the assassin," Krig said "you both met him. See what you can dig up, and get back to me."

For a moment, there was silence.

"You're kidding, right?" Leon demanded, in a low voice. "You want me to work with *her?*"

"Is that a problem?" Krig questioned, eyebrows arched with a hint of danger. "Has she got some highly contagious disease you haven't told me about?"

"Krig, this isn't going to work - we don't get on," Susannah tried.

"We'd picked up on that," David remarked dryly. She rolled her eyes at him, while Mica snickered.

"Oh don't encourage them," Cade sighed. "I think this is a good idea. You can get over your differences and stop bickering." Delilah made a noise of agreement.

"We don't *bicker-*" Leon began.

"You're working together," Krig stated; a tone of finality in his voice. "It's logical, and I'm getting tired of you two fighting. We're a team."

Susannah looked down, an embarrassed flush staining her cheeks.

"I'll try," she agreed, reluctantly. "Though if he comes back with a broken nose, I will not be held responsible for my actions."

"Yeah, I figured violence would be your first answer," Leon muttered. "I suppose you lack the intelligence to work things out any other-"

"Stop!" Krig glared. They both fell silent. "This is an illegal resistance, and we can hardly afford any more divisions amongst ourselves right now...so, you're going to work together on this, get past whatever your issues are, and get back to me when you're done, alright?"

"Alright," they both repeated; exchanging wary looks. This was going to just be horrible, Susannah could tell. Jamie shot her a sympathetic look, behind Krig's back.

"Right, onto the second matter I want to discuss," Krig said. "I want you all to take an Introvertai ward." There was a thick, heavy silence. "We have a traitor, that is clear, and hopefully this will limit the damage they can do as I'm unwilling to disband and we don't know who our resident mole is. I'm extremely sorry for having to do this, but I'm prioritising the resistance above any wounded feelings. It's not that I don't trust you all, I do, which is why our having a traitor is such a problem as there's not one of you who I would have believed capable of betraying me like this...but, nonetheless, the evidence speaks for itself," he sighed. "Anyone who doesn't want to take one, I will erase your memories and you can leave."

Now, the silence seemed suffocating. Susannah swallowed.

"Fair dues," she said, finally. "How do you give the ward? Is it like with the Extravertai?"

Krig smiled at her. Leon was eyeing her suspiciously, almost speculating too.

"Yes, just like that," Krig murmured. "But perhaps a bit more, er, intrusive. Sorry."

"Well, you know I'm in," Cade shrugged.

"Me too," Leola said, shakily. "Definitely. Whatever you need."

Ultimately, everyone was pretty quick to agree, seeing the logic of the idea. There was no clue as to which of them was the traitor, as after the first of them agreed, the rest fell in line.

It felt odd, as if her brain was muffled, enclosed. Krig had assured them the sensation would fade. It was still strange though.

"What about you, boss?" David teased. "Who's doing your ward? Democracy and all that..."

Krig seemed to take the thought seriously though, pausing. "Is anyone here good at Mind Arts?"

"I am," Jamie said. "If you trust me enough to let me fiddle around in your head."

"I trusted you enough to let you in my resistance group, did I not?" Krig returned, indicating for Jamie to come forwards. "Try not to give me a headache," he added, with a somewhat strained smile. Jamie took Krig's head in his hands, firmly, thumbs resting on temples.

"Advanced skill," Jamie replied idly. "I don't leave headaches – I'm probably better at this then you," he grinned. Krig smirked, arching his brows.

"Is that so? Prove it."

After a minute Jamie stepped back, letting his hands drop and Krig blinked. They both studied each other for a moment.

"You're done?" her boss questioned. Jamie flashed a smile. "Yeah. Told you I was good," he replied. "You should be able to feel the muffling sensation, but nothing else." Susannah couldn't help but feel impressed, and Jamie sat down again. "So...on with the meeting. Leola, report."

Susannah wasn't sure if Delilah realised how very nervous she looked, as the meeting ended. Her best friend's hands were trembling slightly, her face white as chalk. Then again, it would have been absurd if Delilah wasn't nervous, after all she could have been getting some proof on whether or not her parents were actually murdered. More than anything, Susannah got the urge to tell her friend all about her own parents being in the Starlight Resistance. Leon looked pale too, his magic flittering anxiously; a tell-tale flash of silver chain around his neck, his key to the hospital was nestled under his shirt, as he strode forward at a relentless pace. The key was the same colour as Leon's eyes, albeit a little less stormy and troubled as a metal wasn't alive to express those emotions.

"Visiting hours are from two to six," he told them curtly. "So let's go, it's already three o clock." As abrupt as his words were, his tone wasn't particularly harsh, not like it would be if he was directing them at her. Leon actually got on quite well with Delilah. Susannah stayed quiet, knowing she was only supposed to be there for moral support, and that Leon wasn't altogether that pleased with her presence. She was actually somewhat amazed that he was allowing it, for whatever reason.

"Becki might not know anything," he warned Delilah, with an uncharacteristic gentleness, sparing her a glare over the blonde's shoulder which dared her to comment. But Susannah felt absolutely no desire to mock him for this, no matter what he seemed to think of her. She hoped her expression conveyed that, and, indeed, it must have done for the slight tip of his head, the fractional softening of his unforgiving posture.

"I know," Delilah replied, biting her lip. "But I have to try." Leon sighed, twirling the key absently between his bony fingers.

"Well, if it counts for anything," he began, "I hope you find your answers. Just don't get your hopes up - I don't even know if she's up for visitors today - through here." They turned down another road, alert for attack. Susannah was silent for a moment, simply following, letting the two walk ahead and doing her utmost best to slip into the shadows. Leon glanced at the two of them again, visibly getting more agitated.

"If you upset her, I'll take your teeth out."

Triple C was a large, white building surrounding by an unforgiving iron fence. From first impressions, it looked more like a prison than a hospital - even a mental one. On second impressions, it was clear that the austere fencing had been added several years after the original, simple but elegant, building had been created. Alone, the hospital looked like quite a nice place. It was merely the added security systems, put in place to contain the criminally insane, that made the place look so bleak. The lines of Leon's mouth hardened. Susannah did, of course, know about this place - who didn't in the city? - but she never really considered it, or thought about the name behind it. Most people just referred to it as 'the loony bin.' She was getting second doubts. She wasn't sure she wanted to go in after all. What if it got really awkward? She looked uncertainly at Leon, who refused to meet her eye now as he strode determinedly towards the gate. She felt a pang of sympathy. He fished for the end of chain around his neck, inserting the silver key into the small lock on the gates.

"Leon Daggey, Delilah Moor and Susannah Skelsby, visiting Rebecca Daggey in Maple Ward," he stated softly into the intercom. There was a crackle, a low buzzing noise, then the gates swung open in a manner quite reminiscent of the silver gates of Anzarkledea. Whoever had added them, must have had modelled them on the large protective spikes of the Demon Lord's manor. They entered.

There was a large garden area, that they crossed it first. It had lots of inmates milling around, with their nurses close at hand. She saw one little girl with red pigtails picking the wings off butterflies and cooing. She could honestly say that it was one of the most disturbing things she'd ever seen, and she'd been witness to horrible things. The grass was kept quite nicely, but it was bare and sparse, plucked out like the poor butterfly's wings. The area was mainly just paving - almost like a retirement garden might look like, which gave her chills. Inside, the halls were brightly painted in an effort to induce some cheeriness to the despondent place. The faerie receptionist hovering at the desk was picking at her nails and looked tired and haggard. There were shadows around her eyes and tiny headphones shoved into her ears. A sign above the small desk said that there were nine wards in the mental hospital.

Maple ward – trauma. Susannah's heart skipped a beat; that was Becki's ward! *Acer ward* – rehabilitation from drugs and addiction. *Cedar ward* – dealing with depression. *Cherry ward* - paranoia, schizophrenia and other delusion based illnesses. *Pine ward* - borderline disorders. *Birch Ward* - short term stay. *Willow Ward* - dealing with magically induced illnesses. *Oak ward* – *Dementia. Alpha ward* – which held the criminally insane. It appeared an odd mixture, and Susannah wasn't entirely certain about the legitimate presence of all the wards, but everyone knew Triple C was more than just a mental hospital. It was an expensive drop off place for everyone the Government didn't know what to do with too.

Maple ward was in between Acer and Cedar, because according to Leon a lot of the trauma induced events could relate to/lead to addictions, obsessive habits or depressions. She found it all quite creepy actually, and, in some cases, excessive. Severity of disorder seemed barely differentiated. There were screams coming from Alpha ward, although Leon said that it was a normal occurrence for one of the long-time residents, Sybil Violet. Apparently she was convinced that she was actually seventeen instead of sixty one and kidnapped by vampires who wanted to force her to be their queen. If let out, she was prone to murdering people in an effort to escape from the 'evil leeches,' never mind the fact that Sybil was actually a vampire herself and had to be told that her daily blood intake was tomato soup or cranberry juice. She was slightly worried about meeting Rebecca Daggey, what if she started screeching or something? She felt really sorry for Leon. It must be awful for him coming here so much, listening to people call the place a loony bin or bedlam when that wasn't necessarily an accurate description. She had asked him what the 'CCC' actually stood for, but he didn't know: no one did. They just called it Triple C.

They turned into Maple Ward.

The ward was painted a sunny blue colour, for calmness and serenity and had lots of different doors. Leon stopped to talk to a rather plump, motherly looking biscuit brown haired woman.

"Leon," she smiled at him. "Who are your friends?" It was clear that they knew each other.

"Delilah," Leon said shortly. "Delilah Moor, and Susannah Skelsby." His expression softened a little bit. "How's she been?" he asked.

"Alright. She had an episode late last night after you left, but she's been okay. We found pills in her room again; they were confiscated, of course. I think the new tablets are really helping with her nightmares," the nurse confided.

"Is she in now?" he asked. "Can I see her?"

"Of course, sweetie. You seem to do her good - just don't pass on any more horror books, she's been spreading ghost stories around the whole ward. She's in her room now, just got back from a meeting with Doctor Seweld a while ago."

"Okay, thanks," Leon nodded. "Come on," he instructed, a bit tersely, walking briskly down the corridor.

"Try not to stare, dears," the nurse whispered as they passed. "He doesn't bring people often." Delilah offered the lady a brief smile. Susannah didn't try, knowing it was more likely to come out as an awkward grimace. They came to a small door, room 29: Rebecca Daggey.

Susannah tried valiantly not to stare; the problem was that she wasn't sure how well she managed it. Rebecca Daggey was a skeletal, emaciated wraith of a girl with the same brown hair as Leon and sickly white features that seemed stretched over her face like some gaunt skull. There was a small smile on her face, a look of delight and the sight of her younger sibling, before her features furrowed a little.

"Leon...who are your friends?" she asked. She had an almost aristocratic voice, slightly melodious and very clear. The room they were in was painted a light, calming blue colour, the same as the ward, and had lots of pictures on the walls of a bunch of people, skulls and note pages scribbled red in a colour disturbingly reminiscent to that of blood. Then there was writing, poems...the efforts of many years of different forms of therapy. There were also books and CDs and posters on the walls. It was very simple. With a bed, a cabinet, a desk and chair - nothing sharp ended or dangerous at all - and endless papers. They were tacked all over the walls like some little child's bedroom. It was clear, from the lack of blank sterile hospitalness, that Rebecca

Daggey was a long term resident.

"Hi Becki," Leon greeted, pulling his elder sister for a very careful, feather light hug. "This is Delilah, do you remember I told you about her? Delilah, this is Becki, my sister. And that's Susannah, she's Delilah's friend."

"Nice to meet you," Delilah smiled automatically, seeming to be able to refrain from staring or acting in some manner rude or uncomfortable just fine. Susannah's insides twisted again. What was she even doing here? She wasn't suited to give moral support anyway, Delilah normally laughed at her attempts of offering comfort. And her dad had said not to encourage this!

Becki was painfully thin and slight, with dark bruises from lack of sleep shadowing her eyes like smudged eyeliner. Her hands were shaking, a constant tremor. Becki stared intently at her, before seeming to accept their presence.

"Hi," she greeted, surprisingly lucidly. Then Susannah felt awful for assuming that she wouldn't be lucid. "It's nice to meet you too. Are you Leon's friends?"

"Something like that," Susannah said. Becki's head tilted, before she focused on Delilah.

"Oh, are you his girlfriend? You're very pretty."

Delilah blushed.

"No! No, I'm not his girlfriend. We go to the same club." She wasn't technically lying, was she? The resistance was a club...of sorts.

"Ah, the resistance," she said. Leon glared at her.

Susannah's eyes widened and she shot Leon a look. What if Leon was an accidental traitor...if he'd told Becki...and then *Becki* was the one who passed it on, not fully aware of the consequences?

"Becki!" Leon hissed.

"What?" Becki asked innocently. "Was I not supposed to

talk about that?" A smile tugged at Delilah's lips, though Susannah didn't see what was so amusing. Becki seemed very...normal, except for the unbearable thinness, bags and tremor. On some level, she couldn't help but wonder what Becki was doing in a place like this. Leon rolled his eyes. "Keep it quiet, guys...Krig would have my head," he muttered. "She won't tell anyone." His mercury eyes bore into her specifically, and she merely raised an eyebrow in response, keeping to the corner of the room, trying not to intrude.

"Um," Delilah began, more hesitant than Susannah had ever seen her "What's, er, why -"

"Severe anorexia and bulimia, cutting - apparently as a way to deal with the lack of control I feel in my own life. Chronic insomnia and suicidal thoughts, along with 'fits'. That's what it says on my file, is that what you wanted to know?" Becki questioned, tonelessly. She lifted her pale hands a little, the sleeves of her top slipping back to reveal a crisscross of scars running up her arms. Leon's eyes narrowed at her, daring her to even think about commenting negatively.

"You were wondering why I seemed to be so normal," Becki stated.

"Yes," Delilah murmured guiltily. "Sorry."

Becki stared at her coldly, her gaze like chips of ice. "Your eyes would look lovely in my collection."

Delilah took a step back, glancing at Leon, and Susannah's aura immediately flared, causing Becki's head to snap to her. They stared at each other. Then Becki's head tilted, suddenly, and she grinned and burst out laughing.

"Your faces!" she giggled manically. "I'm in Maple, not Alpha! Got a bit of control problem there - Susannah was it?" she questioned. "Maybe you should join us...a stint here would sure heal you right off!" the girl peeled into cackles.

"I guess we deserved that one," Delilah murmured, obviously trying to ease the sudden tension in the room. Leon's face, in contrast to her own posture, had inexplicably relaxed.

"You have spent far too much time with Renee," he told his sister, amusedly. Becki smirked.

"If you can't beat 'em, join 'em," she quipped. "Renee's cool anyway - when she's not trying to convince me that she's actually Vanity Carmel and that her brothers will be coming for her any day now." There was a moment of silence. Becki turned slightly more serious.

"Leon said you had some questions for me?" she prompted Delilah. Her best friend shifted nervously, biting her lip and playing with her hair.

"I was, I was wondering if you could tell me about what you saw? Fourteen years ago?"

Becki was silent, her expression slowly shifting.

"No," she replied, flatly, fists starting to clench. "I'm not talking about it. Sorry, but you can't make me, and I won't." Leon held up his hands in a placating manner.

"Okay, okay, just calm down. You don't have to talk about it, I promise," he wheedled. "Just calm down, you don't want the nurses to have to put you under again, do you?" Coming from some people, that statement might have sounded threatening, but not from Leon, bizarrely, and not now. His expression was too tender. He was genuinely asking her to calm down so she wouldn't have to be sedated. Becki calmed down a little, her features dishevelled and her eyes wet with tears that she didn't appear to know she'd shed. Her posture slowly relaxed too, more at ease once more.

"That's right," Leon soothed. "It was just a question; you don't have to talk about it if you don't want to. Delilah, Skelsby, we're leaving."

"But," Delilah started helplessly, pausing under Leon's venomous glower.

"*We're leaving.*"

Susannah suddenly got a bad feeling, a Delilah-is-going-to-do-something feeling that she didn't get very often, because despite doing random things and being rather quirky, Delilah was actually the sensible one out of the two of them.

"Del-" she began.

"I know you don't want to talk about it," the blonde rushed on, quickly, dodging Leon's attempt to pull her out, and completely ignoring Susannah too. "I know it must be horrible and I'm sorry, I really am...but that's the night my parents died, and I *need* to know what happened! Becki please!" she begged. Becki stared at her with wide eyes, her mouth and body trembling as much as her shaking hands.

"I can't help you. Go away," she scrunched up into a ball, defensively, entirely closed off. "Leave me alone, I don't know. Go away. Leave me alone. Go away! I don't know what you're talking about!"

This time, Delilah let Leon usher her out, shoulders slumped, and Susannah followed, turning as she reached the door.

"Thanks anyway," she said quietly, to Becki's too still form. "I know this must be difficult for you...sorry for the memories."

The door to Becki Daggey's door slammed shut. Susannah struggled to keep up with Leon's furious strides, his aura flaring with fury, his fingers tight on her best friend arm, dragging Delilah along with him.

"For Shadow's sake, Moor, what the hell?" he snarled. "Skelsby - why didn't you stop her? Isn't that why you're supposed to be here?"

"I'm sorry!" Delilah murmured. "It's not Suze's fault-" Leon rounded on her best friend again, his features twisted with rage, growing alien.

"Oh, you're *sorry*? That doesn't bloody well cut it! I said I'd help you, let you talk to her. I said she might not tell you anything!"

"I know!" Delilah cried. "I just had to try."

"Don't upset her!" he roared. "I gave you one damn rule. Don't upset her! But no! You just have to go and do that! Do you know how much that could have set her back? *Do you?*" he demanded, shaking her roughly. Delilah's head hung low, tears burning her eyes relentlessly.

"Hey, leave her alone," Susannah said, a little angry herself, stepping forwards. "She didn't mean any harm-"

"No, no, Suze, he's right. It was stupid of me," Delilah whispered. "I'm sorry...I just...I know it didn't excuse what I just did, but I'm sorry. I had to try!" The fury seemed to deflate out of Leon like air out of a balloon.

"I'm sorry you didn't get your information too," he said shortly. "But you *can't* just do that."

"I know," she said quietly. "I wasn't thinking. I was..."

"Yeah, I know," he said softly, staring at her. "Just, look. Don't ever try and contact her again. Okay? She doesn't need the extra stress."

"Thank you for letting me see her," Delilah twisted her hands round her t-shirt. He sighed.

"Don't worry about it. She'll calm down soon enough. I'll see you at the next meeting. You won't...tell anyone?" he pierced them both with a sharp look. Delilah shook her head.

"Of course not," Susannah murmured. "You have my word. He nodded.

"I'll see you around."

"Bye."
One step forward, two steps back. Delilah sighed.

She split from Delilah upon feeling her communicon buzz, and pulled the small orb out of her pocket, watching it grow in her hand back to its normal size. It had been from Jamie, asking if she wanted to meet up. With a smirk, albeit a strained, tired one, Delilah had immediately made her excuses to leave – saying she wanted to be on her own and think things through, despite Susannah's best attempts of assurance regarding the matter. Nonetheless, she'd left, and Susannah found herself meandering through the city in search of the café Jamie had suggested. There was a fluttering sort of excitement in her stomach, despite the events of the day, and while Jamie had in no way indicated that this would be anything like a date, she enjoyed the possibility that it one day might be. Silly perhaps, but the thought made her smile. She raised her eyebrows slightly at the name of the place – Café Diem, before just chuckling and walking in and up to him.
"You sure know how to pick your cafés," she greeted. "Another rebel hot spot?"
Jamie grinned upon seeing her, standing, pulling out a chair absently before sitting down again, causing her to be torn between a pleased flush at the gentleman-like gesture and incredulity.
"I tend to prefer to avoid mainstream places," he replied. "Problem?"
"No, course not, not at all." she shook her head.

This café was less polished than the one with glass tables, cosier and...more intimate. There were lots of pictures and paintings on the walls of places all around the world – the

Golden Falls, Brightpine woods where the trees glittered at night, the Diamond Caves, the Violet marshes...the list continued. She stared at them all, entranced. Whilst she didn't want to travel as much as Delilah did, she'd always itched to see more of the world, but never gone more than five miles from the city (and that was for a school trip to the Silver Hollow which Silver Hollow Park was named after.) They both ordered, and Susannah made sure to pay for herself this time, despite Jamie's joking pout and eye roll. They chatted idly for a bit about films and numerous other things, before Jamie finally gave her a sheepish grin.

"So, I have to admit, I do have a reason for stealing your company," he said.

"Oh?" Susannah grinned. "And there was me thinking you just enjoyed having me around. I'm hurt. Really."

"Sorry," he smirked. "But yeah, do you have any leads of the assassin?" Susannah once again couldn't help but look around again, worriedly, and once more he reached over, taking her hand reassuringly. "Come on, trust me – I'm still alive, aren't I? No one's listening to us."

"Oh, I don't know," Susannah murmured. "That waitress seems pretty focussed on you."

Jamie glanced around, before winking at her.

"Jealous?" he purred.

"No!"

He chuckled.

"Ward the table if you want to, but from my experience that actually just draws more attention because people assume you have something to hide."

Susannah considered this for a moment, thoughtfully, never having looked at it in that way before. It made sense, she supposed.

"No, we don't," she replied, finally. "Should I assume you

do?"

"Redgrave," he said, after a minute or so, softly. "He's got something to do with the name Redgrave."

"How do you know?" she asked, equally quiet, her voice hushed.

"My family dabble in the arms industry," Jamie replied, grimacing. "And they're Carmel supporters. Ergo...you hear stuff, sometimes. Growing up in that environment." His expression became a bit awkward. "I don't know if it's valid, or actually the assassin or anything, but it's a starting place, isn't it?" he offered, squeezing her hand.

"Thank you," Susannah murmured. "It's more than I had. I wouldn't even have known where to start," she admitted. "Probably trawling through newspapers and stuff for days on end."

"Happy to help," he smiled, before the smile turned to more of a grin. "Besides, it means you spend less time with Leon, no?" This time, she was the one who smirked at him.

"Jealous?" she asked. He laughed.

"Incredibly," he stated. That took her by surprise for a moment, but he was already moving on, easily, dismissing the matter even as she tried not to blush. "Be careful though, won't you? Hunting assassins isn't the most carefree past time, especially with people you don't get on with or fully trust. Call me if you get in trouble, or just want help, okay?"

"You don't trust Leon?" she questioned, head tilting to one side. His posture grew more guarded, as he regarded her closely.

"You don't either," he replied. They stared at each other for a moment. Susannah swallowed.

"Do you reckon he's the traitor?"

"I think he's a possible candidate," Jamie admitted.

"He...well, he does seem very eager to pin it on one of us, doesn't he?"

"Doesn't mean he's the traitor though," Susannah said, though not with any great amount of conviction. "He took the secrecy ward."

"Everyone took the secrecy ward," Jamie returned. "Doesn't really say much. Besides, the traitor would have already betrayed us, this just prevents the traitor from doing so again so easily."

"You think they can still betray us?" Susannah's insides tightened and knotted at the thought. "But the Introvertai-" she started, only for Jamie to cut in, eyes dark.

"-*rests on magic.* That's where it draws its power from. Marco Carmel is incredibly powerful; he might still be able to overpower the ward, just by force. You know how wards work, Susannah....a Locksmith can pick them, subtly, but a ward can also just be smashed unrecognizably by brute force, in rare occasions, if one doesn't care about lasting damage or getting caught. That's why professional warders always have so many-"

"-layers, yeah, I know," Susannah murmured, troubled. "Do you think that's what Carmel will do then? Just smash the traitor's mind?"

"If it comes down to it, it's a possibility. He tends to get what he wants, doesn't he?" Jamie returned. Susannah frowned. "He probably wouldn't do it unless as a last resort though," Jamie continued. "And if he does, we can't really worry about it. There's nothing we can do about it."

"Surely Krig would know this," Susannah muttered. He met her eyes.

"Of course he does...but what else can he possibly do if he doesn't want to surrender and disband?"

She grimaced.

"Well, I doubt Leon will do anything to me," she said, finally.

"Probably not," Jamie agreed. "But take care, won't you?"

"Worried?"

"Amazingly enough...*yes*."

The waitress came to take their drinks away.

Chapter Seventeen – Redgraive

It was an odd sight, Susannah concluded, to have Leon Daggey standing on her porch. His expensive, pressed attire left her feeling entirely scruffy and inadequate and her house somewhat untidy and mismatched. She abruptly hurried to grab her bag.

"Come on," she muttered. "Let's just go." It wasn't that she was embarrassed about her home so much; it was that she knew that the conceited snob probably wouldn't appreciate it for what it was. Her parents were reasonably well off - but his parents were loaded, weren't they? And they were Carmel supporters, or at least that was what she'd heard. It was even more reason as to why Leon could be the traitor, and therefore unwelcome to get any details on her family...most kids followed their parents' beliefs, didn't they? Why would Leon be in a resistance against Underworld supremacy when he'd been strongly taught since birth to respect, love and generally worship the Underworld? It was very suspicious. She wished Krig hadn't forced them to work together - he was In the TA and she was in Entry, it just didn't work. Leon turned immediately on his heel, as if disgusted. He didn't look too happy to be there either. It felt even more awkward after the events with his sister...which would imply Leon wasn't the traitor....but if he wasn't, who on earth was? A moment later they were out on the street, and she opened her mouth to apologise about Becki, or something, but he spoke hurriedly, clearly not wanting to talk about.

"So, do you have any idea where to start?" he asked, in a mockingly polite tone of voice. She let the topic drop, and though she felt sympathy for him, she could still feel her hackles rising at his implicit taunt. She'd have thought going with him to see his sister might have changed something between them, made him less of a jerk, but it seemed not.

"I've done some research," she started, tightly.

"Oh, you mean you're actually capable of planning? Instead of rushing straight into the fire? Amazing."

"Will you drop it?" she spat. "Okay, so maybe I made an error of judgement, but it worked out well. We got the information and frankly, Krig already addressed the mission so really it's incredibly bad taste of you to keep bringing it up. What, didn't your parents teach you any manners?" His jaw clenched, nearly white with rage. She regretted the words immediately.

"Don't you talk about them - don't you even *dare*," he snarled.

"Then back off." They continued in a mutually hostile silence.

"What was your research?" he questioned finally.

"I didn't get much," she admitted. "There isn't much to get, at least not without Carmel's clearance." She waited for a snide remark, but Leon just nodded in understanding, seeming to decide that the only way this was going to work was through a façade of civil professionalism. She continued. "It took a bit of digging, and its obscure - Jamie helped, he's in research, well, he gave it to me actually -" Leon snorted, apparently unable to help himself. "-but I think I may have a name...Redgraive."

"Helpful," he drawled. She narrowed her eyes.

"Oh, you have something better then?" she enquired coldly. "Something to add?" she paused. "Or were you just going to coast on Jamie's efforts and make petty remarks that I should have done better?" His sullen silence told her the answer as clearly as if he had spoken. "I didn't think so..." she struggled to bolster her own patience levels. "So, I was thinking that we could head to the Library and start there; look through the records and that type of thing. What do you think?"

"Sounds tedious and time consuming. Lead the way."

There was only one Library in the city: the Carmels liked to monitor the flow of information. Back in Contessa and Damien Carmel's time the reading material had been heavily censored, but it wasn't so much anymore - not since Marco Carmel turned his majority, gaining his full Demon Lord inheritance and control. Most people loved him for it, and his 'liberal' angle on education and information, but Susannah knew it wasn't as much of a free gift as the media had spun it. The information was less censored, yes, and the library had rapidly expanded its shelves, but the information was still controlled. She had to admit that Marco Carmel was clever, far cleverer than his parents before him. He didn't censor the information, but he did keep a very close watch on who was reading what. It was a rather subtle but brilliant way of keeping an eye on the population. If anyone began to look where they shouldn't the Demon Lord now knew instantly; he'd essentially made any underground trade of information visible to his eyes. It also made it a lot harder to slip through the shadows...but over the last two or so years she'd sought and discovered a few tricks to evade the system. The loopholes were there if you were determined enough to find them. For example, if you didn't try and borrow the book, or take it out, the records weren't solid, relying on witnesses rather than any hard evidence.

"If the librarians ask, we're doing a summer project on the city's unsung heroes, okay?" she whispered to Leon, as they ascended the large white steps to enter. The library was a beautiful old building, huge in size with large domed ceilings and a labyrinth of rows. She loved the woody smell of it, and the way the light sloped down from windows hidden high amongst the rafters. A vampire was watching them suspiciously from the information desk.

"Do you know any unsung heroes?" he hissed back. "If they ask?"

"Nope, but I can insist that there was this one amazing demon called Matthias Beaumont who helped sort out the plumbing."

"We're screwed," he muttered. They headed for the records section. It was near the back, crammed between one of the many fiction aisles and a row for shadow puppet magic. The vampire's gaze followed them until they disappeared from sight, as he pressed down on a button to call one of the library assistants. The Underworld didn't generally work in the Library, there were only a couple in the high positions to keep a hold on the situation. Mostly, the place was manned by wood elves. She figured that one of them would be along shortly to check on them, so she pulled out a couple of old records in search of potential unsung heroes. Leon seemed to follow her trail of thought and pulled out a packet of gum which he transformed into a notepad and pen. They pretended to take notes. A wood elf came round the corner a few minutes later, reluctance shadowing her light green skin.

"Do you need any assistance?" she asked. Leon shot her a look, as if to prompt her to deal with it.

"No, thanks," she replied politely. The wood elf stared at them both for a moment with her expressive yellow eyes, before nodding nervously.

"Okay, well, just ask any of the staff if you run into problems."

"We will," Leon agreed, flashing a brief smile. "Thank you."

They waited for her to shuffle out of sight again, before abruptly dropping their files and taking one for addresses. Leon flicked to the 'R' section.

Raymond...Reagan...Redfern...Redgail...Redgraive! They exchanged glances, animosity forgotten. It might, in the end, be nothing of consequence, but the feeling of achievement and progress was a nice one. This had been far less complicated than she thought it would be, for finding an assassin. She read the record hungrily. It was scarce, and the print was long and small but...

"There's a current address!" she said excitedly.

"Yes, I can see that," Leon snapped irritably. "I'm not blind - and keep your voice down, idiot." Susannah rolled her eyes. The Bellevue penthouse, Bellisle Street, belonging to a Miss-

"Katerina Redgraive," Leon whispered, looking at her.

"Who's Katerina Redgraive?"

A quarter of an hour later, they were approaching Bellisle street.

"This is a bad idea," Susannah said, quietly. "We don't even have a plan." Leon waved a dismissive hand, brushing aside the statement for what had to be the tenth time by then.

"Says the girl who ran headfirst into a burning building. Surely, this should be right up your street...after all 'we need the information,'" he goaded, quoting her own words back at her. She gritted her teeth. Was he ever going to stop bringing that up?

"Yes, and Krig hauled me over the rocks for it," she replied. "And, if I remember rightly, you haven't stopped mocking what a stupid idea it was since it happened."

"Yes, but the penthouse isn't a burning building. The receptionist said Redgraive shouldn't be back until tomorrow - there's no danger."

"It could be a trap," she hissed. Leon raised his brows. "Then by all means, stay out here and appease your cowardice...I mean your paranoia," he 'amended.' Susannah was almost certain that the first part hadn't been an honest slip of the tongue.

"And let you go in there alone and get yourself killed? No chance," she spat. He sneered at her.

"Because you'd be able to fight any and all beings that came at us, wouldn't you? You're just so fabulous."

"No, but I'd be able to fight some of them," she muttered. "How exactly do you intend to get up to the Penthouse anyway?" He glanced at her.

"Food delivery." Food delivery -? Oh no. He couldn't possibly...he did. He wanted them to pretend that they'd been sold as livestock, a ready meal.

"This is definitely a bad idea," she moaned. "We should contact Krig -"

"-You have his personal communicon code then?" Leon smiled at her, coolly. Her hands curled into fists.

"No, but-"

"-Well, there you are then. Onwards and upwards." He strode into the grand looking block of flats without waiting for a reply. She hurried to catch up, grabbing his arm and pulling him back. This could go seriously wrong...what if he was the traitor? It was even more reason for it to be a trap. If he was the traitor, it would surely explain his eagerness to rush in without consulting anyone. It was a bad idea...and yet, what if he wasn't the traitor? She couldn't just leave him. This was a nightmare. His eyes flashed as he looked down at the hold she had on his arm, but she didn't let go.

"Why are you so desperate to just rush into this? We have no reason to go in!"

"We do if we don't want to get stuck," Leon returned.

"What's the point of finding leads if we don't properly research and investigate them?"

Susannah grimaced, able to see where he was coming from. "But we don't have to go in *right* now," she said.

"Didn't realise you wished to prolong the amount of time we spent in each other's company so much." Leon shook her off again, this time entering the Reception before she could stop him. She cursed and followed.

"I've been instructed to go up to Bellevue," Leon stated to the snobby looking Dark Angel manning the front desk. Susannah crushed her magic down, warily, not letting it flare and give the game away. Why was she doing this?

"Who sent you?"

"Mr Redgraive," Leon replied smoothly, excitedly. Susannah mentally crossed her fingers that there was a Mr Redgraive. After what seemed like forever, the receptionist nodded, eyeing them both with a hungry distaste.

"Go right up. I'll buzz you in."

"Thank you," Leon murmured, dipping into a small bow. Susannah forced down bile, going for a deferential nod instead. They made their way to the golden lift, their expressions relaxing as the doors slid closed. Leon shot her a smug look.

"We still need to get out," she warned. He shrugged.

"Yeah, but the hard part is over," he said. Susannah disagreed, but bit her tongue because they were soaring up to the Bellevue Penthouse. Her stomach was twisting and fluttering with pangs of terror, and not just swooping due to their fast elevation. This was a bad idea. There was a soft ding as they reached the top, before the doors slid open to reveal the Bellevue.

Susannah's first thought was that she would love to live

245

there. It wasn't one room, but a series of rooms, with one large area for a lounge and a kitchen. The floor was a shiny wood, with thick, soft rugs and the latest equipment. It looked very expensive.

"Wow," she breathed, despite herself. It was truly exquisite; even Leon seemed to be in a state of shocked awe.

"I'll look in the other rooms, search the lounge...you might find something useful," he said.

"Like what?"

"I don't know," he replied, walking away into what looked like a bathroom. "You'll know if you see it. It's why we're in here." That was helpful. With a soft sigh, her muscles knotting, Susannah began to carefully examine the living room. She was wary not to touch anything, even though she realised that nothing they could actually use would be turned up without a deeper search. This was such a stupid, reckless thing to be doing. Yeah, she had run into a burning building...but at least she'd learnt from her mistake! Her gut was churning, her instincts screaming alarms in her head. They shouldn't have been here; especially not on their own. She eyed the coffee table cautiously. It was made of glass, and adorned with several magazines including 'Angel.' There was also a newspaper open with the programme entry for Dark Angel Next Door circled in red ink, along with the words 'please record this for me.' She thought it might be a female's handwriting - Katerina's, possibly? Either way, it was indicative that Dark Angels lived there, and one of them was probably quite young. She turned away, her eyes scouring for more data, though latching onto the state of art music system despite herself. There were speakers all around the room. The smallest burst of envy imploded in her chest. She would have loved to have this music system...music was, after all, her magic medium. It was far too costly though, only really manufactured for the Underworld to afford. She couldn't help but edge towards it slightly, her hand flinching back from skimming over the music collection. There was an odd mix; V.A.M.P and Right Freak-quency albums sitting on the shelf alongside a classical mix and some obscure reggae album. It made it even clearer that there were at least two people currently in residence here. There was a small thump from the other room, and she stiffened. *Please let Leon have only dropped something...*

"Okay?" she called, softly. Her magic flared a little, as she immediately started for the other room at the lack of reply. Her heart thudded in her chest; a hammer and nails rhythm. "Leon?"

She knew this was a bad idea.

Leon was standing in the middle of the room, a young, female Dark Angel holding a blade to his throat. She had another blade pointing out towards Susannah, copper eyes sparking with threat, face white.

"Stay back," she warned. "Or I'll slit his throat..." Susannah froze on the spot, placing her hands slowly in the air, her blood pounding. Oh no. "Who are you?" the Dark Angel continued, her voice shaking slightly. "What do you want from me?"

"Please put your blade down; I'm not going to hurt you," Susannah tried tentatively. The Dark Angel snorted, shaking blonde locks. She looked to be about their age; but you could never really tell with the Underworld. The Underworld aged a year for every ten years that passed, starting from when they reached their coming of age (seventeen for a Demon or Demon Lord/Lady, eighteen for a Vampire, twenty one for a Dark Angel.)

"Oh sure, you're just a couple of friendly Overworld beings, who happen to be breaking into my house," she murmured sarcastically, eyes wide with fright.

"You're Katerina Redgraive..." Susannah realised, stunned.

"Again, who's asking?" Katerina demanded, tightening her grip on the knife. "Are you going to kidnap me?"

"We're looking for the assassin. But we'll just go!" Leon whimpered. Susannah bit back a groan. Maybe Leon didn't even mean to be a traitor; maybe he was just a coward in life threatening situations. A bead of blood formed on his neck, and Susannah wet her dry lips nervously at the sight. She felt almost dizzy in terrified anticipation of what could happen.

"This is the last time I'll ask," the Dark Angel warned dangerously. "Who are you? Start talking if you want your accomplice to live." Susannah drew in a shaky breath.

"Annabelle!" she said quickly. "My name's Annabelle Smith. He's Luke Jones." She would have spun some story about them getting a call to come here, and could the Dark Angel please tell them what it was about, but Leon had already given that away. Katerina's eyes narrowed.

"Liar," she accused, though without the ring of certainty. Another pinprick of blood appeared on Leon's throat as the Dark Angel's hands tightened convulsively on the blade.

"No, don't!" Susannah pleaded, insisting. "My name is Annabelle, Annabelle Smith!" Leon swallowed, hard, his pupils dilated with fear as the blade eased again. Katerina appraised her, seemingly searching for the truth on her face. Susannah couldn't breathe.

"Why do you seek the assassin, Annabelle?" the Dark Angel demanded finally. "And what makes you think he lives here?" Susannah was silent. The blade started tightening again, ruthlessly. Leon made an odd, squeaking noise.

"She found a lead. The name Redgraive was linked to him, so we looked it up in the records and it came up with this address! Please! We didn't mean any harm," he gasped.

Katerina studied them both with suspicious eyes.

"And why would you be seeking him out in the first place?" she asked coolly. "It's classified information."

"Dare," Susannah replied, promptly.

"A dare," Katerina repeated sceptically. "You decided to screw with the Underworld Prince's personal assassin, and thus the Underworld Prince himself, because of a *dare*."

"Yeah. It was stupid really - Mum always said I was an adrenaline junkie - and I never thought I'd actually find anything. Then I did," Susannah purposely made her voice fast and babbling, not caring how ridiculous she sounded so long as they got out of this unharmed. "And this happened. And it all went really wrong...and please will you drop the knife and let Luke go? We honestly didn't mean for things to get so out of hand. We can...er...pay for any damages to your house...just...please..." Katerina stared at her, coldly.

"I'm not stupid," she snapped, sounding offended. "It was NOT a dare. Tell me the truth, or I'll call the wardens on you. I'm sure there are beings out there who would be very interested in this case." Susannah swallowed again, trying to get past the lump in her throat. Her magic flittered with anxiety, frustration, she could hardly think straight.

"Well, obviously," she snapped back, dropping the flustered demeanour she was presenting, "we can't tell you the truth or we would have said it already! And you're probably going to call the wardens on us anyway, aren't you? So it makes no difference if we tell you or not. You're a Dark Angel! You hate us."

Katerina's expression darkened, her posture radiating rage. "And you're a hypocritical, bigoted little human...you probably deserve it. You break into MY house and then make accusations! You don't even know me. How dare you!"

"It's not bigoted," Susannah hissed. "It's experience. That's what you Underworld always do."

"Oh, so you have experience breaking into other people's houses then?" the Dark Angel questioned flatly. Susannah's magic crackled, despite herself.

"Give me Luke," she ordered. "And we'll go. Either that, or just call your precious wardens already and have us arrested...but stop talking, you're giving me a headache."

"Yeah, it must hurt to have your preconceptions challenged. Your brain probably can't take the strain," Katerina spat, grip on the blade tightening once more.

"And I'm supposed to somehow believe you're nice when you're about to turn us over with knives to our throats?" Susannah sneered. "Clearly you're the stupid one if you ever think that would happen. It's not pre-conceptions, it's survival instinct. I know your kind, and I know how you treat us. We don't matter to you, we're just food!"

"Oh, like you lot are so much better to us," Katerina snapped. "Do you campaign superior rights for chicken? No, you don't. Perhaps you expect us to die and starve instead? So don't you even *dare...*"

"Yeah, sure, you need to feed, doesn't mean you lot have to treat us like crap to do it! The Overworld have thoughts and feelings too-"

"Trust me I'm fully aware of that," Katerina said coldly.

"Yeah, fully aware of it when all those emotions just go tunnelling down your mouth like they're cheap and nothing more than sustenance!"

"I don't think that!"

"And yet your kind still feed to full consumption. You

destroy us, so don't you dare preach about eating attitudes-"

"My best friend was a human," Katerina hissed, eyes suddenly filled with tears. "So no, actually, I would never do that and you should think before you just throw accusations!"

A thin line of blood appeared on Leon's neck to mark her fury and her...hurt. Susannah felt her mind ground to a halt.

"Your best friend was a human?" she asked, eyes wide.

"Yeah, actually she was. Don't bother reporting me for breaking the Declarations, she's already dead. They wraithed her for it! So don't you even-"

Susannah's throat felt thick, as she stared at the other.

"I-I'm sorry. I didn't know."

"And you didn't want to know, because to you we're all the same."

"No, no you're not," Susannah shook her head, feeling terrible. She could also feel a thought nagging in the back of her head, as well as an always present survival instinct.

"Your friend – I – what was her name?"

"I don't see why you need to know," Katerina replied stiffly. "It's irrelevant."

"Please...I..." should she say it or not? If she did and was wrong, this could go from disastrous to entirely nightmarish, hellish. Yet...if she said nothing, there was an extremely high possibility that they would die here. "We're friends with Krig, does that...mean anything to you?"

"Kriger Carter?" The Dark Angel questioned, freezing completely.

"Yes," Susannah murmured, inwardly crossing her fingers, breathing shallow with tension as she watched the other.

"You're friends with Krig."

"Yes," Susannah repeated.

"Did he send you here?"

"Not to you, exactly," Susannah explained, warily. "The assassin…we were tracking him for Krig and…well. Now we're here." Katerina stared at her.

"It wouldn't be proper for me to let you go," the Dark Angel stated. "He would kill me for it if he knew."

"He-the assassin?" Susannah's brow furrowed, before leaping on the words anyway, desperately. "He doesn't need to know. We swear we won't come back, ever. I swear, just please – let us go. This was a mistake, a misunderstanding-"

"Is he alright?" she asked. Susannah paused.

"Krig? Yeah…yeah he's okay." Katerina was silent for a while, and Susannah held her breath while Leon seemed about to faint from terror.

"I suppose I could let you go. I highly doubt you'd get past the security anyway."

"Thank you," Susannah gasped. "Thank you so much. I won't forget this. I'm…I'm sorry I misjudged you…you're *Kitty,* aren't you?"

"Shut up," Katerina instructed, but she nodded cautiously in acknowledgement of the words also. "I'll let your friend go once you're out the door. Start walking." Susannah didn't question this, immediately walking backwards towards the lift, keeping her gaze fixed on the Dark Angel. She obligingly didn't speak, but then Katerina did, again. "I don't know what you want with the assassin, what Krig wants with him, or what he's got himself into now but… I'd quit while you're ahead. Nothing good will come from your search." They reached the lift and Susannah turned to it, only to freeze again.

The light was glowing. Someone was coming up.

She spun round to face Katerina, her heart lashing against her chest as if it had done it personal insult.

"You called security?" she accused. She didn't know why that hurt so much; she'd expected it from a Dark Angel. Maybe it was the feeling of having escape torn away when it was so close. Kitty shook her head, eyes wide.

"No, I didn't," she said, sounding frightened. Susannah frowned, panicked.

"Let him go," she pleaded. "For Shadow's sake, let him go, we're dead if they find us here! We need to run!"

Katerina hesitated for the briefest second, no doubt in her own fear of getting 'disappeared'...and the doors slid open with a soft ding. Susannah spun round again, terrified, only to feel her blood run to ice in her veins. It was him. It was the assassin. He stopped at the sight that greeted him, not looking remotely surprised by the scene in front of him.

"Katerina," he murmured. "I didn't realise we had...guests." Copper eyes flashed across the two of them. Crap. "Hello again, Skelsby."

Katerina shot her flabbergasted, uncertain, accusing expression, as the false name she offered was revealed, but Susannah couldn't find the presence of mind to return the look. This was a nightmare. The assassin's gaze trailed once more over Leon, still in a chokehold, before a predatory grin slowly graced his lips.

"My dear niece," he said, amusedly. "You have been busy in my absence. Well done," he praised. "Your mother would be so proud of you...I didn't know you had this in you. It's a welcome change, perhaps your finally getting over your unnaturalness, hmm?"

Katerina looked down, subdued, though there was still a trace of frightened fire in her eyes. Susannah looked between Kitty and the assassin, carefully. No way. This was too strange, too big a coincidence. Krig's *Kitty* could not be related to Marco Carmel's assassin. She resisted the urge to question, suddenly painfully aware that the assassin hadn't thought Katerina was letting them go. If this really was Emiah's friend, she couldn't possibly make trouble.

"Uncle," Kitty mumbled in greeting. "You know these two?"

"We've met," the assassin replied. "These are some of the rebels that our lord was talking about last week." Kitty's eyes widened and her gaze shot to them again. Susannah could tell she was immediately linking Krig with the resistance. "Did they tell you what they were doing here?" the assassin questioned. For a heartbeat, Susannah was terrified that the younger would reveal them, and Krig too, before Katerina's expression slid to something very different entirely.

"No," Kitty lied. "I thought you'd sent them to me for dinner...but they're not really my type," her nose wrinkled. Leon's skin had tinged a waxy, green colour. The Assassin favoured her suspiciously.

"When have I ever sent you humans for dinner? You know I don't trust you around them. You're still on probation."

"I thought it was a test, seeing as I'm a lot better," Katerina replied, expression steeled. The assassin took a step forward, and Kitty shrank back. "Unless you doubt your ability to 'cure' me?" Susannah felt awful for doing this, not wanting to leave the young Dark Angel alone in such a situation...but they couldn't stay. Glancing at Leon, a countdown in her gaze, she reacted a moment later - lashing out with her magic as Leon simultaneously drew his and tore out of Kitty's (admittedly not as tight as it should have been) grip. Redgraive hit the wall of the apartment with a sickening crack, hissing with pain. They both dodged into the lift, slamming a hand on the button for the doors to close.

"Katerina!" the assassin ordered, staggering after them, blood trickling from his temple. The doors smashed closed with a little magical aid just as he reached them. The lift started a smooth descent.

"Okay?" Susannah demanded, to where Leon was wheezing and massaging his throat. Her heart was racing, with both fear and guilt and too many emotions as of yet unrealised. "Y-yes," Leon stammered. "Just about." She nodded. "Come on, out here, hurry! The security will be swarming this building soon - they probably have the lobby covered already." She leapt out at the floor below, tugging Leon into motion by the wrist, spinning round to jam the lift so no one could follow them that way.

"We're twelve floors up," Leon moaned.

"Well, don't tell me you're scared of heights," she snapped, tugging him towards the windows with a panicked look. "I have an idea - Jamie taught me how to make these things called -" she stopped as a wave of dizziness swept over her. Ow.

"Skelsby," Leon croaked. She turned, her heart sinking. The assassin stood behind them, a spray in his hand. With the acidic, burning sensation in her lungs, she had the horrible feeling it wasn't a pesticide. Gossamer. Her eyes watered, her magic already beginning to shred and strip down, painfully ramming into her chest and burying itself beneath her skin. Leon's aura, him having been closer, was almost gone. Shadow, the assassin was fast. Bloody Underworld speed! She'd never hated it more as she felt her knees threatening to buckle beneath her. Deftly, a cruel smile on his face, he squirted another spray of the Gossamer straight into her face. She dropped to the floor, disorientated, black spots blurring her vision. It hurt. Her magic raged against its prisons, rattling her body as if it were cage bars. She felt convinced one of her ribs would snap. Leon collapsed beside her, sweat slicking his fringe to his forehead. The assassin tucked the bottle away again, crouching down to whisper in her ear, his breath as hot as flames.

"Tell your boss that Marco Carmel sends his regards."

Susannah looked up, head like lead, her hands barely holding her weight. Nausea bubbled in her gut as she watched Darren scoop Leon's prone form up off the floor.

"No…" she protested, struggling to rise, reaching for a magic she could no longer access. The assassin sauntered casually away, speaking over his shoulder to the security guards closing on her in a blur of motion. "No need to detain the human, Nikolai," he said. "Toss her on the streets…no, actually, make sure she gets to McKinley road, Middle City…"

Susannah found herself dumped on Krig's street ten minutes later, battered, bruised, but ultimately no worse for wear. She despised it. What was happening to Leon? Why had they only taken him? Bait. Her mind supplied the answer immediately, coolly. Leon was the bait, and she was the messenger to bring Krig running - probably straight into the clutches of Marco Carmel. He said he'd make them disband, and now he was going to tear them to shreds because it wasn't happening fast enough. She scrambled to the door, memories of the last time she was here spinning in her head as she fought her way towards the door of his flat. The floors were narrow, the walls covered in graffiti. It seemed darker than last time. She felt sick. Her magic still hadn't returned. What if it never did? Oh god. She complained about her power and the difficulties of it, but she'd never wanted to lose it. She loved her magic. She'd never willingly give it up; for love or money. She pounded on the door, praying that he was in, half leaning against the wood to stay upright. She could feel the protective wards thrumming against her skin.

"Krig - it's Susannah!" she called, urgently. Please let him answer. Please. She thumped the door again. "Open up!" There was a scuffling, some curses, before the door opened.

"What is it?" Krig started, his tone perhaps a little annoyed, before his expression changed to one of deep concern as he noted the change in her aura...or the lack thereof.

"Krig? What's wrong?" another, sugary voice questioned from within the apartment. Leola. Susannah suddenly felt extremely embarrassed, she was obviously intruding. But this was important. It was more than important.

"They took Leon!" she gasped. Krig yanked her in through the threshold. His magic seemed suffocating in its power now that she herself had none. Her head was reeling. Her whole body ached, her magic throwing temper tantrums inside her chest. Shadow, couldn't Gossamer kill you if you were under its influence for too long? Leola hurried over, her face pale and her eyes red and smudged with mascara. She'd definitely interrupted something. What if they were in the middle of a lover's tiff? It didn't matter. It couldn't. Leon.

"Susannah, are you alright?" Leola asked. Krig hushed the blonde gently, leading her to sit on the sofa.

"What happened?" he questioned. She was thankful for the directness. She didn't think she'd be able to stomach fussing, she felt too guilty. She should have noticed Darren approaching, or found a quicker way out of there, or not spent so much time bickering with Katerina. She felt sick. It was her fault. She should have been able to stop Darren. What was the point in being powerful if she couldn't protect those she wanted to?

"L-Leon. They took him," she stammered, numbly. Leola's eyes widened, flooding with tears. Susannah's insides twisted.

"The Underworld?" Krig verified, his hand firm and grounding on her shoulder.

"Redgraive - that's the assassin, we were working on the assignment you set us -" any victory in their discovery of the assassin's identity was obliterated, and she noticed Krig stiffen at the name. "I couldn't do anything. I-my magic..." the nausea rose in her throat once more. Leola took in her green face with alarm, before she dove to place a bucket-like object in front of her from one the cupboards. Susannah retched, before abruptly hurling out the contents of her stomach. "Sorry," she said weakly.

"Shh," Krig soothed. "It's alright, don't apologise. It's the Gossamer...you know," he added encouragingly. "I think I can feel your magic coming back." Susannah wasn't sure if this was true or not, she couldn't feel it yet, but it was good of him to say so. She felt the bile, the Gossamer hurtle to the surface again, and gave up explaining for the next five minutes as she vomited. Her stomach hurt. She could vaguely hear Krig saying something about "understandable" and "her body rejecting it." She presumed he meant the Gossamer, certainly, the next time the sickness faded she could feel her magic stirring a little. It was weak, but it was there. She felt like collapsing in relief. It wasn't gone. It wasn't gone!

"He said to tell you Marco Carmel sends his greetings," she croaked, remembering. Krig's face was ashen, paper white. His grip tightened reflexively on her shoulder.

"Leola," he ordered, quietly. "Go and send a message that we're holding a meeting at the nearest possible convenience, and that it's urgent." Leola nodded, rushing out the room with an uncertain backwards glance. "Come on, kid," Krig tugged her up onto her feet. "Let's get you to your parents. You look dreadful," he murmured.

"I want to help Leon," she protested. He looped her arm over his shoulders, his cologne enveloping her senses along with his magic.

"Then work on recovering," he replied. "The meeting probably won't be until tomorrow anyway." His worried eyes took in the rather apparent objection on her features. "I can make that into an order," he added. She smiled, just faintly, in response.

"Right, gotcha boss - rest. But I'll be there tomorrow," she said, unyielding. He shook his head slightly.

"Stubborn," he remarked softly. "But, of course, I wouldn't expect you to stay away. Now, let's go. You can't walk through middle city without your magic. You can tell me more about what happened on the way."

Krig left after reiterating that she would make a full recovery, features strained, magic bubbling with fury and fear. Her parents, thankfully, were at work, so she just hid up in her room, clutching her duvet around her with a bucket standing ready. It was cold and she couldn't stop shaking; as if she had a fever. She just knew the Gossamer was to blame. It was vile. She felt far too vulnerable...if she got attacked now the only thing she'd be able to do was vomit at the enemy, and while that could be mildly entertaining, it wasn't the most beneficial or effective defence. Her head was pounding. Someone was knocking on the door. Delilah? She hoped so. She crawled out of bed, dropping the duvet despite the overwhelming desire to stay cocooned in its soft warmth and staggered down to the door. The doorbell shrieked.

"Shut up," she spat at it bitterly. Normally, she would have sent some magic with the command, but her magic felt shaky and strained. What if when she used magic it disappeared again? Back to the beginning of the cycle? Or even gone forever? She didn't dare risk it, even if it was only her senseless paranoia. She opened the door a crack. Jamie? She pulled the door open some more, leaning against it for support. Oh no, she probably looked ugly and pathetic.

"Susannah," he breathed, taking a step forwards, his hand reaching out, before it paused just prior to touching her.

"Are you alright? I heard about what happened." He looked a tad disconcerted, presumably at the feeble aura.

"Fine," she murmured. "Krig tell you?"

"No, Leola," Jamie said, "we ran into each other. I came here immediately." There was an awkward silence. "I'm glad you're okay," he said. She nodded, unsure of how to reply to that.

"Thanks…" He looked at her for a moment, before seeming to jump into action. "I'm dragging you out of bed, I'm sorry. I should-"

"No!" she said loudly, before flushing and lowering her voice. "No, it's alright, really," she said. She didn't want to be on her own. "Come in?" He considered her for a moment, before smiling and stepping through the threshold. She shut the door behind them, watching as he took off his jacket.

"On here…?" he questioned, indicating to the coat rack,

"Uh, yeah, or the banister…whichever…" she replied. He nodded, before studying his surroundings with interest. She realised he'd never been in her house before. "Er, lounge is through there," she pointed. "Kitchen straight down the hall. Bathroom there, and one upstairs. Bedrooms also up, obviously." He glanced at her as if to ask permission, before heading up to the second floor with an easy confidence. She blinked, before following after him. He stopped at the entrance to her room, his eyes scanning across her belongings with curiosity.

"Yours?" he questioned. She nodded, watching his expression. He smiled slightly, glancing at her again, seeming perfectly aware of the scrutiny he was under. He didn't seem bothered by it at all, merely amused if anything.

"It's a mess, I know," she muttered. "Mum's always nagging me to tidy it."

"Well, I don't think I ever imagined your room to be tidy anyway," he replied. He'd imagined her room?

"I'd like to think it's organised in its chaos," she said, grinning. He wandered in further, his hand trailing across the desk, eyes piercing her myriad of notes, half done projects, last year's school books and photo collection. He picked up one of the obscure magic textbooks, raising an eyebrow at her.

"Naughty girl," he remarked. She snorted.

"Says he in an illegal resistance."

"Touché," he said softly, setting the book down again. "Though just for reference, I feel the need to point out I'm still probably more law-abiding than you. You're in the resistance too, troublemaker."

"Don't ever introduce me to your family," she teased. His gaze shot to her, startled. "You said they were Carmel supporters?" she added, tentatively, losing her nerve.

"Oh, right," Jamie said, before shaking his head. "Yeah, no offence but they'd hate you." Her head tilted, her desire for more information surging up to the front of her mind. She sat down on the bed, carefully, still aching all over. She prayed she wouldn't be sick in front of him.

"Do you...did you get on with them?" she asked, remembering too late that most of them had died. Stupid, insensitive question! "If you don't mind me asking," she continued hastily. "It's just I know so little about you." Jamie shrugged, eyes growing dark.

"All families have their issues," he said, before seeming to dismiss the subject. "Guess I'm just your regular tall, dark, handsome stranger then," he winked. She felt her cheeks heat up a bit and looked away. A hot, prickly hand of shame abruptly squeezed her intestines in a chokehold. What was she doing? Leon could be going through hell right now - she shouldn't have been enjoying anything, she didn't have a right to! He seemed to notice the change in her mood, his own playful air fading. "Susannah?" he questioned, approaching her cautiously. "I'm sorry. That was inappropriate -" The words blurted out without her consent, sickening in their truth and their accusation of guilt.

"It was my fault." He slowly sank to sit next to her, gaze fixed on her face.

"What was? Leon?" he questioned. The nausea was rising once more, swelling like some dark wave, unstoppable.

"Yeah," she whispered, her palms closing to tight fists to prevent their shaking. A moment later, he had silently enclosed them in his own. "I should have been able to, I don't know, stop it from happening. If I'd-"

"-No," Jamie interrupted, sharply. "No. Don't think like that. It wasn't your fault. Do you understand me? There was no way you could have prevented it. Darren Redgraive has had years of training and experience that you couldn't possibly compete with...you're not a mind reader; you couldn't have known that Leon would get captured! You couldn't have stopped it." He stared at her intently. "You're powerful,

Susannah, but you're not invincible." She glanced up at him. "The thing is I shouldn't even be stewing in this - self-pity!" she continued, her voice turning angry. "I shouldn't be thinking about myself and how I feel! How could I be so - selfish! - when Leon could be dead or worse..." the colour drained from her face. "Shadow, what if he's dead? What will his parents do? We can't tell them about the resistance, they'd hand us over to Carmel immediately!"

Jamie was silent. Susannah closed her eyes, pulling her hands away, pressing against her eyelids with her fingertips to hold back the sting of tears. She wanted her mum. After a moment, she sucked in a shuddering gasp of air, straightening. "I'm fine," she said, automatically. "I-I'm sorry. You should probably go. I'm a mess right now," she looked at him imploringly. It wasn't that she didn't want him there, but it had been a bad idea to invite him in right at this moment in time. Jamie nodded, offering her a reassuring smile.

"I understand," he said. "Take care of yourself, and get some sleep. You look..." he grimaced. "It's not your best day." She felt mortified. He hesitated for a moment, before pressing a kiss to her cheek. "I'll see myself out." The next second, he was gone.

Her skin tingled.

Chapter Eighteen - The Anzarkledea Cells

Susannah dodged her way to the disused fire station, Delilah at her side. Ever since her best friend had learned of the incident with Leon and the Gossamer, she'd barely left Susannah's side. It was comforting. Delilah had this air about her, soothing and peaceful, that never failed to make Susannah feel better. It was odd, because Delilah herself could be so hyper and excitable, but it was true. Maybe it was because Delilah was at peace with herself - or something, she didn't know. Her magic was coming back, to her utmost relief, though it still wasn't to the level it was before, and greatly limited. It felt odd. She felt completely unbalanced, as if she were missing some vital body part, torn in great hunks from her chest and side.

"What do you think is going to happen?" Susannah looked at Delilah after a moment, realising she had spoken. Her best friend repeated the question, only the slight tremor in her tone suggesting her lack of inward composure. "What to do you think's going to happen? I mean...surely we can't just leave Leon in Carmel's clutches?" The small blonde seemed pained even by the thought. Susannah's insides twisted.

"I don't know," she admitted, before offering Delilah an encouraging smile. "But it will work out, I know it will. Krig will figure it out." Delilah nodded. "We did the right thing, joining," Susannah continued, not allowing herself to wonder whether it was Delilah or herself that she was trying to convince.

No. She didn't need convincing. It was the right thing to do, and she'd known what she'd signed up. Okay, mostly...she hadn't ever thought Marco Carmel would take any kind of interest in them, or at least not for many years. She wasn't soft or innocent or naïve, but the thought of even a potential attack on Anzarkledea made shivers of fear dance like devils up her spine.

She'd never been to the manor - she'd never had any reason to. The first floor was Carmel's base, where everything official took place, and all the floors above that were his home. It felt odd to imagine that the Demon Lord even had a home, and was capable of doing normal activities like listening to music or...well, not sleeping or eating. He didn't have to do either of those the human way...Delilah was watching her carefully. She forced a smile, but the other didn't look away. "

What?" she asked finally.

"It feels kind of strange to walk next to you without your aura," Delilah murmured. "Like there's something missing."

"You're telling me," she muttered. Delilah tossed her a look, to which Susannah grimaced, still feeling subdued. They arrived at base soon enough.

The atmosphere in the disused fire station was tense and grim, with a weight on the air that pressed down at them all in terror, guilt, rage or shame. There was determination too, a steely resolution that lined the faces of the remaining TA sector members in particular. Krig was at the front of the room, his calmness barely masking the troubled thoughts that lurked in his eyes. Susannah sat down wordlessly, hyperaware of everyone staring at her. She studied her fingers with more concentration than was necessarily required, her skin prickling under the scrutiny. Her magic twitched, pathetic in its infant stages. The absence of Leon and his snide remarks seemed like an abyss she could be swallowed by, the gaping jaw of some monster prowling under the skin of the earth, desperate for a meal.

"You all know why we are here," Krig began, quietly. "Carmel has taken Leon."

"We have to get him back," Alice said flatly. "We can't just leave him there." Susannah agreed, but she wasn't sure how much of that was her guilt speaking. There were too many aspects to this that didn't make sense.

"You do realise this is most likely a trap?" Jamie questioned; his features rigid.

"Of course we're aware of that," Leola snarled, eyes glistening with unshed tears and desperation. "Doesn't mean we're going to leave him there."

"You're the head of the bloody TA, Bymalt," Jamie snapped back. "And you're advocating walking into Anzarkledea manor? Are you insane? Or just in love with him?"

"Jamie," Krig said warningly. Jamie glanced at Krig, remorseless.

"Sorry about the love comment," he said, "I know she's your girlfriend...but you're not seriously going to listen to her and walk into Marco Carmel's own home, are you? The security is phenomenal, there's no way it would work."

"Thanks for the vote of confidence," David said dryly. Jamie threw his hands up in frustration.

"Is it only me who sees this is a terrible idea? You're going to risk the whole resistance for one member, that's stupid."

"I agree," Susannah murmured softly, causing everyone to look at her. "It is stupid." Leola and Alice both narrowed their eyes. She shot them a glare in return, silently telling them to let her finish. "BUT," she continued, "I'm in anyway." Delilah was studying her intently, but she didn't look at her best friend.

"Because you feel guilty," Jamie growled, his tone making her stomach to squeeze. "You think it should have been you instead of Leon." She said nothing in response to that, merely watching the other flatly, un-amused that he should be using their discussion against her like this. Krig cleared his throat.

"I understand your concerns, Jamie, and I'm not asking you, or anyone else, to aid me on this particular mission. It will be dangerous, the most dangerous thing we've ever done, and yes, it's stupid, but I will not abandon any members for the sake of a greater good. That's what the Carmels do."

Jamie appeared to very much want to say something, but was ultimately silent, folding his arms, his expression unreadable.

"But what if it is a trap?" Cassie questioned weakly. "You could get hurt."

"Don't worry about me, Cass," Krig reassured, though Susannah couldn't help but notice that he didn't strictly deny either statement.

"So…do you have a plan?" Delilah asked finally.

In the end, it turned out that it was Krig , her, Delilah, Jamie rather surprisingly, Leola, David, Alice and Cade who were going on the actual mission. Everyone else had opted to be more…back up. Well, Mica hadn't technically opted, but Cade had ordered and generally guilt-tripped the other into staying out the line of fire. The same held true for Cassie, who'd volunteered, only for Krig to refuse. They would all come to the execution anyway, as was customary when one was on, and intervene if they had to. A secret back up force. Susannah didn't mind, oddly, that they weren't all directly involved in the mission. After all, it got harder and harder to sneak around Anzarkledea undetected with the more people that entered their group. They'd been having almost constant meetings, to try and plan this out, in the desperate hope of pulling it off. David had been having them memorise all the known routes in and out of the manor - the Bookcase Passages, Hangman's Bridge, the window if preferable to facing certain individuals, the front door, the backdoor...Susannah couldn't help but feel a tight knot of apprehension twisting in her stomach, heavy as lead. Carmel knew of these passages, and would surely be watching them, wouldn't he? But she trusted Krig. Her leader knew what he was doing. So did David. It would be okay. She had to believe that.

When everyone was there, Krig floated a large, blown up poster in front of them. It looked like an enlarged version of a sketch, with annotations and everything. At the top of the page there was the word "hell."

"Is that - is that the Anzarkledea Cells?" David asked, leaning towards the map, for Susannah saw now it was a map, with rapt fascination.

"Yes," Krig said. There was a murmur of interest, everyone craning for a closer look.

"Oh my god, I love you, boss-man," David breathed. There was a weak round of laughter.

"Where did you get it?" Jamie questioned. The tiniest hint of pride coloured Krig's tone in bolder colours as he answered.

"I know some people," Krig said. "One of them drew it up for me; they were in the cells for juvenile delinquency for about six months. Never want go back."

There was a solemn silence at that. Susannah swallowed, hard. Krig continued smoothly, not letting them stew in silence and work into a panic. "The AC - that's the Anzarkledea Cells - are split into five different groups, according to this - can you see the different colours?"

Susannah could, in the large rectangular prison area; there

were at least a thousand different, small coloured squares. She presumed the boxes represented the individual cells and the colours something about the cell or the person in it. There was a red, a purple, a blue, a green and a black.

"Each colour represents a different group, a different type of prisoner," Krig explained. "These groups, named by the prisoners themselves as opposed to by Carmel, are Comms, Double D's, Lutes, Chevy's and PPC." Susannah was hit by the overwhelming urge to take out a notepad and start jotting down notes, as if she were in school. She managed to suppress it, curling her fists tightly. Jamie must have mistaken it as a sign of worry, for he threw her a concerned look. "The Comms are the red area, as you can see they're the majority, taking up around half the cells. They're the ordinary criminals, though their crimes vary in severity from delinquency to, well, murder...not mass, though."

"And they're ordinary?" Delilah questioned, sounding horrified. Krig grimaced in reply.

"By ordinary, I mean they are there for a basic prison sentence."

"Comms..." Cade murmured. "Commoners?" Krig nodded. "Then there are the Double D's," he said. "That stands for Double Dealers. They're the second biggest group in the AC...the blue...they can initially come from any of the other four groups, but are characterised by the fact that they're, well, double dealers. Basically, they're the type of scum who will betray everyone who they've ever known for a chance of freedom, or whatever self-interest they currently have in mind. Everyone else in the cells hates them, for obvious reasons." After a moment, Krig continued once more. "Then you have your Chevy's, the purple. Chevy's are locked up because they have rebelled or disobeyed the Carmels, or one of the leading Underworld variations. Persistent troublemakers. Those Carmel uses as leverage also tend to be lumped with the Chevy's."

"So," Leola said, "that's us, right?"

"Wish I could say 'yes' to that," Krig sighed. "But no. I think we're more likely to fit into the small green area - Lutes. Lutes commit more serious crimes, such as joining illegal resistances. They're the highest you can get without an immediate death sentence, and, even then, a death sentence is likely if the cells get too crowded." Susannah repressed a violent shudder.

"Well, at least that means we're getting at him," she offered, trying to rather ungracefully brighten everyone's gloomy countenance. She caught Krig giving her an appraising look, and returned the gaze, only for Krig to return to his map, looking thoughtful.

"What's PPC then? The black one?" Alice asked, her voice trembling marginally.

"PPC stands for Personally Pissed off Carmel," Krig said flatly. "It's very rare to get into that group, considering a Carmel is more likely to kill you than imprison you if you get on their bad side. It's normally political enemies."

"Very high security then," Cade remarked.

"All of the Carmel security is high," Jamie said, quietly.

"Wouldn't it be brilliant if we could break out all of their top prisoners? Can you picture the look on the Carmels' faces?" David looked dreamy. Susannah smiled slightly despite herself. She knew what David was doing; he was putting the conversation back into normal levels (for them), in an effort to ease the building tension in the room, the fear.

"Dream on," Alice laughed incredulously, but she too seemed wistful.

"For Shadow's sake," Leola snapped, apparently not getting it, "can you all please focus! We're breaking into

Anzarkledea in probably under a week's time; we don't have time to waste!"

"Alright, alright," David put his hands up, frowning slightly. "Bloody hell, don't get your magic in a twist, I was only-"

"-only trying to what?" Leola demanded shrilly. "Goof around like the idiot-"

"I think," Susannah said tightly, interrupting, "that he was actually trying to help and not stress everyone out even more. Working ourselves into hysterics isn't going to be beneficial." There was a moment of silence. Krig was favouring her with that assessing expression again.

"Well said," Delilah said softly. "Leola, I know you're freaking out, we all are, but we need to keep a level head, not turn on each other."

"In case you hadn't noticed," Leola said crossly, "we've already turned on each other. It's called having a traitor, or-"

"Leola," Krig's voice was firm, yet understanding, "that's enough." Leola's lip trembled, her hands curling in her lap, the normally immaculate nails bitten down to ragged stumps.

"Sorry," she conceded after a moment. "You're right, I'm not helping, I just-" Delilah rose from her seat, moving over to hug the older girl, seemingly without thinking of her actions. Leola choked on a sob. The rest of the meeting passed largely without event, all things considering.

"Susannah," Krig called. "Stay behind for a moment." She exchanged a look with Delilah and Jamie, who both hesitated before moving out of the door. Was she in trouble? Again? She hadn't done anything...that she was aware of. Shadow, he'd said she couldn't do field work (like this mission) if he couldn't trust her to follow orders...and it

271

was her fault that Leon got captured. Oh hell. He'd probably just been nice to her at the time before because she was in a total state of shock.

"I'm sorry," she blurted, before he could speak. He looked at her for a moment, then raised his brows.

"Guilty conscience?" he questioned, sounding marginally amused. "What does such a reflexive statement say about our relationship? You're not in trouble." Oh. Well, that was good. What was this about then? "Come and sit," he kicked a chair out towards her, eyes filled with an emotion that she couldn't quite place. She dropped into the offered seat, surveying him intently. "As you know," he began, "this mission is going to be dangerous. Extremely dangerous."

"If you're telling me to stay at home-" Susannah began, warningly.

"Let me finish." Susannah fell silent again, watching her leader for clues as to what this could possibly be about. "If - IF - the worst comes to the worst," Krig was serious now, there was no sign of that trademark friendliness on his features. It caused Susannah's stomach to tighten. "I want you to look after the resistance for me." She blinked. What? Was he saying what she thought he was saying?

"I don't-I-" she started, stammering like an idiot. He leaned forward, staring straight into her face.

"If I die, you're leader," he said, very slowly and clearly, as if knowing exactly the turmoil in her mind. He was saying what she thought he was saying.

"You're not going to die," was her automatic response.

"That's why I said 'if'," he replied, without missing a beat.

"I can't," she said. "I mean, why me? David-"

"David is a great guy," Krig said, "and I'd trust him with my life, but he's...impulsive."

"And I'm not?" she questioned, sceptically. "I ran into a

272

burning building, I - Leola. Leola could…"

"Is this you refusing?" he asked. "Because I can ask someone else if you wouldn't want to do it, but frankly, you're my first choice." She stared at him helplessly.

"I don't understand," she murmured. He laughed, but Susannah really couldn't find anything remotely funny within their conversation.

"No," he said, "I don't suppose you would. You're a bit slow at times." Susannah felt a surge of irritation, and he must have caught onto it because he softened the words with a smile, before turning solemn again. "Susannah, your magic is incredible, this, coupled with what I can only call a natural flair for this resistance, makes you perfect for my job. It was one of the first things I noticed about you, when we met." Susannah could feel a lump growing in her throat. "But you don't see that, do you?" Krig questioned. "It's ordinary to you, all you have is other people's perceptions and jealousy."

"So you're asking me because of my power?" she asked, not sure if it was right to feel just the smallest tinge of disappointment.

"No," he said sharply, "if I cared only for a powerful leader I could just ship you off to Carmel. I'm sure he'd do a stunning job if he had the slightest bit of sympathy for our cause." His voice softened again, coming back under control. "I'm asking you because I think you would do a brilliant job. You talk about impulsive moments; I talk about instincts and reactions that better the resistance. More so, you must have noticed, Susannah…the resistance is becoming more active. You're a warrior, a military leader, practise to my theory and preaching. You *do* and react, and, as a consequence, you inspire those around you to fight and react too. Now, this could be a problem, making you a wild card, but your dedication to the cause is more than apparent, as shown by the fact that you ran into a burning building because the resistance needed it... and, perhaps most importantly, you're...how shall I put this? An odd mixture between idealistic and cynical," he said finally. Susannah's mouth opened, but he waved a hand dismissively. "Yes, you are, don't try and deny it, and frankly, that makes you perfect for this job. Someone too idealistic would not be able to make the decisions needed to run this resistance, and someone too cynical can't genuinely believe, like a leader must, that their resistance can succeed despite overwhelming opposition. A utopia cannot be created if it cannot first be envisioned...so, do you accept?" Susannah stared at him, gob smacked.

"I need time to think," she admitted, her thoughts racing. Surely she couldn't be a good leader is she wasn't confident she could pull it off? A leader had to be confident! Krig certainly seemed pretty damn assured most of the time.

"Of course," Krig agreed. "But please get back to me as soon as possible, so I make the necessary arrangements." He stood, and she rose with him, the silence between them pensive now, each lost in their own thoughts.

"Do you really think that you're going to be killed on the mission?" Susannah asked, troubled. Her gut churned.

"If we get caught," Krig said, regarding her solemnly. "And I think you know why."

"I don't-" she began automatically, before pausing, sighing. "Carmel can't leave you alive, won't leave you alive, he'll make an example out of you, you're a figurehead...your death would be crippling for the resistance, with all the following headless chicken panic of who's in charge." She was starting to see why he was so adamant in settling the morbid issue of his successor.

"Here's to no headless chickens," Krig smiled, thinly. Susannah nodded.

"Here's to not getting caught," she returned. Krig looked tired.

"Hmm, I'll drink to that. Goodnight, Susannah...and thank you."

"Night..."

Susannah closed the door behind her, heading immediately for her guitar. Her parents studied her, silently drawing conclusions, the obvious being that she'd been at a meeting.

"How are you feeling?" her mum asked softly. "Your magic is looking better."

Her aura twitched at the mention, giving her a sense of curling and uncurling. She still felt empty; her insides hollow with some of her power still locked up behind remnant traces of the Gossamer. She had quickly decided that Gossamer was the worst substance she had ever come across, and she'd come across a lot of horrible things.

"I'm alright," she said, smiling thinly. "I do feel be-"

A vivid purple messenger pixie shot in through the window, bringing conversation to an abrupt halt. Susannah had always found it unfair (or maybe it was only that she noticed it unfair due to how her parents had raised her, with their, on retrospect, resistance-inspired attitude) on how they were forced into their roles of mail-deliverers and heralds. They were all over the city - a being could pay one for personal delivery or for the use of a company - but this one was wearing the Carmel crest. An official pixie; there was a whole fleet of them, who flew across the whole city upon order to deliver urgent news.

"Hem, hem. The execution of Leonard Daggey, rebel traitor,

under the command of our Lord, the Underworld Prince Marco Carmel, is to be Friday next week, at 7:00pm at the Anzarkledea courtyard. You are cordially invited, and we look forward to seeing you there. Please remember that any words spoken by our Supreme Lord may not be used without official permission, and that cameras or other recording devices are banned. You will be searched upon entrance. Thank you – Long live the Carmels!" The pixie zoomed out again, to the next house, a tiny whistle around its neck and a scrap of scroll tucked under its arm. There was a moment of silence. Her parents were staring at her, but she felt frozen. This was actually happening. She couldn't believe Carmel worked so fast!

"Leon...is he?" her mum began, carefully. Susannah nodded tightly.

"Are you going to the execution then?" her dad asked, voice neutral, but the dangerous gleam in his eyes suggested the real question behind the relative normality of his words. She nodded again. Yes, the resistance were doing something. "Of course," she smiled, thinly. "We're cordially invited after all. It would be rude to refuse such a summons."

Chapter Nineteen – Parental Guidance

Her mum was surveying her, warily, scrutinising. Several wards shot up around them, silencing, protective, preventing curious ears from noting that not meant for them.

"If I say no, will you stay at home?" she asked, voice even but for the faintest tremor.

Susannah felt a pang of guilt, twisting her insides viciously, like giant hands were wringing her out like a wet cloth.

"Probably not," she replied, before hesitating. "Krig...Krig asked me to...well...I'm his successor." Her dad buried his head in his hands, breathing deeply.

"And did you accept?"

"I said I'd think about it," she said honestly.

"And what exactly are you planning that would make him feel so desperate to name an heir to his...company? That would suggest something is going to happen to him, and consequently, a level of danger which I'm not sure I want my daughter involved in," he continued with a slightly menacing air.

"You always taught me to do what I thought was right," she replied cautiously. "I won't just do nothing, not when I have a chance of being able to help. Leon, he...I was *there*; it's my fault he's in this situation. I should've done more-"

"No," her mum snapped. "No you couldn't have done more, you're lucky to still be alive! Yes, we taught you to do what was right, and doing what's right is standing strong to your own beliefs and instincts, not risking everything in hopes of appeasing a misguided, or even valid, sense of guilt." Her mum took a few steps forward, clasping her shoulders tightly. "You know how it is, Susannah, this city is at war with itself, this *world* is in constant battle. War requires sacrifices for a greater good, and not everyone can survive. Don't throw your life away on the whim of youth; it's far too precious for that." Susannah swallowed.

"My life?" she repeated. "What is my life going to be? Passing school, then probably getting used to death by Carmel for my magic, furthering his empire, with only the sickness of my conscience for company? Or getting some dull job, perhaps, forever hiding everything I can do to avoid the former. That's not life!" she cried, infuriated. "That's just survival."

"Sometimes survival is all we can hope for," her dad said quietly.

"And what if I want more?" she murmured. "I want so much more than that. I want to be able to do what I want, when I want, and be able to walk down the streets without fear of becoming some being's dinner."

"We all want that, baby," her mum murmured. "That doesn't mean we're going to get it any time soon."

"So you've given up?" she demanded, fists clenched. "You're just going to roll over and take it? I'm pretty sure that's not staying strong to your own beliefs and instincts...if you didn't *want* me to be like this, if you just wanted me to stay out of trouble, then why did you raise me to question everything? To see how unfair and unequal this place is? I could have loved the Carmels like every other girl my age."

"Because you're powerful," her dad snapped, seeming to begin losing patience for the first time. "To raise you otherwise was not an option. You would have found far worse trouble and company if we didn't raise you like this. This world's dangerous, we would be terrible parents to try and convince you otherwise."

Susannah deflated slightly.

"Then give me your support in acting how you made me," she said softly. "Because I'm going to do this either way - and you can't stop me."

Her mum looked incredibly irritated, torn between fear and frustration.

"We don't want to see you harmed."

"The world's a dangerous place; I'd rather be harmed fighting for this than from something meaningless."

The silence was heavy, suffocating, and thick like treacle.

"We'll talk about this and get back to you."

David dropped into a seat next to her. They were going over more plans for the resistance, marking out which passageways they would need, and trying to research the guard schedules. The plan, so far, was to use Hangman's Bridge to get to the lower levels of Anzarkledea, and then intercept Leon's path to execution, rescue him, incapacitate the guards surrounding and escorting him, before making their way out again. Cade and Jamie were working overtime, around the clock, even with the help of the other sectors with their attempts to research everything in such a short space of time. Getting into Anzarkledea wasn't really the problem; the problem was getting out. Krig had immersed himself in delving through his numerous connections around the city, struggling to bring everything together in time. Safe houses were organised by the NR, all recruiting temporarily put on hold, for Leon when he managed to escape. He'd be forever more a fugitive...but surely that was better than being dead? He'd be free. Susannah, KT and David were working manically on warding; David's locksmith ability coming handy in plans to counter the sentience of the Demon Lord's manor. Her sector leader cleared his throat, and she looked at him, smiling briefly. He settled back in his chair, studying her intently, his voice low.

"Krig told me that you were next in line," he said. Susannah shifted, glancing around discreetly.

"Does everyone know about that?" she asked.

"Leola does, Cade and Joel do, because they're the originals and Krig's best friends...and I do, because I'm your sector leader. No one else."

"I told him it should have been you," she stated, hoping he wasn't mad at her. He'd been in the resistance longer than her, hell, they all had! They must think she was some arrogant upstart newbie or something!

"Meh. I'm happy where I am. Entry is what I do best," he dismissed. "Do you not want the gig? If not, you better tell boss-man sooner rather than later so that he can settle everything. Not that I'm saying he's gonna die, I hope he don't, but you know, better safe than sorry."

"I don't know if I can do it," she admitted, quietly. "I'm just...what if...surely if I was ready for this, I wouldn't have all these doubts? I want to do it, well, I don't *want*, I like Krig being leader, and I want him to stick around-"

"Yeah, I know," David assured. Susannah's magic twisted with anxiety.

"What if I mess it up? Get you all caught? I – I don't know how to run a resistance!"

"We'll help you out," he said. "All of us will, you won't be going it alone. It's a team effort. It's not like you suddenly can't ask for advice...and as for messing up, well, everyone's scared of failure, that's normal. I reckon you'll be more cautious for your doubts. If you thought you were perfect, you wouldn't take the necessary precautions, that, and you'd be an annoying as hell to put up with." Susannah laughed weakly.

"You don't mind that he asked me? Do you think the other's mind?"

"Nah, I don't think so," David slung an arm around her shoulders, his voice growing conspiring. "Being leader is shit-scary, why on earth would we want the job?"

It broke the tension successfully, and Susannah scowled, a grin tugging at her lips.   "Lucky me."

He laughed, withdrawing his arm.

"Seriously though, Susannah. I think you'd be brilliant, if that counts for anything."

"Thanks." She didn't know what else to say, to express how touched she was by his confidence.

"It's nothing...but get back to him, alright? Now come on, we have a break in to plan."

Krig called them all together again after some time, pulling everything they'd been doing into one more efficient plan, slotting the pieces and fragments as if he was assembling a jigsaw puzzle. Everyone accepted the Entry plan, or the very brief outline they'd been given.

Krig was keeping the overall sections together in his head alone, to limit the damage that their traitor could make. The traitor...that was a thought to keep Susannah awake at night.

She honestly didn't know who it was, though she suspected Leon. Of course, she'd largely kept her concerns private. She knew some people thought it was her.

Temporarily lost in thought, she almost missed Krig's next line of enquiry.

"Would you be willing to use Mind Arts, Delilah?"

Delilah froze on the spot, her cheeks turning pale.

"I-I'd rather not," she murmured. "What did you need it for?"

"It's more a security measure, a back-up, then anything else," Krig said honestly. "But the more control we can have over our surroundings, the better. We might need control over the guards at some point, for example – it depends what comes up."

"I don't think I can do that," Delilah said quietly, swallowing thickly. Leola's brows furrowed.

"Why not?" she asked. "It's not that difficult. I study Mind Arts – and you already take Psychology, don't you? They're not that different, so what's the problem?"

Delilah was silent for a moment.

"It's...wrong," she mumbled. "I don't want to take away anyone's free will. I'd hate it if anyone did that to me. I don't like the thought of controlling people."

"That's very noble of you, Delilah," Krig said, softly. "But most people wouldn't share your view, and our enemies certainly won't. They will use every single one of the advantages they have available to them. I won't...force you to do this, if it makes you so uncomfortable, but I would strongly recommend that you accept. Leola or I can teach you."

"Or I can," Jamie added. "If you want."

"I'll think about it," Delilah muttered, eyes uncharacteristically dark, troubled and stormy.

"That's all I can ask," Krig sighed, though all other remnants of stress or exhaustion were invisible upon his features. Delilah frowned, staring at the floor.

"Krig," Susannah caught up with him, as the meeting ended, and everyone was leaving. She caught David and Delilah, along with Cade, Leola and Joel, watching the two of them carefully. She realised she was going to have to give her answer to his offer, and thought she might have made up her mind. But, first, she had another matter on her mind. He stopped, entering the base again, excusing himself from his conversation with Jamie with a quick smile, who now also studied them both for a few seconds.

"Susannah, everything alright?" he asked.

"I think I – we – I think we met Kitty," she blurted out, though she'd initially intended to approach the topic a bit more subtly. He went still, eyes almost distant. "What...did she die? Is it possible that I met her?" she asked. Krig slowly moved so he was sitting down, his jaw tight.

"What makes you think it was her?" he asked, softly.

"Well, she was a Dark Angel and not completely horrible...and she knew you-"

"Blonde?" he interrupted, looking up at her for a moment. She nodded. His eyes closed, and he inclined his head slightly, his expression seeming nearly pained.

"Sounds like her."

"I didn't know what you wanted to do with this information," she said, a bit awkwardly. "But I thought you should know either way..."

"Thank you," he murmured, opening his eyes again, features smooth once more. She appraised him for a few seconds.

"Were you close? When she was Emiah's-" she corrected herself hastily when she saw him flinch at the name "-your sister's friend..." she trailed off, not really sure what to say. Krig looked at her, his expression unreadable, before he shrugged.

"There was something there," he said, with a faint smile. "Em...died before it went anywhere, but I sometimes thought, if she hadn't..." Krig stopped, shaking his head, any whimsicalness or nostalgia vanishing from his tone. "It doesn't matter. It's the past. We have bigger problems now,

I'll put the NR on the matter of recruiting her after this is all sorted out…have you thought anymore about what I said?" Susannah let the topic drop quite gladly, despite her curiosity – it was a bit uncomfortable.

"I thought about it, yeah," she said.

"And?"

"I'll do it," she said, nodding firmly. For the first time in a while she saw some of the weight slide off him, his face lighting up in stark relief to the exhaustion in his gaze. "But don't take that as an excuse to go dying on us, alright?" she added. He offered her a salute.

"Do my best, Susannah," he replied, "…thanks."

"I hope you know what you were doing, cause I don't," she said honestly.

He started to laugh, shaking his head.

"Still don't trust me and my decisions, huh?" he grinned, no particular spite in his tone. Susannah flushed.

"I do!" she protested. "I just-"

"You just?" he prompted, with some amusement. She scowled.

"I just like to understand decisions, and I don't understand yours," she mumbled. His amusement faded somewhat, as he stood.

"You will, with time," he assured. "To be honest, if you thought you were perfect for the job, you'd probably be over-confident and screw up…as well as being a bit annoying."

"That's what David said," Susannah smiled.

"It's a valid point," Krig returned. "But, anyhow, I'm not personally planning on dying anytime soon, so you should be safe," he teased. She rolled her eyes.

"Good."

"Was that all?" he asked, after a minute or so. "Not that I'm in any mad hurry, but I do still have some stuff to take care of today...

"Yeah," she said quickly. "That was all. Sorry."

"It's no problem," he replied, offering her a lazy smile. "No need to apologize, kid."

They started moving to the door, when a thought seemed to strike him.

"Make sure Delilah's okay with all this Mind Arts stuff, won't you?" It was phrased like a question, but more of an order really.

"Of course," she agreed.

"Is everything alright with her? She's seemed a bit distracted recently," he persisted.

"It's just some...family stuff," Susannah explained. It wasn't her place to go into it, and explain suspicions of murder... "I think she's worried about Leon too. I mean, we all are, but...she's just got a lot going on at the moment."

"Is she going to be able to participate in the mission? I won't have her distracted." The words may have seemed harsh and uncaring, if not for the genuine concern on his face too.

Susannah shook her head.

"She'll be fine. Del's tough, stronger than she looks."

Krig studied her for a moment.

"If you're certain...just make sure she's okay, alright? And remind her to come and find me, if she changes her mind about the Mind Arts."

They split.

The days rolled by, and Susannah couldn't help but notice her parents were still furiously discussing the mission outside of her hearing. She supposed it was quite a big decision to make, and ultimately she took the lack of immediate refusal as a good thing, but the waiting for feedback was still unnerving. Today, however, she had a different reason for being nervous outside of the constant fluttering in her stomach at the fast approaching execution date.

Becki Daggey had contacted Delilah again, apparently more willing to talk now. Delilah had been both thrilled and terrified; Susannah was just disconcerted and terrified. Nonetheless, she was going with her again as Delilah was set on this and, from experience, if her best friend actually did set her mind on something she was even more stubborn about it than Susannah was. Still, she couldn't help but hope Delilah's investigation wouldn't attract the wrong type of attention – be it from Starlight, or from Carmel if it truly had been a murder that was covered up.

"Are you sure this is a good idea?" she asked again, as they drew near the formidable mental hospital once more. It looked no more cheery now than it had in her memories. Delilah ignored her, and so Susannah simply tried to ignore how sick she felt visiting Becki with the full knowledge that Leon wasn't there and was instead waiting to be executed. It just...the whole thing was wrong, from start to finish.

"How are we even going to get in?" she asked. "We don't have a key."

In response, Delilah took her hand out of her pocket, holding it up. A silver key dangled around her fingers.

"It's called a visitors key," she explained. "It'll disintegrate after this one time. I got permission for it, under Becki's request."

"Oh."

"Yeah. Oh. You know, you don't have to come," Delilah added, a bit snappishly, looking completely stressed out. Susannah's eyes softened.

"Of course I'll come, I'm just worried, if they really were murdered, that all manner of things might come crawling out from the woodwork. We've got enough going on already, I just…"

"It'll be fine," Delilah murmured, though she didn't sound completely certain. "Besides, I have to know…I *have* to…you might not understand but I…I need to know. Maybe I'm being selfish, but, I need to be completely focused on what's coming on, I need closure on the past to do that…I…Becki needs to know too. About Leon. I'd want to know if I was her. Oh, my thoughts are a mess…am I making any sense at all?"

"Some," Susannah sighed, heavily. "I can tell it's important to you anyway. Let's go."

Becki Daggey's room was even more of a mess than it had been last time, and the girl's eyes were red-rimmed and raw from tears, white as sheet. Her jaw was hard.

"You're going to save him, aren't you?" was the first thing she said. "He's never missed a visit before…and though we don't get the messenger pixies here…something's wrong, isn't it? Leon needs help. What's happened?"

Susannah swallowed…was this conversation liable to set the eighteen year-old off?

"Tell me," Becki insisted, staring at Delilah. "And I'll tell…an information trade. Their story for his. That's fair, isn't it? I have to know, like *you* have to know."

"You'll tell me what happened with my parents if I tell what happened to Leon," Delilah summarised. Becki nodded.

"Deal," Delilah agreed, instantly. Susannah could feel a headache building, and sank to sit at the desk, trying not to look at all the pictures.

"Leon's been captured by Carmel," Delilah said, evenly, and

with an uncharacteristic bluntness. "He's set to be executed this Friday, at 7:00pm."

Becki's face drained of all colour, bloodless lips pressing tightly together as if to suppress the tears that sprang to her eyes, before her hand clamped over her mouth to cover any noises of horrified shock too. She stared, emptily into the distance for a moment, eyes closing, a lone pearl of sorrow rolling down her pale cheek. She appeared to struggle with her composure for some time.

"You're going to save him, aren't you?" she asked, again, desperately.

"We're going to do our best, yes," Delilah said softly. "Sorry you had to hear it like this...and, um...sorry to rush you but...?"

"R-right," Becki gulped thickly, swiping at her eyes, rocking marginally, trembling uncontrollably. "W-well, I was just seven at the time...when I saw them. They were," her eyes grew distant, and her shaking amplified. "I have to talk about this all the time, really, never like doing it though," she mumbled. "I'm not supposed to...they were murdered, if that's what you wanted to know. Didn't look like an accident to me, at least..."

Delilah inhaled sharply.

"What happened?" she asked, breathlessly. "The bodies...the bodies were never found."

"They probably took them, that's why," Becki muttered. "Massive great fight, I...I presume your parents were the two fighters, not the big group?"

"I assume so," Delilah said, eyes wide. Susannah listened carefully, her insides rolling with the anticipation of new knowledge. If she felt sick, she could scarcely imagine how her best friend felt. Becki gestured at one of the pictures on the wall, and Delilah moved over, taking it down. It was no great piece of artistry, but it quite clearly showed two fighters, a man and a woman. The man's face was clearly etched out, with the same shade of blue that all the family had. The woman's features, presumably those of Delilah's mother, was a distorted blur, like a scribble, not complete.

"The fight went on for some time," Becki continued quietly. "But your parents lost...they...they were torn apart...their *magic* ripped out..." Delilah had turned green.

"Who killed them?" she asked; her voice barely above a whisper. Becki glanced up, appearing haunted, eyes still filled with that awful, lost distance.

"I-" she couldn't seem to speak.

"Vampires?" Susannah questioned. "Demons? Dark Angels?"

"Monsters." Becki stared straight ahead, white as sheet. "People. Humans. Overworld."

...Starlight?

Susannah found her way home, head still spinning. Her stomach was churning. Had Starlight really done this, or was she just leaping wildly to conclusions based on her dad's opinions? She didn't know, but the new information disturbed her either way. If it was the Underworld, it would have been easy to deal with, expected even, as horrible as that was. But humans...Overworld beings...it was unnerving, terrible, and just left the gaping question of *why?* Delilah had gone very quiet; her teeth gritted, and had simply gone home, begging off all discussion until tomorrow after she'd collected her own thoughts.

Her parents were waiting for her when she arrived, calling her through to the living room with stern, haggard faces. She figured they may have finally come to a decision, and her stomach squeezed in anticipation.

"What response did you give to Krig?" her dad asked quietly. Susannah wetted her lips nervously.

"Yes. I told him yes," she stated. They both studied her for a moment, posture rigid.

"Then I don't see how we can do anything other than say yes," her mum murmured. "You're not exactly giving us any choice in the matter, so all we can really try and do is support you and try and stop you from getting yourself killed." Her mum's voice tightened at the last, strained, and Susannah grimaced guiltily. "You've made it more than clear you'll be doing this regardless of our opinion on the matter."

They both looked at her disapprovingly for that.

"It's the right thing to do," Susannah replied, once more. "I'll be careful."

"You always say you are," her mum said flatly. "And you always get into trouble anyway."

"...so, really, actively seeking out trouble for a good cause doesn't make all that much difference, does it?" she offered, with a hopeful smile, aiming to lighten the heavy atmosphere a bit. It didn't seem to work.

Bizarrely, they then promptly sat her down and starting talking tactics and resistance.

Chapter Twenty - After Visiting Hours

Nausea rolled in Susannah's stomach and her knuckles were white-washed in their fists. Her insides twisted. It was mission day: the execution was set for seven o clock that evening. She felt sick. She bet Leon felt a million times worse. They gathered at the Disused Fire Station; it was their closest base to Anzarkledea. She couldn't quite believe that she was doing this. She'd pulled some crazy stunts in her time, joining the resistance most definitely included, but this one had to top them all. The tension in the air was tangible. Delilah was pacing up and down, unable to stop, back and forth as if the room could scarcely contain her restless energy, while Leola sat hunched in the corner staring blankly into the air before her as if it somehow held all the mysteries of the world. Krig was frantically going over last minute plans with David, their voices low so as not to carry. Cade, to Susannah's utter disbelief, was sitting in the corner calmly reading and neither Jamie or Alice had arrived yet. Her hands felt shaky, and watching Delilah pace was making her feel dizzy. She sank into a chair, tapping rhythms on the table. Her stomach knotted, but she remained firmly resolute. This was the right thing to be doing, and she couldn't exactly leave Leon to his fate. It was too cruel, and far too much like a signal of submission to her tastes. She couldn't decide if time was passing frighteningly fast or excruciatingly slowly.

"Nervous?" a voice asked, settling down next to her. She half glanced at Krig, a smile tucking the corners of her lips at the familiar question.

"No," she lied, as was customary. His mouth flashed a smile back at her, before growing grave.

"Seriously now, Susannah, how are you feeling?"

"...alright. Nauseous."

"Well, that's to be expected," he replied quietly. "I'd have been more nervous if you weren't…it's better to do these things when you're anxious, it boosts the adrenaline and makes you careful."

"More likely to survive," Susannah finished.

"Exactly."

"You know, that's not the most encouraging thing to be saying," she murmured, dryly. A laugh startled from him, and Susannah flushed at the attention the sound drew. It seemed too loud and jarring against the tense hush in the room.

"No, but it's probably the most helpful advice I can give you at the moment…though I can try and throw a couple of motivational comments on the topic, if you want?"

Susannah studied him carefully for a moment, her eyes tracing over the unnatural stillness of his posture, the way he appeared almost too casual.

"What about you?" she asked, lowly. "Are you nervous?"

"Me?" he looked surprised. "I'm fine, I always am." She stared at him flatly. He appraised at her, a dark cast to his gaze, before sighing softly. "Of course I am, but I largely don't have the luxury of doubts or other such things."

She nodded once, gratified by his honesty, and the implicit guidance. A leader couldn't afford to be seen as weak. They couldn't crumble beneath that pressure, and they couldn't buckle. They had to be strong. He squeezed her shoulder lightly, before moving to another part of the room, checking on everyone.

Jamie and Alice arrived promptly, and then, all too soon, it was time to leave.

They went in groups of two. Krig and David first, leading the way, followed by Cade and Delilah, then Leola and Alice. At the end, were her and Jamie. They managed to get to

Hangman's Bridge without incident, but, really, that had always been the easy part of the mission. Susannah swallowed. This bridge had always given her the creeps. They made their way under it, avoiding the empty beer bottles and blood bags, and whatever other rubbish had been tossed there. She and Jamie checked the surrounding area, cautiously, to see if anyone had noticed them, before squeezing into the passageway behind one of the stones after everyone else. It was pitch black, and Susannah could scarcely see her hand before her face, and the only sign that this was the way to go was the barest flicker of light ahead. They'd decided against any obvious lighting, choosing instead to feel their way through, in fear of alerting anyone to their presence. It was better to sneak up. They'd cast silencing charms on their feet too, and their breaths. It made everything all too eerie, as if all life had fallen away. They pulled the entry shut behind them.

The tunnel was narrow, uncomfortably so. Susannah was all too glad that she wasn't particularly claustrophobic, and her heart pounded with sympathy for Delilah, who was. She felt Jamie's fingers search out her hand, the grip warm and comforting. Though she couldn't hear his breath, it confirmed that there was life, that she wasn't simply alone in the darkness. Honestly. She mentally scolded herself; of all the things to be scared of during this mission, a gloomy tunnel should have been the least of her worries. Ugh, there were probably all sorts of spider webs in here!
"Come on," he whispered, his breath hot upon her ear. "We can't fall behind, don't worry, I've got you."
She wanted to tell him that she didn't need to be 'got', but her throat was suddenly too dry. She'd barely talked with Jamie since he'd been at her house, and the emotional turbulence, the confusion, wasn't helping the state of her

thoughts. What had he even meant by kissing her on the cheek? Was it just a between friends thing or -? Friends didn't really kiss each other on the cheeks like that, did they? Maybe they did, and she was just reading into it...damn it. It was inappropriate and unprofessional. She forced herself to concentrate, ignoring the tingle of their close proximity. They continued in silence, not daring to speak, but he didn't let go of her hand. For a moment, time seemed suspended, her senses heightened by the shadows. She could suddenly smell his faint cologne, a foreign scent, exotic almost, but familiar all the same. The thumping of her heart seemed all too loud and frantic in her chest. The journey seemed to last forever, but then, all too quickly, they reached the others at the end of the tunnel, waiting. Jamie let go of her hand, leaving her palms feeling slightly cold and empty, with a ghost impression of phantom fingers still entwined with her own. David was working on the wards, his eyes a blue flame in the darkness, a light shimmering web of security around him, sliding in a vast network. There was a small frown on his face, utter concentration. Then, he nodded. The guards would switch their shifts in one minute.

They waited in a stressed, crushing silence, unmoving, crouched beneath the floors of Anzarkledea. Her breathing grew shallow, and she focussed on it - and her magic, stifling it. Viridian would be mad at her for the restriction, but it was necessary this time. She pushed it deep inside until it hurt, until all that was visible was the barest pin prick of an aura, a speck of glitter in the dust. There was a rumbling of voices and heavy footfalls above them.
"Evening Az," a voice grunted. "You hear about the execution? Going to make your way over?"
"Course," 'Az' replied in response, "meeting the missus

there. Some rebel kid, isn't it?"

"Tha's what I heard," the other guard said. There was some shuffling, then a calling of bored goodbyes, along with some grumblings from the guard who'd taken over about how he wouldn't make it. Apparently Carmel was going to make a speech. Susannah swore to herself that the Demon Lord wouldn't get the opportunity if she could help it. The next second, Krig had burst out the tunnel with a sign, bludgeoning the Daemon across the back of the head as he started to morph into his true, monstrous form in alarm. He fell with a heavy slump, mouth half transformed to a wolfish jaw, and for the next few moments, they all crawled out, keeping an eye out for anyone around. The next patrol was in fifteen minutes. David was still concentrating on the wards, white as sheet with the effort of battling the sentient manor, keeping a bubble of broken wards around them, and they patched the space with their own magic, so nothing seemed untoward. KT was outside, not officially with them, but keeping an eye out on all the other entrances, ready to warn them if they became compromised during the execution. Joel was also co-ordinating from the outside; and everyone was doing their best to help, really.

"Let's go - Susannah, lead the way," Krig ordered. Right. She was in Entry. She knew this place like the back of her hand...or was working on it anyway. She prayed she wouldn't get lost, though she shouldn't, with David warding off the sentience and KT a communicon call away if it came down to that. The building shouldn't move around from its default structure. She swallowed, but began walking confidently enough.

It was the first time she'd been in Anzarkledea manor; she'd only seen it in pictures and maps before, and couldn't quite help her awe. It was breath-taking. She'd thought the

Bellevue penthouse flat was impressive, but it held nothing to this place. Everything was so grand, so intricate and beautiful. She'd never seen anything like it. The floor beneath her feet was gleamed to a shining polish, the walls tastefully decorated with pieces of art that she was certain cost a fortune. The ceilings were weaved from elegant and elaborate carvings, with tiny swooping patterns and birds where the wall met the ceiling, accented by stretches of pure white. The closer they got to the cells, the simpler the designs of the house became, though they were in no way ugly or average even in the servants quarters. Perhaps the most magnificent thing, though, was the magic. The whole building hummed with power, and despite David interference, she could feel the intense weight of a colossal system of wards covering every aspect. With Sklis' home, it had been a mild itch, here it was impossible to ignore. It was as if David was physically holding up a massive pressure above them, like a small tunnel capable of collapsing and crushing them if it was given the chance.

She couldn't imagine living in such a place, it was so casually grand.

"Okay," Krig whispered. "We wait here. Leon, plus whatever guards he has escorting him, must pass by this way on the way to the courtyard; it's the only way when the house is fixed."

Susannah was suddenly aware that while they remembered the work of their own sectors, Krig tried to remember them all, even if not to as specific detail – he knew what the TA did, he'd memorised their plans and back up plans, he knew his way around the city and Anzarkledea reasonably well, he'd recruited before and certainly dealt with everyone in the resistance. She'd never considered the true magnitude of his role outside of calling the decisions, co-ordinating all of them into a cohesive whole.

Tense with anticipation, they waited.

Susannah felt like she'd never waited so long before, her stomach was knotted with anticipation and David was startlingly pale with the strain of holding the power of Anzarkledea from crashing down upon their backs. Cade had also joined in the effort to help now, having done some study into warding. Delilah was tense as she used subtle Mind Arts to scan for any approaching mentalities around them. It wasn't intrusive, but she knew her best friend hated every second of it. The blonde had also not had any formal training outside of a few quick, pointed lessons and so the act took far more effort than it did for Krig, whose brow was only marginally furrowed with his sharp attention. Susannah focussed on keeping her magic pressed inside, while everyone else directed their attention to the approach of Leon and the guards. Eventually they heard it, and Susannah's nerves increased two fold. Here came the difficult part; getting Leon and getting *out.*

When they saw him, she almost didn't recognise the haughty brunet. His features were the colour of porridge, waxy, his eyes wild with absolute terror, but there was no fight in his body. Indeed, the proud boy was hunched in on himself, as if shrinking to make a smaller target. He appeared horribly diminished. She didn't have time to contemplate the awful changes further, and the effects of the cells and company that must have made them, before they were attacking. The two demons on either side of Leon were more talented and intelligent than the Daemon guards had been, but no match for them.

Leon gaped at them, trembling, as if he could scarcely believe his eyes.

"K-Krig?" he stammered, his voice drained of his former

confidence, crippled to a shocked stammer. "You came, oh shadow, you all came, I...how-" Krig snapped to attention at his name, with a look to Delilah to keep her focus, he appeared marginally surprised when Leon latched onto him for dear life, sobbing unashamedly, clinging onto his shirt. Krig's eyes flickered, before he took it in his stride.

"Of course we came, Leon, didn't think we'd leave you, did we? Besides, we've wanted to break in here for ages, it's no trouble," her leader joked, gently. "Come on, it's alright, don't cry, you're okay, but we need to get moving now, all right? It won't be long before you're missed."

Leon drew back, embarrassed, scrubbing at his eyes, clearing his throat.

"Thank you," he breathed, and Susannah couldn't help but feel uncomfortable with the painful sincerity with which he spoke. Krig squeezed the younger boy's shoulder with a small, reassuring smile, before looking to her. Right. Leading the way out. Stealthily, they moved out the way they came.

It was a tense business. They crept along; head's nearly spinning with fear of getting caught. There was an occasional servant around, but the halls seemed mostly empty as everyone was filling the courtyard outside. Susannah could hear the roar and bay of the building crowd, the sick, excited clamour and speculations that created a dull rumble in her ears. They kept checking everyone was still with them, not getting left behind as the dove to hiding places whenever anyone came – or fought back when hiding was not an available option.

"Everyone here?" Krig checked, as they neared Hangman's passage again, looking around him, before freezing.

"Where's Leola?"

Susannah's eyes closed for a moment. Everyone was still, too still. Though there was hiding involved, they shouldn't have been going fast enough to actually lose anyone; it was a paranoia check.

"Maybe she got captured somehow," Delilah offered, weakly, desperately. Something like a groan escaped Krig's lips.

"Or maybe she's the traitor..." her leader swore, rather colourfully. "Everyone, assume we're compromised and move faster!"

"But what if we're not?" Alice cried. "What if she got left behind by accident or something, we can't just leave her, I – she's your girlfriend!"

"Actually," Krig muttered, tightly. "She broke up with me. And how likely do you think it is that she got left behind, really?"

Susannah wondered immediately if their breaking up was the scene she had walked in on, when Leon had been captured, before scowling at herself because it wasn't actually any of her business. Unless Leola was the traitor...but, surely, she couldn't be? It was Leola!

"And you didn't suspect something then?" David yelped, incredulously, "When she was breaking up with you right before our mission? Shadow, why didn't you call the whole thing off? You said you were dealing with the traitor thing!"

"I had you all take Introvertai wards, didn't I?" Krig returned, with a sharpness to his voice. "As for Leola, it wasn't an immediate thing. We've been drifting for a while."

"But what if she *is* captured?" Delilah whispered, sounding horrified. Susannah tightened her jaw, noting that a sheen of exertion was beading upon David's forehead, his features strained, as Cade's was too. Sentient wards, she assumed, would fight back.

"I agree with Krig, we need to get out of here," she said.

"We can't just leave her, not here, they'll kill her!" Leon

moaned. Krig tugged a hand agitatedly through his hair. Susannah made a split second decision at the panic in his eyes.

"Look - you guys go ahead, I'll see if I can find her," she bit out. They gaped at her. "Go, now," she ordered, insistently. "We can't just leave her, and there's no point risking all of us getting caught."

"Su-" Delilah began.

"-I know the layout of this place, I'm good with warding so I should be able to hold the sentience back off me...and you know I'm powerful. I can handle most people I run into better than the rest of you, no offence."

"There's no way I'm leaving you here on your own," Krig said flatly. "Especially if Leola is the traitor. Remember that talk we had on doing stupid things?"

And then alarm bells began to shriek.

Susannah didn't know how it had happened, but, somehow, they'd managed to get split up in the chaotic sprint out of Anzarkledea manor. The hit team had swarmed on their location within minutes, and they'd had to duel desperately to stay afloat against superior training. The hit squad seemed to have appeared out of nowhere; in one second they were alone in in the corridor, the next second they were surrounding by darting figures, snarling teeth and the glint of sharp blades. Everything had erupted around her, and she was just running to try and escape. When she stopped for a moment, everything was quiet around her, with no one else in sight. Her heart was pounding furiously. She started to sprint again. The mansion seemed to horribly twist around her, mocking her with the lack of exit. She had the awful feeling that she was going around in circles. The Underworld Prince's team seemed to be enjoying picking them off, one by one - hunting. So far, she'd destroyed the five that had caught up with her, but could feel her focus and energy beginning to lag. She sincerely hoped some of the resistance managed to get out - like David, with his Locksmith abilities. The house shouldn't reveal him as quickly as it betrayed the location of the rest of them. She was okay, her magic and warding classes proved useful in holding back the sentience from telling her position, though she wasn't skilled enough to block the house from warping, labyrinth-like, around her. Only David had been able to do that. She sprinted down another corridor, no longer caring to note or comment on the view around her. This manor was a curse, a beautiful, deadly, trap - a spider's web glittering like diamonds on an early morning. Her feet smacked against the floor like wet fish, taunting her with the echo. She directed some of her magic to silence them. She needed to get out, find Leola and get out, (the second one suddenly felt rather more optional.) Every single one of her instincts were screaming. The next second a hand seized hers, yanking her to the side. Her back hit the wall, her magic flaring, before she caught it just in time, nearly fumbling her control if his power hadn't been smashed back at her to absorb the crash of their magic.

"Jamie," Susannah breathed. "Thank Shadow you're alright - do you know if anyone else got out? - And for crying out loud don't just grab me like that I almost killed you-"

"-Shut up and hide our auras," he ordered, a steel of command in his voice. She followed automatically, seeing the logic, but narrowed her eyes, demanding answer. She was suddenly aware of how close together they were standing, his chest pressing against hers, his arms like cages on either side of shoulders. Inexplicably, a blush crept to her cheeks. She heard the hit team thunder past their recess. They stayed in silence for a moment.

"Come on," he said, more softly this time. "I know a way

out-"

"Leola," she began. He glared at her.

"Don't play the hero, Susannah, it doesn't suit you," he replied. "A life trapped within these walls wouldn't be kind to you." He seized hold of her hand again, strongly, dragging her back the way she came, and she was sprinting beside him.

"Wait - Jamie - this can't be the right way - *we're going up!*" she said, quickly, trying to pull back.

"Bookcase passages, remember? All the other passages will probably be covered by now."

"The others-?" Susannah's eyes widened with horror. "Crap, we need to check-"

He pulled her roughly into another room, a...study? He slammed the door shut behind him, before turning to face her, only to pause at her expression. The floors were a dark wood, gleaming like all the other floors in this place. A large table dominated the scene, the walls lined by *bookcases* filled with books on every topic imaginable. The desk was crammed full of papers, with a reading lamp, and a pot holding about fifty working fountain pens. There was a door, open just a crack, which appeared to lead into what looked to be a whole flat and living quarter.

"This isn't the Carmel Library," she noted, glancing at him.

"No, it's not," he said shortly, striding over to the bookcase, sliding individual books in a complicated order, his back blocking her view. She was once more hit by the certainty that it was easier to get into Anzarkledea than it was to get out. Her mouth felt dry. How did he know that combination?

"Where are we?" she demanded.

"Marco Carmel's study - no, don't touch anything! - come on, through here."

She stared at him.

302

"How do you know all this?" she questioned, warily. "Your family-"

"Susannah," his teeth gritted. "Are you seriously going to start this now, really? *Go!*"

"Answer me," she instructed, folding her arms. He strode back over to her, his face twisted viciously, yet, still so handsome, grabbing her arm again, ignoring the warning flicker of her magic and pushing her towards the passageway.

"Go, *please,* they'll be here any minute."

"J-"

Lips were suddenly on hers in a fierce, crushing kiss, fingers tangling in her hair, not painful, but...she couldn't think. He pulled back after a moment, his eyes dark, so dark and unreadable, yet shining. His fingers traced along her jaw line, the touch leaving a blazing trail to rival the popping-candy tingle upon her lips.

"Why do you have to be so damn stubborn?" he whispered. "You should have just gone."

The hit team burst in in a blur of Gossamer.

Chapter Twenty One - The Carmel Brothers

Susannah's heart was in her mouth, dread clawing a home in her chest. She could feel *his* magic instantly, playing with her senses, intoxicating, drowning her in power. It was powerful. She'd never felt an aura so powerful before. She glanced desperately around her, catching glimpses of a large, ornate room before she was forced down onto her knees, breathing ragged. Her magic tugged inside of her, raging at the Gossamer that entrapped it, feeling threatened. The guards had dragged her back down, Jamie with her, and out of the corner of her eye she could see Delilah, Krig, Jamie, Cade, Alice, David, and Leon on either side of her. Her stomach sank. They hadn't got away! Krig was next to her, Delilah on the other side. Then there was Leola. The blonde was standing in the corner, arms folded, not looking at any one of them, the treacherous bitch. Instead, her attention was on...footsteps, soft, measured. Her head shot up without permission. There he was. Marco Carmel. The Demon Lord. Her breath caught in her throat. It was the first time she'd ever seen the Underworld Prince so close, and she couldn't help but hope that as long as she lived she never saw that feared face again. She couldn't help wishing she would. He was handsome, beautiful, she'd give him that...but he was dangerous.

"Well, well, well, what do we have here then," Carmel mused, mockingly. Obsidian eyes assessed them all, judging them within seconds of observation. He paced before them with a deadly grace, stopping on the hunched figure three down from her. Jamie. Carmel's head tilted, features suddenly seeming both harder and softer all at one. Long, slender, ivory fingers knotted into Jamie's hair, tugging upwards slightly to bring Jamie's face into view. Protests began to swell in her mouth, silenced by the Demon Lord's next words.

"Nicely played, little brother." She could have sworn that her heart stopped. Jamie was a traitor too? Jamie was a Carmel? The other Carmel brother? It felt as if someone had plunged a jagged shard of ice straight into her gut; flooding her with frost…he'd been trying to help her! Hadn't he? Oh, but he'd known everything so well, it made sense, but then it didn't…Jamie arched his brows.

"Are you going to let me stand up or not?" the younger Carmel returned. Marco smirked, slightly, stepping back and gesturing for the guards around Jamie to back away and release him…his brother. Jamie was Marco's brother? She couldn't believe it; he'd seemed so nice, so…he'd kissed her. He caught her gaze for only the fraction of a second, cold, emotionless…the bastard. His lips quirked mockingly. She felt played.

Krig was staring at Jamie in shock, and in…pity. There was pity in his eyes, a warm, dangerous pity that she couldn't help but notice the younger Carmel wouldn't face. The Underworld Prince studied Jamie for a moment too, scanning for something, an unusual and wholly unexpected shadow of concern passing across his features in under a second, so brief that Susannah scarcely caught it, and only caught it due to her intent awareness. Then the Demon Lord was rounding on them again, a small chilling smile gracing his lips, an amused sound escaping his throat.

"You didn't truly think you'd be able to walk around my house undetected, did you?" Marco questioned, pacing before them once more. "With a traitor? Tell me," the Demon Lord laughed; the sound devoid of any genuine mirth or kindness, "are you ridiculously optimistic, or just stupid?"

Leon whimpered, eyes fixed on the figure before them in hazy terror. Neither Carmel spared him a glance. Jamie seemed nonchalant, standing beside his brother, looking every inch as comfortable there as he ever had with resistance, if not more.

"Ridiculously optimistic," a voice said cheerfully. "We can't all be an oppressive misery guts now, can we?" Krig. Marco stopped in front of him and Jamie's eyes fixed on his leader's...ex leader's...features. Susannah winced, knowing exactly what Krig was doing, and despising every second of the sacrifice. If the Carmels were focused on him, they weren't paying attention or trying to harm the rest of them. Marco smirked, deceptively pleasant.

"Mr Carter," he murmured. "Who's been a naughty boy, then? Pray, tell me, how long did you think this silly little insurgence was going to last?"

"Really, Mr Carmel," Krig returned, in acidic mimicry. "How long did you think you'd be able to go unchallenged?"

"Unchallenged?" The Demon Lord laughed again; that terrible laugh. "I remain unchallenged, human, for neither you nor your precious resistance are a challenge to me."

"Except," Susannah bit out, recklessly, not quite able to restrain herself, "we both know that's not quite true. If we weren't a threat to you this whole scenario wouldn't be playing out, unless the Underworld Prince holds audience with all those who break his laws?"

Delilah shot her a warning look, the expression half pleading and half threatening her to keep her mouth shut. Carmel turned slowly to face her, unreadable in his study. He gave his brother a swift glance, before turning back to her once more, prowling closer.

"You're Susannah Skelsby," he stated.

"You're Marco Carmel," she responded, acting calmer than she felt, resisting the urge to scramble back when he was barely a foot away from her; falling to an elegant crouch so they were on the same height level. "See, we know each other's names already, isn't that fabulous? Though I see no reason that you should be familiar with mine."

"Don't you?" he murmured. "Because in some circles your name is starting to become almost as famous as mine...don't look so surprised, Susannah," he chided, placing a slender hand on her shoulder, a fraction too tight in its fire and ice pressure to be as mentoring as it initially seemed. "You have a lot of magic locked up in there, after all."

"Leave her be," Krig spat, tightly. "She's just a kid."

The Underworld Prince gave no indication to having heard this, his gaze intent on hers, as if the whole world had narrowed onto the two of them.

"Do you know why we Demon Lords, or Ladies, are the rulers of this world, despite the numerous candidates there may be for the role?" Marco questioned. Jamie seemed about to move, but in the end was still, not even flinching, so she thought she must have imagined it.

"Because you kill all your opponents?" she offered sweetly.

"We're stronger than normal Demons, faster than the Vampires, more alluring then the Dark Angels and...we have magic. Powerful magic. And, let me tell you a secret..." he leaned forwards, in a parody of children's secret sharing, his breath teasing the shell of her ear. "That's because we *feed* on it." Susannah reared back, unable to take his eyes off him, though his grip remained ruthless on her shoulder. He fed on magic? He *fed* on magic! Her stomach churned, rolling, threatening to spit out everything she'd ever consumed. He could...he could feed on hers, drain her completely and add her power to his own. Okay. She could see why her parents had gone to such lengths to try and conceal the extent of her magic. His smirk broadened. "Challenge me?" he whispered. "Don't flatter yourself, green eyes."

He turned back to Krig without another word, only a mocking wink that had her bristling. Theron Kerr or any gang recruiter didn't compare – she'd never hated anyone so much in her life, and she'd never hated her own vulnerability so much either. Even with the hunting, she'd still always *had* her magic, even if it was limited. The Gossamer was awful, but temporary. This...this was permanent. "So, where were we?" Carmel asked Krig, with that charming shark-smile. Her leader stared back stonily, defiant against offering any information he sought, rhetorical or not.

Marco didn't appear to have been expecting a response, and if he did, he hid his expectations masterfully. "Well, I'd say it's been a pleasure playing with you, but it was only too easy. To whom should I send my condolences? It's just, there's a huge crowd out their waiting for an execution, and it seems such a shame to waste their time."

It was the second time in too short a duration that Susannah was watching Marco Carmel give a speech. He was standing on the execution platform, Jamie in the shadows behind him, only visible if one was intent to find him. Krig was standing next to the Demon Lord, his chin up to stare down the crowd, no fear on his face, just contempt for the Prince at his side. The rest of them were forced into the wings to observe, held still by guards and Gossamer. "Some of you may know Kriger Niall Carter," Carmel began, "you may be his family, his friends...or mere acquaintances." Susannah could see none of the resistance members in the crowd, or her parents or any recognisable face, but she could imagine the horrified shock they were struggling to suppress, the numbness that seeped through their blood as if they'd been submerged in liquid nitrogen, for those were her emotions too. She didn't know what to do, and dared not meet the gaze of anyone else, not even Delilah, in fear that she would lose it completely and shatter. He couldn't die. He just couldn't. "A good student, a worthy friend, on an external level at least. Internally, in his black heart, Kriger Carter is nothing more or less than a traitor." There was a sharp intake of breath from the public. "I have no tolerance for traitors." She saw Cassie shoving to the front of the crowd, screaming, followed by an older auburn haired woman who had to be the Carter Matriarch. "No – no please, please no," Cassie wailed. "Krig!"

She was pulled back, the sight awful to behold as someone quietened her so that Marco could continue talking, and he did, calmly, eyes moving across the Carter family for a moment. "About two years ago, Mr Carter began a resistance that has since then tripled in its membership." Susannah gritted her teeth, trying to ignore Cassie's silenced screams for her brother, Delilah's trembling and that enticing magic that curled around them all, as if searching them for their deepest secrets and fears. Tripled in size…that made the resistance sound a lot bigger and more threatening, and thus made the fact that Carmel had defeated them appear all the more greater too. Any other resistances out there would be cowering. The *bastard.* He certainly knew how to manipulate his audience. The thought tasted bitter on her tongue, like the bile she had to fight to swallow before it choked her. "This resistance say they are fighting for Freedom, but, my people, they would oppress our natures in pursuit of their Utopia. They fight for Equality, but believe they, above all others, have the right to trample our traditions and way of life for their own convenience and motive. They claim they are Justice, but discard the rules of our world for nothing, and stand against the law in impudent righteousness." Carmel paused, letting this sink in. "I will not stand to watch our world be polluted by his twisted ideal, his taint, his filth. Will you?"

Before Susannah could comprehend what was happening, Marco had shoved Krig into the midst of the Underworld before him. For a moment, she held her breath, praying nothing would happen...but it did. Krig disappeared beneath a fury of claws and teeth and wings.

And he didn't come out.

Carmel marched back towards them, but Susannah couldn't think enough to gather herself, her mind frozen on the spot. He didn't come out. The Underworld had just torn him apart...but maybe he was okay? He could still be okay, right? He could be alive, still, couldn't he? And oh Shadow, she was head of the Resistance now, wasn't she, if he didn't? No. No. She couldn't do it! Except, she didn't really have a choice...and she couldn't disappoint Krig in failing. She couldn't leave the resistance in this mess either, and she certainly could not yield to the dictator who swept passed them with dismissive orders to have them jailed - all of them. For the first time, Leola started forwards, tears welling in her eyes as a guard moved to restrain her.

"Wait," she called, desperately, her voice shaky. "You *promised*. We had a deal."

Jamie paused, and after a moment, Marco turned around again too, a glint in his gaze.

"Ah, yes," he murmured. "The rebels in exchange for your father's treatment, wasn't it?"

Susannah blinked, her insides twisting. Her father's treatment? *What?*

"You promised," Leola repeated again, imploring, breathless.

"Indeed I did," Carmel stated, with a thin smile. "Raphael," he began, and a dark-skinned, curly haired vampire stepped up from the vast entourage that had surrounded the

Underworld Prince in a flurry of official business and desire for attention. "Make sure Mr Bymalt gets the medicine he requires."

"Yes sir," Raphael said quickly, dipping his head and near vanishing with the speed he disappeared down the corridor. Both Carmels turned away in unison.

"Wait - what about me - your guards-" Leola began, helplessly, glancing over at them, wide-eyed, fearful, when she wasn't released. Her attention darted desperately back to the Demon Lord. Marco didn't bother turning around this time, seeming to be dismissive of all of them by now, and especially Leola. Susannah surveyed her stonily in response, not knowing the situation, but feeling it was too soon for even an attempt of explanation of forgiveness. She was numb. Her blood was awash with ice.

"What about you?" Marco drawled. "Your request was for your father, I don't believe any part of our deal involved *your* freedom."

Leola gaped, but before she could plead further, the Underworld Prince had vanished with only the echo of his orders left behind. The bureaucrats and representatives too, had disappeared with their lord. Jamie was nowhere in sight, and a knife twisted in Susannah's gut, exacerbating wounds that already cut too deep. They were shunted down stairs and into what seemed to be a like a prison waiting room, roughly, and then left alone. She would have claimed that to be arrogant, but she could feel the wards pressing down and smothering her on all sides, and the complete lack of unlocked magical reservoir inside her. Without magic, they had no chance, and Carmel knew it, he mocked it. Jamie mocked it. For a moment, they all stared at each other in silence.

"Well, that went well," Cade said, with a harsh sarcastic

edge to his voice that betrayed his turbulent emotions, his rage, and his fear. "Thanks Leola, we really owe you one." The blonde girl cringed away from them, looking every inch a cornered and wounded animal, the lines of her jaw hard in contrast to the soft sheen of vulnerability in her scrunching fingers. They picked at her jumper, at her skin, curling in on themselves to form glaring scarlet slits upon white skin.

"You would have done the same thing in my position," Leola spat. "Don't be so hypocritical. If Mica had been dying-"

"Mica might die now, actually, because of you!" Cade accused. "All of our families might. Do you think Carmel will spare them if they didn't know? No. He won't. You've damned us all!"

"I had no other choice-"

"There's always a choice," David snarled. "You could have chosen to talk to us, any of us, instead of betraying us. Krig is dead because of you!" Suddenly, the silence overwhelmed them, broken only by Leola's wretched sobs. Susannah had never heard a sound so awful before, the cries catching in the girls' throat like she was a hooked fish, hysterical, uncontrollable. Leon had not spoken, hunched in on himself, ashen and shaking. He was utterly still, dead looking. She hated it. She wanted him to sneer at her or make some jeering comment, anything that showed a bit of spark. She wanted Krig to be alive. She wanted to go home. She wanted...what did it matter what she wanted? It couldn't. Not now.

"Let's not fight among ourselves," Delilah said softly. "There's no point. It's not what he-it's not what K-Krig would have wanted."

"I'm sure Krig would have wanted his girlfriend to refrain from stabbing him in the back," Cade's lips were drawn back, in a sneer, his muscles bulging with the restraint it was apparently taking him to attack with nothing but words.

"I'm not going to apologise for my actions," Leola hissed, swiping at her eyes furiously. "And nor do I need to defend them to you, so you can stop acting so righteous. I was desperate! Dad was dying, don't tell me it wasn't the best thing to do. Besides, I don't see any of you bitching about Jamie, and he's a bloody Demon Lord!"

"So it's somewhat expected that he would be a total arsehole inside, isn't it?" Alice snapped. "You...I thought you were better than this."

"Sorry to disappoint, I'm not. I guess I'm just as human as the rest of you," Leola growled.

"Human? You have the heart of a-"

"Enough!" Delilah shrieked, nearly crying herself. "Will you stop fighting with each other - *please?* - it's not helping anyone." There was another silence; so loud that it could have been a million screams. Susannah couldn't help but be worried that Leon still hadn't said anything. Perhaps it was a trivial worry in the scheme of their current situation, but she grasped at it desperately, anything to fill her head and keep her away from her own thoughts. Nothing else was quite so poisonous, quite so critical and so condemning. Her own heart knew best how to self-destruct.

"What do we do?" Alice whispered. "What in Shadow's name do we do now?"

Susannah's magic thumped inside her, against the locks of Gossamer, against the prison which they would soon be seeing for possibly the rest of their lives. She couldn't stand the thought of it. Jamie's kiss seemed to burn blazingly hot against her skin.

"We're going to keep fighting," she stated, trying to bolster an authority into her voice, a confidence she didn't feel. Everyone's heads snapped to her, watching her intently.

"We're going to find a way out of this hell hole...and we're going to bring Carmel...both of them...down." She stared them all down, meeting each of their desperate gazes, jutting her chin out. "We're going to win."

"How do you know?" Leon questioned, sounding a shadow of his former self, a mere imitation of the arrogant boy he used to be. She tugged her lips into a smirk just for him, nailing it there with the last dregs of her endurance. "Because I won't give up until we do."

And then the Guards returned again.

Chapter Twenty Two - The Lord of the Manor

Susannah wasn't sure how long she'd been in the Anzarkledea cells; no time seemed to pass here, and no solace could be found. The place was lit by an eerie green glow, with one light for every single, tiny cell that seemed to turn on by motion. It snapped and followed her wherever she tried to move to get away from it, that glaring, sickly light that burned behind her eyelids, casting more shadows than they kept away. Each cell was miniscule and cramped - hers was no different. There was a wall at the back, which she leant against, a toilet cubicle, a rickety, threadbare bed and bars; bars on each side, separating her personal prison from the next. There were bars at the front, some cells even had chains. They'd all been split up, and she had no idea where the rest of resistance was, or what had happened to those of them that hadn't come onto the mission. Or her parents. What had happened to her parents? She thought it might have been a week since she'd seen them, but she wasn't sure. Time didn't seem to pass here. Life in the AC seemed to be a rigid, endless, *tedious* routine. Guards patrolled regularly, sneering at any inmates, particularly Overworld ones, as they went. They wore a uniform of a simple pair of black trousers, a black trench coat with a hood, sturdy hobnailed boots and black leather gloves. It was intimidating, and allowed for little actual skin contact with any of the prisoners (why would an Underworld variation want to touch a filthy inferior, possibly Overworld criminal?) and hid the face, so that when a prisoner was released back into society they couldn't hunt down those who imprisoned them. They were given meals twice a day, and that was how she assumed the passage of time - by taking every second meal and calling it breakfast. Every meal was a tough hunk of bread and a cup of water which left a metallic taste in her mouth for hours on end. She missed her freedom, missed it desperately, and spent most of her time worrying about the fates of everyone else. There wasn't anything to do in the cells but worry, really, to worry about how everyone else was, what was happening, and how memories of sunshine and clean air and silence were slowly slipping away from her. This place could drive you insane. There was nothing to do, aside from think or take part in the needling barbs that the different groups traded. She'd also tried desperately of a way of which to get the resistance out...and to avoid thinking about Krig and Jamie. She couldn't stand to think of either, the first with grief and helplessness and rage, the second with more rage, betrayal, humiliation and sorrow. In a way, both were dead to her now, weren't they?

She had several inmates around her, and none of them were particularly nice. Directly on the cell on her left from her was a pale, bespectacled woman called Jennifer Joby -or the 'White Phantom' as she preferred. She was well-built, with purple, clearly dyed hair back in thick braids, in the cells for burgling with a sentence of two years. Sentences were a big deal in the cells, or so it seemed, as well as how long you'd been there. Long-standing inmates had more prestige, though beings were always being shipped off too. On her right was Kiran, a scrawny, pinched looking werewolf who barely spoke a word except to occasionally make sneering comments. She wasn't even sure his name was Kiran - but she could have just been projecting her own paranoia, when asked, she'd claimed her name was Annabelle again. Maybe it was stupid, most people would have clung to their identity and the scraps of the world outside, but she found it more to her convenience to leave her former self and life behind. She didn't like the thought of being linked to this place, and somehow, acting and giving a false name helped make the situation feel blessedly more temporary. The noise was deafening; the prison an echo of wails and torment, screams and curses and *hatred* and *fear.* It was horrible. She couldn't quite find the words to describe it, the cacophony, the discordant swell of mutual loathing so intense and suffocating that conversation could scarcely be drawn from the chaos. Even when she shut her eyes and clamped her hands over her ears, she couldn't drown the noise out, the reminder that she was prison. Prison...was she a criminal? She didn't think so. Technically, she was rebelling against the Government, against society, but...she was a criminal in the eyes of a system that was in itself criminal and abhorrent. Who was the villain when both sides truly believed in the rightness of their stance? Her stomach churned.

The worst thing about the AC was the Gossamer. The air reeked of it, and her magic burned and spat and writhed inside her, thrashing for its freedom. She normally kept her magic quite restrained, but this was different altogether, and her vulnerability was only exacerbated by her complete lack of ability to call on her powers. In that way, she was terribly glad that the inmates were simply kept in their cages - that was essentially what each cell was - because at least it formed a metal barrier between her and the criminals of this place. She'd heard rumours, horror stories, that if prisoners were giving the guards too much trouble, they'd be plucked out and set to fight each other to death for entertainment, or just sent *elsewhere*. She shuddered, violently. It was extremely different flirting with the law, and being on the receiving end of a brutal justice system,

largely hidden from public scrutiny. She wondered if they were the youngest here, to be held for more than six months of Juvenile delinquency. In a way, she hoped so, because she wouldn't wish this hell of anyone. It was monotonous too, forcing a person to confront every facet of themselves that real-life pushed back in its flurry of activity. Susannah had come to be convinced that she did not like being left with just herself...fantasies stripped aside to leave naught but harsh reality. She didn't look up when she heard the heavy footfalls of the Guard patrol, their batons cracking against prison bars in an ominous beat.
The door to her prison clicked open.

She was hauled down the corridor, panic gnawing on her heart like a slavering Daemon over its prey. Were the rumours true? Was she going to have to fight someone? *Without magic?* She could scarcely breathe, her chest tight, the narrow corridors and walkways of the AC closing in on her, claustrophobic. Faces swam before her, none that she recognised, and once again she wondered over the fate of the rest of the resistance and her loved ones. She clenched her jaw. No. She wasn't going to show her fear, to any opponent they put in front of her...she wouldn't, couldn't, give them the satisfaction. She was tougher than this. She wouldn't let them break her. She would survive. She had to. She was shoved into a room, and it took her a moment to realise that the door slammed closed with no guards behind her. She caught her stumble, shaky on her feet, her magic straining painfully. The room was entirely nondescript, a clinical white...they weren't going to give her therapy or anything, were they? Corrective therapy? Her gut lurched. She wished she hadn't eaten her last meal, for it threatened to come back up again now. There was a single table in the centre of the room, two chairs...oh. She swore mentally. Her heart stopped. Her body locked in place, and if the door had been open for her to run and escape, she wasn't sure she could have unfrozen enough to manage the attempt. Carmel. *What was he doing here?*

He looked exactly the same as last time, with those liquid shadow eyes, dark hair, handsome ivory features that were too inhumanly perfect and similar to Jamie's in bone structure to offer even the comfort of a familiar face. How had she missed the family resemblance? It was striking. Jamie's eyes were differently coloured, his hair perhaps a little lighter, and he was younger...but other than that. Jamie looked more human, that was probably the crux of it. She really didn't want to think about Jamie. They stared at each other for a minute or so, before he arched his brows. "Are you going to stand there gormlessly, or take a seat?" he enquired. His voice didn't feel like it should be so smooth, so velvety, for one so piercing and dangerous. "I'm going to stand here gormlessly," she replied, purely out of defiance. His head tilted. "You don't seem very frightened of me," he stated, She regarded him flatly, with no answer to that and no desire to explain. What did being scared of him get her now? There was no point to it. "What do you want?" she asked, instead. "Don't you have a country to run, more of my friends to kill, autographs to sign...?" "I want you to join me," he said, after a while. Her stomach dropped. "What?" "Gormless *and* deaf apparently, perhaps I should rethink this offer," he returned dryly. Her eyes narrowed before she could help herself, her tone scathing.

"I heard what you said, and personally, I have to say I find your own intelligence suspect by the idiocy of your question! Why would I *ever* want to join you?"

"Because you'll waste away in prison your whole life if you don't," he replied. "And considering your age, that's a very long time to spend behind bars."

True, but ultimately irrelevant.

"I'm not a traitor," she said coldly.

"Everyone has a breaking point," he murmured idly. "And I'm certain I could find yours. It's so obvious I can't believe none of your gang recruiters ever tried it."

Susannah's shoulders stiffened.

"Everyone has a breaking point...does that include you?" she dared. His smirk broadened.

"You wouldn't find it, Susannah, and if you did, it would be of little use to you."

"I'm pretty sure I could find a way to use it," she said. He folded his arms, leaning back in his chair, saying nothing. Susannah couldn't help but be the tiniest bit insulted that he clearly didn't view her to be any sort of threat to himself. It was irrational, he was the Demon Lord, he was famed for his skills, but...she didn't know...she guessed she was used to a level of wariness from anyone who came across her, as arrogant as that sounded. The Gossamer was still in her system though, so there wasn't, if she wanted to be brutally honest with herself, admittedly that much to be threatened by. Without her magic, how could she possible have a chance against him? "Why do you even want me to join you?" she questioned, knowing guiltily that she should have just been walking out - but she'd rather be talking aimlessly with him then being in that prison. If she was out, she might as well remain out as long as possible without it compromising her loyalty to the resistance or anyone else. "Obviously, because I think you could be of some use to me," he stated immediately. "Next question, try not to make it a stupid one."

Susannah's jaw clenched.

"You mean that you'd be able to make use of my magic," she replied, "but you also said that your race gets stronger by devouring the magic of others, so why are you asking me to join you instead of simply adding my power to your own?"

"Now that's a more interesting and intelligent enquiry," he murmured, surveying her. "Well done." She squashed any sense of pride his praise instilled, before it could fully manifest. He was Marco Carmel, the most renowned, powerful and desired being in their world, but that didn't mean she should act star-struck. It was how he ensnared people so easily. "As for the answer, how much do you know about the nature of magic?"

She studied him warily.

"We have individual reservoirs of it, to varying degrees of power; it is uniquely tied to the being who controls it, though a person can also draw ambient magic from their surroundings. It's made to be used, and deteriorates if it is stagnant for too long."

Horror embedded inside her. Did that mean her magic would disappear under an extended period of Gossamer?

"So from that understanding, what would one be able to draw about the nature of your magic?" he probed, his gaze intent. She frowned slightly.

"My magic is like me, and tied to me...but under that presumption, you wouldn't be able to, er, eat anyone's magic."

"Your magic is uncommonly powerful, as I'm sure you are

aware of," he said, his head tilting. "And your personality, from what I've observed, is characterised by rebelliousness." Susannah felt a smile spread across her lips. "My magic would react badly to you," she realised. The sense of utter relief, and even self-assuredness vanished after a few seconds, to be replaced by suspicion. "Why are you telling me this?" He wouldn't give her information, or leverage of any sort, unless it benefited him, surely? There had to be a catch somewhere.

"Figure it out," he challenged. Annoyance began to bubble somewhere in her chest.

"This conversation would go quicker if you would just answer yourself," she told him.

"Perhaps," he stated, "but I don't encourage laziness, especially not in those who will in the future serve me."

"I have no intention of serving you. Ever," she snapped, furious at the assumption of his victory.

"Nonetheless, you will," he replied silkily. "Eventually. You might as well save yourself the dungeon time and do so immediately."

"Careful," she bit out, icily, "you're starting to sound desperate."

"If it helps you sleep at night," he returned idly. She turned away from him, for both a sign of indifference and to hide her expression from him. It was a dangerous move to make, but she found it satisfying anyway, for the implication that *he* wasn't a threat. He was, of course, but at this point looking at him and not looking at him wasn't going to make a difference. He had Underworld reflexes, faster than her eye could see.

"Tut tut, did no one teach you manners? You should learn to respect your superiors better. Come now, don't be a coward, face me."

"Why would I respect a tyrant?" she returned coldly.

"A tyrant," a delighted laugh issued from his lips, velvety music. It was a very Jamie-ish...no. She was doing it again: thinking about him. Damn it. "Is that what you think of me? How adorable, but, nonetheless, I dare say there are a lot of attributes one could admire and respect within a tyrant." She froze, feeling a hand resting on her shoulder with a fire and ice pressure, taunting, his lips by her ear. "You could admire their power, and the skill with which they gain and maintain it."

"By oppression," she spat, tightly. "There's nothing honorable or admirable in that."

"And yet, I'm more liberal than my parents. Most of my people love me as much as they fear me."

"Most people find you attractive, that's not *love.*"

"And you don't?" he questioned, a smirk in his voice. "My looks are an evolutionary trait, Susannah, don't be jealous."

"Jealous-!"

"-And my features are, indeed, admired. Nonetheless, a less aesthetically influenced being could also respect my intelligence, if power doesn't sway them or you under your standards of its normalcy," Marco continued, ignoring her. He circled her, the fluid movement pinning her to the spot. "Or my talent."

"Or your modesty?" she enquired sweetly. "You seem to have so much of that."

"I am confident of my skills," he replied simply. "The point is, that there is very much one could find to respect in a tyrant, depending upon the tyrant in question. There's a reason I'm in control, and you, little girl, are not."

Little girl? He was only three years older than her! The hypocrite. She studied him warily, wishing she could reach out and throttle him, but knowing it would only serve to entertain him.

"I'm not sure whether to be flattered by your eagerness to stress your virtues to me or not," she replied, locking gazes with him as he stood before her, too close. "It makes you come across as rather needy."

Obsidian eyes flashed, before he smiled darkly.

"I go through periods of obsessiveness, and my little brother has told me so much about you, forgive me for indulging in my curiosity."

Her fingers clenched into fists.

"Jamie talked about me?" she asked, trying to sound disinterested, not allowing the flush to grow on her cheeks. Had he told the Demon Lord about how he had played her? How he had *kissed* her? She wanted to hide in absolute mortification if he had.

"You find *him* handsome, don't you?" Carmel smirked. She glared at him. He laughed again, crueler this time, practically gliding away from her once more. She hated him. She really hated him. What had Jamie said to him that piqued his interest so that he would come here himself, and ask for her to join his forces?

"But, alas," he sighed with a mocking mournfulness. "I do not have the time for play without my work, as fun as this is. Would you like to hear the terms of our agreement?"

"We don't have an agreement," she said, turning to keep him in her line of vision. He simply smirked at her again, convinced of his victory.

"Join me, with an oath of your loyalty, and I will guarantee your immediate freedom, and ensure that your family remains unharmed — provided they do not attempt sabotage against me or my regime."

She swallowed. She hadn't expected that last part about her family, and yet, she would have dismissed him outright without it.

"Where are they now?" she asked, softly, not sure he would answer her. He glanced at her, his expression unreadable.

"Under watch," he replied. "They're plotting a similar stunt as your resistance did, to free you. Pray that they do not attempt to follow through."

Susannah's eyes widened, before she could help herself, nervous warmth growing in her chest. Then she tilted her head back, with the conclusion that she couldn't necessarily believe anything he said as fully true. He was a Demon Lord, he couldn't directly lie after his turning – no Demon Lord or Lady could, but that didn't mean he wasn't a master of omission and words games twisted upon his silver tongue. His ulterior motive was to get her to join him, to agree, but she wasn't stupid enough to think he would only have one motive. He didn't seem to be that simple. Why hadn't he arrested them already? She'd have asked him, but was certain that his answer would hardly reveal anything she could use, and would instead only highlight her own ignorance. It was better to stay quiet on that matter.

He still had it as leverage though; he could threaten to have them taken in. On any other family, she dare say that tactic would have worked. Her parents, and herself, had all been in a resistance though. She'd practically been raised on a diet of defiance, with the need to win no matter what (more or less.)

"And the resistance?" she asked, out of curiosity more than anything else. His eyebrows arched.

"What about your resistance?"

"Where do they factor into these terms, would you let them go?"

"Don't be ridiculous."

"Then we don't have a deal."

He stared at her, before leaning forwards, appearing even more intrigued than before.

"You're very attached to them, aren't you? And the late Mr Carter himself, I believe, recruited you." She surveyed him, keeping her expression as closed as she could, the weight of his intense scrutiny flattening across her face. "Not that he was the first to try. You've rejected many a gang recruiter over the years."

"I'm good at refusing people's prisons," she replied, her head raised.

"And yet, you seem to be rather effectively caught in mine, but then, I'm the best recruiter you'll ever come across."

"And the modesty strikes again," she muttered, before raising her voice. "Let my resistance go free and don't arrest them or their families again, with the same terms as you have offered for the safety of my family, and I'll join you." She paused, steeling herself, aware that any deal or words exchanged between them could never be taken back. "With an oath of absolute loyalty."

He stared at her in silence, mouth twisted in something like a smile, predatory, eyes glittering.

"You have neither the standing nor the leverage to make demands of me, Skelsby."

"Then, if you're not interested, I'd like to return to my cell. The food is disgusting by the way," she added, in goading carelessness.

"You can return, if you wish," he shrugged, his gaze still fixed upon her. "It makes little difference to me. Ultimately, you're at my beck and call for the rest of your *imprisoned* life. Think about it. You'll change your mind; the cells are very good at doing that to people."

Susannah defiantly vowed to not even think about Marco

Carmel, but, despite her best intentions, she found his words circling her head anyway. She blamed it on the lack of distractions being in prison afforded a person. The Guards escorted her back, tossing her roughly into the cells. She could feel Jenni and Kiran staring at her, but the weight of their gazes held nothing against the Demon Lord's scrutiny. Those black eyes felt like they could sear right through to her soul, it was really unnerving.

"What was that about?" Jenni demanded, leaning in close to the bars separating them. "You a scummy double D or summin?"

"No," Susannah snapped. "Never."

She hoped. She wouldn't. She would never betray her resistance, her friends, her family – and the only reason she would ever work for Carmel was if their safety and freedom was ensured. She highly doubted he would accept her offer, as he had said, she had no leverage or standing...except his apparent desire for her allegiance. Her power over him correlated directly to how eager he was to have her on side, and his own advantages far outweighed her own as he had far more incentives to offer her. Like freedom, or the safety of her friends and family. Except, Marco underestimated the fact that her parents had always preached loyalty to a cause, if you joined it, no matter what.

"Then what was it about?" Kiran questioned quietly. "You haven't fought, your magic is still shackled and you have no physical wounds to indicate battle."

"I *could* tell you...but it's none of your business."

"Oh come on Anna," Jenni rolled her eyes, a dangerous glint starting to grow in her gaze. "Tell us, yeah? We're mates, right? We could make things very difficult for ya round here, 'specially if you're a Double D."

"I'm not a Double D," Susannah repeated irritably. Was she?

A Double D was someone who made deals...wasn't that was she was just doing? She sighed.

"Well, who were ya talking to then? Redgraive? Cobre? Press?"

"Carmel," she replied, just to shut them up. They stared at her for a moment, before Jenni burst out laughing, clutching her sides with mirth.

"Yeah, sure you did, honey, sure you did. Who'd ya really talk to? One of the guards take a liking to you or something?"

Susannah grimaced, in complete horror and disgust. Kiran was studying her intently, more verbose than she'd ever seen him.

"You actually *did* talk to Demon Lord..." he murmured.

Jenni's laughter came to an abrupt halt.

"There is no way she did! The Prince never comes to the cells himself, and certainly never lowers himself to talk with one of the prisoners."

"Indeed, he doesn't normally," Kiran stated, eyeing her.

"What did you say your name was, girl – Annabelle? Annabelle who?"

"Private."

"Annabelle Private," Jenni's lips pursed. "Nope, I'm getting nothing...you famous or summin?"

Kiran rolled his eyes.

"Private, Joby, *private,* she's not telling us her name you moronic comm."

"I aint no moron, sweetcheeks," Jenni immediately flared up. "I robbed the Carmel Head Gardener and made 'im think he was crazy, that takes brains, that does. Not your run of the mill thug crime, is it? I ain't a comm."

"Common, cheap and nasty," Kiran muttered.

"Well, what are you here for then? Being a sour puss in

civilized society?"

"Resistance, actually."

Susannah's jaw nearly dropped.

"You're in a resistance?" she demanded, her interest caught. He glanced at her, tersely.

"As are you, 'Annabelle,'" he sneered. "Though I don't know what type of half-arse club takes kids like you, or what you've done if Carmel wants to talk to you...you a murderer?"

Jenni looked disturbed.

"Anna can't be a murderer, she's too nice, she's just a kid, aint she?" the Comm surveyed her suspiciously, as if suddenly uncertain. "Besides, if it's some leech or Dark pigeon, I'm reckoning they deserved it!"

"I'm not a murderer," Susannah said tightly. They simply studied her for a moment.

"Then how come he's interested in you?" Kiran questioned distrustfully.

Susannah had the bizarre thought that if the Gossamer wasn't in place, they probably wouldn't be asking. She'd many times wondered what it would be like to not have magic as potent as hers, but now she was experiencing the sensation, it was somewhat disconcerting. Most people just assumed things about her because of it, she wasn't used to having to explain...and she wasn't going to explain to them. "I have no idea," she replied. Jenni scowled.

"Well, that's helpful, ain't it?"

"None at all?" Kiran questioned, appraising her, his pupils luminescent moons in the darkness. She wondered, absently, what happened when he changed into a wolf. His cell was one of those that had chains in, so she could probably guess. She wasn't looking forward to having her theories confirmed though. A transformed werewolf could be vicious at the best of times, and a caged beast was no doubt even worse.

"What resistance were you in?" she asked, suddenly. "The werewolf rebellion?"

His lips thinned, and she became certain he wasn't going to answer.

"Yes," he replied, finally, his tone clipped. "And yourself?"

"None that you'd know of," she said, honestly.

"Are you their leader or something? Is that why he's interested?" Jenni asked. Susannah remembered, with a start and a pang of crippling grief, that she *was* a resistance leader, though the point was currently moot. Another guard was circling down the aisle towards them, on patrol.

"I already said I don't know why he's interested," she replied.

"So you *are* a resistance leader!" Jenni declared, triumphantly. "You never said you weren't, that means you are."

Kiran rolled his eyes.

"Whether she is or isn't doesn't matter, Joby," he sneered. "If she is, she'll be dead soon, and if she's not, well, that's hardly something Carmel would be interested in either way. No, there has to be something else – something you're not telling us," Kiran insisted, glaring at her. "What is it?"

"It's because she's powerful," the Guard said, having come to a stop in between their cells, face cloaked in shadow by the uniform's hood. Susannah's heart stuttered to an abrupt halt, her mouth dry. "Probably one of the most powerful people you'll ever meet," the guard continued, "and, somehow completely hopeless and lacking practical escape instincts despite that. You should have picked the TA. Hello Susannah."

She would have recognised his voice anywhere.

Chapter Twenty Three – Fight and Flight

"Jamie?" Susannah asked, confused, wary, not even sure what she was feeling. Her stomach churned; her heart pounded. The prison door slid open at his touch – the Carmel touch - and he gestured for her to come forwards. She hesitated, before doing so. "What are you doing here?" she hissed. Was he here on Marco's behalf?

Jamie didn't reply, tightly grabbing hold of her arm, towing her down the corridor at a relentless pace; ruthlessly ignoring her struggle to pull back. The other inmates stared when they passed. A few walkways away Jamie paused, glaring at her with those far too familiar eyes.

"Calm down," he ordered, meeting her gaze. "I'm not going to hurt you – believe it or not, I'm saving your life."

She stared at him, shocked. *What?*

"What about everyone else – Delilah? David?" she began, numbly. His jaw clenched.

"Regrettably, we don't have time for a tour."

She tugged away from his hold, furiously, trying to stand her ground as firmly as she could.

"I'm not leaving without them," she stated. His eyes narrowed.

"Yes, you *are,*" he growled. "I won't be able to pull this stunt again, if you don't leave now, there's a strong chance you won't leave at all."

"How can you just leave them?" she demanded. "They were your friends!"

"Susannah-" he started, dangerously, sounding frustrated. She folded her arms, jutting her chin out stubbornly. He tugged a hand agitatedly through his hair. "You're so stupid," he muttered. "Let's just go, *please.*"

"Is loyalty stupid?" she questioned coldly.

"It is when you're going to get killed for it!" he snapped. "Tell me, is such blind devotion an Overworld trait, or just one common to annoying rebels?"

"If I'm an annoying rebel, why are you *helping* me then?" she asked angrily. "Why did you ki-" Susannah stopped, biting her lip. Jamie's expression was hard, but, remarkably, his eyes softened slightly after a moment.

"Do you know where they are? We have half an hour at the most before someone notices my absence and yours."

"Somewhere in the cells, from what I've gathered, they're in the green or purple areas." Chevy's or Lutes. His eyes flashed, his head tilting, considering.

"Most of them will be purple, maybe a couple of green," he murmured, seizing hold of her arm again, dragging her with him.

"I can walk," Susannah muttered. He shot her a sharp glance.

"You look more like a prisoner like this," was all he said. "Especially from a distance."

That made sense.

"Oh, and your magic's coming back," he added. "So try and suppress it, by all rights, if you were a prisoner, I should have you under more Gossamer."

With an excruciating slowness – at least it appeared so with the silent tick of the countdown clock and increasingly small possibility of escape as time wore on – they tracked down the other members of the resistance. She'd never appreciated quite how huge the Anzarkledea Cells were: they were like a whole separate floor of the manor, and its grounds, on their own. A prison hidden in the earth; like hell. She'd never be able to walk across the ground above in the same way again. Jamie gripped her forearm tightly, and in another scenario she would be pushing away anyone who tried that, but...he was strong. He wasn't...Underworld strong, she didn't think, she assumed he hadn't undergone his full inheritance, but he was still stronger than the average human. She winced slightly at his grip, but made no protest. It was...awkward enough between them already, without the whole 'knight in shining armour' thing, and damn it, she wasn't supposed to be some faint hearted maiden that needed rescuing anyway! Urgh. Her skin tingled under his touch. It was still hard to reconcile Jamie with everything she'd ever heard about the younger Carmel brother.

"How did you even get down here?" she whispered.

"I had some help, Kitty's creating a distraction with Marco," he replied, a worried tint to his eyes. Susannah blinked.

"Kitty as in Katerina Redgraive? As in, Kitty the Dark Angel who knew Emiah? You know her?"

"I've met her at a few functions. She came and found me immediately after Krig's...after his death." She noted he didn't say 'execution.'

"...and she's distracted Marco?"

"Yes," Jamie didn't elaborate, eyes scouring the cells distractedly, before cutting into her. "I heard you two met again." She couldn't read his expression, or his tone.

"Yes," she replied tersely. "Charming fellow, your brother."

"I've been told," he murmured.

"You...you said, once, that you got on with your brother, that he practically raised you." She was furious with him, embarrassed with herself, but so very, very curious. His jaw tightened fractionally.

"Is this going to fuel Overworld gossip?" he questioned. She narrowed her eyes.

"No, actually," she replied coldly. "Forgive me for showing

an interest…oh, but I forget, you watch your words so carefully that all that comes out is lies. I thought your kind couldn't lie anyway?"

"I haven't come into my full inheritance yet," he said, equally cool. "And of course I watch my words carefully, I'm a Carmel."

"Right yeah, probably joined to betray us - Leola help you out? I always thought you two were quite *close-*"

"-Seriously, you want to do this now?" he hissed, grip tightening on her arm, pulling her flush against his chest as they ducked out of sight of a guard patrol. He studied her, flatly. "Yes, I joined the resistance with the sole purpose of destroying you. That's *my job.* You're not the first rebellion I've destroyed. Get over it and look at it from my side. Besides, I'm helping you escape now - illegally - I might add."

"Why?" Susannah couldn't help but question, challengingly. "This is punishable by death…you could be accused of breaking the first act of the Declarations. "No Underworld Variation and Overworld Variation shall ever possess feelings of-"

"Shut up, Susannah," he ordered tightly. "Don't you even dare quote them at me; I was raised and practically fed on a diet of this world's rules before you could even walk, so just – just shut up, alright? I know what they say!"

"Then why did you do this?" she asked, more softly now, as they sped through the corridors in search for the rest of the resistance. Jamie was like a coiled up spring, a volcano about to erupt from brewing tension at any given moment.

"I don't know," he said, darkly. "But your incessant questioning is making me regret the decision…"

Susannah fell silent.

It went surprisingly smoothly, with only a few mishaps to speak of – and even with her limited magic, those were easy enough to deal with. Jamie also proved to be rather ruthless at combat, he was clearly extremely well-trained. If the situation wasn't so dire, she would have considered it interesting to duel him. As it was, she just felt exhausted and desperate, dragged down by everything that had happened and the weight of everything that hadn't sunk in yet, or was still to come. They managed to gather up all the resistance, but their time was now extremely strained. There had been varying reactions to Jamie; some, like David, had to be restrained from punching the younger Carmel brother in the face, whilst others, like Delilah, had simply expressed their gratitude for the aid and continued as if the whole scenario wasn't completely messed up. Actually, that had only been Delilah really – though others had expressed gratitude, like Cade, it was marginally stiff and lacking in warmth. Sincere, but cool. Jamie had been remote in response, more concerned with getting the whole thing over and done with as quickly as possible...not that she couldn't understand that desire.

It became harder and harder the closer they got to success, due to the larger gathering and thus greater commotion. An escorted prisoner was highly unlikely, and too many cells that should have held those prisoners were empty. The pattern of who was missing was also clear to anyone with a brain, which was why they were all now sprinting and fighting their way out the manor.

With Jamie's aid and command of Anzarkledea, exiting was actually plausible, however, though he'd informed them in a stressed tone of voice that the second Marco got involved his own jurisdiction and control of the house ended. Apparently, as the actual Underworld Prince, Marco had veto over the mansion, and its surrounding areas.

Delilah had ended up using Mind Arts again after all, to stop the Guards from causing more of a disturbance or alerting anyone to the impeding escape. She'd since gone absolutely silent and deathly pale with the barest green tinge to reflect her apparent self-loathing at having done so. Jamie had far less qualms about using Mind Arts, and was, as a consequence, far more effective in his usage of the magic as his compulsions didn't shake with doubt. He was in total, iron, control. He'd also conjured and slipped a mask over his face, edgily, under the Guard hood.

They finally found their way to the grounds, a disquieting trail of incapacitated beings at their wake, silenced in their efforts to raise the alarm, defeated in intentions of preventing them from leaving. It was there that it all went wrong.

Once again, alarm bells began to scream.

Jamie's eyes widened with horror, and he shoved them all forwards, favouring her with a 'told you so' expression. Despite all they'd done to try and buy time for the time they'd spent gathering everyone else, time had ran out on them.

"They know, the hit team will be out here within the minute – go – GO!" he ordered.

"How-" she began, before pausing. Of course. "The Flights."

"The Flights," he agreed quickly. She nodded at him, sending him a smile.

"Jamie-" she began, helplessly all of a sudden in the face of his departure, and the realisation that there was a high chance she might not see him again after everything he'd done to help them. At that very moment, the fact he was an Underworld and a damn Carmel didn't even matter.

"I need to go," he said, already turning around. "I'll try and-" all of a sudden, Jamie stopped, blank neutrality sliding and locking upon his features. Susannah whipped around to where his gaze rested. Marco. Her mouth ran dry as he approached them, something rather predatory in his smooth gait. She glanced at the rest of her resistance, thinking furiously. Flights. Yes, that had been the plan. Flights. She traded a look with Delilah, receiving a nod of understanding in return, before silently summoning her own.

Sky Cat, I need you.

"Make sure everyone gets out," she instructed quietly. Delilah opened her mouth to protest, and then quelled it under her fierce stare. This wasn't negotiable. Krig had made her leader, so, for now, it was her priority to lead and make sure everyone else got out safely. David nodded, determinedly, overhearing the exchange and then there was no more chance to talk as the Underworld Prince was almost upon them, so close, power crackling like thunder. She could see the specks of the Flights, Sky Cat, Bluebird (and others too?) growing on the horizon, dark and vibrant flecks against a bloody sky. She turned to face the Demon Lord, resolute, drawing her magic in anticipation. Her heart was thrashing against her ribcage, adrenaline streaming through her veins like icy fire. She had never been so thankful that the Gosammer had worn off, even though she still felt utterly sick. It seemed, after the first time, her magic was getting more used to recuperating from this threat too.

"Jamiesius," Marco greeted, with an air of soft menace. Susannah felt her mind jar at the odd name, and noted Jamie flinch at it too.

"Mar-"

"I'll deal with you later, little brother. Go to your room now, and don't stray from your destination if you know what's good for you."

Jamie shot them all a look, unreadable, violet eyes blazing with emotions, and, for one wild second Susannah thought he might stay, but then he dipped his head towards the elder Carmel, heading back towards the manor. Under the terrible threat, not so much in the Demon Lord's words, but in his stance, she wasn't entirely certain she could blame him.

"Hello again," she greeted with a false cheeriness.

"Susannah," Marco murmured, favouring her with a somewhat wolf like smile. She dared not flick her gaze to the oncoming Flights, fearing the consequences of removing her attention from him – even for an instant. "You are indeed good at rejecting people's prisons."

"It's a talent," she shrugged, innocently.

If she could only keep him talking, then maybe the others could get away, if she could just distract him somehow. He merely gave a thoughtful sort of hum, in response, and then, without any indication or pre-warning, his magic was bulleting towards her, fierce and strong. She leapt out the way on instinct, drawing her own power out, firing back. He shielded, deflecting her spell back at her, and she dissipated it immediately, turning the ground around him to ice, thanking her elemental studies teacher profusely in her head. He used the sudden slipperiness and skid to glide closer and faster, a harder target by human standards, but it impeded his ability to use his Underworld speed to defeat her outright, limiting him to magic until he reverted the floor back to normal. The ground beneath her own feet split in response, forming great chasms to remove her ability to dodge. Susannah's heart hammered in her chest, her mind almost spinning with adrenaline. Without even considering it, not really having a choice if she wanted to have any hope of success — she unleashed her magic. All of it. It screamed in her ears, and she saw his posture immediately change, a frightening grin tearing at the edges of his elegant façade.

Drawing back from offensive, Susannah focussed on smoothing the earth again, before blasting raw power at him in a hope of gaining some breathing space. It was terrifying. She could easily see why the name Marco Carmel struck such fear into his opponents, despite his relative youth — he was brilliant. She was searching frantically for weaknesses in his seemingly flawless duelling skills, but could find none. She needed to find a way to unsettle him, and pushed back harder, hoping to force him away from the offensive. He had a very offensive style, much like her, not naturally relying on defence and instead attempting to reject the need for such a thing by not giving opponents the space to form an offensive they would need to defend from. Even when they did use defence, they both, she noticed, tending to favour deflected shields, which turned the defence into an offense. She really didn't want to look into the psychology of that. She dodged out the way, sending back a volley, shuddering as their magic clashed and entangled in a battle for dominance. She'd never felt so scared, or so exhilarated. She'd never had to fight this hard before to keep up, everything else seemed to pale in comparison to his intensity. He was just as powerful as her, maybe even more so, she didn't know. All of her natural advantages or brute strength was stripped from her, leaving her to rely on instincts, technique and duelling talent alone. To an outsider, the whole attack may have appeared choreographed as they danced around each other, slipping beneath attacks and lashing out with their own. He'd stopped trying to remove the ice beneath his feet, for she only returned it the second he did. The area itself had become her battlefield. She'd lost track of everyone else, consumed by the effort it was taking her, lost in the fight and the blistering sensation of their magic.

This time, she wasn't sure if she cared about Viridian's cautions that her magic was lethal and more that of a war veteran – it worked in her favour. Her mind raced as she toed the edge of death. If any of their spells had actually hit and made impact as they were supposed to, she honestly would not have known what would happen. Her blood was roaring with determination for victory; she couldn't lose against him, she just couldn't, the stakes were far too high and her pride was rejecting the concession. Her body ached, but her magic sung, delighted in its utter lack of constraint. She had to use everything in her arsenal. Some part of her wished fervently that it was the same for him, a challenge, and that he wasn't merely toying with her in sadistic mind games. Every second the power between them was building, and she wasn't sure how much longer it could do continue doing so, reaching a crescendo, until something either had to give way and splinter, or explode. They twirled around each other, completely focussed, the very air seeming charged as they switched magic arts and tactics nearly constantly. She could win...could she win? It was too early to tell, but there was a possibility – and a hand caught her wrist – Delilah.

She nearly freaked out to have her friend there, and Marco's target immediately switched onto the blonde girl, to which Susannah desperately had to try and adjust her style. It was like the bubble of solitude between them had burst, and now chaos reigned. His eyes burned black.

"We need to go!" Delilah hissed, tugging her away, and Susannah wasn't entirely sure she would have had the presence of mind to leave right now if her best friend wasn't dragging her. "The Flights are here, come on...and don't sodding well say that we should go ahead and leave you, we've lost Krig already! Come on!"

Susannah shot the Underworld Prince one last glance, calling up everything she had left, hoping it was enough, and blasting it in his direction, but not at him, picturing the effect she wanted, knowing her magic would comply - trusting it explicitly.

As the explosion happened, they sprinted in the opposite direction, Susannah onto the front of Sky Cat where David immediately moved aside to let her steer her flight – they were so personal and tuned to the maker, it probably would have been immensely difficult for him to control it – while Delilah leapt onto Bluebird. There was also a dragon (Jamie had lent them his flight!?) which Cade was steering and a Dog, whose owner she didn't have a clue about. Did one of the other members have a Flight?

She didn't have another moment to think of it, as the Demon Lord's magic soared towards them, ensnaring, ready to tear them to pieces, and she didn't dare look behind her.

The next second, they were flying, the wind tearing against her skin as much as her magic was.

Free.

Interlude – Jamie

Jamie stared out the window of his study, into the thick sheets of rain that broke and splintered the sky. He'd seen Susannah, Delilah's, Kitty's and his own Flight soaring into the sky, and knew Marco would arrive in his quarters before the minute was out. He was still trying to wrap his head around everything that had happened...and Krig. Kriger Carter was dead. It shouldn't have bothered him in the slightest, but it did. It did, and that disturbed him. It was wrong, unnatural – illegal. It was never supposed to happen this way. He'd been told to infiltrate the resistance, and had done so successfully, as always. It should have been perfect, a clean job and cut, especially with Leola acting as a traitor too. It was easy; it was supposed to be easy! The Overworld were supposed to be pathetic, *human*, utterly inferior to him in every single possible way. That's what he'd always been taught and told. The Overworld were there for food and amusement, and for them to expect anything else was ungrateful. It had all been a lie; they'd fallen for a fabricated 'Jamie Cutta.' They'd never really been friends. It would have been entirely different if he approached them as Jamie Carmel. Yet...

He hadn't gotten attached. That was impossible, illegal. The thought revolted him, but he feared it may have been true even more. Especially near the end. Krig's expression when his true identity had been revealed was so...open, accepting, *pitying*, not full of hate at all. It was as if he somehow knew how much the whole thing was tearing him up inside, pitifully. Polo, he swore, this was pathetic. This shouldn't have been a problem. His work wasn't supposed to be infected by sentiment. The memories raced through his head nonetheless, sickeningly. Just for a few seconds, as his time with the resistance closed to an end, he'd almost believed in their cause...believed in them. For just an instant, he'd wanted to be Jamie Cutta. Ridiculous.

He felt the furious magic before he looked around, and the next second his brother was next to him, expression hard.

"Explain yourself," Marco ordered; his tone dangerously soft. He'd thought about this too.

"You said they were my mission," he began, hoping this would sound convincing – he could never admit to treacherous feelings of...sentiment, he could barely comprehend them himself right now. It went against everything he'd ever learned.

"Yes, and you fulfilled your part of the mission, little brother," the Demon Lord said tightly. "So I honestly don't know what you were thinking with this *stunt.*"

"She's famous now," he interrupted, quietly, heart pounding.

"And liable to turn to our side if you'd given me a bit more time to work on Miss Skelsby...I presume she's the one you're talking about? Honestly, if you were that *charmed* by her aesthetics, you could have kept her then!"

He shot Marco a dark look, before he could stop himself. "Not what I was talking about," he hissed. "Just let me finish, alright? She'll be resistance-famous for this escape; all the other resistance groups are going to flock to her...like Starlight? She's the perfect bait now."

"That would only require freeing her, why the others?" Marco demanded harshly,

"What, you think they're a threat? Besides, she refused to leave them," Jamie said defensively. He turned to face his brother finally, making sure his expression was smooth, professional, everything else wiped away. Marco appeared absolutely livid, his posture ramrod straight and contained as he sought for self-control against a violent and deadly rage. His magic swirled around him, curling around Jamie too, like the flat edge of a blade – capable of flipping and inflicting damage at any given movement. He stood up from where he was sitting, putting them on a more even height level, though he was still shorter, placing a hand on Marco's arm. "Believe it or not, I did do this for you," he said. "I haven't turned traitor, if that's what you're thinking. She's just…useful, convenient. Besides, you find her fun to play with too. I know you do."

He stopped at the warning look the Underworld Prince gave him, grimacing.

"Regardless of the potential benefits of this situation," Marco said coldly. "You still went behind my back, Jamie. You went out of your way to deceive and lie to *me,* your own brother! Why did you hide this from me?"

"…I didn't think you'd agree with me."

"And yet you did it anyway."

"Sorry," Jamie murmured. "It won't happen again?"

"It better not," his brother warned, almost gently now. "I'd hate to think there was a more…emotional reason behind your actions." Jamie barely caught himself from stiffening, meeting Marco's intent scrutiny evenly enough. His brother knew him too well; sometimes. He could read him too well.

Marco knew there was more to this story; of course he did, he just didn't want to or dare to look due to the necessary consequences. If his brother truly believed Jamie's actions broke the Declarations, by the laws that upheld their world, he was to be executed instantly and without question.

Except he hadn't broken the Declarations. This was logical, this was all about logic, and nothing so foolish or forbidden as love or affection.

"Don't be absurd," he replied, "of course there isn't. That would be illegal, and, really, the *Overworld?* I'm a Carmel; we have better taste than *that.* The Declarations are absolute."

"Make sure it stays that way, Jay," Marco cautioned softly, eyeing him for a moment longer, before turning away once more. "I'll have someone send dinner up; I won't be joining you today, sorry. It seems I suddenly have rather a large amount of extra work to do."

Jamie felt a pang of guilt twisting his insides, and grimaced. "I'll help you with the paperwork..." he hesitated for a moment, careful to keep his tone neutral as he continued. "You're not going to be sending the hit team after them, then? You'll let me handle this? It's my mission?"

"For now."

The door slammed shut behind him.

Jamie winced.

Epilogue

The first week passed in a flurry of fear and paranoia, of packed bags and plans of escape. Susannah spent every second expecting Carmel's hit team at her door, but the only change that had occurred since their escape was that the border patrols around the city had been significantly strengthened. No one could leave. They were trapped in the city. But no one came for her or any of them. She didn't understand it; it made no sense, and only unnerved her more because of it. Carmel – Marco – had no reason to just give up. Yet, for some inexplicable reason, it almost appeared as if he had. Except, he hadn't...that would be completely illogical. Moreover, just sometimes, she could feel herself being watched, and her mum and dad had reported the same sensations at their work places. It wasn't mere paranoia on her behalf; they were under some form of surveillance. Her parents had been overjoyed and more than little shocked to see her back. Her dad had bashed his head against the bathroom cupboard apparently because he was so startled to hear her voice again. They'd taken and reacted to it surprisingly well though – no fainting, barely any crying, just a crushing hug and an immediate brainstorm of next moves, tactics and plans for survival. They, too, had been suspicious of the strange circumstances. The hit team weren't at their door, which frankly, just seemed ominous. It suggested the Demon Lord's plans had changed, and highlighted her ignorance over his actions and why he was behaving in this way. Maybe it was because capturing them would mean admitting they had escaped in the first place? She didn't know.

The cells still haunted her sleep; she couldn't purge her mind of the yells in her ears, or that sickly green light, however hard she tried. It permeated her waking hours too, dogging her footsteps with the threat of return, causing bile to claw up her throat at the thought.

Why was no one coming? They couldn't leave, they were sitting ducks. Maybe that was the point. He didn't have to round them up; he had such a close eye on them all that anything they did was forfeit for return. She hadn't seen the resistance members since either.

The resistance…she was in charge of the resistance. If there was to be a meeting, apparently she would now be the one to organise it. She didn't even have a clue where to begin, or even if she had any right to be leading it. Her parents were rather more supportive of the idea now, paradoxically – though she thought that may have been because everything had already gone pear-shaped, so continued resistance didn't actually make much difference anymore. Fifteen years of hiding and cover: blown. There was no point hiding her magic from the Carmels now, they were both fully aware of her existence. Her heart squeezed.

She wanted Krig back. Krig would have known what to do about this whole situation, about everything. His funeral was later today, though there wasn't actually a body to bury. A shudder crawled up her spine. Even if it was maybe stupid to attend when the funeral was so obviously going to be a hot spot for rebellion and Carmel's guards to observe them, or if she wasn't welcome there, she would go anyway. She had to. It felt too disrespectful not to. She left a note to her parents, even more protective since her return, to explain where she'd gone.

They were all there – all of the resistance, despite no plans made to meet. They stood some way away from the actual 'service' due to the glares and filthy looks tossed their way by Henry Carter, Krig's father. Krig's mother and Cassie just stood frozen, with their heads bowed, over the empty, burning casket. It wasn't even a proper funeral, those weren't granted to 'traitors of the state.' No words were spoken, there was no one to speak them, and Krig's parents didn't seem to be in the mood to address a congregation of fellow rebels. So they stood some way away, quiet, the wind racing through their ears and their hair, tears forming on white, hard faces. In the distance, she could see the Underworld, watching the proceedings closely too. It made Susannah's insides clench with hot fury. Was even a funeral not untouchable anymore? Delilah stood next to her, unspeaking, though her hand found Susannah's and squeezed, reassuringly. Susannah herself stood stoically, only her gaze and magic blazing. She felt utterly numb all over, as if all grief had been scrubbed ferociously out her, leaving her skin and soul raw and achy, with only the smallest blisters of sorrow, pain or anger. She still couldn't believe he was gone, and her fists clenched as Cassie began to wail all over again. The coffin slowly burnt to cinders and ash, and grief grew more muffled along with it, as if that was fading too, or at least silenced. Susannah couldn't see how the grief would ever fade. It had all been too sudden, too abrupt; she couldn't wrap her head around the fact that he was truly gone. She kept expecting to see him miraculously saunter up them to explain his amazing escape and then to fill them in on what happened next.

Except...that was her job now, wasn't it? What came next? Maybe it was time to call another meeting.

Calling a meeting turned out to be far easier than she'd anticipated, at least this time around. They all simply approached her after the funeral, regarding her expectantly. She had to swallow down her nerves, keeping her features composed. Right now, they needed a strong leader, not a lost girl.

"He made you leader," Cade stated. "I know, he told me. He told all of us, before the end."

"Are you guys all okay with that?" she asked, seriously, trying to ignore the terrible dryness in her mouth. If she was to lead them, they needed to want her to lead them, or this would *never* work.

"I trusted him to always make the right decisions for us," Leon said quietly. "If that includes you, then I suppose so, yeah."

That this was coming from Leon, more than anyone else, made the first sparks of self-confidence start to bloom in her gut. The rest of them all murmured their affirmative too, and she couldn't help but smile at it, faintly. Delilah beamed at her, albeit shakily, her cheeks still wet with her mourning. That helped too.

"Thank you," Susannah replied, softly.

"Well," Jess mumbled, "it's not like we could ignore a dead

man's last wish, is it?"

Susannah nodded, taking a moment to gather her composure, really hoping she wasn't going to make an idiot of herself. It just seemed so fundamentally wrong to be taking control of Krig's resistance when she was standing by the side of his grave – she could never hope to fill his shoes, just struggle not to do a terrible job and make him proud of how she did things.

"So," David said, with a sort of faux cheerfulness belied by the black bags under his eyes, and the tension in his shoulders. "What's the plan, boss?"

She wouldn't let him down.

58500578R00210

Made in the USA
Lexington, KY
12 December 2016